Cultural Encounters with the Arabian Nights in Nineteenth-Century Britain

Edinburgh Critical Studies in Victorian Culture
Series Editor: Julian Wolfreys

Recent books in the series:

Rudyard Kipling's Fiction: Mapping Psychic Spaces
Lizzy Welby

The Decadent Image: The Poetry of Wilde, Symons and Dowson
Kostas Boyiopoulos

British India and Victorian Literary Culture
Máire ní Fhlathúin

Anthony Trollope's Late Style: Victorian Liberalism and Literary Form
Frederik Van Dam

Dark Paradise: Pacific Islands in the Nineteenth-Century British Imagination
Jenn Fuller

Twentieth-Century Victorian: Arthur Conan Doyle and the Strand Magazine, *1891–1930*
Jonathan Cranfield

The Lyric Poem and Aestheticism: Forms of Modernity
Marion Thain

Gender, Technology and the New Woman
Lena Wånggren

Self-Harm in New Woman Writing
Alexandra Gray

Suffragist Artists in Partnership: Gender, Word and Image
Lucy Ella Rose

Victorian Liberalism and Material Culture: Synergies of Thought and Place
Kevin A. Morrison

The Victorian Male Body
Joanne-Ella Parsons and Ruth Heholt

Nineteenth-Century Settler Emigration in British Literature and Art
Fariha Shaikh

The Pre-Raphaelites and Orientalism
Eleonora Sasso

The Late-Victorian Little Magazine
Koenraad Claes

Coastal Cultures of the Long Nineteenth Century
Matthew Ingleby and Matt P. M. Kerr

Dickens and Demolition: Literary Afterlives and Mid-Nineteenth-Century Urban Development
Joanna Hofer-Robinson

Artful Experiments: Ways of Knowing in Victorian Literature and Science
Philipp Erchinger

Victorian Poetry and the Poetics of the Literary Periodical
Caley Ehnes

The Victorian Actress in the Novel and on the Stage
Renata Kobetts Miller

Dickens's Clowns: Charles Dickens, Joseph Grimaldi and the Pantomime of Life
Johnathan Buckmaster

Italian Politics and Nineteenth-Century British Literature and Culture
Patricia Cove

Cultural Encounters with the Arabian Nights in Nineteenth-Century Britain
Melissa Dickson

Novel Institutions: Anachronism, Irish Novels and Nineteenth-Century Realism
Mary L. Mullen

Forthcoming volumes:

Her Father's Name: Gender, Theatricality and Spiritualism in Florence Marryat's Fiction
Tatiana Kontou

The Sculptural Body in Victorian Literature: Encrypted Sexualities
Patricia Pulham

Olive Schreiner and the Politics of Print Culture, 1883–1920
Clare Gill

Victorian Auto/Biography: Problems in Genre and Subject
Amber Regis

Culture and Identity in Fin-de-Siècle Scotland: Romance, Decadence and the Celtic Revival
Michael Shaw

Gissing, Shakespeare and the Life of Writing
Thomas Ue

The Aesthetics of Space in Nineteenth-Century British Literature, 1851–1908
Giles Whiteley

Women's Mobility in Henry James
Anna Despotopoulou

The Persian Presence in Victorian Poetry
Reza Taher-Kermani

Michael Field's Revisionary Poetics
Jill Ehnenn

Contested Liberalisms: Martineau, Dickens and the Victorian Press
Iain Crawford

Plotting Disability in the Nineteenth-Century Novel
Clare Walker Gore

The Americanisation of W. T. Stead
Helena Goodwyn

Women's Mobility in Henry James
Anna Despotopoulou

For a complete list of titles published visit the Edinburgh Critical Studies in Victorian Culture web page at www.edinburghuniversitypress.com/series/ECVC

Also Available:
Victoriographies – A Journal of Nineteenth-Century Writing, 1790–1914, edited by Diane Piccitto and Patricia Pulham
ISSN: 2044-2416
www.eupjournals.com/vic

Cultural Encounters with the Arabian Nights in Nineteenth-Century Britain

Melissa Dickson

EDINBURGH
University Press

Edinburgh University Press is one of the leading university presses in the UK. We publish academic books and journals in our selected subject areas across the humanities and social sciences, combining cutting-edge scholarship with high editorial and production values to produce academic works of lasting importance. For more information visit our website: edinburghuniversitypress.com

© Melissa Dickson, 2019, 2021

Edinburgh University Press Ltd
The Tun – Holyrood Road, 12(2f) Jackson's Entry, Edinburgh EH8 8PJ

First published in hardback by Edinburgh University Press 2019

Typeset in 11/13 Adobe Sabon by
IDSUK (DataConnection) Ltd

A CIP record for this book is available from the British Library

ISBN 978 1 4744 4364 7 (hardback)
ISBN 9781474443654 (paperback)
ISBN 978 1 4744 4366 1 (webready PDF)
ISBN 978 1 4744 4367 8 (epub)

The right of Melissa Dickson to be identified as the author of this work has been asserted in accordance with the Copyright, Designs and Patents Act 1988, and the Copyright and Related Rights Regulations 2003 (SI No. 2498).

Contents

List of Illustrations	vi
A Note on the Text	viii
Series Editor's Preface	ix
Acknowledgements	xi
Introduction	1
1. 'For a time their world made mine': Childhood Encounters with the Arabian Nights	19
2. Underground Palaces and Castles in the Air: The Realms and Ruins of the Arabian Nights	61
3. The Magical Metropolis	108
4. Magic and Machines at the Great Exhibition	141
5. Epilogue: A New Arabian Nights	174
Bibliography	188
Index	209

List of Illustrations

Figure 1.1   Title Page of 'The History of Aladdin, or The Wonderful Lamp' by William Henry Brooke (Illustrator), c.1840s. Renier Collection. © Victoria and Albert Museum, London.   25

Figure 1.2   'Webb's Characters and Scenes in Aladdin, or the Wonderful Lamp', accompanying W. Webb, *Aladdin: or, The Wonderful Lamp, a Romantic Drama, in Two Acts. Written expressly for and adapted only to Webb's Characters and Scenes in the Same.* Author's own copy.   30

Figure 2.1   'Washing Before or After a Meal'. Edward William Lane, *An Account of the Manners and Customs of the Modern Egyptians.* London: John Murray, 1871, p. 181. Courtesy of the Bodleian Libraries, The University of Oxford.   97

Figure 2.2   'A Party at Dinner or Supper'. Edward William Lane, *An Account of the Manners and Customs of the Modern Egyptians.* London: John Murray, 1871, p. 182. Courtesy of the Bodleian Libraries, The University of Oxford.   97

Figure 2.3   'Dancing-Girls'. Edward William Lane, *An Account of the Manners and Customs of the Modern Egyptians.* London: John Murray, 1871, p. 88. Courtesy of the Bodleian Libraries, The University of Oxford.   97

Figure 2.4   'Whirling Darweesh'. Edward William Lane, *An Account of the Manners and Customs of the Modern Egyptians.* London: John Murray, 1871, p. 153. Courtesy of the Bodleian Libraries, The University of Oxford.   97

Figure 3.1   The British Museum, Room 4 - Colossal bust of Ramses II, the 'Younger Memnon'. Author: Mujtaba Chohan. Courtesy of Wikimedia Commons. CC BY-SA 3.0, https://commons.wikimedia.org/w/index.php?curid=1545133.   112

Figure 3.2   'Mode in which Memnon's head was removed by Belzoni and his team of labourers'. *Plates Illustrative of the Researches and Operations of G. Belzoni in Egypt and Nubia.* Agostino Aglio, 1820. Rawpixel free CC0 Image ID: 399667.   113

Figure 4.1   'All the World Going to See the Great Exhibition of 1851', George Cruikshank, in Henry Mayhew and George Cruikshank, *1851; Or, the Adventures of Mr. and Mrs. Sandboys and Family, Who Came up to London to 'Enjoy Themselves' and to See the Great Exhibition.* London: David Bogue, 1857. Credit: Internet Archive.   148

Figure 4.2   The opening of the Great Exhibition by Queen Victoria at Crystal Palace. 1851. Engraved by H. Bibby. Credit: Wellcome Collection. CC BY 4.0.   151

A Note on the Text

The collection of stories known in Arabic as *Alf Layla wa-Layla* has taken many guises and many names over time, from *Les Mille et Une Nuits* to *The Thousand and One Nights*, *A Thousand Nights and a Night*, *The Arabian Nights' Entertainments* and many other renderings. For the sake of consistency, I have used the term 'Arabian Nights', without italics, to refer to the tales collectively, as that vast accumulation of texts that have, since the eighteenth century, been translated by many scholars into European languages from Arabic sources. This terminology is also intended to reflect the emergence in the nineteenth century of the Arabian Nights as an abstract concept, or set of concepts, as well as a story collection. Where the title appears in italics, I refer to a specific edition or play.

Series Editor's Preface

'Victorian' is a term at once indicative of a strongly determined concept and an often notoriously vague notion, emptied of all meaningful content by the many journalistic misconceptions that persist about the inhabitants and cultures of the British Isles and Victoria's Empire in the nineteenth century. As such, it has become a by-word for the assumption of various, often contradictory habits of thought, belief, behaviour and perceptions. Victorian studies and studies in nineteenth-century literature and culture have, from their institutional inception, questioned narrowness of presumption, pushed at the limits of the nominal definition, and have sought to question the very grounds on which the unreflective perception of the so-called Victorian has been built; and so they continue to do. Victorian and nineteenth-century studies of literature and culture maintain a breadth and diversity of interest, of focus and inquiry, in an interrogative and intellectually open-minded and challenging manner, which are equal to the exploration and inquisitiveness of its subjects. Many of the questions asked by scholars and researchers of the innumerable productions of nineteenth-century society actively put into suspension the clichés and stereotypes of 'Victorianism', whether the approach has been sustained by historical, scientific, philosophical, empirical, ideological or theoretical concerns; indeed, it would be incorrect to assume that each of these approaches to the idea of the Victorian has been, or has remained, in the main exclusive, sealed off from the interests and engagements of other approaches. A vital interdisciplinarity has been pursued and embraced, for the most part, even as there has been contest and debate amongst Victorianists, pursued with as much fervour as the affirmative exploration between different disciplines and differing epistemologies put to work in the service of reading the nineteenth century.

Edinburgh Critical Studies in Victorian Culture aims to take up both the debates and the inventive approaches and departures from convention that studies in the nineteenth century have witnessed for the last half-century at least. Aiming to maintain a 'Victorian' (in the most positive sense of that motif) spirit of inquiry, the series' purpose is to continue and augment the cross-fertilisation of interdisciplinary approaches, and to offer, in addition, a number of timely and untimely revisions of Victorian literature, culture, history and identity. At the same time, the series will ask questions concerning what has been missed or improperly received, misread or not read at all, in order to present a multi-faceted and heterogeneous kaleidoscope of representations. Drawing on the most provocative, thoughtful and original research, the series will seek to prod at the notion of the 'Victorian', and in so doing, principally through theoretically and epistemologically sophisticated close readings of the historicity of literature and culture in the nineteenth century, to offer the reader provocative insights into a world that is at once overly familiar, and irreducibly different, other and strange. Working from original sources, primary documents and recent interdisciplinary theoretical models, Edinburgh Critical Studies in Victorian Culture seeks not simply to push at the boundaries of research in the nineteenth century, but also to inaugurate the persistent erasure and provisional, strategic redrawing of those borders.

Julian Wolfreys

Acknowledgements

This project grew out of my PhD at King's College London (KCL), which would not have been possible without the award of a Freda Bage Fellowship of the Australian Federation of Graduate Women and a King's International Graduate Scholarship. The vibrant academic communities at KCL and at Goodenough College, London, were constant sources of inspiration and support during my doctorate, and my work benefitted especially from the wisdom and the extraordinary generosity of my supervisor, Clare Pettitt. Research on this project also overlapped with my time as a postdoctoral researcher on the Diseases of Modern Life Project at St Anne's College, Oxford, and received funding from the European Research Council (ERC) under the European Union's Seventh Framework Programme ERC Grant Agreement number 340121. I am indebted to Sally Shuttleworth for her keen critical attention, unfailingly good advice, and staunch support of junior scholars. I would also like to thank my fellow 'Diseases' postdocs, Amelia Bonea, Sally Frampton, Sarah Green, Jean-Michel Johnston, Hosanna Krienke, Emilie Taylor-Brown and Jennifer Wallis, for creating such a supportive and stimulating academic environment, as well as dramatically expanding my knowledge of nineteenth-century technology and print culture. My current academic home at the University of Birmingham has provided me with a new and dynamic research culture, and I am thankful for the many galvanising conversations that have helped me to bring this project to completion.

I am grateful to John Holmes, Sally Shuttleworth, Mark Turner, Ian Henderson and Ruth Livesey, who read parts of this work in various iterations, and to those scholars who suggested possible sources or new avenues of exploration: Marina Warner, Kirsten Shepherd-Barr and Gavin Budge. The readers appointed by Edinburgh University Press also offered immensely valuable comments, which I have endeavoured to take on board.

I note in this text the profound impact that the stories and dreams of our childhood have on later life, and I thank my parents, Paul and Margaret Duthie, for filling my own early years with books and possibilities. I also thank Colleen, Gordon and all the Gunthorpes and Dicksons, who have been unfailingly generous in their support of both my career and my marriage since they first welcomed me into their family in 2006. Finally, this book is dedicated to Gareth Dickson, my personal jinn, whose endless emotional and intellectual support has been nothing short of magical.

Some of the material in Chapter 1 has appeared as 'Jane Eyre's "Arabian Tales": Reading and Remembering the Arabian Nights', *Journal of Victorian Culture* 18.2 (2013), pp. 198–212.

Introduction

In the fourth issue of the short-lived Pre-Raphaelite journal *The Germ*, the art critic and theorist Frederic George Stephens, writing as Laura Savage, enjoined modern painters and poets to 'go out into life' and to exploit the aesthetic and poetic possibilities of the modern city. Instead of 'living only in the past world', Stephens insisted, the artist might discover a great deal of beauty in the workings of daily life in Victorian Britain:

> And there is something else we miss; there is the poetry of the things about us; our railways, factories, mines, roaring cities, steam vessels, and the endless novelties and wonders produced every day; which if they were found only in the Thousand and One Nights, or in any poem classical or romantic, would be gloried over without end; for as the majority of us know not a bit more about them, but merely their names, we keep up the same mystery, the main thing required for the surprise of the imagination.[1]

For Stephens, the technological and industrial achievements of modern life are rendered both poetic and magical because the science that underpins their operations cannot easily be understood by the non-specialist observer. The invention of the steam locomotive and the coming of the railways and telegraphy in the mid-century might, in this way, be perceived as marvels akin to the wondrous events that fill the pages of the Arabian Nights. The inner workings of the factory, the boiler and the steam engine are seemingly wonderful, and their effects upon the material world not only are surprising, but have the capacity to generate aesthetic pleasure. Indeed, Stephens notes, the splendours of the modern age have, in many ways, surpassed those mysteries familiar to readers of Oriental fiction, for 'the long white cloud of steam, the locomotive pours forth' not only escapes 'like the spirits Solomon put his seal upon, in the Arabian Tales', but comprises even 'mightier spirits' that have been bound 'in a faster vessel'.[2] The railways, too, now shake the earth with 'the footfall of the Genii man has made'.[3] They are the material realisation in England of a phenomenon that, until recently, could only be imagined.

Stephens's celebration of Britain's recent technological innovations as a source of both wonder and poetry was part of the widespread rhetoric of the magic of modernity that was emerging across nineteenth-century literature, technology, science and the periodical press.[4] Faced with profound structural shifts, commentators of the period frequently deployed the language of magic, genii and the Arabian Nights in order to communicate and make sense of the dramatically changing nature of their urban, industrial environments. 'When we hear the word Lamp', declared one article in Dickens's periodical, *Household Words*, 'we involuntarily recall that beloved lamp of our childhood, burning in the secret mountain-cavern, and throwing its magic radiance over so many of our winter nights – the Wonderful Lamp of Aladdin.'[5] That fictional lamp, whose own origins and workings were shrouded in mystery, became a common reference point for the marvels of scientific and technological innovation in Victorian Britain. The Scottish chemist and religious writer George Wilson (1818–59), for example, declared, in the opening paragraph of his study of electricity and the electric telegraph, that 'a deeper truth than its author probably intended, or than most of his readers have discovered, is shadowed forth in Aladdin's story'.[6] The evocation of 'an almost omnipotent genie', central to that well-known tale, had, Wilson argued, found an equivalent in the modern age not by rubbing a magic lamp but by rubbing a piece of amber, and thus bringing into being an invisible agent that 'in our hands has done far more wonderful things than the genie of Aladdin's Lamp did, or could have done, for its possessors'.[7] Not only does this tale from the Arabian Nights provide a useful analogy to the mysterious workings of science in producing electrical currents, but science itself seems to co-opt the magic of the East, to demonstrate magic, and to make magic 'real' and available in the modern world. A writer for *The Museum of Science and Art*, edited by the Irish scientist and popular lecturer Dionysius Lardner, similarly endowed the cables and wires that comprised the electric telegraphic circuit with magical properties, declaring that 'compared with all such realities, the illusions of Oriental romance grow pale', as 'the slaves of the lamp yield precedence to the spirits which preside over the battery and the boiler'.[8] It seems that the technological advancements of this rapidly growing and increasingly urbanised population were impressing themselves upon their participants as nothing short of magical.

While the realities of many technological and industrial developments of this period were far from corresponding to such enthusiastic appraisals, the language of magic and genii testifies to the enthusiasm and excitement that they generated.[9] Wonder, Philip Fisher reminds us, occupies the horizon between the familiar and the unfamiliar. It is an 'impassioned state', underpinned by novelty, pleasure and surprising new facts.[10] In the context of British industrial and technological modernity, this wonderment was expressed in the recurrent correlations being drawn between notions of progress and the realisation of Eastern magic. An increasing number of references to genii, sprites, magicians, wonderful lamps and, in particular, to the Oriental magic of the Arabian Nights, can be found throughout and beyond the nineteenth-century press, serving as a popular gauge of the extent to which Britain had realised the impossible while, paradoxically, continuing to provide a space of wish-fulfilment, fantasy and escape from an increasingly hectic modern life. In this book, I seek to explore some of these constructions, ranging from developments in children's literature and child psychology, travel writing, theatre and exhibitions, to fictional speculations as to what lies ahead for Britain once it has become, literally, a magical metropolis. My concern is to situate the Arabian Nights in relation to specific sites of social and cultural experience, in order to interrogate its dynamic role within such negotiations. As Stephens's impassioned call to poetic engagement with industrial modernity suggests, the great discoveries and developments of this era were believed to be transforming Britain's industries, economy and population, and called for new ways of thinking about itself, its past and its position in the world. Industrialisation, urbanisation and technological innovation inspired deep reflections on the nature of human relationships and communications – individual, global and imperial – and the role of new machinery and new technologies in daily life. In many cases, this involved the evocation of the Arabian Nights as a familiar version of the old, the other, the magical, the Oriental and the traditional, in order to distinguish nineteenth-century Britain as new, exciting and modern. In so doing, however, that fantastic other against which Britain so frequently measured and defined itself became an integral component of that self, its imagination, its memories and its dreams.

The Arabian Nights was a useful and evocative metaphorical device for describing moments of intense joy and wonder, sudden reversals of fortune, magical transformations, and the realisation or manifestation of the seemingly impossible in much nineteenth-century writing. It was a rhetorical strategy that was very much in keeping with the unsettled, shape-shifting quality of the tales themselves, which have no known creator, no clear linguistic or geographical origin, and no fixed length, structure, shape or contents. The collection of stories generally known in Britain in the eighteenth and nineteenth centuries as *The Arabian Nights' Entertainments* was not a unified anthology of tales, but a culturally diverse assortment of narrative fragments that have been traced to Arabic, Egyptian, Persian and Indian storytelling traditions of ancient and medieval times. There is a ninth-century Arabic version of the famous frame tale, in which the despotic Sultan Schahriar becomes so engrossed in his new wife Scheherazade's nightly, unfinished storytelling that, each morning, he postpones her intended execution in order to hear the end of her tale. However, the most substantial extant manuscripts are believed to have emerged from Egypt and Syria in the fourteenth and fifteenth centuries. Alongside these two core collections, many of the source texts are known to have been circulating in oral form throughout and beyond the Arab world for centuries.[11]

This unstable palimpsest of narratives first arrived in Britain not from the 'East', but from France in the form of the French Orientalist and archaeologist Antoine Galland's *Les Mille et Une Nuits*, which was published in Paris in twelve volumes between 1704 and 1717. The first volume of this collection was translated into English by an unknown Grub Street translator, and published in London by Andrew Bell only two years after its publication in France. Galland's translation drew on an Arabic version of the Syrian manuscripts, and it was augmented by several tales that he had independently sourced from Baghdad and Cairo, as well as eight 'orphan stories' – including Aladdin and Ali Baba – which were possibly invented by Galland himself, as they were not found in any of the original manuscripts.[12] In this undertaking, Galland had, as Jorge Luis Borges observes, 'established the canon, incorporating stories that time would render indispensable and that translators to come – his enemies – would not dare to omit'.[13] His creative translation work became, by default, the basis of all English versions of the Arabian Nights for more than a century, until Edward Lane's new 1839–41 translation from Arabic appeared, and the first printed versions of the authoritative Arabic texts were published between 1841 and 1842. Lane endeavoured to resist Galland's canon, failing to include the stories of either Aladdin or Ali Baba in his work. Developed and modified across regions and throughout different historical and cultural periods, the Arabian Nights comprised an array of genres, languages, customs and religions. Fables, fairy tales, histories, adventures, romances, crimes and family anecdotes are drawn together through the figure of Scheherazade in a seemingly infinite and inherently unstable sequence of narratives.

Britain's deep and sustained engagement with the Arabian Nights in the first half of the nineteenth century was unquestionably facilitated by the technological innovations that gave rise to an expanding print culture in this period. In the year 1800, there were already at least eighty editions of the Arabian Nights, and the English version of Galland's tales had reached its eighteenth edition. Over the next thirty years, following the mechanisation of paper manufacture, the creation of the steam-powered press and the abolition of various newspaper and advertisement taxes, this rate of publication doubled. With the steady rise in general literacy rates from 1800, printed material was now available on a mass scale, to a large range of audiences. Newspapers became increasingly prolific, and public access to reading materials was significantly improved through the growth of circulating libraries, public libraries and railway bookstores. The Arabian Nights was part of this easily circulated, un-copyrighted material, and it came to enjoy even greater prominence in Britain than it had held before. The tales appeared regularly throughout the century as extracts and selections across different periodicals, in a range of chapbooks and in illustrated penny and pocket series, as new and revised editions, adaptations for children and creative continuations. There were new volumes of the Arabian Nights especially designed for railway travel, and new short reprints of popular individual tales. Imitations in prose and verse, moralistic re-writings, as well as satires such as Dickens's 'Thousand and One Humbugs' (1855), filled the pages of the periodical press. In his extensive review of nineteenth-century criticism of the Arabian Nights in British periodical culture, Muhsin Jassim Ali has identified the range of new editions and revisions of the tales that appeared in the first decades of the nineteenth century alongside numerous reprints of the English translation of Galland. These include William Beddoes's translation of some additional tales in his *Miscellanies* (1795), the antiquarian Richard Gough's edition of 1798, the Reverend Edward Forster's translation from the French in 1802, G. S. Beaumont's translation from Galland's work in 1811, 1814 and 1817, Jonathan Scott's *Arabian Nights' Entertainments* in 1811, Henry Weber's composite edition of *Tales of the East* in 1812,

George Lamb's translation of Joseph Von Hammer's *New Arabian Nights' Entertainment* (1826) and Henry Torrens's unexpurgated first volume of the work in 1838.[14] Such was their extraordinary appeal to readers, as Leigh Hunt declared in an 1839 review of six recently published editions of the tales, 'that at this present writing, the "Arabian Nights" is the most popular book in the world' and 'the only book of which it can be said, that it is a favourite with all ranks and times of life'.[15] Victorian print culture, itself a sign of the new steam-powered age, had become a vehicle for the transmission of ideas concerning the Orient, and for multiple, divergent encounters with the world of the Arabian Nights. The very ease and speed of circulation newly enjoyed by these tales served to highlight the dramatic transformations that were being undergone by the industrialising nation, while offering a means of imaginative escape into, and explicit comparison with, this fictional other world. In so doing, the Arabian Nights became a kind of measure of the shifting nature and preoccupations of nineteenth-century Britain itself, as well as a complex marker of personal and cultural identities.

The present volume is, in many ways, less concerned with what the Arabian Nights actually were than with what they meant in the nineteenth century. The temporal and structural openness of this story collection invites diverse application in multiple locations, and the tales of the Arabian Nights have been evoked and manifested themselves in a variety of social, cultural and political worlds throughout history.[16] This book traces some of the ways in which the Arabian Nights was used throughout the nineteenth century to reflect and refract new materials and ideas, offering different ways for British readers to interpret and to frame their experiences. While the tales are, of course, many and varied, their fundamental appeal in the early decades of the nineteenth century related, I will argue, to their ongoing associations with magic, wonder, sudden transformations and supernatural manifestations.

It is not my intention here to catalogue the numerous manifestations or textual variations of the Arabian Nights that appeared throughout the nineteenth century. Muhsin Jassim Ali, in *Scheherazade in England* (1981), has already conducted an extensive review of nineteenth-century criticism of the Arabian Nights in British periodical culture, and identified the range of new editions and revisions of the tales that were appearing at the time. More broadly, Robert Irwin's seminal study, *The Arabian Nights: A Companion* (1994), has traced systematically the textual developments of these stories from prehistoric India and Pharaonic Egypt to modern times, while exploring the various moments in which the contents of the collection were altered, added to, plagiarised and imitated. My focus here is upon the ways in which these various tales provided familiar forms of expression with which to structure and articulate new experiences in nineteenth-century Britain. My outlook is deliberately interdisciplinary, drawing upon discourses of science, psychology, history, archaeology, ethnography, stagecraft, reading and book history as I strive to tease out the variety of operational fields in which a potent series of metaphors derived from the Arabian Nights became implicated in the conceptual frameworks of British modernity. This diverse range of source material highlights the often close dialogue that took place across disciplines, in discussions that dovetailed with the constructions of childhood and the modern self in historicist, psychological, social, cultural and literary spheres. This project, then, is not one simply about the influence of one text on others, but a demonstration of the ways in which texts are culturally, and often materially, enmeshed.

The period that this study addresses largely falls between two significant events in the history of British imperialism and 'academic' Orientalism. Napoleon's Egyptian expedition from 1798 to 1801 and subsequent chronicling of all aspects of Egyptian customs, society and culture in *Description de l'Égypte* (1809–28) marked, in Edward Said's words, a 'truly scientific appropriation of one culture by another, apparently stronger one'.[17] This historical moment of burgeoning antiquarian exploration was a critical turning point in the European imagination of the Orient and has been cited by Said as the definitive beginning of 'Orientalism', when 'One could speak in Europe of an Oriental personality, an Oriental atmosphere, an Oriental tale, Oriental despotism, or an Oriental mode of production, and be understood.'[18] It marked, too, a significant shift in the reception of the Arabian Nights, as the tales increasingly came to be understood not simply as the fantastic fictions of childhood, but as narratives of infiltration, excavation and discovery that contained historical 'truths' about the East and could provide a familiar set of literary tropes for articulating the psychological, emotional and material experiences of Eastern exploration. As the conquering nation in Egypt, Britain expropriated countless monuments and relics (including the famous Rosetta Stone) as the spoils of war, and Britain's triumph in military conquest became intertwined with an impulse for the exploration and documentation of the ancient world. As British travellers, archaeologists, geologists and ethnographers increasingly worked to infiltrate, examine and possess both the living East and the ancient relics it contained, the tales of the Arabian Nights provided a rich narrative template for communicating those efforts, in a style and structure that were already familiar to British readers.

Half a century later, the Great Exhibition of the Works of Industry of All Nations, held at the Crystal Palace in Hyde Park from 1 May to 15 October 1851, staged a celebration of the achievements and primacy of British industrial technologies, as well as the commercial success of its colonial expansion. Tens of thousands of objects were removed from their social and cultural contexts in the colonial peripheries and placed on display in the imperial centre. Although 1851 was not the height of the territorial expansion of the British Empire, it has been seen as the pinnacle of Victorian power and self-confidence, and it was one of the last decades in which Britain's technological and economic primacy was uncontested. A fantastic construction that, like Aladdin's own palace, promised access to seemingly magical objects and far-away kingdoms, the Crystal Palace also registered the removal of such fantastic spaces from the distant Orient to the very landscape of London itself. This transmigration of the Arabian Nights to the very heart of the British Empire, which was followed by new translations of the tales from the Arabic by John Payne and Richard Burton in the 1880s, as well as Robert Louis Stevenson's collection of stories aptly titled *New Arabian Nights*, marked a further change in the collection's representative status. While late-Victorian engagements with the Arabian Nights continued the tradition of identification with the magic of these tales, they also frequently registered the removal of such magic from the Orient to the metropolis. Britain had, it seemed, not only realised but surpassed the magic of the Arabian Nights, as its magic was diffused within the modern, urban landscape itself. London had replaced Baghdad, Cairo and Delhi in the popular imagination as a city of enchantment and a source of potentially infinite, wonderful stories.

Discussions of the role of the Arabian Nights in Britain during this key period in its formation of an imperial consciousness have been largely dominated by scholarship on the production and active maintenance of difference between Occident and Orient put forward by Edward Said in *Orientalism* (2003 [1978]). In examining the ways in which Eurocentrism not only influences and alters, but also produces other cultures, Said presents Orientalism as a systematic discipline by which European culture was able to know and to control the Orient during the post-Enlightenment period. The Oriental fantasies of the Arabian Nights were, as has often been noted, compelling sources for constructions of the East as morally, politically and culturally other. The tales were a substantial component of what Rana Kabbani calls 'Europe's myths of the orient' and, as Saree Makdisi and Felicity Nussbaum have claimed, a proliferation of European derivations and imitations of the Arabian Nights and its tales of Eastern opulence, sensuality, supernatural intervention, amoral freedoms and sexualised violence during this period 'helped, especially in its later nineteenth-century redactions, to provide ideological fodder for imperial conquest'.[19] Such an approach to the tales in the nineteenth century inculcated repulsion, horror and morbid fascination in their readers in order to emphasise the East's alterity. It was an approach, however, that was significantly undercut by the inherent multiplicity of the work in question, a work that does not represent a clearly defined, single 'reality', but rather numerous forms of time, space and culture. This multiplicity allows for difference, contradiction and diversity, and it facilitates moments of recognition, experimentation, surprise and suspense, while at the same time delineating social and cultural differences. A work comprising infinite narrative possibilities and stories within stories, the Arabian Nights was also an avenue for diversion, distraction and the pleasurable immersion of the reader in the stories and spaces of the East. Just as the despotic Sultan Schahriar finds himself captivated and ultimately transformed by an ongoing engagement with the fictions of the Arabian Nights, so might imperial readers of these tales also be detained, entertained and strangely altered by their imaginative experiences.

It is this latter approach, resistant to an imposed homogeny, with which *Cultural Encounters* is concerned. As Marina Warner has shown, as a work of 'multiple transformations, putting on different guises and exciting different effects in various circumstances', the Arabian Nights reveals 'how much translations between cultures can alter and even mitigate the costs of protracted and entrenched hostilities'.[20] Resisting readings of the tales as evidence of the West's static, imperialist constructions of the Orient, Warner has identified moments of profound inter-connectedness between the stories and myths of the East and the West in her study, *Stranger Magic* (2011). Seeking to uncover 'a neglected story of reciprocity and exchange' between East and West, and between Islam and Christianity, she traces the persistent strains of magic and magical thinking in modern Western societies to the continual adoption and adaptation of Oriental materials like the Arabian Nights, which functioned as a 'stranger' space on to which might be projected those fantasies and desires that have remained taboo in 'Enlightened', domestic Western contexts.[21] Magic, Warner shows, may open up new possibilities of thought, of invention and of sympathy in a self-consciously rational, secular world, as 'an imaginary Orient, stimulated by the *Nights*, profoundly interacted with modernity's most characteristic expressions, cultural and social, even as it was being disparaged and repudiated, falsified and invented'.[22]

Like *Stranger Magic*, *Cultural Encounters* approaches the Arabian Nights not as an instrument of imperialist ideologies, but as a dynamic site of cultural exchange, receptive readership and cross-cultural transmission. Unlike Warner's, my focus is on the Victorian everyday rather than the contemporary world, and my analysis is embedded in the dynamic array of texts, characters, images and objects from the Arabian Nights that permeated nineteenth-century literature and culture, resonating not only with the transgressive fantasies of those deemed somehow socially or morally aberrant, but with British fantasies and dreams more openly held within evolving practices in archaeology, geology, ethnography and geography, and in theatre and museum cultures. Throughout, I illustrate how the Arabian Nights was actively and self-consciously drawn upon across multiple emergent disciplines in order to support nineteenth-century Britain's conceptions of its own, changing world.

My analysis of the dynamic relationship between nineteenth-century Britain and this collection of stories as both texts and objects responds to recent scholarship on the material culture of the Victorian period. How we ask things 'to make meaning, to make or re-make ourselves, to organize our anxieties and affections, and to sublimate our fears and shape our fantasies' is one of Bill Brown's fundamental questions at the outset of *A Sense of Things* (2003).[23] Following Arjun Appadurai's *The Social Life of Things* (1986), Brown's work on 'Thing Theory' has called attention to the myriad ways in which materiality is implicated as a constitutive force in both literary culture and social life. In the specific context of Victorian Britain, Elaine Freedgood, in *The Ideas in Things: Fugitive Meaning in the Victorian Novel* (2006), has further revealed the imperial and industrial histories of 'things' that appear in canonical Victorian texts, in order to demonstrate the histories and the individual and cultural knowledge potentially 'stockpiled' in such objects, resonating throughout the texts in which they appear. Suzanne Daly, in *The Empire Inside* (2011), similarly exposes the history and politics behind material goods imported to Britain from India in the eighteenth and nineteenth centuries, while questioning their subsequent troubling status 'at home', and the extent to which they were domesticated or remained other within British fiction. 'One universally acknowledged truth about the Victorians', as John Plotz has observed, 'is that they loved their things,' and things, the work of these critics shows us, are not passive agents.[24] They have a tendency to acquire a life of their own, to accumulate multiple meanings, and to stand in for a great many other things. As Bill Brown has declared, 'Things quicken. What you took to be the inanimate object-world slowly but certainly wakes.'[25]

The Arabian Nights overflows with such things that quicken, and it has contributed countless objects to the repository of British literature and culture, from wonderful lamps to flying carpets, enchanted rings, magic statues, buried treasures, talismans and potions. These objects seized the nineteenth-century imagination and enchanted the everyday. They emerged throughout the period as referents for the workings of imperialism, industry, commerce and scientific and technological processes, as provocations to debates about race, gender, class, history and childhood, and as means of articulating the workings of the natural world. A source of and a stimulant to fantasy, travel, narrative, poetry, drama, art and music, these objects, and the tales in which they appeared, were a rich component of those 'disparate and fragmentary, unevenly developed, even contradictory images of the material everyday' in nineteenth-century Britain.[26]

Part of the function of this book is to draw recent scholarship on thing theory into the history of reading practices, and in particular, of childhood reading practices, in order to register the potentially transformative powers of reading in the context of the emotional, psychological and material relationships forged with the Arabian Nights in nineteenth-century Britain. Childhood reading of the Arabian Nights was, this book will demonstrate, a familiar phenomenon in the Britain of the late eighteenth and early nineteenth centuries, and engagement with the Arabian Nights at this stage of life was not only conceptual and imaginative, but it was also material. The books themselves became personal property and treasured objects, which were fondly remembered and frequently referred to in later life, actively contributing to individual and cultural memory, and to the shaping of the individual and cultural consciousness. 'It is the active accrual of meaning over time', as Clare Pettitt argues, 'that makes things cherished and luminous with meaning,' and the stories and objects of the Arabian Nights, familiar to many nineteenth-century readers since childhood, became similarly charged with various new meanings in adult life, as their contents seemed to spill over from their texts to be seen, re-interpreted and re-imagined across Victorian literature and culture.[27]

Reading is, as Rachel Ablow notes in her introduction to *The Feeling of Reading* (2010), as much an affective, psychological and tactile experience as it is a means of communicating printed material to the mind:

> Texts . . . serve not just as sources of information or even as objects of identification. Instead, they function as barriers, windows, screens; as affective, erotic, and aesthetic objects; and as temporal and rhythmic experiences that may have no real-life substitute or corollary. Reading emerges . . . as one of the most intriguing and mysterious of practices not just because of its apparent privacy or individuality, but also because of the significance of its consequences, and because those consequences – affective, cognitive, social, and political – can never be fully determined in advance.[28]

Socially and culturally inflected readings of the Arabian Nights in the nineteenth century undoubtedly fit this paradigm, rendering those texts at various times affective, erotic and aesthetic objects as they endured and multiplied across time and in memory. Affective reading is, as Ablow's edited volume suggests, an ongoing exchange between reader and text, in which the reader finds his or her emotions stirred, and oscillates between distance and closeness, identification and alterity. There is in this movement the potential for an active exchange of identities, sympathies and ideas in the imaginary projection of the reader into the space and time of the narrative. It is a model that, as Ros Ballaster has noted in the context of an imperial and colonial power working to reinforce its sovereignty, demonstrates an unusual willingness 'to project outward' and 'imagine itself serially in the place of the "other"'.[29] However, in so doing, it also draws that other into the place and the life of the actively engaged reader.

It is this dynamic relationship between reader and narrative/narrator that underpins the current volume. Framed by questions of affective reading and material memory, I seek to interrogate the highly mutable state of the curious, responsive reader in nineteenth-century Britain, the extent to which readers were transported and transformed by their reading, and the ways in which they applied that reading to their everyday lives. The following chapters illustrate how tales and interpretations of the Arabian Nights both structured and were constituted in relation to new fields of scientific, historical and cultural practice. Chapter 1 focuses on acts of reading, and on the nature and circumstances of childhood encounters with the Arabian Nights in Britain, both as a collection of narratives and as a series of material objects such as books, pictures and toy theatres. Despite their continual association with the innocent joys of childhood throughout the nineteenth century, the tales of the Arabian Nights were neither written nor designed for children, and they were far from educational or institutionally approved works in the late eighteenth and early nineteenth centuries. Instead, these tales belonged to the more obscured histories of storytelling in the school yard, the nursery and the study or library, into which the curious child intruded uninvited and generally unsupervised. Operating in such spaces, which were largely held to be separate from the demands of parents and teachers, young readers were granted a temporary escape from the highly regulated, adult worlds of their daily lives, while inculcating a sense of agency and heightened importance in moments of self-directed play, diversion and experimentation with magical possibilities and newly discovered imagined worlds. It was the abiding attraction of these tales for children that led to their designation (and subsequent expurgation) as children's literature, and also to their continued use as metaphors for adult fantasies and constructions of childhood. As the time and space of childhood were increasingly associated with the time and space of these Oriental tales, this chapter argues, the Arabian Nights came to operate not only as a material and psychological souvenir of childhood, but as metonymic of childhood itself: exciting, unpredictable and culturally and temporally other. Ultimately, childhood reading invested in the Arabian Nights turned that material from something treated as other, to a distinctive part of the British psyche.

Moving from the work performed by the Arabian Nights in individual memories and personal histories to its influence in the construction of national and regional histories and ethnographies, Chapter 2 explores the use of the Arabian Nights as a familiar cultural narrative through which the burgeoning practices of archaeology, geology, geography and ethnography might be communicated. An inherently diffusive and unstable work, the Arabian Nights allegedly manifested itself and was witnessed by European travellers in a variety of cultures, religions, societies and spaces across nineteenth-century Egypt, India, China and the Middle East. These tales clearly had force in the social world, in that they were capable of informing and shaping cultural and political relations. The imaginary voyages and adventures of the Arabian Nights, known since childhood, profoundly interacted with actual voyages above and below the ground, providing a narrative template and structure for approaching new experiences that were already familiar to British readers. It was a means by which travellers and scientists might communicate their discoveries in strange lands and familiarise their readers with the new sciences. At the same time, I will argue, this narrative strategy infused those emergent sciences with an enduring form of magic, or magical thinking, in the adult world, which informed processes of thinking about the physical laws of nature, the elements that comprise the globe, and new technological developments of the period. The magical possibilities and treasures of the Arabian Nights held an irresistible fascination for Western readers, who did not want to relinquish themselves fully to the emergent disciplines of science, history, archaeology or ethnography, the potential meanings and possibilities of Eastern exploration above or below the ground.

Chapter 3 turns to the science of stagecraft, and to the endless recreations and adaptations of the wonders, magic and treasures of the Arabian Nights that took place within the shows culture of nineteenth-century Britain. These authorless, ownerless tales presented ideal theatrical opportunities to display the rich landscapes, domestic interiors and dazzling treasures of the East within the public spaces of Britain. In so doing, they facilitated a kind of 'virtual' tourism, whereby audiences might participate in the adventurer's narrative of discovery, infiltration, exploration and safe return, without ever leaving England. At the same time, however, such performances fostered a self-reflective, inward movement, as an imaginative destination of childhood became a physical space that might be stepped into, examined and explored. Performances of the Arabian Nights had a disturbing capacity to evoke and to disrupt childhood memories simultaneously, as they were reliant upon a substantial amount of labour and technical expertise in order to realise fully the workings of magic and the apparently spontaneous eruption of the supernatural on stage. As a vehicle for exploring the material and technological limits of nineteenth-century stagecraft, the wonder and enchantment of the Arabian Nights thus became inextricably intertwined with the wonder of machinery and technical ingenuity, as new techniques were developed for representing fantasy and manufacturing magic.

Chapter 4 turns to the accumulation of goods at the Great Exhibition of 1851, which was frequently understood as another theatrical manifestation of the Arabian Nights, within the 'fairy-tale' Crystal Palace in the heart of Britain. A new and innovative architectural form, the palace and its content challenged the viewer's vision, judgement and sense of scale to such an extent that recourse was made to the language of magic in an effort to represent its unfamiliar effects. The palace and the objects it contained had apparently materialised like the stuff of dreams, seemingly conjured by the rub of a magic lamp. Within this transformative space, the magnificence of Britain's industrial resources became truly apparent only by way of comparison, by the jostling together of old and new, of fictional and material, and of machinery and magic. Here, an anxious meta-narrative emerged about the nature of modern production and consumption. Casting those products originating from India, China and elsewhere within a framework of magic and the Arabian Nights was, this chapter argues, a part of the rhetoric of British modernity, which made the comparison between nations and their wares more palatable by insisting that supposedly 'inferior' nations had employed the agency of magic. Such a narrative generated wonder both for the beautiful, often hand-crafted productions that had supposedly been wrought by magic, and for the advancements of British civilisation, which had apparently gained, through science and technology, all the powers of Aladdin's lamp.

The Arabian Nights, conflated at various moments with the experience of nineteenth-century childhood, travel, exploration and theatre, provided a paradigmatic space of dreaming and fantasy, which was serially delved into and at least in part created by the Victorian psyche. It had an active agency on its readers, who, like the Sultan Schahriar, found themselves captivated and ultimately transformed by an ongoing engagement with its tales. Such, as Ros Ballaster has argued, is the cumulative power of Scheherazade's narrative enterprise, which lies not in the contents of the tales themselves but in their ability to endure and multiply across time. Scheherazade need not 'husband or manage her resources particularly, but rather simply keep them in circulation and her symbolic capital magically grows'.[30] The tales are ever-burgeoning and expanding, and, 'like the woman who tells them', they 'transform the world around them by repetitive acts of simple accretion'.[31] In the case of nineteenth-century Britain, repeated encounters with the tales across time and in different formats allowed readers to gaze upon, define and revel in its psychic landscape, while at the same time re-defining and re-creating itself. The brief epilogue to this volume offers some concluding thoughts on this process, while identifying the emergence of a new vision of the Arabian Nights in the latter decades of the nineteenth century, which celebrated the transformation of the modern metropolis into a dynamic space of magic and mystery that supposedly far excelled its Eastern counterparts. The increasing permeability of national boundaries, coupled with an increasingly global commodity culture in late-Victorian London, intensified fantasies of the modern city as a place of adventure with a now internalised, potent Oriental presence. In many ways, this centre of commerce, industry and science became that fantastic, unpredictable and ever-alluring space of a new Arabian Nights.

The findings of this volume show that the Arabian Nights provided an imaginative field for experimentation, creativity, self-reflection and self-definition in Britain during the first half of the nineteenth century. Alongside the more familiar narrative of its prevalence as material with which to manage the Orient, it points to moments of readerly exchange, immersion in and receptivity to the realm of the other, and to narratives shared and adapted across cultures. Such moments were often deeply personal, but not hermetic, as they played an essential role in the broader cultural system and became constitutive building blocks of nineteenth-century modernity.

Notes

1. Stephens, 'Modern Giants', pp. 170–1.
2. Ibid. p. 171.
3. Ibid. p. 171.
4. For further discussion on the role of science in *The Germ*, see John Holmes, 'Pre-Raphaelitism, Sciences, and the Arts in *The Germ*', pp. 689–703.
5. Anon., 'Eternal Lamps', p. 185.
6. Wilson, *Electricity and the Electric Telegraph*, p. 3.
7. Ibid. p. 3.
8. Anon., 'The Electric Telegraph', p. 116.
9. It has often been noted that new modes of transport, machinery and communications technologies and the expansion of print culture in the nineteenth century were met not only with this kind of enthusiasm, but with ambivalence, as they prompted concerns about the new stresses and strains of modern life, and the velocity necessary in human thought and action in order to keep pace. The jarring effects of new modes of transport, machinery and technological advances have been explored, for example, by Rabinbach in *The Human Motor* (1990), by Andreas Killen in *Berlin Electropolis* (2006), and in the more recent edited collection by Salisbury and Shail, *Neurology and Modernity* (2010). Now 'classic' texts in the field, such as Schivelbusch's *The Railway Journey* (1986), are also instructive in considering how contemporary technological and scientific developments could alter perceptions both of the world and of the individual's place within it.
10. Fisher, *The Vehement Passions*, p. 12.

11. For a detailed analysis of the potential sources and derivations of the tales of the Arabian Nights, see Mahdi, 'The Sources of Galland's *Nuits*', pp. 122–36.
12. Mia Gerhardt famously designated these eight tales 'orphan stories' in *The Art of Story-telling* (1963). The eight tales were 'Aladdin', 'The Awakened Sleeper', 'Ali Baba', 'Prince Ahmed and the Fairy Peri Banou', 'The Envious Sisters', 'Nocturnal Adventures', 'Ali Khwaja' and 'Khudadad'. There is as yet no decisive evidence as to their origin.
13. Borges, 'The Translators of *The Thousand and One Nights*', p. 92.
14. Ali, *Scheherazade in England*, p. 42. Ali's book provides an extended bibliography of appearances of the Arabian Nights in print across eighteenth- and nineteenth-century periodicals.
15. Hunt, 'New Translations of the Arabian Nights', p. 106.
16. That the Arabian Nights had a remarkable propensity to proliferate and to evolve nationally and internationally within multiple literatures and cultures has been thoroughly documented in recent years. Nishio and Yamanaka's *The Arabian Nights and Orientalism* (2005) traces the history of these tales in Japanese culture, while Marzolph's edited collection of essays, *The Arabian Nights in Transnational Perspective* (2007), draws upon Hawaiian newspapers, Sicilian folk traditions, early German cinema and Greek and Balochi oral traditions, amongst other sources, to attest to the influence of the tales upon a range of visual and print cultures, as well as upon other oral traditions. The essays collected by Makdisi and Nussbaum in *The Arabian Nights in Historical Context: Between East and West* (2008) similarly analyse adaptations and uses of the tales in fiction, poetry, music, theatre and religion in order to show that 'European and Arabic worlds are not easily separable, but overlap and intersect culturally and intellectually' (p. 12), while Nance's *How the Arabian Nights Inspired the American Dream, 1790–1935* (2009) provides a fascinating social and cultural history of Eastern stories and performances in America up to the Great Depression, arguing that the leisure and opulence that many imagined typical of Eastern life were equally used to define the great American Dream.
17. Said, *Orientalism*, p. 42.
18. Ibid. p. 32.
19. Kabbani, *Imperial Fictions: Europe's Myths of the Orient* (1994). Makdisi and Nussbaum, 'Introduction', p. 12.
20. Warner, *Stranger Magic*, p. 25.
21. Ibid. p. 26.
22. Ibid. p. 26.
23. Brown, *A Sense of Things*, p. 4.
24. Plotz, *Portable Property*, p. 1.
25. Brown, 'Reification, Reanimation, and the American Uncanny', p. 175.
26. Brown, *The Material Unconscious*, p. 4.
27. Pettitt, 'Peggotty's Work-Box: Victorian Souvenirs and Material Memory'.

28. Rachel Ablow, 'Introduction', pp. 9–10.
29. Ballaster, *Fabulous Orients*, p. 14. The experience of being 'carried away' by the act of reading, in the sense of projecting oneself emotionally and psychologically into other spaces and times, is also taken up by Kate Flint in 'Traveling Readers', pp. 27–46. This psychological movement in and out of the narrative space also recalls the critical 'break in time' that is built into all serial publication cycles and, as Mark Turner has argued, is a 'constitutive feature of periodical-ness, of all periodicities'. See Turner, 'Periodical Time in the Nineteenth Century', p. 183.
30. Ballaster, *Fabulous Orients*, p. 108.
31. Ibid. p. 108.

Chapter 1

'For a time their world made mine': Childhood Encounters with the Arabian Nights

> In another moment I was within that apartment. There was every article of furniture looking just as it did on the morning I was first introduced to Mr. Brocklehurst: the very rug he had stood upon still covered the hearth. Glancing at the bookcases, I thought I could distinguish the two volumes of Bewick's British Birds occupying their old place on the third shelf, and Gulliver's Travels and the Arabian Nights ranged just above. The inanimate objects were not changed: but the living things had altered past recognition.
>
> Charlotte Brontë, *Jane Eyre*, 1847

On Jane Eyre's return to her aunt's house at Gateshead, the sight of the old furniture and books in the breakfast room immediately brings memories of a lonely and unhappy childhood to her adult mind. Each of the works she re-discovers on the bookcase holds special significance for Jane within the context of her memoir: in the opening scenes of the novel, her perusal of the illustrations in Thomas Bewick's *A History of British Birds* (1797–1804) precedes her cousin's attack upon her and her famous incarceration in the red room; Bessie brings *Gulliver's Travels* (1726) to distract and comfort her during her subsequent illness. Most vividly remembered, however, as the culmination of her childhood woes, is the morning of her indignant outburst against her aunt after Mr Brocklehurst's interrogation of her upon the very rug still by the hearth, and her retreat to the familiar pages of 'some Arabian Tales' in this very room.[1] The sudden immediacy of these unchanged objects generates and recalls the sensations of that past time, while marking the temporal remoteness of the experience and the emotional and psychological alterations in Jane herself. The Arabian Nights is referenced throughout Brontë's novel, remembered but apparently never re-read by Jane in later years. Her material and emotional connection both to the tales themselves and to the physical books that contain them is established in childhood, only to be re-ignited in this scene. The collection of tales, a kind of material and psychological souvenir, becomes metonymic of her childhood and all her miseries at Gateshead.

The Arabian Nights has often been cited as a literary influence upon *Jane Eyre* and it is certainly useful to consider it as a source for a novel so much concerned with authority and who has the power to tell their story.[2] However, its 'physical' presence in the narrative draws our attention to the work it performs in material culture and memory, and to the time and space dedicated to reading the Arabian Nights. This chapter explores the operations of that space in nineteenth-century Britain, and its deepening associations with the time of childhood. Saree Makdisi and Felicity Nussbaum rightly introduce the Arabian Nights in their recent study as a 'vertiginously unstable' work, which operates less as a unified narrative than as a 'loose cluster of texts', and their edited collection of essays has effectively established the 'hybrid, translinguistic, and transnational tendencies of the *Nights*' in an imperial context.[3] Placing Jane's collection of books within the context of the unstable proliferation of these tales across nineteenth-century print culture illustrates the workings of this fluctuating matrix of texts within the domestic setting, where it draws the reader's imaginative movement in and out of the fictional realms of the Arabian Nights into the rhythms and the increasingly regulated temporal structures of nineteenth-century Britain.

Material Conditions of Reading

Jane's childhood reading was a familiar phenomenon in the Britain of the late eighteenth and early nineteenth centuries. As they materialised and multiplied across British print culture, the tales of the Arabian Nights permeated British literary traditions and captivated their readers. Eighteenth-century writers such as Samuel Johnson, Alexander Pope, Jonathan Swift, Horace Walpole, Oliver Goldsmith and Thomas Gray were among the work's earliest European admirers. Later, the Romantic poets demonstrated a profound emotional and intellectual attachment to the tales, which was shared by ensuing literary generations. It is well known that writers such as Tennyson, Dickens, Thackeray, Hardy, Robert Louis Stevenson, the Brontës and De Quincey also read the tales in their youth and returned to them in maturity in their own writing. As Robert Irwin observed in his 1994 companion to the Arabian Nights, rather than listing all the European writers of the eighteenth and nineteenth centuries who were influenced or in some way inspired by this work, it would be far easier to identify the very few who were not.[4] Studies such as Peter Caracciolo's *The Arabian Nights in English Literature* (1988), Mushin Jassim Ali's *Scheherazade in England* (1981), and *Oriental Prospects* (1998) by C. C. Barfoot and Theo D'Haen indicate the validity of this claim by tracing the use and meaning of references to the Arabian Nights across the British canon. So ubiquitous was this reading material that, as Robert Mack has observed, the practice of reading the Arabian Nights in moments of leisure is replicated in Smollett's *The Expedition of Humphry Clinker* (1771), Mary Hays's *Memoirs of Emma Courtney* (1796), Maria Edgeworth's *The Absentee* (1812), Brontë's *Jane Eyre* (1847), Thackeray's *Vanity Fair* (1847–8) and *Pendennis* (1848–50), Dickens's *David Copperfield* (1849–50), Gaskell's *Cranford* (1853) and Collins's *The Woman in White* (1860), *Armadale* (1866) and *The Moonstone* (1868). The fictional readers represented in these novels are most commonly discovered 'at moments when they are either thoroughly absorbed in the world of the *Nights* and its imitations, or . . . in the act of invoking Oriental tales'.[5] Their choice of reading material becomes, I would argue, symbolic of their rich imaginative life and emotional sensitivity, while identifying them as characters of interest within their texts.

The Arabian Nights was undoubtedly an active force in Victorian literary culture, and a pervasive touchstone for the Oriental tale and representations of the East. However, the question of what was actually being read and experienced in childhood, and subsequently remembered and referenced in adulthood, still requires further scrutiny. Surprisingly little is known of the formats and the transmission of this work within the domestic sphere, or of the ways that its publication history affected its reception in relation to individual and cultural memories. What is certain is that the authorless, ownerless cluster of tales bound together under the rubric of the Arabian Nights underwent exponential growth within the expanding print culture of the nineteenth century. While the general phenomenon of discovering and reading the Arabian Nights during childhood was commonplace, the sheer number of versions and editions of the tales in this period, outlined in the introduction to this volume, rendered this process a very individual and discontinuous reading experience.

A child's encounter with the tales may or may not have involved the famous frame narrative, adult supervision, illustrations, toy theatres, editorial commentaries, individual stories or larger collections. Linking adults to their particular childhood version of the tales is fraught with difficulty and in many cases impossible. In her section of the *Companion to Romance*, Leonée Ormond unequivocally claims (although she does not demonstrate) that 'we know that, as a boy, Tennyson read *The Arabian Nights* in Galland's French translation'.[6] If true, this means that Tennyson was versed in Galland's twelve-volume *Les Mille et Une Nuits*, which was an unillustrated collection of the tales intended for adult readers. Ulrich Marzolph and Richard van Leeuwen similarly note in passing that 'Dickens read the Arabian Nights in his youth, probably in Jonathan Scott's 1811 edition.'[7] This assumption, though reasonable, seems to be based on little more than the fact that Scott's six-volume edition (which included Scott's own lengthy introduction to the tales, his notes on Muslim religion and customs, and a new series of stories that were not contained in Galland) was circulating during Dickens's childhood years.[8] Robert Louis Stevenson recalls that he read the tales in the form of 'the fat, old, double-columned volume with prints', which is suggestive perhaps of a periodical form, while Winifred Gérin claims that the edition 'accessible to the Brontë children was a translation of the French text by Antoine Galland, published in 1706'.[9] This, despite its seeming specificity, might refer to any one of the numerous editions in English until Lane's new translation from the Arabic in the late 1830s. No version of the Arabian Nights survives today in the Brontë Parsonage Museum.

Each of these youthful reading experiences has an implied connection to a very specific childhood object, which becomes representative of the child's knowledge of the Arabian Nights story collection, and the parameters of his or her acquaintance with the kind of 'Orient' contained within it. There is often a very palpable sense of ownership deployed in these accounts, as both the intellectual and the material conditions of discovering the Arabian Nights are recalled, and the physical books become personal property and treasured objects. In her collection of sketches published collectively under the title *Traits and Trials of Early Life* (1837), for example, the English poet and novelist Letitia Elizabeth Landon recounts in some detail the moment of her introduction to the Arabian Nights, in the form of a paternal gift of what was clearly an illustrated, adult version of the tales. Landon demonstrates an intense sensory and emotional connection both to the volumes themselves and to the narratives they contain:

My father produced four volumes, and for me. How delicious was the odour of the Russian leather in which they were bound, how charming the glance at the numerous pictures which glanced through the half opened leaves. The first reading of the Arabian Nights was like the first reading of Robinson Crusoe. For a time their world made mine – my little lonely island.[10]

Like Jane Eyre, Landon allows fictional and actual worlds to merge in her childish consciousness and they assume meaning in relation to one another. Later, in a poem addressed to her brother, Landon wrote of the transformative powers of this kind of childhood reading, when 'any favourite volume was a mine of long delight', and facilitated her imaginary projection into new, fictional worlds. It also induced a distinct physical response, as her 'pulse danced those light measures that again it cannot know'.[11] Although the later complaint put forward by Landon's brother, that the Arabian Nights had occasioned him 'many a weary day' for 'I had to hear all!', undercuts this nostalgic memory of communal reading practice, it also provides us with a momentary glimpse of the transmission of these tales in the domestic sphere.[12] Landon seemingly read the tales aloud to her (apparently unmoved) brother over a lengthy period of time, embodying the figure of Scheherazade in her own serial performances. The Arabian Nights was clearly a substantial physical presence in her childhood in the form of these leather-bound volumes, and the 'delicious . . . odour' and 'charming . . . glance' of the pages are powerful sense memories attached to the unique objects of her account, providing a tangible connection to past, imagined spaces of colour and delight.

Wordsworth's reflection in the fifth book of *The Prelude* indicates a very different process of discovery and immersion in the world of the Arabian Nights. However, it is one that equally emphasises the materiality and individuality of the experience:

> I had a precious treasure at that time
> A little yellow canvass-covered Book,
> A slender abstract of the Arabian Tales;
> And when I learned, as now I first did learn,
> From my Companions in this new abode,
> That this dear prize of mine was but a block
> Hewn from a mighty quarry – in a word,
> That there were four large Volumes, laden all
> With kindred matter – 'twas, in truth, to me
> A promise scarcely earthly.[13]

The yellow volume Wordsworth refers to here remains unidentified, although its canvas cover and slenderness are suggestive of a popular chapbook edition. Chapbook versions of the Arabian Nights were certainly plentiful, and they were, as Wordsworth's poetic memory indicates, an extremely limited introduction to the story collection. Often sold by wandering pedlars to the servants of middle-class households, it was quite possible that such works entered the domestic sphere and were brought to the attention of young children without any adult supervision.[14] These small pamphlets generally contained only one or two stories with accompanying engravings, and they gave no indication of the famous frame tale, or of the fact that they had been drawn (and very often adapted) from a larger work.

An example of this kind of Arabian Nights chapbook, *The History of Aladdin, or The Wonderful Lamp*, published by John Limbird's Mirror Press in the early nineteenth century, demonstrates not only the degree of variation apparent in different renditions of this story, but also the importance of the material aspects of the book in configuring the fictional Orient encountered in childhood.[15] Like Wordsworth's, it is a small and slim book, only 14 cm by 9 cm, with stitched, pale yellow wrappers. The upper wrapper (see Figure 1.1) is very ornate, with detailed flowers and greenery woven around a classical frame and an absent-minded young woman reading beside a lute in a pastoral English scene. This use of landscape may simply be due to the limited range of woodblock figures used by the publisher, or it may be the result of an ignorance of authentic 'Eastern' scenery on the part of the illustrator, William Henry Brooke. It does, however, suggest an idyllic, non-industrial world of leisure and tranquillity. Is this young woman a fair Scheherazade, performing her tales with musical accompaniment in a new environment? Is she Aladdin's beloved princess of the story, transported to a new world of delight by the powers of the magic lamp? Presented as a 'history' rather than a fiction, the work seems to allude to an earlier, unspecified time that has been lost to British modernity. It offers a brief, fantastic escape from daily realities.

The mere eleven pages of text within this pamphlet contain eight small engravings by Matthew Urlwin Sears, the illustrator of the long-running *Mirror* periodical. The minimal use of background or landscape and the nondescript, classical outfits of the characters throughout give the appearance of stage sets and emphasise the performative nature of the work.[16] There is undoubtedly something of the theatrical about this volume, which indicates a very active, participatory kind of reading. The story itself accentuates the

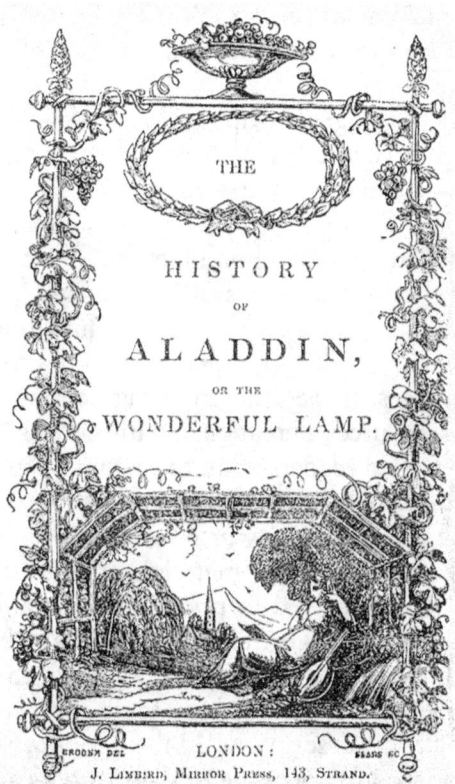

Figure 1.1 Title Page of 'The History of Aladdin, or The Wonderful Lamp' by William Henry Brooke (Illustrator), c.1840s. Renier Collection. MB.ALAD.LI. © Victoria and Albert Museum, London

sensual nature of the Orient through a series of vivid descriptions of the magician's perfume, the fine-tasting fruits in the subterranean cavern, the multiple colours of Aladdin's glittering treasures, and the melodious singing and dancing performed before the princess at the palace. The illusory quality of such a stimulating environment is brought to the fore in the concluding sentence of this version of the story: 'Aladdin was seated on a throne under a canopy of gold; the crown was being placed on his head, when – he awoke, and found that he had been fast asleep on his father's shop-board.'[17] Revealing that Aladdin's adventures were but a dream is a critical alteration to Galland's text, in which we are told that Aladdin, who has been raised 'after a very careless and idle manner', is 'wicked, obstinate, and disobedient to his father and mother' and yet successfully employs magical means in order to live happily ever after with Princess Badroulbadour.[18] Limbird's chapbook introduces a moralistic injunction into an otherwise amoral tale. In his version, hard work rather than idle wishing is the key to happiness, for there is no magic in the grown-up world.

The concept that such a work is, in Wordsworth's words, 'but a block hewn from a mighty quarry' emphasises the degree of craft involved in the production of new editions and variations of the tales by way of a very material metaphor. Like Landon's comparison of her beloved childhood books to mines of 'long delight', it illustrates the nature of the book as a physical treasure of childhood, while rendering the story collection itself a kind of literary repository that might be delved into for images, tropes and enduring fictional characters. The Arabian Nights is a source of great imaginative riches for Wordsworth, Landon and other child readers, akin to the 'real' repositories of treasures and relics that, as the next chapter will show, were being excavated in the same period. Wordsworth's own treasured 'block' clearly facilitates his discovery of further materials in the vast quarry of tales, and it is specifically connected to processes of meaning-making and personal development. It is worth noting, too, that while Wordsworth and Landon both mention four-volume editions of the tales, this does not necessarily mean that they read the same version. There were, in fact, several that fit this description.[19] Like Landon, Wordsworth was clearly ignorant of the history of the Arabian Nights up to the moment of its intrusion upon his consciousness in this particular format. The immediacy of this yellow volume and whatever visual images it contains inculcate a private world of response and imagination. Reading itself is an embodied experience that stimulates not only intellectual, but physical, emotional and psychological responses.

The significance of the material possession of the Arabian Nights to establishing a childhood identity and a space for the embodied reader to inhabit was readily apparent at Haworth Parsonage. Here, extensive reading, which included the Arabian Nights, famously inspired the Brontë children not only to invent and perform their own stories, but to create material representations of them in the form of miniature story books.[20] These tiny books, lovingly and painstakingly sewn together in the style of chapbooks, were later described by Elizabeth Gaskell as 'an immense amount of manuscript, in an inconceivably small space; tales, dramas, poems, romances, written principally by Charlotte, in a hand which it is almost impossible to decipher without the aid of a magnifying glass'.[21] Like a chapbook, the size of these objects implicitly associates them with the diminutive world of childhood. They are microcosms of secret, imagined worlds and, in their pages, the Brontës undertook the wholly uncensored creation of the kingdoms of Glass Town, Angria and Gondal, each with complex social and political structures that were explored through multiple narrative voices. In Glass Town, they re-created themselves as powerful genii named Tallii, Brannii, Emmii and Annii in the manner of the continually interfering, capricious genii of the Arabian Nights. In the world of Angria, Caroline Vernon makes explicit reference to the story of Aladdin in her childish wish that 'a fairy would bring me a ring or a magician would appear & give me a talisman like Aladdin's lamp that I could get everything I want'.[22] More than imaginative childhood play, these books signify the active participation of four ambitious young readers in appropriating narratives and other printed matter such as newspapers and travel writing, and constructing their own episodic chronicles, dialogues and illustrations. They mark an experimental, transitional phase between reading and authoring (and the manufacture of books) in a liminal form that is both escapist and self-reflexive.

In her study of constructions of identity in Charlotte Brontë's juvenilia, Christine Alexander notes the significance of the material dimension of the children's early games and narratives. After quoting Charlotte's well-known diary entry describing her father's return home from a trip to Leeds with twelve wooden toy soldiers for Branwell, and the children's immediate adoption and naming of them for their play, Alexander writes:

> What interests me here is the way possession of the character followed possession of the object, and the way that character then split into a variety of narrative voices. 'It shall be mine!' represents not only physical possession of a toy soldier, but the assumption of a persona, a mask that allowed the child author to speak.[23]

If, as Alexander argues, the toy soldiers were physical manifestations of new authorial identities, then I would add that the careful construction of books to contain and illustrate their stories (apparently designed to be read by the 12-inch soldiers) indicates the children's material possession and assumption of control over the tales themselves in a minute level of detail. The miniature scale of the books is suggestive of a rich interior world beyond their fragile construction, impenetrable to outsiders and fully apprehended only by the four children. In language that emphasises the concrete efforts of literary creation as a kind of craft, Heather Glen has noted that these miniature story books serve physically to capture a common childhood dilemma, 'the attraction to powers which one does not possess; the need to carve out a sphere within which agency is possible, yet the awareness of the self as powerless and others as powerful; the apprehension that one inhabits a world that one does not control'.[24] The physical objects of childhood play are, as Glen suggests, important corollaries, or indeed starting points, for configurations of narrative and fantasy.

The Brontës' miniature book-making and associated domestic theatrics facilitated very active games of 'make-believe' through their intellectual and material participation in continually evolving narratives. Their childhood experiments with narrative find a parallel in the juvenile dramas and toy theatres that began to emerge as a form of entertainment for domestic consumption in the late eighteenth and early nineteenth centuries.[25] The toy theatre – an accurate, miniaturised representation of contemporary theatrical productions and their actors – comprised a series of cardboard sheets or templates, which were either commercially coloured or black and white so that they could be coloured by children. It generally included characters, scenery and stage wings, and was often accompanied by a small pamphlet or story book, which both facilitated and prompted childhood play. The child may or may not read the pamphlet in order to direct the drama, but must physically move the characters and change the backgrounds, manipulating the time and space of the theatre in order to create their own adaptations in concrete form. The embodied nature of this experience is emphasised by Robert Louis Stevenson in his essay, 'A Penny Plain and Twopence Coloured' (1884), in which he vividly recalls how he 'handled and lingered and doated [sic] on these bundles of delight' in the stationery shop, for 'there was a physical pleasure in the sight and touch of them'.[26] For Stevenson, 'every sheet we fingered was another lightning glance into obscure, delicious story; it was like wallowing in the raw stuff of story-books'.[27] In another material metaphor akin to Wordsworth's 'mighty quarry' of tales, this 'raw stuff' of story books might, Stevenson implies, be endlessly mined, manipulated, formed and re-formed.[28] The toy theatre was a site, like the Brontë children's miniature story books, in which the child attained a kind of agency, control over a tangible, miniaturised world that served as their own dramatic and literary experiment. The influence of such theatrical world-making upon Stevenson's own formation of identity was, it should be noted, equally profound and embodied, as he believed himself to have been 'but a puppet in the hands of Skelt', who 'stamped himself upon my immaturity' through his collection of *Skelt's Juvenile Dramas*.[29] The Skelts were one of the most prolific publishers of toy theatres in the period.

The Arabian Nights was well represented in nineteenth-century commercial collections of juvenile dramas, and it is impossible to know how many similar stage sets and associated characters were simply made at home.[30] It is safe to assume, however, that the mass product was designed, at least in part, in recognition of the toy theatre's existing appeal to children. It is known, for instance, that as well as Robert Louis Stevenson, Dickens, John Everett Millais, William Powell Frith and Ellen Terry played with toy theatres as children. Dickens certainly included tales from the Arabian Nights in his childhood play-acting, recalling in 'The Ghost in Master B's Room' (1859) how he and the other children determined to 'have a Seraglio' and act out the adventures of Haroun Alraschid.[31] Alraschid (r.786–809), the legendary Abbasid Caliph of the Islamic Golden Age, features in many tales of the Arabian Nights, and his magnificent court in Baghdad provides a frequent narrative setting for the tales of Scheherazade.[32] His was, as Dickens's youthful narrator observes with considerable nostalgia, a name 'scented with sweet memories' for the early nineteenth-century British child reader.[33] The sensory metaphor employed here in evoking Dickens's childhood memory illustrates the immersive and embodied experience of his youthful performances.[34]

Like the childhood encounter with the Arabian Nights in general, the toy theatre was a common but highly individual phenomenon. The use and choice of colours, settings, characters and even plots were open to endless variation, according to the wishes of the child in question, as well as their prior knowledge (if any) of the production that it was tied to, or of the Arabian Nights in general. Encouragement of improvisational 'free-play' is clear, for example, from Webb's juvenile drama of Aladdin, which contains six plates of characters, eleven scenes of generic caves and streets with palm-trees, Chinese-style buildings and a bridge, three wings, and an eighteen-page play book (see Figure 1.2).[35] There is no indication of the frame story, and there is no image of the pivotal magic lamp or any other treasures from the cave. The only visual indication of magical transformation is the fact that Aladdin is presented in increasingly elaborate costumes. The landscape itself appears to be a curious fusion of Chinese and African influences, bringing far-reaching lands of the Eastern world into the domestic spaces of nineteenth-century Britain to be imaginatively explored, crafted, coloured and physically manipulated.

The possession and physical manipulation of a diminutive object places its owner in a position of authority that, Susan Stewart has argued, implies the possession and mastery of the diminished (in this

Figure 1.2 'Webb's Characters and Scenes in Aladdin, or the Wonderful Lamp', accompanying W. Webb, *Aladdin: or, The Wonderful Lamp, a Romantic Drama, in Two Acts. Written expressly for and adapted only to Webb's Characters and Scenes in the Same*. Author's own copy.

case, Oriental) world contained within. According to Stewart, 'the miniature book frequently served as a realm of the cultural other' and served to 'collapse the significance of the Orient into the exotica of a miniaturized volume'.[36] More recently, Megan Norcia has analysed the role of home theatricals, games and improvised play in promoting a culture of imperialism by allowing children to 'experiment with Other identities and to produce Otherness as an amusing spectacle for English entertainment'.[37] In controlling the scenes, lives and events of, for example, the unnamed African magician, the beautiful princess or Aladdin himself, the child potentially participates in the imperial domination of nameless, geographically nebulous and clearly other landscapes and cultures. In the case of the Arabian Nights, however, such undeniably troubling distinctions between the British child and his or her Oriental subjects are not so clear-cut, as Scheherazade's extraordinary web of tales was increasingly correlated with childhood identity throughout the century. In this way, the Arabian Nights not only recalls the time and materiality of a childhood in early nineteenth-century Britain, but it comes to be conceptualised in the same way as that childhood. I turn now to the ways in which the materials and tales of the Arabian Nights, which were deeply constitutive of childhood fantasies and narrative experiments, came to operate not only as the treasured materials and psychological souvenirs of childhood, but as metonymic of childhood itself.

The Arabian Nights and Fantasies of the Self

It has often been noted that nineteenth-century recollections of childhood encounters with the Arabian Nights functioned as sentimental tributes to the simplicity and naivety of youth, and to childish fancies that are quickly outgrown in maturity. Edward Said observes that the Arabian Nights are 'regularly associated with childhood, beneficent fantasies, it is true, but ones occurring in a sense so that they may be left behind'.[38] Robert Irwin has similarly argued that in the work of the Romantic poets and of Victorian writers like Dickens and Brontë, 'the linkage between the stories of the *Nights* and the lost delights of innocent childhood is strong indeed'.[39] Nostalgia is undoubtedly a significant aspect of the presence of these stories in adult memory, as individuals recount their powerful sensory and material engagement with both the texts and the objects of the Arabian Nights as a way of illustrating what was lost in their progression from childhood to adulthood. Nevertheless, it is important to recognise that, despite their continual association with the innocent joys of childhood, the tales of the Arabian Nights were neither written nor translated for children. The proliferation of these tales in British print culture did coincide with the introduction and establishment of children's literature as a distinct, commercial product with a specific target audience. From the 1740s to the 1830s, the number of books written and published specifically for children expanded at an extraordinary rate.[40] However, far from being educational or institutionally approved works in the late eighteenth and early nineteenth centuries, the tales of the Arabian Nights generally belonged, as we have seen, to the more obscured histories of reading and storytelling in the school yard, the nursery, and the study or library into which the curious child intrudes, uninvited and generally unsupervised. The increasingly frequent designation of the Arabian Nights as children's fiction throughout the century, and the emergence of a range of heavily expurgated, selected and bowdlerised versions of the tales explicitly for children, were doubtless in response to the extent to which these tales were already being seized upon by enthusiastic child readers. It was the abiding attraction of the tales for children that led, I would argue, not only to their designation as children's literature, but also to their continued use as metaphors for childhood itself.

The nature of the adult's investment in children's literature, and precisely what constitutes the 'child' of children's literature, are the fundamental questions of Jacqueline Rose's work, *The Case of Peter Pan, or the Impossibility of Children's Fiction* (1984). Rose's argument that all children's literature is, by its very nature, an adult's projected fantasy of childhood posits the socially, culturally and politically constructed identity of 'the child', while illuminating the use of fiction as a means by which adults may produce and affirm that construct. Through a fascinating reading of J. M. Barrie's Peter Pan stories, Rose argues that this kind of writing is not a matter of responding to a child's wants or needs, but rather of responding to the adult's desires regarding what a child is, should be and should know. Children's fiction thus 'sets up the child as an outsider to its own process, and then aims, unashamedly, to take the child *in*'.[41] In those works consciously written by adults for children, the implied reader is an impressionable youth who finds himself or herself subtly manipulated – or, to use Rose's terminology, solicited, chased or seduced – by the text, while the physical child and the mind of the historical child reader remain troublingly inaccessible.

Rose's representation of children's literature as a dynamic space in which adults and young readers may negotiate and define childhood identity is certainly an illuminating approach to works such as *Peter Pan*, but it is significantly complicated by the reading history of the Arabian Nights, and other instances in which the realm of what constitutes children's literature is defined by the reading choices of children themselves. There is, in the above memoirs and accounts, a deliberate adoption of the tales of the Arabian Nights by the children in question, in a manner that resists the figure of the 'conscripted child reader', who is 'forced to read, to read particular texts, and to read in particular ways', whom Matthew Grenby has posited as the norm in the history of reading in Britain.[42] Here, the fantasy of the innocent, delighted child reader drawn to the world of the text still emerges, but it has not been projected by an adult writer who has a vested interest in the nature of the child. Rather, it is projected by the child readers themselves in later, more mature years. This fantasy, too, is not of childhood as it was experienced. It is of childhood as it is remembered, and the remembered reading practice becomes a far more personal, individualised fantasy of the self and its meanings, akin to Valerie Krips's reflection, in a different context, on the special status of the miniature story books of Beatrix Potter:

> This is not the child of childhood, but the child the adult was and is. The child of childhood is an abstract entity, a fantasy of self to which the children's book stands as a metaphor. Potter's little books, which for some grown-up children may have a special place in their individual economy of remembrance, represent a genre that is emblematic of selfhood, and speaks to the adult's past of object relations, and to a fantasy of childhood in which the culture as a whole is implicated.[43]

In memoir and other accounts of childhood reading, the remembered stories and objects of childhood become deeply associated with the adult's own constructed identity. They serve a metaphorical purpose in making claims about themselves, their personality and their aesthetic preferences. More than a symbol of childhood innocence and delight, the colourful, non-linear and unempirical world of the Arabian Nights becomes, in this manner, metonymically associated with childhood itself.

Childhood was, throughout the nineteenth century, increasingly marked as a sphere of existence apart from adulthood, and increasingly made the subject of scientific, medical and philosophical scrutiny. 'We know nothing of childhood,' Jean Jacques Rousseau had declared in the preface to his enormously influential treatise, *Émile, ou de l'Éducation*, published in France in 1762 (and in Britain in 1763).[44] By devoting themselves to 'what a man ought to know, without asking what a child is capable of learning', Rousseau argued that educationalists were imposing their own adult ideals and imperatives upon childhood, and thus seeking to accelerate the child's progression into adulthood by 'always looking for the man in the child, without considering what he is before he becomes a man'.[45] Childhood, however, comprised an existence that was emotionally and psychologically other to that of adulthood. The child, Rousseau declared, 'has its own ways of seeing, thinking, and feeling', and he insisted that 'nothing can be more foolish than to substitute our ways for them'.[46] As Sally Shuttleworth has observed in her study of nineteenth-century child psychology, Rousseau's primary interest here lies not in delineating those ways of seeing, thinking and feeling in any great detail (the later child study movement would devote many hours to that undertaking), but in segmenting and defining childhood simply 'as a space and time that was not adult'. As such, Shuttleworth notes, 'his childhood is a peculiarly empty space', defined largely in terms of what it lacks.[47] Thus differentiated from the rest of the population, the child occupied a mode of existence that was understood to be fundamentally separate from, and yet defined and controlled by, the adult world.

Rousseau's instructions for rearing the fictitious young boy Émile urged the protection not only of the time and space of childhood, but also of the child's supposedly 'natural' state of innocence and purity. A child, Rousseau argued, must not be treated as an already rational human being or a miniature adult. Rather, the young mind should be protected from the influences of reading materials or of formal education, and 'left undisturbed until its faculties have developed' organically, preferably whilst physically removed from the corrupting influences of cities and from society in general.[48] This Rousseauvian model of education, while generally cited and upheld by educational treatises of the late eighteenth and early nineteenth centuries, was a source of great anxiety for Wordsworth and the Romantic vision of the imaginative, sensitive child as source of knowledge and wisdom.

While Rousseau advised that, with the sole exception of Daniel Defoe's *Robinson Crusoe* (1719), a child should not be introduced to any reading material until at least the age of twelve, Romantic poets, including Wordsworth, Coleridge, Southey, Bryon and Shelley, enjoyed repeated readings of the tales of the Arabian Nights in their formative years.[49] In later life, as Tim Fulford has argued, their youthful engagement with, and heightened emotional susceptibility to, the Arabian Nights became 'a constituent element of the Romantic Ideology, that self-mythologization by which the poets distinguished themselves from others in contemporary British society'.[50] As they developed their poetry in the context of a vital interest in Orientalism, the Arabian Nights became a standard by which such figures might define themselves, their art and their aesthetic preferences as acutely sensitive, formally innovative and socially transgressive. Moreover, it seemed, in later constructions of their autobiographical selves, that the creative life of the Romantic poet had developed organically from youthful readings of this intoxicating material. Coleridge's recollection in a letter of 1797 of his discovery of an unidentified, though evidently adult version of the Arabian Nights in his family home at the age of six is testament to its transformative effects upon his psyche:

At six years old I remember to have read *Belisarius, Robinson Crusoe*, and *Philip Quarll* – and then I found the *Arabian Nights'* entertainments – one tale of which (the tale of a man who was compelled to seek for a pure virgin) made so deep an impression on me (I had read it in the evening while my mother was mending stockings) that I was haunted by spectres whenever I was in the dark – and I distinctly remember the anxious and fearful eagerness with which I used to watch the window in which the books lay – and whenever the sun lay upon them, I would seize it, carry it by the wall, and bask, and read. My Father found out the effect, which these books had produced and burnt them. So I became a dreamer.[51]

The affecting tale referred to here by Coleridge is that of 'The History of Prince Zeyn Alasnam', in which the King of the Genii tells the profligate and debauched young Zeyn that, in order to gain a great treasure for his kingdom, he must seek out a beautiful fifteen-year-old virgin who has never once lusted after a man and deliver her unmolested to the island of the Genii.[52] The anxious and fearful eagerness induced in Coleridge by this tale was doubtless in part due to its erotic elements, as the young boy's reading clearly trespassed upon the distinctly adult territories of sexuality and horror. The hero's struggles to subdue his sexual passions for the young maiden he removes from her father's house in Baghdad might well have produced an 'effect' that was alarming to the child's guardian, and prompted the dramatic removal of the works from his household. Such content clearly belongs to those pernicious materials that Rousseau had deemed disruptive to a 'natural' childhood. Coleridge, however, cites this event as the moment when he became a dreamer, deliberately committing himself to the imagination and its fancies.[53] The child's susceptibility to experiences of sensuality, horror and the sublime serves, it seems, a specific autobiographical purpose in his treatment of them as necessary to the later production of his poetry. The Arabian Nights operates as a stand-in, representing the temperament and aesthetic sensitivities of the child in question.

Like Coleridge, Thomas De Quincey also noted that a lasting imprint had been made upon his childhood imagination by the Arabian Nights – in this case, by the story of 'Aladdin' – and he, too, used that experience as metonymic of his childhood self. In the 'Infant Literature' section of his *Autobiographic Sketches* (1853), De Quincey notes the intense dislike he and his sister shared for the tales of Sinbad and Aladdin, which they deemed the worst stories of the entire Arabian Nights collection. After this indication of some kind of communal readership or enactment of the tales within the domestic spaces of his family, however, he identifies a particularly thrilling moment in the story of Aladdin that, in his own words, 'fixed and fascinated my gaze, in a degree that I never afterwards forgot, and did not at that time comprehend'.[54] As he reprises this story, which he claims to have read at the tender age of six (the same year that Coleridge gives for his initial discovery of the tales), it becomes clear that De Quincey's Aladdin was not the usual idle and disobedient young Chinese boy of most nineteenth-century renditions of the tale. Rather, he is a 'solitary infant', an 'innocent' playing on the banks of the Tigris, who finds himself the unwitting victim of an evil magician's plot. In this, as Judith Plotz has observed, De Quincey's 'peculiar and terrifying Aladdin of solitary innocence pursued' has less in keeping with traditional versions of the Arabian Nights than it does with the Wordsworth circle's Romantic reconstructions of childhood.[55] Although unusual, De Quincey was not alone in fashioning Aladdin as a form of Romantic innocent. In *Stranger Magic*, Marina Warner identifies 'a little-known monument of Northern Romanticism', a poetic drama of Aladdin that was written by a young Danish playwright named Adam Oehlenschläger in 1805. Here, a 'Faustian dilemma about the limits of permitted knowledge' is played out between Aladdin, a naturally innocent and wise Romantic child, and the wicked magician.[56]

Although most editions of Aladdin offer no explanation for the magician's motives in employing Aladdin to retrieve the lamp, De Quincey dwells at length upon the nature both of the child and of the terrifying magician who exploits him. Living 'in the central depths of Africa', the magician of De Quincey's account has learned, through his demonic 'secret art', of an enchanted lamp imprisoned in a series of underground chambers that can be released only by the hands of an innocent. The magician's solution to this difficulty is a demonstration of impossibly heightened sensory perception and receptivity as he renders the entire globe an accessible and 'readable' object:

> Where shall such a child be found? Where shall he be sought? The magician knows: he applies his ear to the earth; he listens to the innumerable sounds of footsteps that at the moment of his experiment are tormenting the surface of the globe; and amongst them all, at a distance of six thousand miles, playing in the streets of Bagdad, he distinguishes the peculiar steps of the child Aladdin. Through this mighty labyrinth of sounds, which Archimedes, aided by his *arenarius*, could not sum or disentangle, one solitary infant's feet are distinctly recognised on the banks of the

Tigris. . . . These feet, these steps, the sorcerer knows, and challenges in his heart, as the feet, as the steps of that innocent boy, through whose hands only he could have a chance of reaching the lamp.[57]

It is this conceptualisation of the world as a dizzying sequence of underground tunnels filled with magic and the macabre possibility of live burial that is truly terrifying for the young reader and, according to De Quincey, the discovery of 'the sublimity which [this scene] involved was mysterious and unfathomable'.[58] The subterranean, labyrinthine spaces of the Gothic are suggestive here not only of problems associated with communication, noise and receptivity in the modern world but also of the multiple layers of the mind, and the palimpsest of the child's developing psyche, which in turn reflects the proliferating, mutating network of tales in the Arabian Nights. Patrick Bridgwater has analysed in detail the image of the subterranean chamber as it pertains both to the Gothic genre and to representations of the mind, as a dominant leitmotif in De Quincey's work. In so doing, he explicitly traces its origins to this encounter with Aladdin. Bridgwater even identifies the evil magician who deliberately leaves Aladdin to die in the underground cavern as De Quincey's own 'Gothic (Satanic) self or id' – a repressed figure of guilt and shame.[59] The image of the subterranean cavern will be discussed in greater detail in the following chapter. Certainly, De Quincey himself presents his youthful reading of the tale, or perhaps more accurately, his adult recollection of that reading, as a nightmarish encounter with the Gothic sublime and a critical developmental phase in the life of the imaginative writer:

> It was, in fact, one of those many important cases which elsewhere I have called *involutes* of human sensibility; combinations in which the materials of future thought or feeling are carried as imperceptibly into the mind, as vegetable seeds are carried variously combined through the atmosphere.[60]

Susceptibility to the realm of the Arabian Nights in childhood provides a rich source for the later dreams and writings of the opium eater. It is material that can be consciously and unconsciously drawn upon, re-shaped and re-invented as it merges with the highly subjective and personalised chronology of his autobiographical 'sketches'.

The shifting temporalities of childhood impressions and adult memories are even more complicated because this formative reading experience is not, it seems, from the Arabian Nights collection at all.

Rather, it is highly likely that the young De Quincey's nightmarish encounter with the sublime in 'Aladdin' is a false memory, an adult and perhaps opium-inspired invention. Having reviewed seventy-five versions of 'Aladdin' that were extant during De Quincey's lifetime, Judith Plotz suggests that the memory he recounts here is, in fact, a false one, inspired perhaps by a particular night on Denmail Rise in 1808 during the Peninsular War, when, as De Quincey claims in *Recollections*, he observed Wordsworth laying his ear to the ground so that he might catch any sound of wheels, signifying news from the rim of Europe. For Plotz, the relationship between Aladdin and the magician of De Quincey's account comes to symbolise the relationship between these two Romantic writers.[61] However, the strategic deployment of this possibly false memory in De Quincey's autobiography also points to his use of the Arabian Nights as a means of illustrating his own innocent and highly susceptible childhood character. In this context, the story of Aladdin, as it mutated in his memory, becomes for De Quincey a convenient but powerful metaphor for the Romantic's childhood experience and emergent poetic consciousness.

Such connections between the child and the Orient of the Arabian Nights serve to reflect the broader shifts in Orientalism in Britain that took place during the Romantic period in response to European imperial expansion. During this time, as Saree Makdisi notes, the Orient 'overlapped and gradually fused with other integral processes of modernization', such as modern imperialism, industrial capitalism, evolution, and modern constructs of race and gender, and it produced 'an altogether new discourse on otherness'.[62] As Eastern territories came to be identified more and more with so-called primitive governments, which were perceived as inherently inferior to new forms of European colonial administration, local populations were increasingly regarded as intellectually and morally limited subjects in need of instruction and civilisation. The Orient, in other words, came to symbolise the 'anti-modern', 'a backward, debased, and degraded version of the Occident', and its people were to be treated and controlled like children by their adult European counterparts.[63]

In this historical moment, self-consciously aligning the unconventional childhood of the Romantic poet with immersion in the tales of the Arabian Nights is perhaps a further illustration of those imperial anxieties and instabilities that Nigel Leask has shown to be deeply embedded in the Romantic discourse of the Orient. The 'exotic, composite Orient of the Romantic imagination' is, Leask argues, 'an Orient invested with an uncanny power to disturb'.[64] It is at once familiar and strange, attractive and repulsive, and, like De Quincey's tortuous relationship with opium, it inculcates a growing sense of escapism and dislocation from the modern metropolis, alongside the threat of dependency and cultural, racial and sexual degeneration. Explicitly delineating this tension in relation to the Arabian Nights, Rana Kabbani has noted that 'although Islam continued to be regarded with suspicion and distaste' throughout the century, 'its sublunary aspects as reflected in the *Les Mille et une nuits* produced a passionate desire for additional narrative of this kind'.[65] The Romantic Orient was, in Kabbani's words, 'a sublimated location, with no connection to the Real East'.[66] It was a space of the imagination and of fantasy. Explicitly associating the dangers and the freedoms of that location with the sensitivities and proclivities of youth, I would suggest, located the nineteenth-century child, a figure already in a constant state of physiological change and mental flux, within the realms of the Romantic Orient.

In her study of the emergent field of child development in the nineteenth century, Sally Shuttleworth has noted the comparatively slow emergence of child psychology in Britain within the broader developments of psychiatric and paediatric practice. This, Shuttleworth argues, should not be attributed to a lack of medical or scientific interest in the mental state of the nineteenth-century child, but rather to 'a fundamental uncertainty as to how to define and demarcate the sphere of childhood'.[67] For later evolutionary psychologists, the child remained separate from the adult world and the structures of middle-class Britain, and represented an earlier phase of evolutionary development. The child was, like other supposedly lesser creatures, a more primitive being that had not yet transitioned into adulthood – specifically into white, European adulthood – and thus 'real' humanity. As Shuttleworth observes, this alarming alterity existed at the very core of British social and domestic institutions:

> The figure of the child, I would suggest, lies at the heart of nineteenth-century discourses of gender, race, and selfhood: a figure who is by turns animal, savage, or female, but who is not located in the distant colonies, nor in the mists of evolutionary time, but at the very centre of English domestic life.[68]

Through the figure of the child, which seemingly re-enacted the phases of humanity's evolution in its progression to adulthood, both the distant Orient and the 'mists of evolutionary time' existed within the new temporal structures of industrial modernity. As the English anthropologist Edward Burnett Tylor noted in his 1871 study of *Primitive Culture*, the child, an undeveloped and basic form driven solely by instinct, occupies an almost mythic status as a kind of primordial being in British culture: 'In our childhood we dwelt at the very gates of the realm of myth.'[69] Childhood, in such constructions, is a phase of existence that inhabits a different temporality from the adult world.

Robert Louis Stevenson, exploring the mental condition of the child in his 1878 essay 'Child's Play', similarly conceptualised childhood as a separate phase of existence from the adult world. 'Surely', he declared 'they dwell in a mythological epoch, and are not the contemporaries of their parents,' explicitly situating the adult and child within different moments of anthropological time.[70] This world of childhood is, his essay shows, one of semi-literacy and partial understanding, in which visual images and physical objects have an increased potential to distract and to capture attention. In keeping with Burnett Tylor's suggestion that animism – the personification of inanimate objects and a distinctive mark of 'primitive' psychology – 'makes its appearance as the child's early theory of the outer world', Stevenson emphasises the importance of material objects to the world of the child, and to their processes of making sense of that world.[71] Drawing upon memories of his own childhood, he demonstrates the manner in which the child relates to the world through animism and, in his case, through objects transformed by an early knowledge of the Arabian Nights. He recalls his excitement as a young boy hollowing out calves' feet jelly with a spoon and imagining that sooner or later he would reach the secret golden tabernacle: 'There, might one find the treasures of the *Forty Thieves*, and bewildered Cassim beating about the walls'.[72] Here, the time and space of childhood merge with the Oriental tales. Children, in other words, seemingly dwell within the mythological epoch of the Arabian Nights, and the world of the child is understood in the same manner as the world of the Arabian Nights: temporally and culturally other, primitive and fantastical.

Earlier, in his 1850 essay, 'A Christmas Tree', Dickens describes in considerable detail the child's impressions of his or her immediate environment as an experience of the glittering objects and illusionistic possibilities of the Arabian Nights. Witnessing a 'merry company of children' playing around a Christmas tree in adulthood evokes the author's psychological return to his own childhood Christmases. This introductory, intimate domestic scene is placed firmly within a Western context; not only is it a Christian celebration but Dickens specifies that the house is filled with French tables, domestic furniture from Wolverhampton and 'that pretty German toy,' a Christmas tree.[73] Nevertheless, the succession of toys and objects that fill this remembered space impinge upon the child's consciousness and are read in the same way as the Arabian Nights. They are fantastic and mesmerising:

> Oh, now all common things become uncommon and enchanted to me! All lamps are wonderful; all rings are talismans. Common flower-pots are full of treasure, with a little earth scattered on the top; trees are for Ali Baba to hide in; beef-steaks are to throw down into the Valley of Diamonds, that the precious stones may stick to them, and be carried by the eagles to their nests, whence the traders, with loud cries, will scare them.[74]

The list of magic objects continues as Dickens describes the powers of food, jewellery, live animals and his own nursery toys. The Arabian Nights becomes a dynamic source of meaning-making as, in the eyes of the receptive child, the imagined realm of the stories seemingly manifests itself within their actual world, as everyday objects appear as material relics from the East. It stimulates the imagination and becomes a psychological and material 'reality' that appeals not only to the visual, but also to the auditory:

> When I wake in the bed, at daybreak, on the cold dark winter mornings, the white snow dimly beheld, outside, through the frost on the window-pane, I hear Dinarzade. 'Sister, sister, if you are yet awake, I pray you finish the history of the Young King of the Black Islands.' Scheherazade replies, 'If my Lord the Sultan will suffer me to live another day, sister, I will not only finish that, but tell you a more wonderful story yet.' Then, the gracious Sultan goes out, giving no orders for the execution, and we all three breathe again.[75]

The darkness of a cold English morning filled with blank, white snow emphasises the colour and excitement provided by the Arabian Nights. The time of day, which was popular with Dickens because of its associated potential for confusion between sleeping and waking, not only posits that 'disposition to dreaminess' that has long been associated with the tales, but also facilitates the possibility of crossing between different states of being and different modalities of time.[76]

Within literature, too, we are presented with children whose reading facilitates an ability to cross these temporal boundaries. Jane Eyre's status as temperamentally other within the Reed household (where her cousin uses her reading material as a weapon), for example, is emphasised by her repeated mental escape from the daily realities at Gateshead through the medium of stories. Immersed in her books, Jane feels herself to be free from social restrictions and, we are told, she 'feared nothing but interruption, and that came too soon'.[77] Her choice of reading location plays with the notion of temporary escape into an imagined, magical Orient:

> I mounted into the window-seat: gathering up my feet, I sat cross-legged like a Turk; and, having drawn the red moreen curtain nearly close, I was shrined in double retirement. Folds of scarlet drapery shut in my view to the right hand; to the left were the clear panes of glass, protecting, but not separating me from the drear November day.[78]

There is perhaps something of Scheherazade's seraglio in this liminal space enclosed by red drapes, where wonderful stories are endlessly told but regularly interrupted. As in Dickens's tale, the dreary English afternoon, filled with a 'pale blank of mist and cloud', emphasises the colour and excitement of the world of the Arabian Nights, as well as Jane's episodic psychological movement between the two worlds in search of imaginative relief.[79] The short periods of time Jane devotes to pursuing the Arabian Nights represent the stay of activity and the punctuation of the rigid temporal structures and rules of behaviour at Gateshead with another kind of time: the non-linear time of the childish Orient. It is also a time and space that adults cannot enter, or experience in the same way as a child, but which they none the less continually interrupt.

The Lost Worlds of Childhood

Such was the relationship between the child reader and the Arabian Nights that the Arabian Nights itself was ultimately not other, but fundamental to the formation and understanding of British childhood. In repeatedly representing childish impressions and fanciful thoughts, the tales become representative of that childish state of being, seeing and knowing the world, which is either lost or consciously rejected in the progression to adulthood. An 1819 theatre review in *Blackwood's Edinburgh Magazine* examines this phenomenon with the claim that 'these delightful fictions are never read but in early youth, and never forgotten afterwards'.[80] The Arabian Nights is the 'paradise of our boyhood', an Eden before the fall, and, for this reviewer, the realities of existence and such intoxicating fictions are ongoing impediments to one another:

> About fifteen or sixteen years of age, we begin to cherish a kind of contempt for what then appear to be such monstrous fictions. We learn to 'know better' than to be delighted with them; and, besides, our associations with them begin to stand in the way of our growing intimacy with the actual world in which we live. The next ten years is pretty sure to correct this overweening affection for the realities of life and to throw us back upon our old love. But it is now too late. We have been faithless to both, and both reject us.[81]

According to this trajectory, there is no psychological continuity in the individual life-span; rather, the young adult operates in a coherent and intelligible manner counter to or even against the dynamics of the child's world and psyche, represented by the Arabian Nights. Using the Arabian Nights to signify the unbridgeable gap between child and adult seemingly relates less to the actual content of the tales, which were clearly read in both childhood and adulthood, than to the psychological and emotional state of the child, as opposed to the adult, reader. Not only is childhood a time and space separate from adulthood, but, as a world that is at least in part created through acts of imagination and play, it, like the tales used to represent it, follows different rules and logic from adult realities.

It is for this reason, Robert Louis Stevenson tells us in his 'A Penny Plain and Twopence Coloured', that his grandfather envied his own childhood immersion in the tales:

> I was just well into the story of the Hunchback, I remember, when my clergyman-grandfather (a man we counted pretty stiff) came in behind me. I grew blind with terror. But instead of ordering the book away, he said he envied me. Ah, well he might![82]

Stevenson's terror on being discovered reading this story is suggestive of the child's unsupervised choice of reading materials, as well as his awareness that the story (which recounts the death by choking of a hunchbacked man, whose corpse is subsequently shifted from house to house, repeatedly assailed and disposed of) contains disturbingly adult content.[83] The child anticipates punishment for his transgression, through the forceful circumscription of his imaginary realm by an adult authority figure. However, the clergyman's recognition and envy of the child reader's pleasure not only points to the treasured place that these stories must have held in his own childhood, but also illuminates the degree of distance across which this recognition occurs. The experience of reading the Arabian Nights as a child is, he makes clear, ultimately irrecoverable.

In her analysis of Jean Baudrillard's definition of nostalgia in his *The System of Objects* (1968), Susan Stewart argues that childhood, for Baudrillard, is 'not a childhood as lived; it is a childhood voluntarily remembered, a childhood manufactured from its material survivals', and she compares the resulting mythologised childhoods to the types of collaged personal history contained in souvenir collections like photo albums and scrapbooks:

> The past is constructed from a set of presently existing pieces. There is no continuous identity between these objects and their referents. Only the act of memory constitutes their resemblance.[84]

The mechanics of memory are creative and revisionist, reinforcing the adult's sense of self and the distance and irretrievability of their childhood. Above all, constructions of memory and personal history are always selective and produce a version of reality based upon chosen materials and their associations. While the unconscious mind undoubtedly plays a role in this process, the materials selected must conform to the autobiographical subject being constructed. At the end of the childhood section of the novel, Jane Eyre herself emphasises her mediating role (which is, of course, created and mediated by Brontë) in claiming that her story is not a 'regular autobiography' because 'I am only bound to invoke memory where I know her responses will possess some degree of interest.'[85] Much like Stewart's scrapbook, the narrative of *Jane Eyre* is a sequence of those images and objects Jane chooses to report and reflect upon in the form of a meaningful and accessible temporal sequence. They are self-affirming and give definite form to personal memories.

Given their size and fragility, objects of memory like juvenile dramas, toy theatres, children's books and chapbooks most likely did not survive outside memory and so are not often enduring material relics of childhood like scrapbooks or photographs. Nevertheless, the ephemera of childhood persist in adult recollection and the remembered object functions in a manner similar to the genuine souvenir, which, as Susan Stewart has argued, 'moves history into private time'.[86] It personalises public events and shared narratives, and functions as an important marker within the individual life-cycle: 'The memento becomes emblematic of the worth of that life and of the self's capacity to generate worthiness.'[87] Personal time is measured by and against such precious objects as toy theatres and story books, which are intimately associated with the subjective narrative of a (remembered) past. In this way, Wordsworth's emotional attachment to his yellow chapbook as a material memento of his youth contributes to the wider narratives of origin and development that drive *The Prelude*. 'That time' when he possessed this volume was, the poem indicates, during his period at Hawkshead, when one of his schoolmasters drowned. His excited ownership and reading of some magical Arabian tales are deliberately contrasted to the harsher realities of the rational adult world. The yellow book is a 'precious treasure' that, in adult memory, has come to symbolise an irrecoverable childish naivety, imagination and delight in a fantastical 'promise scarcely earthly'. It is only over time and in memory that such objects accrue meaning and symbolic status. Stewart points to the importance of both narrative and subjectivity in this ongoing process:

> The souvenir replica is an allusion and not a model; it comes after the fact and remains both partial to and more expansive than the fact. It will not function without the supplementary narrative discourse that both attaches to its origins and creates a myth with regard to those origins.[88]

The elusive time of Wordsworth's youth is remembered not as it was, but in light of subsequent events and transformations, and the Arabian Nights assumes an almost mythic status as an object and a text representative of the childish realm of magic and dreams.

Interestingly, Elizabeth Landon's first reading of the Arabian Nights, recollected in intense detail, is also counterpoised by death. Outlining the wonderful 'world of wishes' and the 'dreaming world' she finds within the tales, she goes on to describe the day when, while reading in the woods, she hears a gunshot and subsequently discovers the mangled body of her beloved dog, Clio. This shocking spectacle is an object of horror and of the 'real', and it 'shook to its very foundations my fairy-land'.[89] The nature of magical illusion has been revealed and, she insists, any future reading of the tales will now be influenced by this experience. For Landon, there is an unbridgeable gap between the pleasures of fantasy and any knowledge of such harsh realities:

> The delight of reading those enchanted pages, I must even to this day rank as the most delicious excitement of my life. I shall never have the courage to read them again, it would mark too decidedly, too bitterly,

the change in myself, – I need not. How perfectly I recollect those charming fictions whose fascination was so irresistible! How well I remember the thrill of awe which came over me at the brazen giant sitting alone amid the pathless seas, mighty and desolate till the appointed time came, for the fated arrow at whose touch he was to sink down an unsolved mystery bidden by the eternal ocean![90]

The adult cannot re-capture the excitement of such a first reading but suffers an ongoing sense of loss, incompletion and regret. Landon's nostalgic recollection of a time of lost dreams and wishes parallels Raymond Williams's notion of the 'myth functioning as memory' in his analysis of the literary idealisation of rural England as a pre-lapsarian community.[91] In this instance, childhood itself is the former, pre-lapsed condition; immersion in the Arabian Nights and its non-linear, atemporal culture of fantasies and spectacles represents (at least for adults) an unstructured innocence and uninhibited freedom that can never be fully replicated in later years.

As the Arabian Nights permeated British culture, novelists, dramatists and poets demonstrated a sustained engagement with its complexities of structure and genre, and its multi-voiced narrative content. This was undoubtedly made manifest in their own artistic productions.[92] However, in establishing the Arabian Nights as a special place and psychological experience of childhood, into which only the child may enter fully, this fundamentally unstable collection of tales, despite appearing in numerous versions and editions throughout the nineteenth century, was increasingly simplified and essentialised in narrative allusions and popular accounts. While it was safe to assume that the general reader was familiar with, or 'knew', the Arabian Nights in some form, the specific details of this encounter clearly varied immensely. Therefore, deployed metaphorically as a vehicle to represent Victorian childhood, the physical books, as well as those narrative features that were best known and largely common to the entire corpus, such as the magic lamp, the magic carpet, the treasure trove of the forty thieves and the figure of Haroun Alraschid, came to represent the whole. Just as Jane observes at Gateshead that 'the inanimate objects were not changed; but the living things had altered past recognition', the unchanged volume of tales is a reminder of the passing of time around it and of the reader's developing maturity and inescapable mortality.[93] We see this construction at work, too, throughout the novels of Dickens, for whom, as Michael Slater notes, the Arabian Nights was representative of a wonderful and magical world resistant to utilitarian empiricism, such that 'an ability still to delight as an adult in the wondrous tales that had enchanted one as a child is always a sure sign of a good and kind heart'.[94] When Tom Pinch, for example, beholds 'the rare Arabian Nights – with Cassim Baba, divided by four' in a children's bookshop in *Martin Chuzzlewit* (1844), the memories of this multi-volume collection of tales 'did so rub up and chafe that wonderful lamp within him' that 'he lived again, with new delight, the happy days before the Pecksniff era'.[95] In *A Christmas Carol* (1843), the miserly Scrooge finds himself 'in ecstasy' to discover the figure of Ali Baba visiting the schoolroom, 'wonderfully real and distinct to look at', in a Christmas, significantly, past.[96] In such instances, the Arabian Nights represents an earlier time in life that momentarily disrupts the experience of the present, while emphasising its status as 'other' within the adult world.

In his volume on *The Victorians* (2002), Philip Davis has noted the Romantic conceptualisation of childhood as a moment of 'feeling and imagination prior to both the jadedness of ageing and the scepticism of the times'.[97] What childhood came to represent in this historical moment, Davis argues, 'found a form of its own in the Victorian fairy tale', and he notes in passing that 'the translation into English of the works of the brothers Grimm, of *The Arabian Nights*, and of the works of Hans Christian Andersen in the first half of the century helped create a foundation for the child-writing of the second'.[98] Davis rightly notes the formal, generic links between these texts and the later construction of childhood as a realm of lost innocence and potential. However, I would argue that the very construction of this realm, its rules of existence and its metaphoric associations with the Arabian Nights had further implications for later children's literature, beyond these questions of form. The childhood world that came to be associated with the Arabian Nights, much like the later worlds of Wonderland, Neverland and Narnia, comprises a space apart from, and generally closed to, the interference of adults. It is a world of enchanted objects, magical transformations and flying carpets with its own logic, temporal structures and laws of motion and physics. It is also a world that must be left behind as one grows to maturity. In other words, it was a significant literary precursor to those recurrent magical spaces of canonical children's literature, into which only children may pass.[99]

It is worth noting that Lewis Carroll, J. M. Barrie and C. S. Lewis were all well acquainted with the tales of the Arabian Nights. Carroll's private library included the Reverend George Townsend's revised 1866 edition of *The Arabian Nights' Entertainments*, as well as Robert Louis Stevenson's *More New Arabian Nights* (1885), Charles

Morell's famous imitation of the Arabian Nights entitled *The Tales of the Genii* (1764), and George Meredith's later Oriental pastiche, *The Shaving of Shagpat: An Arabian Entertainment* (1856).[100] Barrie noted that when he was a boy, after reading *Robinson Crusoe*, he purchased a copy of the Arabian Nights for a penny to read with his mother. He was dismayed, however, to discover that 'they were nights when we had paid for knights', and he had 'curled my lips at it ever since', this negative experience perhaps contributing to the later creation of his own dream-like realm, filled with great adventures.[101] Like Barrie, C. S. Lewis insisted upon a childhood aversion to the Arabian Nights, which persisted into adulthood.[102] None the less, he reportedly re-read the tales in order to equip himself for the task of supervising a doctoral thesis at Oxford between 1945 and 1948, which focused on eighteenth-century translations into English from Arabic.[103] As he later explained in a letter to a young child in 1952, Lewis explicitly drew on this reading when he was creating the world of Narnia, remarking that 'I found the name [Aslan] in the notes to Lane's *Arabian Nights*. It is the Turkish for Lion.'[104] In his introduction to *The Arabian Nights in English Literature*, Peter Caracciolo has traced Lewis's references to the tales of the Arabian Nights throughout the *Chronicles of Narnia*, noting his complex allusions to individual stories such as Prince Ahmed and the Peri Banou, as well as his 'implied reminiscences' of more familiar tales like Aladdin.[105] In adulthood, each of these writers, in their turn, (re-)imagined the spaces and places of childhood, creating playful alternatives to an adult-dominated world that reflected the essential emotional and psychological differences between the adult and the child. While the tales of the Arabian Nights were a convenient trope for nineteenth-century poets, novelists and commentators to express the childhood capacity for joy, experiment and imagination, the later realms of Wonderland, Neverland and Narnia were spaces that allowed that capacity free rein.

Spaces of Resistance

As nineteenth-century child readers repeatedly allied themselves with the Arabian Nights, in opposition to the increasingly mechanised, industrialised world and rules of British adulthood, their sphere of existence was disrupted and inhibited time and again by anxious adults. New children's editions of the tales throughout the century were a clear attempt to monitor children's reading more closely and to impose order and moral purpose upon this apparently childish realm of magic. Manipulation of format and content were the principal methods of control. As early as the 1790s, abridged versions of the collection and individual stories within it were being published. Many of these had the explicit intention of harnessing the materials of popular culture and transforming them from sinful indulgences into lessons in virtue and religiosity for children. John Newbery and, later, Elizabeth Newbery were key figures in the production of story books specifically designed for children. These included *A History of Sindbad the Sailor* in 1784 and *Tales from the Arabian Nights* in 1791. In 1790, Elizabeth Newbery published Richard Johnson's *The Oriental Moralist, or the Beauties of the Arabian Nights Entertainments Translated from the Original and Accompanied with Suitable Reflections Adapted to Each Story*, with six engraved plates. Writing with an assumed religious authority under the pseudonym of 'Reverend Mr Cooper', Johnson uses the preface to assure readers that his stories, which he refers to as 'fables', are utterly devoid of any material that might offend even 'the most delicate reader', and that he has altered the content of those tales he has chosen to include in order to 'promote the love of virtue, to fortify the youthful heart against the impressions of vice, and to point out to them the paths which lead to peace, happiness, and honour'.[106]

Despite his claims to the utmost discretion and exercise of moral principles, Johnson has not significantly altered the plot of any of the stories he presents. His volume contains strangulations, poisonings, beheadings, the loss of eyes and limbs, cannibalism, and the illogical punishment and transformation of people into animals by evil genii. The perceived 'offence', then, is not the violent content of the tales or their potential to disturb or upset young readers, but the absence of any kind of moral framework underpinning them. In his brief version of the frame tale, the Sultan's motivation for murdering his new wife each morning is unequivocally condemned by the narrator as gratuitous violence: 'it too often happens, that the passion of revenge unhappily carries us beyond the bounds of justice and humanity'.[107] In order to correct the work's lack of moral direction, Johnson introduces his own reflections at the end of each tale. Thus, we read that 'the history of [the second] Calender furnishes a striking example, that there is no condition in human life, however exalted it may be, which is not exposed to the reverses of fortune', and that Sinbad was continually saved not by chance but by the hand of Providence for, 'into whatever calamities he was thrown, he always resigned himself to the will of God, who supported him in a miraculous manner'.[108] In the imposition of a Western, Christian moral order upon the tales, the figure of adult authority and reason emerges to regulate the potentially sporadic images of childhood and to transform them into meaningful but far more circumscribed narratives.

Discovering and remembering the Arabian Nights in such a format would be extremely different from, for instance, remembering the chapbook editions circulating in the same period. For Johnson, the Arabian Nights is an ill-defined and irrational threat that will potentially corrupt young minds. Children, he insists, must be protected and guided by reason. The infinite magical possibilities invoked by other editions have been severely curtailed by his seemingly evangelical attitude towards religious instruction and the salvation of children's souls. Thus, the Story of Amine, a married woman who allows a merchant to kiss her cheek and is subsequently whipped repeatedly by her enraged husband, becomes a lesson in the avoidance of temptation and the sinful nature of humanity:

> We must not quit this chapter without remarking, that in the Story of Amine the youthful reader will see, what fatal consequences may arise from the most trifling indiscretions. Though there was nothing criminal in any part of Amine's behaviour, yet her conduct in the silk merchant's shop was thoughtless and indiscreet, and was attended with the most serious consequences. I would advise my readers of either sex, carefully to avoid the commission of small crimes, if they wish to shun those of a greater magnitude.[109]

Such attempts to regulate reading material and to guide the child's developing emotional, spiritual and intellectual life point to the psychological stimulation and amoral freedoms associated with the Arabian Nights that are potentially disturbing to adult authority figures. In these tales, the boundaries between lies and fantasies, and between reason and insanity, are often disturbingly blurred. To adults like the Reverend Cooper, the tales represent a fantastical world of magic, imagination and, quite often, illogical cruelty that stands in direct opposition to Western morality.

The Reverend Cooper's attempts to regulate the evolving narratives of the Arabian Nights might usefully be compared to the figure of Mr Brocklehurst in Brontë's novel. Based partly on the historical Reverend William Carus Wilson, who ran Cowan Bridge School when Charlotte attended with her sisters in 1824–5, the evangelical Brocklehurst insists upon the importance of young children saying their prayers and reading the Bible night and morning. The text of the Bible functions in this way as a method of control, supposedly over the child's mind and body, and therefore over her soul. Jane's retort that 'Psalms are not interesting' not only is in keeping with her status as a 'discord' in Gateshead Hall, where she is driven by her childhood passions and imagination, but it also emphasises her tendency to disturb those who exercise power over her.[110] The 'Child's Guide', which Brocklehurst gives Jane to teach her the dangers of telling lies, contains 'an account of the awfully sudden death of Martha G– , a naughty child addicted to falsehood and deceit', and is a further attempt to inculcate good Christian behaviour through narrative engagement.[111]

In his essay 'Mr Barlow', included in his *Uncommercial Traveller* series for *All The Year Round* in 1869, Dickens offered some reflections on what he considered to have been the major influences on his own childhood reading and appreciation of literature. His portrait of Mr Barlow is of an 'instructive monomaniac' and rationalist seeking to implement rigid logic in all matters and to destroy the fantasies of innocent youth, with an 'adamantine inadaptability', with 'all other portions of my life'.[112] Dickens's resistance to the displacement of his 'favourite fancies and amusements' by reason and logic is figured primarily through his celebration of the worlds of the Arabian Nights:

> What right had he to bore his way into my Arabian Nights? Yet he did. He was always hinting doubts of the veracity of Sindbad the Sailor. If he could have got hold of the Wonderful Lamp, I knew he would have trimmed it, and lighted it, and delivered a lecture over it on the qualities of sperm oil, with a glance at the whale fisheries. He would so soon have found out – on mechanical principles – the peg in the neck of the Enchanted Horse, and would have turned it the right way in so workmanlike a manner, that the horse could never have got any height into the air, and the story couldn't have been.[113]

This image of Mr Barlow 'boring' into the Arabian Nights in order to deploy his mechanical principles in a workmanlike fashion draws very explicitly upon the language of industrialisation in order to demonstrate the ways in which childhood fancies are continually threatened and even engulfed by the unromantic structures of adulthood. The fact that it is 'my Arabian Nights' points to Dickens's sense of possession over the tales and the intimate, individualised nature of his connection to them. It is his own sense of childhood identity, with its associated intellectual and imaginative freedoms, that is under attack here, and he responds with declared hatred of his attacker.

In memory, the Oriental world of the Arabian Nights becomes metonymic of both childish fancies and childhood itself. However, as the story collection is dispersed, repeated and altered over time, visions of that past proliferate in the present to create an open-ended model of memory as fluid and organic, much like the genre of endless inter-connected yet self-contained stories that the work itself presents. In adulthood, although the child reader's experience can never be fully re-discovered, the short periods of time devoted to viewing and engaging with the Arabian Nights nevertheless represent a setting aside of adult duties and a celebration of the childishly wonderful. Dickens makes clear this pattern of episodic reading as an escape from a world of industrial, scientific and technological change in his analysis of the 'Manchester men at their books' in an article in *Household Words*:

> The [Manchester Free Library] is crowded in the evening by working men; and their great delight and refreshment appears to consist in an escape from routine life to dreams of romance or peril, in relieving the monotony of toil with tales of battle, shipwreck, or adventure. In a word, the imagination, even in Manchester, refuses to be crushed. The pleasure book most read, during the first six months after the library opened was – the Arabian Nights. The weary warehousemen, mill-hands, and shopkeepers spent their evenings with Haroun al Raschid.[114]

The Arabian Nights, readily available in popular culture throughout the century, represents the stay of activity and the refreshing punctuation of the industrialised time of an intensive working day with alternative temporal structures, and the field of play of the childish Orient. The act of reading these tales becomes almost a badge of honour to Dickens, as, like the fictional Tom Pinch or Ebenezer Scrooge, their ability to delight in them marks these working men as responsive and imaginative.

Dickens's celebration of the endurance of imagination amongst the working classes of Manchester prompts comparison to the fictional working class of Coketown in *Hard Times*, published only a year after the above article. Different kinds of time also stand in opposition to, and interrupt one another, in the workings of Coketown society. The 'deadly-statistical clock' in Mr Gradgrind's observatory measures every second of the day 'with a beat like a rap upon a coffin lid', drawing time and death together to represent the uncompromising industrial efficiency of his utilitarian ethos.[115] Gradgrind's notion of time works through fragmentation and a kind of tabulation that is almost violent in its precision. In this room, we are told, 'the most complicated social questions were cast up, got into exact totals, and finally settled – if those concerned could only have been brought to know it'.[116] In contrast, time, 'the great manufacturer', is 'the greatest and longest-established Spinner of all', and operates more delicately on a much grander scale.[117] It 'made the only stand that ever *was* made in the place against its direful uniformity', working subtly and creatively in the manufacture of 'human fabric' and the weaving of destinies.[118] This is the time of fancy and of the construction and evolution of narrative – that alternative temporal framework so often represented in this period by the Arabian Nights.

We see the deliberate violation of imagination very clearly in the opening pages of the novel, through an explicit reference to the Arabian Nights. When the teacher Mr M'Choakumchild 'went to work on his preparatory lesson', we are told that his method was 'not unlike Morgiana in the Forty Thieves: looking into all the vessels ranged before him, one after the other to see what they contained'.[119] In a very material metaphor that represents education as a kind of physical acquisition, an act of pouring information into a child's mind, the children in M'Choakumchild's class are likened to homogenous empty vessels in need of filling. However, like Morgiana, the clever slave-girl who ultimately murders the thieves hiding in jars in Ali Baba's newly discovered cave by pouring boiling oil on them, this is a very violent process, designed to destroy fancy in favour of logic and reason: 'When from thy boiling store, thou shalt fill each jar brim full by and by, dost thou think that thou wilt always kill outright the robber Fancy lurking within – or sometimes only maim and distort him!'[120] Such a forceful removal of a child's ability to dream is, Dickens is clear, mentally and physically damaging.

Catherine Gallagher, in her study of *The Industrial Reformation of English Fiction* (1985), argues that Dickens uses the concept of 'fancy' to establish a metaphoric connection between the adult working population of Coketown and the Gradgind children as comparable victims of the Gradgrind philosophy. In this sense, the Gradgrind family is a mirror of an exploitative society, its lack of imagination pointing to an extreme state of social crisis:

> [*Hard Times,*] therefore, has an excessively metaphoric style, as well as a metaphoric structure, and its style becomes one of its themes. We are told, for example, that if the little Gradgrinds had been allowed to develop metaphoric imaginations, they might have seen their teacher as an ogre . . . or their schoolroom as a 'dark cavern' . . . . Similarly,

workers with imaginative faculties would be able to see their illuminated factories as 'Fairy Palaces' . . . . But the emphasis on fact in Coketown allows no such fanciful escapes for workers or children.[121]

Gallagher's implication that the novel's working classes are, to some extent, perpetual children who have never developed their imaginative powers highlights Dickens's own case for the fundamental importance of fantasies, like those of the Arabian Nights, within industrial modernity. The harsh realities of a rational, utilitarian world can be relieved by the imagination and the memory of childhood tales and dreams. Reflecting upon the way that Louisa should have been raised by her father, the narrator emphasises the importance in adulthood of the memories of childish fancies:

> The dreams of childhood – its airy fables; its graceful, beautiful, humane, impossible adornments of the world beyond; so good to be believed in once, so good to be remembered when outgrown, for then the least among them rises to the stature of a great Charity in the heart, suffering little children to come into the midst of it, and to keep with their pure hands a garden in the stony ways of this world, wherein it were better for all the children of Adam that they should oftener sun themselves, simple and trustful, and not worldly-wise – what had [Louisa] to do with these? Remembrances of how she had journeyed to the little that she knew, by the enchanted woods of what she and millions of innocent creatures had hoped and imagined; of how first coming upon Reason through the tender light of Fancy, she had seen it a beneficent god, deferring to gods as great as itself; not a grim idol, cruel and cold, . . . what had she to do with these?[122]

The wonderful dreams of childhood nurture a childish belief in the ideal and the fantastic that cannot be sustained in adulthood. Rather, they are held in memory and converted into a kind of spirituality, or 'Charity in the heart,' that celebrates the imaginary while accepting the rational. Imagination is a powerful force in insulating oneself against 'cruel and cold reason', cultivating sympathy and allowing for the possibility of new realities. It is for this reason, I would argue, that Sissy Jupe reads stories from the Arabian Nights to her father between his circus performances, distracting him from his financial difficulties and helping him, at least temporarily, to ward off his depression. To read, to see or to hear the Arabian Nights in adulthood is to be detained and momentarily returned to the emotional, psychological and tactile experiences of childhood or, perhaps more accurately, to a reconstructed, mythologised childhood.

It is almost axiomatic that the act of reading transports the reader – emotionally, psychologically and imaginatively – to other times and places, into other bodies and other lives. Affective, embodied reading facilitates an ongoing exchange between the reader and the text, in which the reader finds his or her emotions stirred and oscillates between distance and closeness, identification and alterity. Ros Ballaster has made such a claim for the transformative powers of reading in the specific context of the circulation of the Oriental tale in Europe in the eighteenth century. Declaring quite simply not only that narrative moves, or migrates, from one culture to another but that 'narrative moves its reader', she elaborates:

> Lovers of the oriental tale talk of being 'transported' into other worlds. They are also 'taken up' by the story, find their emotions stirred; they are prompted to sympathy or revulsion. Stories about shape-shifting or transmigration also 'move' their reader by fostering the experience of imaginary projection into the psyche and culture of an other. [. . .] Fiction makes distinct narrative moves – political, social, emotive – which serve to prompt desired responses in the reader.[123]

Immature, in a state of continual flux or development, and inhabiting a world strictly defined and controlled by adults, the figure of the nineteenth-century child reader was one such lover of the Oriental tale, who was repeatedly stirred, moved and transported into the alternative worlds represented by the Arabian Nights. So frequent was this association that nineteenth-century childhood itself was figuratively and conceptually (re-)located to within the Oriental realm, and understood to share its ways of thinking, seeing, knowing and responding to external stimuli. Childhood reading invested in the Arabian Nights thus rendered that material a distinctive part of the British psyche.

Notes

1. Brontë, *Jane Eyre*, p. 38.
2. See, for example, Robert L. Mack, 'Cultivating the Garden: Antoine Galland's *Arabian Nights* in the Traditions of English Literature' (2008); Patricia Ingham, *The Brontës* (2003); Heather Glen, *Charlotte Brontë: The Imagination in History* (2002); and Muhsin Al-Musawi, 'The Taming of the Sultan: A Study of Scheherazade Motif in *Jane Eyre*' (1988).

3. Makdisi and Nussbaum, 'Introduction', pp. 1–2, 18.
4. Irwin, *The Arabian Nights*, p. 290.
5. Mack, 'Cultivating the Garden', pp. 79–80.
6. Ormond, 'Victorian Romance: Tennyson', p. 326.
7. Marzolph and Van Leeuwen, *The Arabian Nights Encyclopedia*, vol. 2, p. 539. Jalal Uddin Khan also links Jonathan Scott's 1811 translation to Herman Melville. See *Readings in Oriental Literature: Arabian, Indian, and Islamic*, p. 45.
8. For an outline of Jonathan Scott's alterations to the Grub Street translation of Galland's Arabian Nights as a response to 'a changed climate and expectations concerning the representation of the passions', see Ballaster, 'The Sea-Born Tale', pp. 38–40. Scott's translation was, in the words of Robert Irwin, 'the first literary translation into English of Galland's work', and it was widely used as a basis for later bowdlerised and popular editions of the Arabian Nights in English for children (see Irwin, *The Arabian Nights*, p. 22).
9. Stevenson, 'A Penny Plain and Twopence Coloured', p. 218. Gérin, *Charlotte Brontë*, p. 26.
10. Landon, *Traits and Trials of Early Life*, p. 233.
11. Landon, 'Captain Cook', p. 337.
12. Blanchard, *The Life and Literary Remains of L. E. L.*, vol. 1, p. 21.
13. Wordsworth, 'The Prelude', p. 446.
14. Tucker, 'Fairy Tales and Their Early Opponents: In Defence of Mrs Trimmer', p. 107.
15. The Victoria and Albert Museum's National Art Library Catalogue dates the publication of this chapbook to between 1823 and 1852. This has presumably been deduced from the period of activity of the printer at the given address.
16. These illustrations are in keeping with the confusing melange of classicism, pastoralism and Eastern archetypes that, Robert Irwin has shown, filled the pages of illustrated editions of the Arabian Nights throughout the eighteenth and nineteenth centuries. See Irwin, *Visions of the Jinn: Illustrators of the Arabian Nights* (2010).
17. *The History of Aladdin, or the Wonderful Lamp*, p. 11.
18. Galland, 'The Story of Aladdin; or, The Wonderful Lamp', p. 651.
19. Consider, for example, Anon., *Arabian Nights Entertainments Translated into French by M Galland and Now Done into English*, 4 vols, 10th edn (London: Harrison and Co, 1785); and *Arabian Nights Entertainments Translated into French by M Galland and Now Done into English*, 4 vols (London: C.D. Piguenit, 1792). The Rydal Mount List published in *Transactions of Wordsworth Society* also includes Jonathan Scott's *Arabian Nights' Entertainments*, as well as Galland's *Les Mille et Une Nuits* amongst its late acquisitions.
20. For a detailed list of the books read by the Brontë children, see Alexander and Smith, *The Oxford Companion to the Brontës*, pp. 54–6. They do not reference any particular edition of the Arabian Nights.

21. Gaskell, *The Life of Charlotte Brontë*, p. 64.
22. Brontës, *Tales of Glass Town, Angria, and Gondal*, p. 256.
23. Alexander, 'Autobiography and Juvenilia: The Fractured Self in Charlotte Brontë's Early Manuscripts', pp. 155–6.
24. Glen, 'Configuring a World: Some Childhood Writings of Charlotte Brontë', p. 228.
25. In his seminal study, *The History of the English Toy Theatre* (1969), George Speaight traces the emergence of the toy theatre from a range of earlier material forms, including portraits of theatrical figures, children's paintings, and story books with cut-out characters.
26. Stevenson, 'A Penny Plain and Twopence Coloured', p. 217.
27. Ibid. p. 98.
28. Stevenson's own re-working of the narrative materials of the Arabian Nights led to his 1882 story collection, *New Arabian Nights and Other Stories*, discussed in the epilogue to this book.
29. Stevenson, 'A Penny Plain and Twopence Coloured', p. 225.
30. In his detailed appendices, George Speaight lists twelve known juvenile dramas based on 'Aladdin' and fourteen based on 'Ali Baba' produced in the first half of the nineteenth century in London.
31. Dickens, 'The Ghost in Master B.'s Room', p. 28.
32. Both Alraschid and his prime vizier, Giafar, are well-known figures in Islamic history. For a study of the relationship between their historical and fictional representations, see Clot, *Harun al-Rashid and the World of the Thousand and One Nights* (2005).
33. Dickens, 'The Ghost in Master B.'s Room', p. 28.
34. Dickens also drew on the figure of Haroun Alraschid in his mature writing. In *Dombey and Son* (1848), for instance, the titular Paul Dombey, a wealthy owner of a shipping company, is likened several times to a powerful Eastern potentate, and at one point the narrator wryly observes that had his assistant Mr Perch 'called him by some such title as used to be bestowed upon the Caliph Haroun Alraschid, he would have been all the better pleased' (p. 143).
35. The Victoria and Albert Museum's theatre archives date this piece to 1813, which coincides with a performance of Aladdin at Covent Garden Theatre.
36. Stewart, *On Longing*, p. 43.
37. Norcia, 'Playing Empire', p. 295.
38. Said, *The World, the Text and the Critic*, p. 271.
39. Irwin, *The Arabian Nights*, p. 269.
40. Matthew Grenby has provided a detailed study of the origins of children's literature as a distinct branch of British print culture over the course of the long eighteenth century in his study, *The Child Reader, 1700–1840* (2011).
41. Rose, *The Case of Peter Pan*, p. 2.
42. Grenby, *The Child Reader*, p. 9.
43. Krips, *The Presence of the Past*, pp. 39–40.

44. Rousseau, *Émile*, p. 1.
45. Ibid. p. 54.
46. Ibid. p. 54.
47. Shuttleworth, *The Mind of the Child*, p. 5.
48. Rousseau, *Émile*, p. 54.
49. The tutor in Rousseau's *Émile* unequivocally celebrates *Robinson Crusoe* as 'the most felicitous treatise on natural education ever written' and a valuable guide for proper living (p. 147).
50. Fulford, 'Coleridge and the Oriental Tale', p. 215.
51. Coleridge, *Selected Letters*, p. 59.
52. This story, which Robert Irwin has identified as one of Galland's so-called 'orphan stories', so designated because they are not found in any surviving manuscripts of the Arabian Nights, was often reproduced in early-nineteenth-century books and stage adaptations as 'The Ninth Statue'.
53. Allan Grant has outlined the powerful association between childhood, the Arabian Nights and Coleridge's later explications of fancy and the imagination in 'The Genie and the Albatross: Coleridge and the *Arabian Nights*' (1988).
54. De Quincey, *Autobiographic Sketches*, p. 120.
55. Plotz, 'In the Footsteps of Aladdin', p. 122.
56. Warner, *Stranger Magic*, p. 365.
57. De Quincey, *Autobiographic Sketches*, pp. 121–2.
58. Ibid. p. 120.
59. Bridgwater, *De Quincey's Gothic Masquerade*, p. 71.
60. De Quincey, *Autobiographic Sketches*, p. 121.
61. Plotz, p. 122.
62. Makdisi, *Romantic Imperialism*, p. 113.
63. Ibid. p. 113.
64. Leask, *British Romantic Writers and the East*, p. 4.
65. Kabbani, *Europe's Myths of Orient*, p. 29.
66. Ibid. p. 30.
67. Shuttleworth, 'The Psychology of Childhood in Victorian Literature and Medicine', p. 87.
68. Shuttleworth, *The Mind of the Child*, p. 4.
69. Tylor, *Primitive Culture*, vol. 1, p. 257.
70. Stevenson, 'Child's Play', p. 357. Shuttleworth discusses the psychology at work in Stevenson's essay in *The Mind of the Child*, pp. 68–9.
71. Tylor, *Primitive Culture*, vol. 1, p. 258.
72. Stevenson, 'Child's Play', p. 357.
73. Dickens, 'A Christmas Tree', p. 289.
74. Ibid. p. 291.
75. Ibid. p. 291.
76. Dickens was, as Kate Flint has argued, a keen explorer of 'the dialogue between consciousness and world, and the incessant interaction

between the conscious and the unconscious mind', and scholars such as Rosemarie Bodenheimer and Louise Henson have offered compelling readings of his ghost stories in light of this broader cultural context, as illustrative of those possibilities suggested by nervous and bodily disorders and altered or troubled states of mind and body. See Flint, 'The Middle Novels', pp. 34–48; Bodenheimer, *Knowing Dickens* (2007); and Henson, 'Investigations and Fictions', pp. 44–66.

77. Brontë, *Jane Eyre*, p. 9.
78. Ibid. pp. 7–8.
79. Ibid. p. 8.
80. Anon., 'Notices of the Acted Drama in London', p. 320.
81. Ibid. pp. 320–1.
82. Stevenson, 'A Penny Plain and Twopence Coloured', p. 218.
83. Caracciolo notes that Stevenson's use of the word 'hunchback' here suggests that he was reading a version of Galland's translation of the tale. Elsewhere, however, Stevenson uses vocabulary from the translation of the British Orientalist Edward Lane. See Caracciolo, 'The Shakespearean Nights of Robert Louis Stevenson', p. 21.
84. Stewart, *On Longing*, p. 145.
85. Brontë, *Jane Eyre*, p. 83.
86. Stewart, *On Longing*, p. 138.
87. Ibid. p. 139.
88. Ibid. p. 136.
89. Landon, *Traits and Trials of Early Life*, pp. 234–5.
90. Ibid. pp. 233–4.
91. Williams, *The Country and the City*, p. 43.
92. On the influence of the Arabian Nights upon the formal structure, genre, motifs and narrative content of eighteenth- and nineteenth-century British fiction see, for example, Caracciolo, 'The House of Fiction and *Le Jardin anglo-chinois*' (2004), which appears in a special issue of *Middle Eastern Literatures* that traces the movement of the Arabian Nights more broadly from culture to culture, and from language to language. Also in this vein, see Irwin, 'The *Arabian Nights* and the Origins of the Western Novel' (2013); Mack, 'Cultivating the Garden' (2008); and Ballaster, 'Playing the Second String' (2013).
93. Brontë, *Jane Eyre*, p. 228.
94. Slater, 'Dickens in Wonderland', p. 133.
95. Dickens, *Martin Chuzzlewit*, p. 65.
96. Dickens, *A Christmas Carol*, p. 31.
97. Davis, *The Oxford English Literary History*, p. 338.
98. Ibid. p. 338.
99. For a detailed study of metaphorical and physical spaces and locales in children's literature, see Cecire et al. *Space and Place in Children's Literature* (2016).

100. Lovett, *Lewis Carroll Among His Books*, pp. 317, 298, 216, 209. As evidence of Lewis Carroll's engagement with the Arabian Nights, William A. Madden has noted that the structure of the Alice stories, with their tales within tales and doors within doors, resembles the formal structure of the Arabian Nights cycle. Borges also posited the influence of the Arabian Nights upon the multi-layered dream structure of *Sylvie and Bruno*. See Madden, 'Framing the Alices', (1986); Borges, *Seven Nights*, p. 53.
101. Barrie, *Margaret Ogilvy*, p. 47.
102. Lewis, 'On Juvenile Tastes', pp. 45–51.
103. Lindskoog, *Surprised by C. S. Lewis, George MacDonald and Dante*, p. 21.
104. Dorsett and Mead, *C. S. Lewis's Letters to Children*, p. 29.
105. Caracciolo, 'Introduction', pp. 50–2.
106. Cooper, *The Oriental Moralist*, p. viii.
107. Ibid. p. xi.
108. Ibid. pp. 144, 262.
109. Ibid. p. 210.
110. Brontë, *Jane Eyre*, pp. 33, 15.
111. Ibid. p. 35. Shuttleworth has noted that Brocklehurst's tract is likely to be an allusion to the Reverend Wilson's children's magazine, the *Children's Friend*, which was filled with many tales of children who were struck down dead if they flew into a passion or told lies. See Shuttleworth, *The Mind of the Child*, pp. 61–2.
112. Dickens, 'Mr Barlow', p. 156.
113. Ibid. p. 156.
114. Dickens, 'Manchester Men at Their Books', p. 378.
115. Dickens, *Hard Times*, p. 95.
116. Ibid. p. 95.
117. Ibid. pp. 90–5.
118. Ibid. p. 69.
119. Ibid. p. 15.
120. Ibid. p. 15.
121. Gallagher, *The Industrial Reformation of English Fiction*, p. 160.
122. Dickens, *Hard Times*, p. 191.
123. Ballaster, *Fabulous Orients*, p. 8.

Chapter 2

Underground Palaces and Castles in the Air: The Realms and Ruins of the Arabian Nights

> My admiration for the 'Arabian Nights' has never left me. [. . .] They have had no little influence upon my life and career; for to them I attribute that love of travel and adventure which took me to the East, and led me to the discovery of the ruins of Nineveh.
>
> Austen Henry Layard, *Autobiography*, 1903

In the early chapters of his autobiography, published posthumously in 1903, the archaeologist and politician Sir Austen Henry Layard (1817–94) draws upon the Arabian Nights as a familiar vehicle to represent his own childhood fantasies of wonderful adventures in exotic lands. Citing the story collection as 'the work in which I took the greatest delight', Layard recalls how he became accustomed to spending hours 'poring over this enchanted volume' until 'my imagination became so much excited by it that I thought and dreamt of little else but "jins" and "ghouls" and fairies and lovely princesses'.[1] The use of the Arabian Nights in this context is, as we saw in the previous chapter, typical of the deliberate construction of the autobiographical self as responsive, imaginative and unconventional in nineteenth-century Britain. The Arabian Nights was commonly understood to inculcate a private world of childish responses and imagination while, at the same time, operating as a stand-in for the volatile nature of childhood itself. However, Layard's claim that it was his childhood reading of an unknown single-volume version of the Arabian Nights that ultimately led him in the 1840s to unearth the ruins of the ancient Assyrian city of Nineveh directly links the Arabian Nights of his childhood memory with the histories and the hidden spaces of the ancient East.[2] It is an analogy that firmly draws the fictions of his boyhood into a dynamic and interactive relationship with the developing professional disciplines of archaeology and ethnography.

Drawn to the East by his own imagined relation to it, 'to realise the dreams that had haunted me from my childhood, when I spent so many happy hours over the "Arabian Nights"', Layard's self-conscious search for some kind of manifestation of the Arabian Nights in the East positions those stories not only as a convenient metaphor for his adventures, but also as a source for a unique kind of historical practice.[3] There is, he seems to suggest, an ethnographic, or 'truth-telling' dimension to these tales, which was materially realised during his excavations in the East in the form of extensive subterranean palaces with spectacular bas-reliefs, the colossal statues of winged, human-headed bulls guarding the palace of Ashurnasirpal II (dated to 883–859 BC) and, later, the cuneiform tablets containing *The Epic of Gilgamesh*, which were discovered in the library of Ashurbanipal in Nineveh in 1853. On one occasion, when he found himself floating down the Tigris away from the ancient ruins of Tikrit, Layard wrote, 'I thought that I had never seen anything so truly beautiful, and all my "Arabian Nights" dreams were almost more than realised.'[4] In his own self-reflexive account of his excavations, the remembered dreams and stories from his personal past actively contributed to the recovery of a past civilisation.

If the tombs and crypts of the ancient world were stunning subterranean repositories of the treasures of the Arabian Nights, then it seems that, for Layard, the dynamics streets and marketplaces of contemporary Eastern cities held its characters. He notes in the same volume that, above the ground, the wonders of the Arabian Nights might be beheld across Egypt, Asia and the Middle East, for 'they give the truest, the most lively, and the most interesting picture of manners and customs which still existed amongst Turks, Persians and Arabs when I first mixed with them'.[5] Here again, the tales serve as a kind of historic record, for, Layard insists, those customs are evolving and 'passing away before European civilisation and encroachments'.[6] Because of the childhood reading invested in the Arabian Nights, which, as we have seen, came to understand that material as a distinctive part of the British psyche, these wonderful tales provide the traveller with a narrative template and structure already familiar to British readers. It becomes a means by which one can describe new experiences in strange lands and allow for moments of recognition, surprise and suspense, while at the same time delineating social and cultural differences. Such references to the Arabian Nights were, this chapter will demonstrate, a common rhetorical strategy of nineteenth-century travel writing. As the tales manifested themselves in a variety of social, cultural and political worlds, the dreams, images and fantasies that they contained became intrinsically bound up with the practice of archaeology, geology and ethnography as professional disciplines, while revealing the enduing influence of magic and fantasy within the structures of British industrial and technological modernity.

Excavating the Arabian Nights

Layard's aspiration to unearth the treasures of ancient Assyria formed part of the broader Victorian impulse to penetrate and often to possess the language, histories and material relics of the East. It was an impulse that coincided with the European age of revolutions, which inculcated not only a wave of physical displacement but a general sense of rupture from the past. The past, represented in France by the *Ancien Régime*, was suddenly distant, obscure and provisional. As Republicans endeavoured to erase material traces of history and the monarchy through the destruction of churches, castles and the graves of the kings at Saint-Denis, a new consciousness of periodicity arose, which distinguished historical epochs and rendered history more malleable and contingent upon individual and social memories. Across Europe, this sense of the fragmentation of time was further heightened by the dramatic developments of industrialisation and urbanisation. As trains, factories and steam engines created new concepts of speed and movement, a new feeling of busyness emerged and individuals increasingly found themselves 'stranded' – to use Peter Fritzsche's helpful expression in his study of European perceptions of time and history – in a rapidly industrialising, modernising present that was increasingly disconnected from its own past.[7]

History and memory became increasingly contested categories in this overarching, but strictly European, temporal narrative. As a consequence, access to the past, as Margarita Díaz-Andreu observes in her analysis of the impact of the birth of nationalism upon the practice of archaeology, became a source of prestige and of symbolic capital.[8] Attempts to locate material traces of the remote past flourished in the late eighteenth and nineteenth centuries as British scholars, historians, antiquarians, archaeologists and Orientalists journeyed to Egypt and the Middle East in order to bear witness to, and unconcernedly ransack, the ancient world.[9] Narratives of exploration and discovery abound in the early decades of the nineteenth century, filled with accounts of surveillance, occupation, observation, categorisation, and the removal of newly unearthed buried treasures. In 1812, the Swiss explorer Johann Ludwig Burckhardt unearthed the extensive ruins of Al-Khazneh, an elaborate sandstone temple in the ancient Jordanian city of Petra; in a series of relatively minor excavations in Persia's ancient capital Persepolis, Robert Gordon discovered a stone slab depicting a charioteer in 1811, and in 1826, Colonel John Macdonald Kinneir discovered a stone relief of a sphinx during excavations of the Palace of Artaxerxes. Between 1815 and 1819, the Italian-born Englishman Giovanni Battista Belzoni (discussed at greater length in Chapter 3) located the bust of Ramses II in Thebes, excavated the temple of Abu Simbel in Nubia, where he also located the tomb of Seti I, and found the entrance to the second pyramid of Giza, successfully infiltrating its elaborate underground network.

Alongside these efforts to examine and to claim possession of the past physically, scholars were working to decode and narrate its mysterious messages. In 1822, the French classicist Jean-François Champollion, drawing on the earlier insights of Thomas Young, published the first correct translation of the famous Rosetta Stone hieroglyphs and a guide to the Egyptian grammatical system. The linguist and antiquarian Claudius James Rich mapped the ruins of Babylon in 1813, and in 1818 published his *Memoir on the Ruins of Babylon*, and the Egyptologist Sir John Gardner Wilkinson spent twelve years in Egypt surveying archaeological sites before producing his major work, *Manners and Customs of the Ancient Egyptians* in 1837. Through such labours, the past, a potential source of arcane wisdom, was now physically accessible and able to be reconstructed by nineteenth-century science and, significantly, the exercise of the imagination. Ancient worlds became strangely new and exciting while their material relics made the past both present and tangible, to be apprehended and narrated in very concrete ways.

The excavation site is, by its very nature, a field of multiple temporalities. Descent into the layers of the earth, bands of rock and sediment formed over vast periods of time, allows the investigation of both the geological and the human past. In the movement between surface and depth, the material traces of earlier times are physically (re-)located to the present in the form of unearthed artefacts, relics and ancient ruins. This, as Mike Pearson and Michael Shanks have argued in their work on interpretative archaeology, leads not to a reconstruction of the past, but rather to its 're-contextualisation' within the social, cultural and psychological formations of the present.[10] Nineteenth-century accounts of archaeological expeditions followed this movement through time and re-contextualisation within the narratives and cultural structures of the present. In her discussion of travel narratives and truth claims, Gillian Beer, although chiefly concerned with the voyages of natural historians, has argued that the genre and structure of the non-fiction travel narrative allow the reader to share the traveller's movement into new spaces and times, the experiences undergone, the knowledge attained, and, finally, their return home, to the present. The delivery of the narrative itself affirms the traveller's re-entry into their own culture, a space that is shared by the implied reader. 'After a spell as alien', Beer notes, 'the narrator is again homely, caught into current society's processes of exchange and affirmation.'[11]

There is, as Beer notes, a very long literary tradition of imaginary voyages to strange and distant lands, and she demonstrates the ways in which nineteenth-century natural historians found themselves operating within the rhetorical modes and narrative strategies of that rich tradition. While this existent framework was enabling for travel writers, it was also dangerous because 'such description was easily melded into fantasy and received as playful exaggeration, not controlled observation'.[12] In cases of archaeological expedition, when the sought-for prize was not scientific knowledge but literal treasure, this danger was, I would suggest, even more pronounced. This is because such narratives of exploration, excavation and discovery were informed not only by the imaginary voyages of fiction, but also by the marvellous localities, shifting temporalities, glittering fortunes and enchanted objects of the fairy-tale tradition.[13] The survey of Sir Frederick Henniker's *Notes, During a Visit to Egypt, Nubia, the Oasis, Mount Sinai, and Jerusalem* (1823) in the *Eclectic Review* demonstrates how such diverse modes of literary, geographical and scientific writing might figure in the observer's struggle to articulate the psychological, emotional and material experience of the ancient world's eruption into the present:

> YOUNG ENGLAND is running to look at old Egypt, the sleeping beauty of two thousand years ago, upon whom Time, the great Enchanter, turned the key, when we, a nation of yesterday, were a mere embryo, – our ancestry scattered over the wilds and woods of Germany, or sweeping the Northern seas. All her caverns, and temples, and pyramids have been shut and sealed during the great part of this long interval; and now, behold the charm is dissolved, and the whole of their furniture – gods, mummies, and amulets, are found as they were left, the very colours of the paintings as fresh as ever! Why, what is Pompeii to this spectacle? That is only an exhumated city; but here is a whole country brought to light, after having been invisible to Europeans for nearly a score of centuries.[14]

The temporal variance at work in this narrative is very clear: enchanted, 'Old Egypt' is buried in obscurity, shrouded by darkness and hermetically sealed from the linear chronology and the scientific, technological and cultural contexts of modern, 'Young England'. From the perspective of the European traveller or reader, the world of ancient Egypt is akin to a wonderful castle in a faraway land that has been frozen in time and lies dormant, awaiting the outsider's discovery. It is the passive, feminine 'Sleeping Beauty' of fairy tale, and the power to dissolve the charm and re-animate this ancient culture clearly lies with Britain's virile, male archaeologists and Egyptologists.[15]

The journey from Britain to Egypt is represented in this narrative as an outward movement of temporal and magical transformation, which is in some ways comparable to the kinds of anachronistic space identified by Anne McClintock in *Imperial Leather: Race, Gender and Sexuality in the Colonial Contest* (1995) as a regulatory function of Victorian culture. The ideological inflections of this passage from West to East, from imperial centre to conquered peripheries, derive, McClintock argues, from prominent Victorian theories of evolutionary progress, which produce a global history of discontinuous cultures from the privileged perspective of a European 'Ur-narrative'.[16] However, the archaeological expedition is also a journey underground, a search for hidden depths and structures, which promises the recovery of lost knowledge, access to the past stages of all human development and, potentially, to the geographical origins of the human race. These enclosed spaces are, therefore, deeply entangled in the construction of Western – and, indeed, global – history and identity. In this sense, the East–West binary is disrupted by a potentially narcissistic movement inwards, for the purposes of self-reflection and self-discovery.

If we consider Layard's own rather grandiose account of his excavations in his best-selling work, *Nineveh and Its Remains* (1849), it is clear that, from the outset, his expedition involved a fascinating amalgamation of the factual, the fictional and the collectively and individually remembered. Layard's primary intention was to unearth a vast, unknown realm that he had previously encountered only in his dreams and in the tales of the Arabian Nights. He wrote of his first evening at the excavation site:

> Hopes, long cherished, were now to be realised, or were to end in disappointment. Visions of palaces underground, of gigantic monsters, of sculptured figures, and endless inscriptions, floated before me. After

forming plan after plan for removing the earth, and extricating those treasures, I fancied myself wandering in a maze of chambers from which I could find no outlet.[17]

In his nervous excitement before the dig, Layard's focus was not upon the ancient city of Nineveh as a once-populated, socially and culturally meaningful urban space, but upon the intricate maze of tunnels and trenches beneath the earth. It is these unseen spaces that captivate his imagination, offering the potential for wonder, horror, death and the attainment of material wealth. The boundaries between the dream realms of his childhood and the material structures that have lain buried for centuries become increasingly fluid and confused, as Layard populates these underground spaces with visions of palaces, monsters and sculptures. The unstable, continually mutating collection of stories comprising the Arabian Nights becomes a kind of imaginative template for the archaeologist's drama of discovery, articulating the processes of excavation and the vast, ancient realms that are now to be opened to the modern world.

Following this model, the *Edinburgh Review*, reflecting in 1888 on the potent connection between European travel writing and childhood reading in Britain, suggested that readers of the Arabian Nights would be irresistibly drawn to Layard's work, and would find both his rhetorical mode and his material discoveries strangely familiar:

> The record of Sir Henry Layard's early adventures ... will greatly interest all those whose imaginations, like his, have been excited by visions of the renowned cities of the East, called up by the early and engrossing perusal of the 'Arabian Nights', and whose curiosity in maturer years has been stirred by the narratives of travellers, few and far between, of buried cities, of strange monuments, of inscriptions in an unknown character.[18]

The similarity between the narrative forms of the Arabian Nights and Layard's travel writing not only enables a similar imaginary projection of the reader into other spaces and times, but also induces certain generic expectations in the reader regarding the archaeological expedition, the physiological and sensory experience of the journey underground, and the materials to be discovered. Actual and imagined voyages, real and imagined cities, become blurred as the underground cavern emerges as a site of memory and of dreaming, as well as a materially realised repository of ancient relics.

Like the wonderful findings and buried treasures that pervade accounts of nineteenth-century archaeological excavations, the tales of the Arabian Nights are filled with rich interiorities and immense, underground caverns. Within the enclosed space of the sultan's bedchamber, which is itself nightly filled with Scheherazade's wonderful tales, vast realms are continually opened up to, or indeed infiltrated by, outsiders. Aladdin famously descends into a cave, which leads him on to a large, vaulted underground palace divided into three great halls, each filled with treasures of intense and beautiful colour: 'The white were pearls; the clear and transparent, diamonds; the deepest red, rubies; the paler, bastard rubies; the green, emeralds; the blue, turquoises, the purple amethysts; and those that were upon the yellow cast, sapphires, &c.'[19] Ali Baba one day comes upon a band of forty thieves as they alight at the entrance to a cave, opening its stone door with the magic words 'Open Sesame'. Ali Baba later enters the cave, noted in Galland's version to have been 'cut out in the form of a vault by men' by the same means, discovering 'all sorts of provisions, and rich bales of merchandizes, of silks, stuffs, brocades, and fine tapestries, piled upon one another, and, above all, great heaps of gold and silver, and great bags, laid upon one another'.[20] In 'The Story of Prince Ahmed and the Fairy Pari Banou', the titular prince performs a similar movement through the earth. Pursuing the path of his arrow, Ahmed descends through a small aperture in the rock face to discover the fairy palace of Pari Banou, the daughter of one of the most powerful and distinguished of genii. He had at first thought, we are told, that he 'was going into a dark obscure place', but presently 'a quite different light succeeded that which he came out of, and entering into a large spacious place' he 'perceived a magnificent palace'.[21] When Zeyn Alasnam ascends the throne of his father in 'The History of Prince Zeyn Alasnam' (discussed in relation to Coleridge in the previous chapter), he has a series of dream-visions, the last of which shows him that there is an underground cavern filled with treasure beneath his own palace. On waking, Zeyn Alasnam finds concealed subterranean vaults within his father's former chambers, which house numerous urns filled with gold, and eight statues each cut from a single diamond and mounted on pedestals of solid gold, with a ninth pedestal left empty. This prompts his journey to recover the final, greatest treasure for his collection.

Physical movement from above to below ground becomes, in such tales, the point at which adventure and fantasy begin. Occupying the threshold to an unknown subterranean world, the caves open out on to new kingdoms, new landscapes and new spatio-temporal fields of play. This movement, it must be noted, is not always one of wonder and delight, for descent into the underground can quickly become the stuff of nightmares. This is made clear during the fourth voyage of Sinbad the Sailor, when the shipwrecked protagonist is buried alive in a deep pit alongside the corpse of his recently deceased wife, for local custom in this distant kingdom dictates that a spouse must be immured with his or her partner when they die. For some time, Sinbad survives by killing and eating the still-living partners of the dead as they are dropped into the pit, before he eventually escapes via a small opening in the cavern through which, he discovers, a sea-monster periodically enters to consume the fresh bodies it finds. Infiltration of an underground cavern leads to carnage, too, in 'The History of the Third Calender', when the young Prince Agib descends through the crevice in a rock face only to discover and accidentally to slaughter a young boy who has been confined in a subterranean dwelling in the attempt to thwart the prophecy that he will die at the hands of a man named Agib. It is within the dark reaches of such caves that the bizarre, the surprising and the macabre take place.

The use of caves as sites of emotional and imaginative investment is, of course, far from unique to the tales of the Arabian Nights. For centuries, the cave has operated upon the imagination as a provocatively dark, obscure space filled with mystery.[22] From at least the time of Greek and Roman mythology, caves have consistently provoked fear, awe and religious dread, as they were frequently supposed to be populated by gods and demons, monstrous beings and the spirits of the dead. Homer's *Iliad* and *Odyssey* and Virgil's *Aeneid* feature many journeys to such worlds. 'Men in all times and in all countries', reflected *Chambers's* magazine in 1880, have tended to 'regard anything in the shape of a cavernous opening in [the earth's] crust with superstitious awe.'[23] The author conjectures that it is for this reason that, in the 'multitudinous fairy tales in all countries', caverns become the 'homes of goblins, gnomes, and other beings with whom we made early acquaintance in those golden hours when a fairy tale had a bright reality'.[24] Arguing that caves have consistently represented the pleasures and dangers of the unknown throughout history, the article turns by way of illustration to a familiar collection of tales:

> Let us take, for instance, the *Arabian Nights' Entertainments*, and see how constantly caverns are employed to give colour to its wonderful pages. What would the story of Aladdin be without its cave of jewels?

> Where too would Ali Baba have obtained his riches, if he had not stumbled upon that wondrous cavern with its magic pass-word? Would not the story of Sindbad have lost somewhat of its charm if the travels of that remarkable voyager had all occurred on the upper earth?[25]

The caves of the Arabian Nights are regions of charm, colour, mystery and romance, to which both the tales' characters and, by extension, ourselves as readers descend from the realities of the upper earth into fantastic spaces, physically and imaginatively held apart from daily life.

In the nineteenth century, as geology, palaeontology and archaeology emerged as new scientific disciplines, the interior conditions of the globe became the subject of intense scrutiny, and the act of journeying underground drew ancient and continuous stories of prehistoric monsters, mountainous landscapes and lost worlds and civilisations into a new popular scientific discourse. The fusion of emergent scientific practice with mythology and spectacle resulted in what Ralph O'Connor has termed the 'romance of Geology' in Victorian England, which, he claims, by 1846 was often likened to the Arabian Nights.[26] Exploring the use of poetry and spectacle in the promotion of popular science, O'Connor shows that geology's success owed much to the literary techniques of its authors, as scientists popularised their theories and discoveries by way of a dramatic *mise-en-scène*. It was in their 'literary productions – in books, journals, magazines, and newspapers – that these geologists and their followers reached most of their increasingly variegated public'.[27] It was their capacity to stir readers' imaginations through spectacle and sensation while remaining within a scientific frame, thus, 'eliciting wonder without compromising the "factuality" of their claims', that ensured the success and circulation of works such as John Mill's *The Fossil Spirit: A Boy's Dream of Geology* (1854), the London educational publisher John Darton's *The Little Geologist* (1840), *The Little Mineralogist* (1838) and *Peter Parley's Wonders of the Earth, Sea, and Sky* (1837), and Gideon Mantell's *Wonders of Geology* (1838). According to O'Connor, scientists transported their readers into fantastic realms peopled with monsters and the supernatural, rendering science itself a kind of spectacle by way of mythical and literary allusions. In *The Fossil Spirit*, for example, John Mill introduced the figure of a Hindu fakir, whose supernaturally enhanced memory enabled him to recall the various animal forms he had assumed over time as his soul transmigrated across geological history. In *The Wonders of Geology*, Gideon Mantell deliberately borrowed narrative techniques from the Arabian Nights in order to introduce an ancient extra-terrestrial traveller who had visited the earth in different epochs and reported on all the wonderful changes he had seen. Both texts, O'Connor notes, include this 'mediating (and exotically Oriental) narrative layer' in order to 'enhance the descriptions' immediacy'.[28] Such familiar tropes and aesthetic forms actively constituted the practice of geology and became means of familiarising Victorian readers with the new sciences.[29] They also led on to broader literary explorations of the subterranean: for example, in the later scientific romances of Jules Verne, H. G. Wells, Arthur Conan Doyle and Edgar Rice Burroughs.[30]

The Arabian Nights occupied a significant place within the conceptual structures of early archaeological and geological practice, and the lure of its underground networks and caverns was instrumental in shaping accounts and interpretations of nineteenth-century archaeological digs. In her *Narrative of a Journey Overland from England* (1830), Anne Katharine Elwood, the wife of Major (later Lieutenant-Colonel) Charles William Elwood of the East India Company, explicitly draws on the story of Aladdin to describe an underground chamber in the Valley of the Kings, near Thebes:

> At the head of this valley were the Tombs, and we entered that of King Sesotris, or Amun Mai Ramses, lately discovered by Belzoni, by a steep descent or staircase at the bottom of which was a door. . . . I thought of Aladdin and his cave, as from a painted corridor we passed into a room filled with spirit sketches, and then by another staircase we found ourselves in a large subterranean hall, and a handsome arched room, where stood the alabaster sarcophagus.[31]

In his *Scenes and Impressions in Egypt and in Italy* (1824), the British army officer Joseph Moyle Sherer also used Aladdin to describe the very same tomb in the Valley of the Kings. Uncomfortable with the splendour and the sheer magnitude of the space that had been dedicated to just one man's tomb, Sherer imposes the image of Aladdin's ornate banqueting hall upon the excavated site:

> It really is like a scene of magic; the sudden transition from the naked solitude of the silent, unpeopled, scorching desert, into chambers, all adorned with brilliant and vivid paintings. Is this a tomb? It cannot be. Come, come, Aladdin, rub thy lamp and order supper; these halls are suited to the banquet and the song: but it is a tomb, these are the chambers of the grave – the embalmed body of a monarch lay here once.[32]

The abrupt change in landscape and architecture from the aboveground desert to the underground tomb is made sense of by recourse to a familiar childhood story. For both Elwood and Sherer, descent into the tomb of Sesotris in Thebes mirrors Aladdin's descent into an underground cavern, despite the fact that, at least in Galland's version of the story, this cavern was located 'between two mountains of a moderate height and equal size, divided by a little valley' somewhere in an unnamed province in the Kingdom of China.[33] This shift in geography and cultural context, though potentially disturbing in its projections of a fixed and easily transposed image of the East, is in keeping with the magical relocations and transformations of Aladdin's palace that occur within the story.[34] This is an otherworldly fantasy space that can be exported across the Eastern world to connect and mediate between antiquity and British modernity. It is also a space that encourages certain ways of thinking about the past. The magical possibilities of the ancient Aladdin's palace unearthed in Thebes are now clearly dormant; the 'brilliant and vivid sketches' on the cave walls are only shadows of what they once were and the space is generally one of death and decay, reinforced by the focal point of the alabaster sarcophagus. This 'scene of magic' from a bygone era belongs to a society that can only be partially reconstructed through narratives and its material remains.

In his *Notes, During a Visit to Egypt, Nubia, the Oasis, Mount Sinai, and Jerusalem* (1823), Sir Frederick Henniker – a business-minded antiquity hunter who had been present at the opening of the Soter tomb in 1821 – describes a similar adventure of rather more brazen treasure hunting on a mountainside somewhere 'between Siout and Girgeh', which provides some startling literary and temporal juxtapositions. First, Henniker describes the location in terms of its immediate beauty and the religious significance of its cavernous interior:

> About half way towards the summit is a large quarry or grotto; a few steps onward the path turns down into the heart of the mountain, it presents a romantic crater, in the hollow of which is the cell of Saint Eredy. Saint Eredy is held in great veneration by the Arabs, and in consequence of repeated pilgrimages, the rugged rocks have been worn into a tolerable path.[35]

This sublime landscape with its 'romantic crater' is, I would suggest, reminiscent of the 'deep romantic chasm' in Coleridge's 'Kubla Khan', a place that is both 'savage' and yet 'holy and enchanted', haunted by the 'woman wailing for her demon-lover'.[36] Like that in Coleridge's Oriental fantasy, Henniker's mountainous cavern is a hypnotic dreamscape, a point where the sublime and the human seem to converge. For Henniker, the romance of this landscape is heightened by its association with the religion and history of the East. A site of pilgrimage, the tomb held within the crater is a medium of collective memory in Egyptian tradition and a metonym of continuing, ancient practices. Henniker recognises that it is dedicated to a particular Arabian version of the past and that this past, a source of Old Testament stories, has the capacity to intervene in the present.

As he ascends the mountain, however, Henniker moves from the biblical and the Romantic sublime to Eastern oral traditions, as he actively directs and participates in a scene from the Arabian Nights:

> I climbed to the very summit of the mountain; the Rockham, large vulture, flying round in every direction, and the surface covered with chrystal [sic] here is at once the scene of Sinbad's valley of diamonds and the rock bird. I am as pleased as if I was reading the Arabian Night's Entertainments, and like a child too, load myself with chrystal, till my handkerchief and pockets burst.[37]

In this account, Henniker casts himself as Sinbad, the merchant sailor from Baghdad, who, through a series of accidents on his second voyage, finds himself alone on a desert island in an unnamed sea, in 'a very deep valley, encompassed on all sides with mountains so high that they seemed to reach above the clouds' and 'so full of steep rocks, that there was no possibility to get out of the valley'.[38] That valley is filled with diamonds and Sinbad ultimately escapes with the stolen treasures by way of his own cunning and the help of a giant eagle. Immersing himself in this story, Henniker changes his account from the past to the present tense in order to convey his uncontrollable excitement and his sudden psychological return to a childish state of joy and wonder. He equates his actions in the valley with the act of reading the story in his youth, imagining himself in the place of the Eastern hero and effectively accessing and 'reading' the surrounding landscape like a text. This imaginative projection of himself into an oral tradition and into a fictional body within that tradition creates a complex dialectic: the mountainous landscape surrounding the tomb of Saint Eredy is clearly foreign, yet it is not unfamiliar to Henniker because it belongs to a well-known tale from his own English childhood. His movement through this landscape represents a mode of exchange between individual memories, literary characters and the ancient languages and civilisations of the East.

There is, it must be noted, a troubling imperialist undercurrent to the persistent analogies made between the Arabian Nights and the infiltration of underground caverns. The story of Aladdin, like that of Sinbad, Ali Baba and many others in the Arabian Nights collection, is one of violence, theft and intrigue, in which wonderful treasure troves are discovered and entered by outsiders, often of dubious character, who seize ownership of them for their own material and social gain. The doubled-edged desire to possess and dispossess the East that is embedded in imperialist institutions undoubtedly finds resonance in these narratives at this particular historical moment. Indeed, Shawn Malley's study of the coverage of Austen Henry Layard's exploits in the East, in British newspapers, religious and scientific debates, exhibition halls, theatres and contemporary literary works, in *From Archaeology to Spectacle in Victorian Britain* (2012), is extremely compelling (though rather totalising) in its argument that the story of Victorian archaeology is one of blatant symbolic conquest and imperial expansion. At the same time, however, the complex cultural and intellectual interactions taking place through the use and construction of narrative in these excavated spaces require careful attention because of their discursive power in the development of historical practice, and in the excavation and interrogation of Western cultural identity and memories.

Like the 'real' repositories of minerals and ancient relics being excavated in this period, the Arabian Nights is a quarry, a work of extraordinary fecundity celebrated by periodical writers as a 'rich repository of the splendid and the marvellous', an inexhaustible source of melodrama and a 'well-known source of stage spectacles'.[39] It is a magical fountain of wealth that has the power to effect personal and social change.[40] Wordsworth's description of his childhood version of the tales as a 'block hewn from a mighty quarry' (*The Prelude* V. 487–8), cited in the previous chapter, is a very appropriate metaphor for this infinite source of raw materials that was endlessly 'mined' for stories, facts, magic possibilities and treasured objects throughout the nineteenth century. The underground is a source not only of material goods, but also of many myths and metaphors through which the Western imagination has sought to interrogate and to excavate itself. The following section will take up some of those ways in which physical descent through the layers of earth mirrors a psychological descent through the layers of the mind, and thus a return to the solipsistic realm of childhood and the Arabian Nights.

Buried in the Mind

Sites of excavation unequivocally exposed the geological layers of past epochs to Victorian modernity. However, through references to the Arabian Nights and its associated fantasies of buried treasures, enchanted palaces and supernatural beings, that past became a magical space between history, memory and fiction where different times and narratives might co-exist. The convergence of these different narratives allowed for a moment of 'dipping into' fantasy from the viewpoint of history, in which, as the above examples illustrate, science might partake of literary and popular culture. This moment is made very clear in the *Illustrated Review*'s 1873 presentation of Layard's expedition in Syria as a contemporary re-enactment of the tale of Aladdin. Here, the excavation site is imagined as a 'hinged valve' in the earth, which promises access to magical kingdoms and underground adventures strangely reminiscent of those magical spaces of childhood associated with the Arabian Nights:

> What was thus accomplished was quite as astonishing in its way as the feat of necromancy performed by the magician in the opening of the wonderful story of Aladdin, when in the wilderness, after a few weird incantations, 'the ground slightly shook and, opening, disclosed a square stone of about a foot and a half placed horizontally, with a brass ring fixed in the centre for the purpose of lifting it up!' Virtually it was as if there had been discovered precisely such a hinged valve as that to the realms of Wonderland. There, again, in the midst of the desert, exactly as Aladdin descended into the bowels of the earth, and, after traversing the garden of jewels, came face to face with the geni of the ring and the geni of the lamp, Layard, like another Aladdin, passed through the halls and galleries of the subterranean palaces of Sardanapalus and Sennacherib . . . . He found strewn around him in profusion delicately carved ivory panels, gilt and enamelled; colossal sphinxes hewn out of alabaster; copper mirrors and lustral spoons; trinkets in agate and amethyst and lapis lazuli and cornelian; . . . gigantic and ponderous sculptures, twelve feet high, of winged lions in solid marble, awful looking forms with human faces, crowned with tripled-horned caps or tiaras, and having their pedestals and the slabs around them covered all over with mystic inscriptions in the antique wedge-shaped, arrow-headed, or cuneiform character.[41]

The range of figures evoked throughout this passage suggest that Layard's descent into the earth is a movement not only from surface to depth, but also from present to past, from history to folklore, from the physical to the psychological, and from the known to the unknown. Journeying beneath the earth in search of buried treasures, Layard discovers the lost palace of Sennacherib, the King of Assyria from 705 to 681 BC, and, in a move from the historical to the mythological, that of the legendary figure of Sardanapalus, who supposedly lived in the seventh century BC in a state of decadence. The actual and the imagined are increasingly confused as these discoveries are explicitly set within the narrative frame of Aladdin, allowing the author to adopt the persona of the storyteller Scheherazade and to draw upon that tale's use of wonder, magic objects and weird incantations in order to illuminate the physical and sensory pleasures of this underground space.

The archaeologist's passage into an excavation site that is also a kind of Aladdin's palace posits the practice of archaeology itself as a mode of recovering and reconstructing not only the distant past, but also the individual's childhood experiences. Archaeology is, in this sense, a wonderful 'adventure underground' with the capacity to unearth past, or repressed, knowledge and experiences. This is emphasised in the above passage by the deployment of yet another narrative frame: like the curious young Alice falling down the rabbit hole, Austen Henry Layard has found a physical portal to 'the realms of Wonderland', another dream realm associated with childhood where time and logic follow different rules.[42] Lewis Carroll's *Alice's Adventures in Wonderland* (1865), which, significantly, was originally called *Alice's Adventures Underground*, was published eight years before the above review, and it deliberately utilised a potent archaeological metaphor in suggesting Alice's movement from consciousness to unconsciousness – her 'falling' asleep – as a literal fall through the rabbit warren that opens out into Wonderland.[43] The cave, or the rabbit hole, represents the threshold between waking and sleeping, for just as the relics of ancient civilisations are buried within the layers of the earth, so, it seems, the contents of the psyche are preserved within its depths. Conflated with the magical spaces of both Lewis Carroll's Wonderland and the Arabian Nights, the practice of archaeology facilitates a deeply self-reflexive exploration of both the ancient East and the Western self, as the two become increasingly entwined.

Archaeology, as Julian Thomas has argued, took shape within the conceptual frameworks of Western modernity, and the discipline has provided an extremely potent series of metaphors for evoking notions of the repressed, the subconscious, the stratification of the mind and the drama of psychological discovery, each of which is 'often spatialised in terms of the relationship between depth and surface'.[44] In *Archaeology and Modernity* (2004), Thomas has demonstrated that the historical emergence of the discipline of archaeology, widely understood as being concerned with 'uncovering and revealing structures and artefacts that have been hidden for centuries', was connected to fundamental shifts in the character of knowledge, which drew attention to the hidden structures underpinning reality, and led to the development of structural thought in the nineteenth and twentieth centuries.[45] Moreover, archaeology 'provided a metaphor through which that thought could articulate itself'.[46] Sigmund Freud's own fascination with archaeology and his ongoing collection of prehistoric and classical artefacts have been well documented.[47] Archaeology, like psychoanalysis, was figured by Freud as a potential mode of recovering and reconstructing the individual's childhood, the distant past, the mysterious and the mythic. As Donald Kuspit has observed, the distinctions that Freud made throughout his career between 'surface and depth, manifest and latent, adult and infantile, civilised and uncivilised, historic and prehistoric', in his descriptions of the mind as a series of psychic layers built up within the individual from childhood, explicitly drew upon the language of archaeology.[48] However, Thomas shows, drawing on the work of Frederic Jameson, that these affinities were also apparent before Freud, in such diverse contexts as the identification of organic functions, economic forces and linguistic structures.

Literary explorations of the darker recesses of the human psyche in this period are, of course, most readily apparent in the Gothic mode, in which fictional expeditions into haunted houses, castles, dungeons, cloisters, caves and crypts become physical manifestations of psychological operations. The Gothic, as Jarlath Killeen has noted, is 'the literature of hesitation and hyphenation', and it is a particularly apt form to use to explore dissolutions, crossings and mergings.[49] Here, boundaries are crossed and binaries are disrupted, as the buried or forgotten past refuses to remain fixed, and erupts instead into the present in order to expose the repressed desires, fears and fantasies of the modern British subject. At times, it is an analogy that is explicitly connected with imagery from the Arabian Nights, as the workings of the mind are made manifest through allusion to familiar childhood tales. Thomas De Quincey, as we saw in the previous chapter, drew on the labyrinthine spaces of the Gothic in exploring his childhood memories of Aladdin and reflecting upon the return of this material in his later writing. In Mary Shelley's *Frankenstein* (1818), the ambitious young scientist describes his great moment of realisation, when he first became capable of 'bestowing animation upon lifeless matter', in terms of darkness, light and underground passageways. This discovery was not, he insists, 'like a magic scene' that 'all opened upon me at once', but rather the identification of a new way of directing his intellectual endeavours. Seeking to explain the workings of his mind at this moment, Frankenstein refers to Sinbad's moment of live burial during his fourth voyage. 'I was', he explains, 'like the Arabian who had been buried with the dead and found a passage to life, aided only by one glimmering and seemingly ineffectual light.'⁵⁰ The notion of live burial here points, perhaps, not only to the bodies that Frankenstein steals and operates upon in order to conduct his experiments, but also to the latent recesses of his own mind, which he must reach into in order to re-direct himself and, figuratively, to find the correct path away from the realm of the dead.

Later, in Mary Elizabeth Braddon's *Lady Audley's Secret* (1862), the eponymous, bigamous heroine, who was abandoned by her husband when he left to seek his fortune in Australia, and then worked as a governess until the wealthy Sir Michael Audley proposed to her, sits in her boudoir to reflect upon her precarious situation. The apartment, we are told, is an 'enchanted chamber', littered with 'fairy-like embroideries of lace and muslin, rainbow-hued silks, and delicately-tinted wools', cabinet pictures, gilded mirrors and 'all that gold can buy or art devise'.⁵¹ Having recently attempted to murder her first husband in order to maintain her new life and conceal the 'secret' of her hereditary insanity, the lady struggles to order her thoughts and to reach any definite conclusions. Here, an allusion to the Arabian Nights offers the reader some insight into her turbulent state of mind:

> She was no longer innocent, and the pleasure we take in art and loveliness being an innocent pleasure had passed beyond her reach. Six or seven years before, she would have been happy in the possession of this little Aladdin's palace; but she had wandered out of the circle of careless pleasure-seeking creatures, she had strayed far away into a desolate labyrinth of guilt and treachery, terror and crime, and all the treasures that had been collected for her could have given her no pleasure but one, the pleasure of flinging them into a heap beneath her feet, and trampling upon them and destroying them in her cruel despair.⁵²

At first glance, the allusion to Aladdin here seems to be a fairly straightforward reference to Lady Audley's sense of wish-fulfilment: just as Aladdin was able to penetrate the underground cavern and utilise its magic objects to become wealthy, Lady Audley has, at least for the moment, successfully effected a material transformation of her life circumstances. Significantly, though, her enchanted boudoir is filled with objects of colonial origin, resonating with the theft and intrigue in the tale of Aladdin, for she has secured her comfort and wealth at the expense of others. Moreover, having lost the youthful innocence and childish outlook that would have allowed her to take pleasure in such a realm, Lady Audley remains burdened by guilt and the horror of her past deeds, as she figuratively loses herself in the labyrinth of an over-active mind, and 'the dark intricacies of thoughts which wandered hither and thither in a dreadful chaos of terrified bewilderment'.[53]

It is worth noting that, more than a passing reference to magical caverns and youthful delights, the Arabian Nights actively informs the unfolding of Braddon's novel. Lady Audley's chief pursuer, Robert Audley, takes on the roles of judge and genie, as his cousin Alicia predicts that he will suddenly re-appear at Audley Court 'like an awkward genie just let out of his bottle'.[54] His part in the novel is that of a capricious spirit, intervening in human affairs and meting out punishments as he sees fit. As he begins to gather evidence against his uncle's new wife, whom he suspects of murder, Robert explicitly aligns himself with the despotic Sultan Schahriar in his vicious complaint against female 'mischief' and its ability to undermine patriarchal structures:

> The Eastern potentate who declared that women were at the bottom of all mischief should have gone a little further and seen why it is so. It is because women are *never lazy*. They don't know what it is to be quiet.[55]

Robert's deployment of the gendered dynamics that drive the frame narrative of the Arabian Nights emphasises, as Nancy Knowles and Katherine Hall have noted, 'the comparison between women's status as oppressed under patriarchy and the status of the colonized under imperialism'.[56] This is underscored, I would suggest, by his association of Lady Audley's victim, George Talboys, with the clearly emasculated 'marble-legged prince in the Eastern story'.[57] The story in question, 'The History of the Young King of the Black-Isles', as it appears in Galland's collection, is a further exposition of female cruelty and infidelity. While tracking his adulterous wife across his kingdom, the titular young King successfully deals her lover an incapacitating wound. In retaliation, however, his wife transforms the lower half of his body into black marble and turns his kingdom into a lake. Such women resist existing power relationships and disrupt class and social structures; in the context of Braddon's novel, they must be overpowered and safely shut away from the world. The initial means by which Robert investigates his new aunt are also telling, as he utilises the secret passageways of Audley Court in order to infiltrate her locked chambers, or her 'little Aladdin's palace' within the house, and examine the relics of her past lives that lie within. This, while inviting a Freudian reading of his act of penetration into the clandestine, female spaces of the house, also points to his forceful intrusion into and excavation of her labyrinthine mind, as well as his ultimate recovery of her repressed past.

In their edited special issue of the *Journal of Literature and Science*, focusing on 'The Nineteenth-Century Archaeological Imagination', Alexandra Warwick and Martin Willis explore 'numerous different kinds of imagining taking place in the widest of engagements with archaeology' in the nineteenth century, often within an already existing cultural imaginary.[58] The Arabian Nights was, I would suggest, one such framework, whose tales of wondrous underground caverns filled with sublime objects provided a familiar cultural narrative through which the processes of archaeology might be communicated. Pursuing the analogy between the Arabian Nights and Wonderland presented by the *Illustrated Review* at the beginning of this section offers us a useful model for conceptualising this physical and psychological movement between history and fantasy, as well as the integration of this fantasy into British modernity. The rabbit hole is, like an excavation site, a physical portal to a temporally other, underground realm, but Carroll's text also posits the psychological notion of dreaming as a kind of portal to an infinite realm that can be endlessly revisited through the simple acts of opening and closing the eyes. When, at the end of the tale, Alice is awakened and has finished recounting her fantastic dream to her sister, the potentially dull 'reality' of their existence continues to be interrupted and mediated by the imagination. Alice's sister is able to share and partake of Alice's dream through narrative, and, once it becomes a communal story, she is able to immerse herself in Wonderland simply by closing her eyes:

> So she sat on with closed eyes, and half believed herself in Wonderland, though she knew she had but to open them again, and all would change to dull reality – the grass would be only rustling in the wind, and the pool rippling to the waving of the reeds – the rattling teacups would

change to tinkling sheep-bells, and the Queen's shrill cries to the voice of the shepherd boy – and the sneeze of the baby, the shriek of the Gryphon, and all the other queer noises, would change (she knew) to the confused clamour of the busy farm-yard – while the lowing of the cattle in the distance would take the place of the Mock Turtle's heavy sobs.[59]

Fantasy and reality are brought into immediate proximity to one another in this very disciplined and self-aware exercise of the imagination. It is only upon awakening that the dream has become 'wonderful' to Alice but, as her sister effectively re-dreams her adventures in Wonderland, she is able to remain partially awake and is therefore in control of the dream, knowing that she has only to open her eyes in order to shift, for example, from the sound of rattling teacups at the Mad Hatter's party to the sound of the shepherd's bells or from the Mock Turtle's sobs to the lowing cattle in the English countryside. As James Whitlark has noted, this kind of controlled dreaming seems for Carroll to achieve an ideal relationship between fantasy and reality, 'neither atoss among the terrors of dreamland nor bored by "dulled reality," but just musing about childhood on a summer afternoon'.[60] The ability to 'hold' and to negotiate this space consciously – literally in the form of a book or, as we will see in the next chapter, in the space of a theatre, exhibition or stage set – and to move in and out of it at will without succumbing to it as one's worldview becomes, I would contend, a sign of British modernity itself. Those who inhabit this illogical and, at times, terrifying dream world cannot escape it, but those who live outside the dream, in a newly scientifically verifiable, rational world, merely visit it and, for that very reason, can negotiate it and own it in ways that perpetual dreamers never will. That the tales of the Arabian Nights feature so many underground spaces, and that archaeology is in itself an adventure underground akin to falling down the rabbit hole, allows each to facilitate this kind of slippage from history into fantasy and back again.

Conflated with Wonderland, the Arabian Nights, itself so mutable, thus becomes not so much a beloved dreamscape as the paradigmatic space of dreaming itself. Though other, Wonderland, like the realms of the Arabian Nights, is at least partly created in the Victorian psyche and we are told that it will be cherished and periodically revisited in later memory. Alice, her sister and their descendants will continue to share their stories and define, take ownership of and enter this wonderful world whenever they choose to do so. The final sentence of

Carroll's tale illustrates the future interpolation of Wonderland into their adult lives:

> Lastly, she pictured to herself how this same little sister of hers would, in the after-time, be herself a grown woman; and how she would keep, through all her riper years, the simple and loving heart of her childhood: and how she would gather about her other little children, and make *their* eyes bright and eager with many a strange tale, perhaps even with the dream of Wonderland of long ago: and how she would feel with all their simple sorrows, and find a pleasure in all their simple joys, remembering her own child-life, and the happy summer days.[61]

This re-imagined and repeatedly retold 'dream of Wonderland' returns the dreamer to the innocence and delights of her youth, but it also actively contributes to adulthood and mediates various familial and social relationships. The time of fantasy and dreams remains other to this existence but it is nevertheless integral to nineteenth-century modernity, as memories of the dream play an important part in creating and sustaining a sense of individual identity and the individual's orientation within their social and cultural environment.

Travellers in an Antique Land

European excavations of the lost treasures and underground palaces of the ancient world were, in reality, not the simple fairy-tale adventures of Sinbad, Aladdin or Ali Baba. Rather, they operated within a context of war and an expanding British Empire. Nineteenth-century Egypt, which was formally independent of European control until the Anglo-Egyptian war of 1882, was a site of ongoing competition between France and England.[62] It was also a nation undergoing radical social, political and economic change. Rather than return to its former, more passive position in the Ottoman Empire in the aftermath of Napoleon's defeat on the Nile, Egypt entered a new phase of industrialisation under the leadership of Muhammad Ali, who came to power in 1805 and ruled until his death in 1848. During this time, Ali, later celebrated as a great innovator and the 'founder of modern Egypt', reformed Egypt's systems of education, agriculture, irrigation and administration; he invaded and conquered Sudan in 1821, fought unsuccessfully against the Greeks in 1827, and defeated an Ottoman army at Nezib in 1839.[63] In *Edge of Empire: Lives, Culture and Conquest in the East 1750–1850* (2005), Maya Jasanoff shows how popular enthusiasm in Britain for ancient Egypt significantly raised the profile of this modernising, imperially ambitious nation, while at the same time deepening the divide between Egypt as a 'site of political and imperial intervention' and Egypt as a mode of entry into the glorious moments of pharaonic past, which were 'increasingly embraced as part of the Western tradition'.[64] There were, at least in the British imagination, two Egypts: the modern world above the ground and the ancient realms below, and each belonged to vastly different times and cultures.

Unlike their archaeological expeditions beneath the surface of Egypt and the Middle East, European voyages above the ground were concerned less with taking possession of material prizes and buried treasures than with occupation, observation, categorisation and control. None the less, despite the clear spatio-temporal, political and imaginative distinctions being drawn between these projects, the Arabian Nights served as a popular narrative framework in descriptions and definitions of both spheres of activity. The collection's ability to cut across ancient and modern worlds derived, I would argue, from its own temporal and structural uncertainty. It is clear that the collection of stories that accumulated within the Arabian Nights tradition was always deeply unstable and culturally and historically diverse. Although the frame story is set in a Persian palace during the Sassanid Empire, which was the last pre-Islamic Persian Empire (AD 224–651), several of the tales are explicitly set several centuries later, in the prosperous Baghdad of the illustrious fifth Arab Abbasid, Caliph Haroun Alraschid (786–809), discussed in the previous chapter, while several others are set in Cairo amongst the common peoples of Egypt. Scholarship by Ulrich Marzolph, Richard Van Leeuwen and Hassan Wassouf, in their extensive *Arabian Nights Encyclopedia* (2004), indicates that these latter Cairene stories probably originated in the medieval period during the Mamluk Sultanate (1250–1517) and were included at a later date, some as late as the eighteenth century.[65] Developed throughout centuries and across regions, the Arabian Nights is a syncretic set of texts, and it features an array of genres, cultures, languages and religions. From its very inception in written form in eighteenth-century France, it was always already world literature. To apply David Damrosch's words, the Arabian Nights is an extremely 'dramatic case of a work that first enters the field of literature only after it has traveled beyond its region of origin'.[66] A continually shape-shifting narrative that celebrates change and diversity, it is inherently diffusive, cross-cultural and trans-historical.

References to the Arabian Nights by European travellers across the East (and, indeed, across various parts of Europe) reflect both the protean nature and temporalities of the stories themselves, and the significant emotional and imaginative investment on the part of the West in those stories. In the *Mirror* in 1825, for example, an extremely verbose description of the city of Damascus and its 'exquisite luxuries', such as coffee houses, beautiful costumes, waterfalls, moonlight and music, includes the declaration that 'if ever the Arabian Nights' enchantments are to be realised, it is here'.[67] It is a potential geographical setting or starting point for the wonderful occurrences of those tales. In 'Mount Arafat and the Pilgrimage to Mekka', quoted in the *Mirror* in 1829, the traveller is suddenly reminded of 'some descriptions in the Arabian Tales of the Thousand and One Nights', when he beholds an Egyptian campsite filled with beautifully embroidered, ornate linen tents.[68] Similarly, the American writer Washington Irving and the artist David Wilkie, 'in their rambles about some of the old cities of Spain', were also, according to the *Mirror*, 'more than once struck with scenes and incidents which reminded them of passages in the "Arabian Nights"'.[69]

Again and again, extraordinarily vivid scenes encountered and reported by travellers in the East recall their past reading experiences in the nurseries of Britain: the bazaars of the city of Isfahan in Iran realise 'many of the scenes so familiar to us in the Arabian Nights'; the tale of a princess threatening to have a confectioner beheaded because he did not put pepper in his tart becomes truly meaningful only when sampling 'the pastry of the East' in Delhi; the colourful sweet stores in Constantinople are believed to be 'like a scene in the Arabian Nights'; and the 'elegant and fanciful creations' within the palace and gardens of Shubra, located a few miles outside Cairo, demonstrate to one writer that 'all the splendour of the Arabian Nights is realised in the Court of Egypt'.[70] In 1823, the *Mirror* provided a lengthy 'Description of an Eastern Caravan', depicting men smoking opium from their pipes, sitting around the fire listening to (unidentified) stories from the Arabian Nights. The author notes that this group both authenticates and performs a scene from the Arabian Nights, even as it listens to those tales:

> Other travellers were smoking their pipes at the door of the Khan, chewing opium and listening to stories. Here were people burning coffee in iron pots; there hucksters went about from fire to fire, offering cakes, fruits, and poultry for sale. Singers were amusing the crowd; Imans were performing their ablutions, prostrating themselves, rising again, and invoking the prophet; and the camel-drivers lay snoring on the ground. The place was strewed with packages, bags of cotton,

and couffs of rice. All these objects now distinct, now confused and enveloped in a half shade, exhibited a genuine scene of the Arabian Nights.[71]

Confronted with the unfamiliar, the traveller makes sense of the scene before him through recourse to a familiar text, extending his memory and reading of a collection of tales to an analysis of social life in an Eastern caravan. In so doing, he deploys a rhetorical mode that allows for rich aesthetic and sensory descriptions while framing the whole as a surreal or confused and dream-like experience.

The tales of the Arabian Nights had force in the social world, in that they were capable of shaping cultural and political relations. Nearly thirty years later, in 1852, an article in Dickens's *Household Words* was far more self-aware in describing the discursive power of the tales to influence and define British constructions, in this case, of India. These potent and very well-known fictions, the article claims, have been so confused with historical truths, and its characters so often conflated with India's existing population, that it almost seems an 'ungracious task' to dispel the fiction with an accurate account of that country's terrible poverty:

> The annals of our kingdom in the East have been written in blood with a pen of gold. They read very like stories from the Arabian Nights Entertainments; and thus many people indulge in the belief that, in India, the population is exclusively composed of caliphs, nabobs, jugglers, rajahs, bankers, fakeers, nautch girls, Brahmin priests, dacoits, and magicians. The name of India is intimately connected with all sorts of wealth and luxury.[72]

The Arabian Nights was clearly a powerful discursive influence in European portrayals of Eastern realms, appropriated for and implicated in historically embedded social, cultural and psychological formations of the nineteenth century.

It is undeniable that much nineteenth-century British travel writing is underpinned by imperialist ideologies, which uphold a system of West/East and male/female binaries. Deployment of the Arabian Nights as a commonplace convention within this genre seems at first to be an instance of what Edward Said has termed the 'textual attitude', which refers to the fallacy that one might 'apply what one learns out of a book literally to reality'.[73] This practice, Said insists, is achieved only at the expense of eliding the 'swarming, unpredictable, and problematic mess in which human beings live'.[74] It is an attitude deliberately inculcated in the reader of Orientalist writings, and one that is instrumental to the imperial and colonial enterprise:

> There is a rather complex dialectic of reinforcement by which the experiences of readers in reality are determined by what they have read, and this in turn influences writers to take up subjects defined in advance by readers' experiences. . . . A text purporting to contain knowledge about something actual . . . is not easily dismissed. Expertise is attributed to it. . . . Most important, such texts can *create* not only knowledge but also the very reality they appear to describe.[75]

Within the Orientalist framework Said expounds, by their claims that the various sites that they visit can be understood in terms of the Arabian Nights, European travellers are effectively using this set of texts not only to create knowledge, but to uphold a static 'reality' that negates the geographical, historical and cultural differences of the East. Beneath the gaze of the European traveller and their reader, the entire Orient, Ros Ballaster notes, 'is telescoped into the confined chronotope of the harem, indeed to the sultana's bedchamber', as, despite Scheherazade's endless propagation of diverting narratives, uniformity and stasis are ultimately affirmed.[76] The story collection was then, in many ways, to use Rana Kabbani's pithy epithet, a case of 'the text as pretext', a means of upholding and disseminating communal European myths about the Orient, which culminated in Edward Lane's version of the tales, discussed in the following section.[77]

The Orientalist's 'textual' attitude, and reliance on a vast body of writing that supported their own, imaginative portrayals of the East is, however, complicated in this instance, firstly by the Eastern origins of the text in question, and secondly by its inherent instability as a reference point. While the travel writers who cite this story collection purport to represent the 'reality' of the East, the Arabian Nights, as we have seen, does not represent a clearly defined, single 'reality'; nor can it 'contain' even itself, as it not only represents multiple forms of time, space and culture, but it exists and is known by these travellers in multiple fragments from various remembered, misremembered or half-remembered versions. As Ros Ballaster remarks in her study of *Fabulous Orients* (2005), the Arabian Nights offers access to continually shifting experiences and histories:

Against the pressure toward a fixed and unified image of the East, the collection can open up difference, diversity, contradiction, and difficulty: a constantly shifting set of tropes of 'easternness' serving many different roles – social satire, attacks on priestcraft, critiques of absolutism and luxury, debates over the female sexuality, explorations of the supernatural, the representation of subaltern experience.[78]

The effect of multiple references to the Arabian Nights, then, is not necessarily one of imposed homogeny. There is also a sense of multiplicity and, Ballaster goes on to suggest, it is an avenue for the pleasurable immersion of the self in the stories and spaces of the East. Like the despotic sultan who becomes so engrossed in his wife's nightly stories that he continually suspends the fulfilment of his violent promise, Ballaster argues, the West's admiration of and receptive desire for Eastern narratives create a sympathetic and imaginative engagement with otherness that implies a sincere disinvestment of the self rather than a uniformly confident expression of imperial ambition.

It is significant, too, that allusions to the Arabian Nights in nineteenth-century travel writings were not confined to journeys in the so-called Orient. In his *American Notes* (1842), for example, Dickens wrote of the rapid fortunes and devastating losses that were made on the New York stock exchange, noting that some of the bankers 'have locked up Money in their strong-boxes, like the man in the Arabian Nights, and opening them again, have found but withered leaves'.[79] The vagaries of finance in this city, he is suggesting, are like the magical reversals of fortunes in those tales. In contrast to New York, Dickens noted that, 'to the admirers of cities', Washington is a 'Barmecide Feast', a reference to the imaginary feast served to the beggar Schacabac in 'The Story of the Barber's Sixth Brother', and a symbol of, in Dickens's words, 'a pleasant field for the imagination to rove in'.[80] Of a man encountered on the American railway, Dickens notes, 'the black in Sinbad's Travels with one eye in the middle of his forehead which shone like a burning coal, was nature's aristocrat compared with this white gentleman'.[81] Four years later, in his *Pictures from Italy* (1846), Dickens again used the Arabian Nights as reference point in communicating his experiences, comparing a scene of stately old houses and sleepy courtyards in Avignon to 'one of the descriptions in the Arabian Nights'.[82] In fact, 'the three one-eyed Calendars might have knocked at any one of those doors', Dickens observes, 'and the porter who persisted in asking questions . . . might have opened it quite naturally'.[83] Later, while walking in the city of

Carrara, where men were working to clear blocks of marbles from the Tuscan hills, Dickens observes that 'I could not help thinking of the deep glen (just the same sort of glen) where the Roc left Sindbad the Sailor; and where the merchants from the heights above, flung down great pieces of meat for the diamonds to stick to.'[84] In such cases, then, the tales operate as an organising principle within the traveller's testimonies, through which the range of new and unfamiliar experiences he describes can be understood.

Like Ballaster's, recent studies on nineteenth-century British encounters with Eastern lands and peoples have emphasised the significance of travel writing in reflecting and exposing a more fragile, open or insecure British self. Jonathan Lamb, for example, has analysed the competing constructions of British identity evident in accounts of European explorations of the South Seas; Linda Colley's work on British relationships with India and North Africa in the two and a half centuries preceding its imperial expansion reveals its smallness and vulnerability; and Nigel Leask has emphasised the highly unstable discourse of curiosity in the Romantic obsession with 'antique lands'.[85] While understanding the imperial undercurrents of nineteenth-century travel writing is essential to any informed analysis of the genre, it is increasingly being recognised that the formal properties and structures of these narratives, as well as their intersection with other dominant categories such as gender, race, class and religion, call our attention to potential disjunctions between different literary and cultural–political forms, as they overlap, but also interrupt and alter one another. The uneasy relationship between the literary, social and cultural–political forms in which the Arabian Nights was mobilised throughout the nineteenth century is, I would suggest, illustrative of Caroline Levine's recent position on 'strategic formalism'. Levine's call for a social criticism that addresses the 'cultural–political field' as a site 'in which literary forms and social formations can be grasped as comparable and overlapping patterns operating on a common plane' seeks to resist the deployment of 'crude binaries', such as those inherent in Said's 'textual attitude', in favour of locating a web of competing attempts to impose order upon social, cultural and economic worlds.[86] Nineteenth-century travel accounts conveyed through the formal properties, figures and tropes of the Arabian Nights illuminate these kinds of tensions and overlaps, and demonstrate how literary forms can, to use Levine's words, 'participate in a destabilizing relation to social formations, often colliding with social hierarchies rather than reflecting or foreshadowing them'.[87]

This potential for the activation of multiple social hierarchies and tensions was greatly facilitated in the case of the Arabian Nights by the work performed by these tales in the nurseries and school yards of Britain. The frequent claims that various incidents and scenes in Eastern lands 'recalled' to mind, 'realised' or 'reminded' travellers of the Arabian Nights not only support the model of a more uncertain and individualised kind of engagement with the East posited by Ballaster, but also suggest a far more intimate connection with that other, as a trigger to autobiographical memories and the potential recognition of a former, youthful self. In the above examples, travellers describe certain objects, peoples and landscapes that bring to their mind – whether voluntarily or involuntarily – a past time of fictional adventure and romance, as well as the emotional and psychological contexts of that time. The vividness of the experience prompts an intense recollection of the moment in which such a scene or object was first encountered: in Britain, during one's childhood. This is not the magical, amorphous past of ancient civilisations being unearthed through excavation, but the intensely personal, magical past of childhood disrupting a publicly consumed travel story. The public/historical narrative intersects here with both personal memories and Eastern oral traditions.

In 1868, the Reverend Alfred Charles Smith demonstrated the powerful relationship between the city of Cairo and the long-held personal and cultural memories of Western travellers:

> What continually came uppermost in the minds of us all, and I suppose of most of our fellow-countrymen in Cairo, was the strong feeling we had that we were living in the midst of scenes so familiar to us in childhood from that favourite book, the 'Arabian Nights' Entertainments', but never realised till now.[88]

Smith suggests that as his party enters the city, memories of the Arabian Nights and of the child's material encounter with that 'favourite book' of the nursery are brought to the fore by the aural and visual stimuli of the surrounding environment. There is a moment of interaction in which the viewer responds to and is psychologically transformed by his surroundings in a highly emotional experience driven by individually nuanced personal and cultural memories. These are, of course, constructed, extremely self-centred memories, which enable the traveller to experience and to explore the city of Cairo both as an exciting new place and as a vital part of his own identity and development. The social and cultural spaces of Cairo become an imaginative resource that, though unfamiliar, is intimately connected to and reflective of the British self. Thus, the artist and engraver William Henry Bartlett describes his arrival in the 'city of Saladin and of the Arabian Nights' – that is, a city of medieval history and an Eastern oral tradition – in *The Nile Boat, or, Glimpses of the Land of Egypt* (1849).[89] For Bartlett, this is a magical moment in which the dreams and fantasies of the West might be materially realised. Cairo becomes a 'flitting phantasmagoria' with 'creations which, once so fanciful and visionary, seem to kindle into life and reality as we gaze upon every object that surrounds us'.[90] The surrounding objects draw and hold the traveller's fascinated gaze, mediating between their own social, cultural and commercial history in Cairo and the magical histories of their fictional counterparts in European versions of the Arabian Nights.

The emotional encounter with objects and figures from the Arabian Nights is a creative and self-authenticating exercise, contingent upon the traveller's receptiveness to the present and remembrance of the past. The American traveller George William Curtis's work, *Nile Notes of a Howadji* (1856), demonstrates the degree to which travellers might engage in a performance of recollected fiction. Curtis describes 'all the pageantry of Oriental romance quietly donkeying into Cairo' in a theatrical display that includes some very familiar characters:

> Abon Hassan sat at the city gate, and I saw Halroun Alrashid quietly coming up in that disguise of a Moussoul merchant. I could not but wink at Abon, for I knew him so long ago in the Arabian Nights. But he rather stared than saluted, as friends may say, in a masquerade. There was Sinbad the porter, too, hurrying to Sinbad the sailor. I turned and watched his form fade in the twilight, yet I doubt if he reached Bagdad in time for the eighth history.[91]

There is, perhaps, in Curtis's dream-like encounter with these figures, something of the delight of Ebenezer Scrooge, who is thrown into ecstasy when he encounters the figure of Ali Baba visiting the schoolroom in his foreign garments in a Christmas past. Through Curtis's eyes, the social and political realities of nineteenth-century Cairo overlap with the popular and immediately recognisable figures of his own childhood reading. He winks at the man he has cast as Abon Hassan and uses only his first name in a very familiar fashion because, as he says, 'I knew him so long ago' in childhood.

Curtis's choice of stories here is telling. Both tales he references are concerned with the use and power of fiction to verify reality. In 'The Story of Sinbad the Sailor', the eponymous hero tells Sinbad the porter a series of unverified, incredible accounts of the seven voyages that led to his material wealth and high social status in Baghdad. Abon Hassan, in 'The Story of the Sleeper Awakened', is given a powerful sleeping potion by the disguised Abbasid Caliph Haroun Alraschid and, on awakening, he is fooled into believing that he has somehow become caliph himself. In this brief moment, his dreams of wealth and power are apparently confirmed by reality and the wonderful riches that appear before him are clear wish-fulfilment. Abon Hassan's pleasure and amazement are complicated by his confusion between illusion and fact: while all that lies before him is 'real', it has been carefully orchestrated by the Caliph and is, at the same time, a meaningless fabrication. Neither of these stories is set in Egypt, but their use by Curtis suggests his awareness of the convergence of fact and fiction, or fantasy and history, in his account and experience of Cairo. He seems aware of the element of deception contained within the elaborate 'masquerade' he presents to his readers. Abon Hassan, he notes, does not 'play along' by saluting or returning Curtis's mischievous wink, and simply meets his gaze in silence. It is the traveller, not the Egyptian, who willingly participates in the unfolding drama of the Arabian Nights.

Curtis's construction of the Orient as a form of theatre is another much-observed commonplace in nineteenth-century travel writing. When Harriet Martineau travelled up the Nile in 1848, for instance, she wrote that 'one had to rub one's eyes to be sure that one was not in a theatre' for 'it was like a sublimated opera scene'.[92] A *Household Words* article on 'Old Cairo and Its Mosque' in 1851 describes the traveller's sensations as he or she moves through the city in a sequence of disjointed dramatic 'scenes'. These landscapes, it is noted, include a 'succession of palm-groves and white palaces' that 'remind one of many scenes in the "Arabian Nights"'.[93] The city of Cairo seemingly stimulated, mesmerised and entertained its visitors as an open-air theatre of spectacle and illusion. According to Said, the concept of representation is itself intrinsically theatrical and, within Orientalist modes of construction, 'the Orient is the stage on which the whole East is confined'.[94] Derek Gregory observes that in nineteenth-century travel writing, this extended theatrical metaphor 'staged Egypt as an enframed exhibit set up before a privileged audience' and that one of the most popular methods of constructing the exhibit was 'through the illuminated screen of the *Arabian Nights*'.[95]

Such a construction is undoubtedly deeply egocentric in its failure to acknowledge the history of an East that is independent of the traveller's gaze, childhood memories and desire for entertainment. Curtis himself hints at the tension between performance and performer when the man he has cast as Abon Hassan fails in his role as mischievous merchant. We are given no indication of this Egyptian man's true social role and personal history in Cairo; he is simply a trigger for Curtis's own memories and personal history in England. Similarly, *Household Words* notes that beyond the sequence of dramatic scenes leading to the bazaar, the 'only aspect of Old Cairo which visitors usually witness', there are 'many parts of the place which it is not easy to see unless you go with a very positive determination to do so'.[96] This is a world that is difficult to access and even more difficult to understand. The American traveller and novelist Charles Dudley Warner evinces fear of this world in his description of the streets of Cairo as a marvellous masquerade that nevertheless causes unease because 'there is a mask of duplicity and concealment behind which the Orientals live'.[97] For some travellers, such as Edward William Lane, the key to accessing that 'real' life of the Orient was to move beyond celebration of the Arabian Nights as a fictional realm associated with British childhood, by attempting to place the tales more firmly within their historical and sociological contexts.

The Ethnographer's Nights

In the first draft of his unpublished work, 'Description of Egypt', the British traveller, translator and Orientalist Edward William Lane (1801–76) described his first arrival in that country on 19 September 1825. Believing that he was able to move freely and without prejudice from one cultural space to another, Lane assumed the (implicitly patriarchal) authority to lift the veil of secrecy and theatricality that he believed concealed the 'true', clearly feminised Orient:

> As I approached the shore, I felt like an Eastern bridegroom, about to lift up the veil of his bride, and to see, for the first time, the features which were to charm, or disappoint, or disgust him. I was not visiting Egypt merely as a traveller, to examine its pyramids and temples and grottoes, and, after satisfying my curiosity, to quit it for other scenes and other pleasures: but I was about to throw myself entirely among strangers;

to adopt their language, their customs and their dress; and, in associating almost exclusively with the natives, to prosecute the study of their literature.[98]

Lane uses extremely emotional and theatrical language here in order to illustrate his supposedly objective, scientific intentions. The veil is, as Meyda Yegenoglu has aptly demonstrated, a dominant trope through which 'Western fantasies of penetration into the mysteries of the Orient and the access to the interiority of the other are fantasmatically achieved'.[99] Its deployment in this context of the metaphysical will to know is both gendered and deeply sexual, as the all-encompassing veil demarcates a physical barrier between the hidden body of the Oriental woman, figured by Lane as a virginal bride, and the desirous, Western male gaze. In refusing to yield to that gaze, the veiled figure is understood as simultaneously threatening and seductive, an enigma that, when penetrated, may ultimately charm, disappoint or disgust.[100]

Lane believed that immersing himself in this role of bridegroom to an Eastern nation, with all its associated fantasies of penetration and knowing, would make him privy to the most intimate details and realities of Egyptian public and private life. He dedicated two and half years to this performance, living almost exclusively in the Muslim areas of Cairo, wearing local dress and speaking fluent Arabic. His first published work, *An Account of the Manners and Customs of the Modern Egyptians* (1836), is a detailed analysis of what Lane considered to be the finer nuances of nineteenth-century Egyptian society, based upon his own observations and first-hand experiences. It is worth noting, however, that the imagined figure behind the veil continued to elude Lane, and he considered his work to be incomplete because he did not have access to the women-only areas of Egyptian society. To that end, his sister, Sophia Lane Poole, also travelled to Egypt, and in 1844 a collection of her writings from this period, selected and edited by Lane, were published as *The Englishwoman in Egypt: Letters from Cairo, Written During a Residence there in 1842, 3, and 4*.

There was, however, another form of cultural immersion and role play that Lane believed could afford the same degree of insight into and intimate knowledge of Eastern life, including its provocative female spaces. This immersion was not physical, but imaginative, with the potential none the less for movement, process and acts of creation and identification. In the preface to *Modern Egyptians*, Lane provides a short survey of the literature on Egypt currently available to the British reading public in English. Noting a dearth of adequate and accurate information in this field, he suggests that there is a hitherto unappreciated yet extremely rich source of ethnographic data on the Egyptian people:

> There is one work, however, which presents most admirable pictures of the manners and customs of the Arabs, and particularly of those of the Egyptians: it is the 'Thousand and One Nights', or Arabian Nights' Entertainments: if the English reader possessed a close translation of it with sufficient illustrative notes, I might almost have spared myself the labour of the present undertaking.[101]

Unlike his predecessor, Antoine Galland, for Edward Lane, the Arabian Nights was no mere entertainment destined for the nursery. Rather, the stories told by Scheherazade to divert the Sultan were serious sociological documents for studying the manners and customs of the East. This had certainly been the view of the British civil servant in India, Henry Torrens (1806–52), who noted in the preface to his own translation of the tales in 1838 that he had rendered the Arabic in English as literally as possible, for his object had been less to give 'the incident of a tale' than 'the manners of a people'.[102] Lane evidently concurred with such an object, although he was convinced that the Arabian Nights did not represent multiple geographical locations and cultures, but that it was a specifically Egyptian tradition. As he wrote in the copious notes accompanying his own translation of the tales, it is in Egypt especially 'that we see the people, the dresses, and the buildings, which [the Arabian Nights] describes in almost any case, even when the scene is laid in Persia, in India, or in China'.[103] There is, Lane is suggesting, a profound historical 'truth' about Egypt that is so deeply embedded in this collection of stories that one might read either a 'close translation' of the Arabian Nights, or his own study of *Modern Egyptians*, to almost equal effect as scientific studies of Egyptian culture.

The notion that the Arabian Nights was a potentially valuable source of cultural information was, in fact, quite well established by the early nineteenth century and, as Rana Kabbani has observed, it was 'one manifestation of the quest for the historical origins of the tales' in this period.[104] As Leila Ahmed has shown in her biography of Edward Lane, the supposed accuracy of the representations of Eastern life that filled the pages of the Arabian Nights had been 'proclaimed on the work's title-page almost since the *Arabian Nights*' first appearance in England', and it was frequently emphasised in prefaces and introductory essays to the many versions of the tales appearing in the early nineteenth century.[105] A piece entitled 'On the Tales and Fictions of the East' in the *New Annual Register* of 1812 similarly reflected upon the different kinds of encyclopaedic knowledge that might allegedly be gained from the stories:

> By the perusal of the Arabian Nights' Entertainments, ... we obtain, in a manner the most impressive on the memory, and the most pleasing to the mind, a perfect insight into the private habits, the domestic comforts and deprivations of the orientals; we are led to participate in their favourite amusements, and acquire a knowledge of their religious sentiments and superstitions: and it thus happens that a boy who has been indulged in the perusal of these ingenious fictions, is made as well acquainted with the peculiarities of oriental manners, and of the tenets of the Mahomedan faith, during the time of relaxation, as he is, during his school hours, with the customs and mythology of the Greeks and Romans.[106]

As noted in Chapter 1, the wonderful events of the Arabian Nights generally occupied childish moments of imaginative play outside the official hours and structures of British education. However, in adult memory, these fictions became as valued and authoritative a source of information on the East as the history texts that had been studied during school hours. The tales are at once entertaining and educational, or, in the words of the *London Magazine*, 'brilliant and faithful', a veritable '*granary* in themselves', which is 'ever new – ever wondrous'.[107] Story and history, and the actual and the imagined, thus inform and are brought into tension with one another, in the attempt to place the collection within a clear historical and ethnographic framework.

This volatile convergence of fantasy, memory, magic and ethnography is readily apparent in the series of studies that comprise Lane's *Modern Egyptians*. As its title suggests, *Modern Egyptians* focuses almost exclusively upon the people of Egypt. In its more than 600 pages of detailed description, there is only a very brief outline of the physical layout and architectural structures of Cairo, and this is mainly confined to the introduction. No map of the city is provided, and of the 130 illustrations, very few are images of streets, houses or mosques, none of which is identified by name. Instead, despite his ethnographic intentions, Lane presents an almost de-historicised exhibition space filled with movement, gestures and colourful experiences. Opening with studies of domestic Arabian life, Lane provides illustrated accounts of men and women bathing, praying, eating, gathering for meals, and performing the various daily tasks of running a household in Cairo. In each instance, close attention is paid to the movements of the body, its clothing and adornments, and the social status communicated by its position in relation to other bodies. From these intimate domestic interiors, which are nevertheless usually pictured without walls or any other marker of space, Lane moves on to discussing the flow of people in the public areas of the city. Here, his focus is on parades, funerals, bridal processions and religious festivals – seemingly undifferentiated masses of people who behave in seemingly uniform ways. Finally, Lane turns his attention to studies of specific individuals who are nevertheless unnamed types, such as snake-charmers, scribes, dancers, jugglers and storytellers.

In the illustrations accompanying *Modern Egyptians*, the city itself is reduced to a mere backdrop, or stage set, and sometimes it is entirely absent (see Figures 2.1, 2.2, 2.3 and 2.4). Throughout this work, it is the people, or perhaps more accurately the characters, who inhabit and move through the streets of Cairo that are important. They confirm Lane's fantasies of the city as a kind of public exhibition space or a mass, improvised performance of the Arabian Nights. For Lane, the Arabian Nights is not simply a reflection of Egyptian life; rather, life in Egypt imitates and illuminates the Arabian Nights. Thus, when describing the characteristics attributed to genii, an 'intermediate class of beings between angels and men' who may inflict irrational punishments upon a whim and must therefore be continually placated, he notes that 'these customs present a commentary on the story ... in which a merchant is described as having killed a gin'nee by throwing the stone of a date which he had just eaten'.[108] Similarly, he observes that 'very curious measures, such as we read of in some of the tales of the "Thousand and One Nights," were often adopted by the police magistrates of Cairo to discover an offender', and he quotes directly from a passage in the Arabian Nights in order to elaborate upon social attitudes surrounding a second marriage.[109]

Lane clearly intended his own translation of the Arabian Nights and his studies of Egyptian culture to be mutually illuminating. His translation firmly embeds all the tales of the collection within nineteenth-century Cairo by the inclusion of extensive and detailed notes relating them to the various customs and practices he had observed during his travels. The meticulous detail of these notes was such that they were later published by his grand-nephew, Stanley Edward Lane-Poole, as an independent collection of essays. In his biography of his great-uncle, Lane-Poole wrote that by taking on this major translation project, Lane was determined to render the Arabian Nights 'an

The Realms and Ruins of the Arabian Nights   97

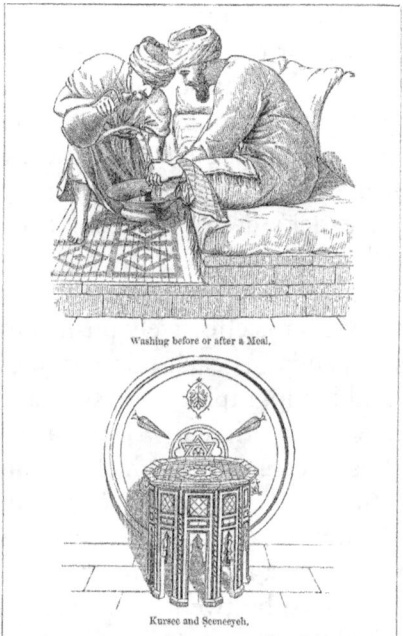

Figure 2.1 'Washing Before or After a Meal'. Edward William Lane, *An Account of the Manners and Customs of the Modern Egyptians*. London: John Murray, 1871, p. 181. Courtesy of the Bodleian Libraries, The University of Oxford.

Figure 2.2 'A Party at Dinner or Supper'. Edward William Lane, *An Account of the Manners and Customs of the Modern Egyptians*. London: John Murray, 1871, p. 182. Courtesy of the Bodleian Libraries, The University of Oxford.

Figure 2.3 'Dancing-Girls'. Edward William Lane, *An Account of the Manners and Customs of the Modern Egyptians*. London: John Murray, 1871, p. 88. Courtesy of the Bodleian Libraries, The University of Oxford

Figure 2.4 'Whirling Darweesh'. Edward William Lane, *An Account of the Manners and Customs of the Modern Egyptians*. London: John Murray, 1871, p. 153. Courtesy of the Bodleian Libraries, The University of Oxford.

encyclopaedia of Arab manners and customs', and the result was certainly encyclopaedic in both scale and format: over 1,000 pages of translation, annotation and commentary organised into distinct and complete chapters.[110] By removing the divisions imposed upon the work by Scheherazade's nightly interruptions, Lane dramatically altered the fundamental structure of the tales. No longer driven by narrative suspense or by the sultan's/reader's desire for resolution, the work becomes an anthology of Eastern stories continually dissected and disrupted not by Scheherazade, but by Lane himself. The impending fate of the clever young storyteller is effectively pushed to the margins in favour of Lane's own agenda, as each tale becomes an opportunity for cultural critique and ethnographic analysis. Lane believed that what was 'most valuable in the original work' was its 'minute accuracy with respect to those peculiarities which distinguish the Arabs from every other nation, not only of the West, but also of the East', and he sought to demonstrate this accuracy in his notes.[111] The collection's frame story, for instance, is presented by Lane in fifteen pages, but it is then followed by twenty-seven pages of explanatory notes dealing with such matters as the principal tenets of Islam, the duties of a devout Muslim, rituals of prayer, fast-giving, pilgrimage, alms-giving and cosmography. When a male child is born in 'The Story of Noureddin and his Son', Chapter 4 in his first volume of tales, Lane provides a six-page essay about the relationship between Islamic doctrine on child-rearing practices, celebratory feasts, the ritual sacrifice of animals, traditions surrounding family names, the power hierarchies of the traditional Islamic family, the ways in which children were protected from supernatural powers, and cultural attitudes towards fertility, circumcision, education and child-rearing.

Edward Said has written that Edward Lane's 'uninspired' and rather insipid translation of the Arabian Nights 'consolidated the system of knowledge inaugurated by *Modern Egyptians*' and allowed his individuality to disappear entirely 'as a creative presence', together with 'the very idea of a narrative work'.[112] For Said, Lane's version of the Arabian Nights transformed that collection from an unstable and proliferating narrative to a static, 'monumental form of encyclopedic or lexicographical vision' that typified the Orientalist will to power over the Orient.[113] Certainly, the desire to define and delimit Egyptian culture is palpable throughout Lane's study. In many ways, he 'bores' into the Arabian Nights like that 'instructive monomaniac' Mr Barlow, discussed in the previous chapter. However, the tales themselves, while altered, are not entirely subsumed or rendered mute by an overtly ethnographic project. Rather, what emerges, as

Jennifer Schacker-Mill has noted, is an ongoing formal and structural tension between the translated text of Lane's Arabian Nights, and the accompanying 'countertext' of his extensive commentaries. This structure, Schacker-Mill argues, exhibits a genuine fascination for the place of storytelling, magic and the imagination in the Eastern culture that Lane believed had produced the Arabian Nights, while his detailed annotations provide a 'metalevel commentary for the translated tales in which storytelling and fantasy emerge as signs of Egyptian otherness'.[114] Here, as in the archaeological expeditions to Egypt and the Middle East discussed above, the convergence of story and ethnography facilitates the possibility of 'dipping into' fantasy, and the time and space of the Oriental tale, from the viewpoint of British imperialism. In other words, Lane's readers might be imaginatively transported into the realms of the Arabian Nights and, with the help of Lane's commentary, be able to negotiate those realms from the perspective of British industrial and technological modernity and its emerging scientific disciplines of archaeology and ethnography, before returning to their own social and cultural structures.

This narrative, readerly motion of transportation, exploration, adventure and safe return, augmented by new knowledge and experience, posits a rather more complex model of cultural entanglement and cross-fertilisation than any simple binary between fantasy and history, or between the rational and irrational, allows. In many ways, it is a model of self-discovery and self-reflection, pertaining less to the history of the Middle and Near East than to the imagination and dreams of Britain itself. The Arabian Nights was not valued in the Arab world at the time of Galland's translation, nor during its proliferation and diffusion in British culture throughout the nineteenth century. Lane himself notes in *Modern Egyptians* that recitations of tales from the Arabian Nights were extremely rare in Cairo, and he attributes this to the scarcity of copies of the work available in Egypt at the time.[115] In fact, recent scholarship indicates that it was the vigorous interest in the tales in Europe that led to the belated attention paid to them by Arabic scholars of the twentieth century, such as Suhayr al-Qalamawi.[116] According to C. Knipp, 'the obscurity and humble status of the work' were such that if Galland had not acquired and translated the tales, the Arabian Nights 'not only might never have become well known to westerners, but also would remain despised, little known, and unread in the Arab countries'.[117] Lane's translated stories, then, are not so much a sign of Egyptian otherness, as they are symptomatic of the absorption of Eastern narratives by the West, and the potency of the tales in British memory and imagination.

Interestingly, this movement between fantasy and history, or magic and realism, which is facilitated by the structure of Lane's text, was also deliberately engineered by George Eliot in the opening of her first novel, *Adam Bede* (1859). Famously, the novel begins with Eliot stepping forward in the character of author:

> With a single drop of ink for a mirror, the Egyptian sorcerer undertakes to reveal to any chance comer far-reaching visions of the past. This is what I undertake to do for you, reader. With this drop of ink at the end of my pen, I will show you the roomy workshop of Mr Jonathan Burge, carpenter and builder, in the village of Hayslope, as it appeared on the eighteenth of June, in the year of our Lord 1799.[118]

This anti-realistic moment of sorcery, which seems markedly at odds with Eliot's broader realist project, is in fact a direct response to her reading of the works of Edward Lane. Lane's *Modern Egyptians* contains a lengthy description of a magician conjuring the past in just such a manner, from a single drop of ink. Eliot's own notebooks record the moment in Lane's text: 'I asked the magician whether objects appeared in the ink as if actually before the eyes, or as if in glass, which makes the right appear left. He answered, that they appear as if in a mirror.'[119] Taking up this practice at the start of her first full-length novel, Eliot's narrator adopts the guise of an Egyptian sorcerer and storyteller, who is busily creating a world, and thus lends a magical, fantastical frame to the realist narrative that follows.[120] Much has been written on Eliot's brand of literary realism, but it is worth reflecting here on her explicit introduction of magic and the imagination at the outset of her narrative. Rather than bringing history and fantasy into conflict with one another, she seems to be presenting the act of writing as a form of conjuring that is itself powerfully affective: it affects the reader, and it answers a moral purpose in terms of accessing, representing and engaging sympathetically, in this instance with the ordinary lives of the people of Hayslope.

The faculties of the imagination, as Marina Warner writes in her reflection on the persistence of magical thinking in contemporary Western societies, 'are bound up with the faculties of reasoning and essential to making the leap beyond the known into the unknown'.[121] Not only, Warner adds, is the one faculty intimately associated with the other, but imagining something can 'and sometimes must precede the fact or the act'.[122] It was in this manner, as this chapter has demonstrated, that the imaginary voyages and adventures of the Arabian Nights profoundly interacted with actual voyages above and below the ground in Egypt and the Middle East throughout the nineteenth century, and, indeed, with the realist structures of British fiction. The tales provided familiar forms of expression, and a shared language with which to structure and articulate new experiences, while also prompting moments of recognition and recollection, as well as repulsion and disavowal.

The Arabian Nights, which was so often associated with childhood dreams and imagined experiences, was explicitly positioned as a precursor to the adult structures of reason and enlightenment. None the less, those structures, as the poet and essayist Leigh Hunt observed in his 1840 review of Lane's translation, rather than 'putting an end to all poetry and romance', had revealed a world as filled with magic and undetected energies as the jinn-filled romances of the Arabian Nights. What, Hunt asked, 'do you know of the thousand and one causes of the unknown and invisible world which is as close as the air you breathe?'[123] There is, Hunt insists, an enduring kind of magic in the adult world, which informs adult processes of thinking about the physical laws of nature, the elements that comprise the globe, and the new technological developments of the period. Such is the 'pervasive, magical thinking' that Warner has argued is 'structural to naming and language, ideas of self and property, and to visual representation'.[124] It was such magical thinking, the *Dublin University Magazine* indicated in an 1837 review of Persian and Turkish poetry, that inculcated an ongoing openness to the magical possibilities represented by Aladdin's lamp:

> Imagination feels averse to surrender the paramount jewel in the diadem of its prerogatives – a faith, to wit, in the practicability of at some time or another realizing the Unreal. . . . [S]o long as the Wonderful Lamp, the dazzler of our boyhood, can be dreamed of as still lying *perdu* in some corner of the Land of Wonders, so long must we continue captives to the hope that a lovelier light than any now diffused over the dusky pathway of our existence will yet be borne to us across the blue Mediterranean.[125]

The 'Wonderful Lamp' in this passage becomes metonymic of the world of the Arabian Nights in its entirety. It is magical; it is an eruption of the supernatural into the everyday; it is a source of knowledge; it effects dramatic transformations; and it has an active agency upon its users and readers. Such a world holds an irresistible fascination for the Western reader, who does not want to relinquish fully, to the emergent disciplines of science, history, archaeology or ethnography, the potential meanings and possibilities of Eastern exploration above or below the ground. It was this ongoing interaction between history and fantasy that, I will argue, underpinned the construction and celebration of artificially re-created Oriental spaces within Britain, described in the following chapter.

Notes

1. Layard, *Autobiography*, vol. 1, p. 26.
2. Layard in fact mistook the ancient city of Nimrud for Nineveh, and the city was incorrectly identified in all his excavation publications. It was the French Consul in Mosul, Émile Botta, who later began excavating the actual site of Nineveh, which was located just across the River Tigris from Nimrud, in 1842.
3. Layard, *Autobiography*, vol. 1, p. 102.
4. Ibid. p. 325.
5. Ibid. p. 27.
6. Ibid. p. 27.
7. Fritzsche, *Stranded in the Present* (2004).
8. Díaz-Andreu, *A World History of Nineteenth-Century Archaeology*, p. 11.
9. For a detailed account of the diversity of interests and practices amongst these groups, and the professional ascendancy of the figure of the archaeologist, see Levine, *The Amateur and the Professional* (1986).
10. Pearson and Shanks, *Theatre/Archaeology*, p. 11. Pearson and Shanks are very vocal advocates of the so-called post-processual archaeological practice, which approaches the discipline as both physical and creative process, reliant upon subjective interpretation and the construction of incomplete narratives about the past. In other words, the meanings of the unearthed material object are always culturally embedded. For works on post-processual archaeological practice, see, for example, Tilley, *Interpretive Archaeology* (1993), *Material Culture and Text* (1991) and *Metaphor and Material Culture* (1999); Thomas, *Time, Culture and Identity* (1996); and Hodder, *The Meaning of Things* (1989) and *Reading the Past* (1986).
11. Beer, *Open Fields*, p. 55.
12. Ibid. p. 56.
13. For a broader analysis of the variety of literary forms and visual media through which travel records were conveyed in this period, see Henes and Murray, *Travel Writing, Visual Culture and Form, 1760–1900* (2015).
14. Anon., 'Notes, During a Visit to Egypt, Nubia, the Oasis, Mount Sinai, and Jerusalem', p. 1.

15. Many writers alluded to the tale of Sleeping Beauty (which was first published by Charles Perrault in his *Histoires ou contes du temps passé* in 1697) in discussions of the excavation work that was being conducted at Pompeii during the nineteenth century. For detailed examples of this trend, see Zimmerman, *Excavating Victorians*, pp. 108–12.
16. McClintock, *Imperial Leather*, p. 37.
17. Layard, *Nineveh and Its Remains*, vol. 1, p. 25.
18. Anon., 'Early Adventures in Persia, Susiana, and Babylonia', p. 519.
19. Galland, *Arabian Nights' Entertainments*, p. 659.
20. Ibid. p. 766.
21. Ibid. p. 834.
22. For a brief overview of the persistent presence of caves in fiction, myth and legend throughout history, see Steward, 'Caves in Fiction', pp. 421–4, and Steward, 'Folklore, Myth, and Legend, Caves in', pp. 321–3.
23. Anon., 'Caves', p. 231.
24. Ibid. p. 231.
25. Ibid. p. 231.
26. O'Connor, *The Earth on Show*, p. 363.
27. Ibid. p. 2.
28. Ibid. p. 366.
29. More recently, Melanie Keene has traced the use of fairy tales, in particular in popular science writing and educational texts for children, in *Science in Wonderland: The Scientific Fairy Tales of Victorian Britain* (2015). Keene identifies fairies, dragons and monsters as entities that provided different means of communicating new and introductory theories in etymology, palaeontology, microscopy and evolution. The Arabian Nights appears in the discussion of L. M. Budgen's *Episodes of Insect Life* (1849) in Chapter 2, which, Keene shows, explicitly draws on the quotidian rhythm of that collection in order to present Budgen herself as a kind of 'Nature's Scheherazade' while illustrating the stories to be found in the natural world.
30. Consider in particular Jules Verne's *Journey to the Centre of the Earth* (1864) and his later work, *The Child of the Cavern* (1877), also known in English as *The Underground City*; H. G. Wells's *The First Men in the Moon* (1901), which features underground exploration of the moon; Bram Stoker's *The Lair of the White Worm* (1911); and Edgar Rice Burrough's *At the Earth's Core* (1914).
31. Elwood, *Narrative of a Journey Overland from England, by the Continent of Europe, Egypt, and the Red Sea, to India*, vol. 1, pp. 195–6.
32. Sherer, *Scenes and Impressions in Egypt and in Italy*, pp. 107–8.
33. Galland, *Arabian Nights' Entertainments*, p. 657.
34. In many versions of Aladdin, the palace is transported from China to central Africa by the magician before Aladdin recovers the lamp and returns it to China.

35. Henniker, *Notes*, p. 107.
36. Coleridge, 'Kubla Khan: Or, A Vision in a Dream', p. 249, lines 12–16.
37. Henniker, *Notes*, p. 108.
38. Galland, *Arabian Nights' Entertainments*, p. 148.
39. Anon., 'Theatrical Journal', *European Magazine, and London Review* (April 1806), p. 289. Anon., 'Theatrical Register', *Gentleman's Magazine, and Historical Chronicle*, p. 672.
40. Interestingly, in keeping with the metaphor of the Arabian Nights as a quarry, at the Great Exhibition of 1851, a display of specimens from a rich copper mine in Burra Burra, South Australia, which 'restored the fortunes of that colony, and rendered it one of [England's] most flourishing possessions', was deemed an 'Aladdin's lamp of a coppermine'. See Tallis, *History and Description of the Crystal Palace and the Exhibition of the World's Industry in 1851*, vol. 1, pp. 52–3.
41. Anon., 'Austen Henry Layard', p. 294.
42. It is worth noting that nineteenth-century visual fantasies of Alice and Aladdin potentially shared a common, contemporary source: Sir John Tenniel, famous for his whimsical and brilliantly comical illustrations of *Alice's Adventures in Wonderland*, contributed a number of engravings to the Dalziel brothers' series of *Illustrated Arabian Nights' Entertainments*, published in the same year.
43. Gillian Beer, in *Alice in Space* (2016), and Robert Douglas-Fairhurst, in 'Working Through Memory and Forgetting in Victorian Literature' (2016), have identified this moment in Carroll's text as the first narrative hint that Alice's experience might be a dream. On the Victorian fascination with the underground more generally, see Douglas-Fairhurst, *The Story of Alice: Lewis Carroll and the Secret History of Wonderland*, pp. 121–4.
44. Thomas, *Archaeology and Modernity*, p. 149.
45. Ibid. p. 149.
46. Ibid. p. 70.
47. For work on Freud's interest in archaeology, see, for example, Paul Ricoeur, *Freud and Philosophy: An Essay on Interpretation* (1970); Sarah Kofman, *The Childhood of Art: An Interpretation of Freud's Aesthetics* (1988); Suzanne Cassirer Bernfeld, 'Freud and Archaeology' (1951); and Donald Spence, *The Freudian Metaphor: Towards Paradigm Change in Psychoanalysis* (1987).
48. Kuspit, 'A Mighty Metaphor', p. 135.
49. Killeen, *The Emergence of Irish Gothic Fiction*, p. 70.
50. Shelley, *Frankenstein*, p. 96.
51. Braddon, *Lady Audley's Secret*, p. 250.
52. Ibid. pp. 251–2.
53. Ibid. p. 256. Certainly, Braddon herself understood the Arabian Nights as belonging to 'the delight of youth', and especially of 'the imaginative child', for whom 'they seem more real than the common things of this

work-a-day world', as she explained in the preface to her own revised edition of Aladdin, Sinbad and Ali Baba, published in 1880.
54. Ibid. p. 280.
55. Ibid. p. 177. Emphasis in the original.
56. Knowles and Hall, 'Imperial Attitudes in *Lady Audley's Secret*', p. 42.
57. Braddon, *Lady Audley's Secret*, p. 211.
58. Warwick and Willis, 'Introduction', pp. 1–2.
59. Carroll, *Alice in Wonderland*, p. 123.
60. Whitlark, *Illuminated Fantasy*, p. 120.
61. Carroll, *Alice in Wonderland*, pp. 123–4. Emphasis in the original.
62. On the Anglo-French rivalry in eighteenth- and nineteenth-century Egypt and India, see Jasanoff, *Edge of Empire* (2005), and Manley and Rée, *Henry Salt* (2001).
63. See Dodwell, *The Founder of Modern Egypt* (1931).
64. Jasanoff, *Edge of Empire*, p. 221.
65. Marzolph and Van Leeuwen, vol. 1, p. 708.
66. Damrosch, *What Is World Literature?*, p. 138.
67. Anon., 'The City of Damascus', p. 364.
68. Anon., 'The Selector, and Literary Notices of New Works', p. 190.
69. Anon., 'The Alhambra, in Spain', p. 338.
70. Anon., 'Some Account of the City of Isfahan', p. 163; Anon., 'Delhi', p. 252; Anon., 'Bazaars of Constantinople', p. 413; 'The Court of Egypt', p. 207. The tale of the pastry-cook who fails to put pepper in the tart is also referenced by Becky Sharp in Thackeray's *Vanity Fair* (1848). Suffering from the shock of a particularly spicy curry that has been made with chili fresh from India, Becky observes, 'I ought to have remembered the pepper which the Princess of Persia puts in the cream-tarts in the *Arabian Nights*' (p. 30), again positing those tales as a frame of reference for historical and cultural realities.
71. Chateaubriand, 'Description of an Eastern Caravan', pp. 381–2.
72. Anon., 'The Peasants of British India', p. 389.
73. Said, *Orientalism*, p. 93.
74. Ibid. p. 93.
75. Ibid. p. 94. Emphasis in the original.
76. Ballaster, *Fabulous Orients*, p. 12.
77. Kabbani, *Europe's Myths of Orient*, pp. 37–66.
78. Ballaster, *Fabulous Orients*, p. 17.
79. Dickens, *American Notes for General Circulation*, p. 92.
80. Ibid. p. 130. Interestingly, Dickens employed the same metaphor in his fictional description of Tellson's Bank by Temple Bar in London, in *A Tale of Two Cities* (1859), which had 'a Barmecide room, that always had a great dining-table in it and never had a dinner' (p. 56). For a detailed analysis of this allusion to the Arabian Nights in the representation of a banking institution, see Wolfreys, *Dickens's London*, pp. 35–40.
81. Dickens, *American Notes*, p. 151.

82. Dickens, *Pictures from Italy*, p. 19.
83. Ibid. p. 19.
84. Ibid. p. 104.
85. See Lamb, *Preserving the Self in the South Seas, 1680–1840* (2001); Colley, *Captives: Britain, Empire and the World* (2010); and Leask, *Curiosity and the Aesthetics of Travel Writing, 1770–1840: 'from an Antique Land'* (2002).
86. Levine, 'Strategic Formalism', p. 626.
87. Ibid. p. 626.
88. Smith, *The Nile and Its Banks*, vol. 1, p. 50.
89. Bartlett, *The Nile Boat*, p. 46.
90. Ibid. pp. 55, 46.
91. Curtis, *Nile Notes of a Howadji*, pp. 2–3.
92. Martineau, *Eastern Life, Present and Past*, vol. 1, p. 108.
93. Anon., 'Old Cairo and Its Mosque', p. 332.
94. Said, *Orientalism*, p. 63.
95. Gregory, 'Scripting Egypt', pp. 115–16.
96. Anon., 'Old Cairo and Its Mosque', p. 332.
97. Warner, *Mummies and Moslems*, p. 48.
98. Lane, *Description of Egypt*, p. x.
99. Yegenoglu, *Colonial Fantasies*, p. 39. On the enduring appeal of the harem in Western art and literature, see Yeazell, *Harems of the Mind* (2000).
100. Interestingly, Eva Sallis notes that the male violence and power structures associated with the gaze are deliberately suspended by Scheherazade's sequence of narratives, as they are converted into an auditory experience. Just as violence is converted by and into fiction, the Sultan's scopophilia gives way to intense auditory pleasures. See Sallis, *Scheherazade through the Looking Glass*, p. 103.
101. Lane, *Modern Egyptians*, vol. 1, p. vi.
102. Anon., *The Book of the Thousand Nights and One Night, from the Arabic of the Aegyptian M. S.*, p. iii.
103. Lane, *The Arabian Nights' Entertainments*, vol. 1, p. viii.
104. Kabbani, *Europe's Myths of Orient*, p. 37.
105. Ahmed, *Edward W. Lane*, pp. 128–55.
106. Anon., 'On the Tales and Fictions of the East', p. 222.
107. 'The Drama', *London Magazine*, p. 483. Emphasis in the original.
108. Lane, *Modern Egyptians*, vol. 1, pp. 283, 284.
109. Ibid. vol. 1, p. 144.
110. Lane-Poole, *Life of Edward William Lane*, p. 93.
111. Lane, *Arabian Nights' Entertainments*, vol. 1, p. viii.
112. Said, *Orientalism*, p. 164.
113. Ibid. p. 240.
114. Schacker-Mill, 'Otherness and Otherwordliness', p. 167.
115. Lane, *Modern Egyptians*, vol. 2, p. 150.

116. Suhayr al-Qalamawi was the author of the first comprehensive analysis of the Arabian Nights in Arabic, which was published in Cairo (in Arabic) in 1976.
117. Knipp, 'The "Arabian Nights" in England', p. 48.
118. Eliot, *Adam Bede*, p. 5.
119. Eliot, *A Writer's Notebook, 1854–1879, and Uncollected Writings*, p. xxiii.
120. Eliot's allusion to an act of sorcery through a drop of ink perhaps anticipates Wilkie Collins's depiction of Eastern divination in *The Moonstone* (1868), when 'the Indian took a bottle from his bosom, and poured out of it some black stuff, like ink, into the palm of the boy's hand' in the attempt to scry the whereabouts of the infamous diamond (pp. 17–18).
121. Warner, *Stranger Magic*, p. 23.
122. Ibid. p. 23.
123. Hunt, 'New Translations of the Arabian Nights', p. 108.
124. Warner, *Stranger Magic*, p. 27.
125. Anon., 'Literae Orientales', p. 275. Emphasis in the original.

Chapter 3

The Magical Metropolis

> Every eye, we think, must be gratified by [Belzoni's] singular combination and skilful arrangement of objects so new, and in themselves so striking. The vivid freshness of the tints, as rich and unchanged after three thousand years . . . must affect the mind of the cultivated spectator with strange and mingled views respecting that unknown people of whose history, nay, of whose positive existence, the mansions of their dead are the melancholy but almost exclusive records.
>
> Anon., 'The Discovery Ships Are Completely Ready to Leave Deptford', *The Times*, 1821

In 1821, the Italian-born Englishman Giovanni Battista Belzoni held a popular exhibition of Egyptian antiquities in London's Egyptian Hall, Piccadilly Circus. Formerly a sideshow giant and strongman at the London circus of Sadler's Wells, Belzoni offered a different kind of theatrical experience through the large-scale reconstruction of archaeological sites as he had first encountered them in Egypt. This was, as the above review in *The Times* indicates, an interactive public entertainment, which was designed to gratify viewers through a range of visual stimuli that incited powerful emotional responses. The central attraction of the exhibition was the alabaster sarcophagus of the Pharaoh Seti I, which had been found in an underground tomb some 328 feet long. Belzoni made a 50-foot model of the tomb to scale in order to display its intricate sequence of subterranean stairs and corridors, and he also created full-size plaster casts based on the wax impressions he had made on-site of what he deemed to be its two most impressive chambers, the 'Room of Beauties' and the 'Entrance Hall'. Dispersed throughout were smaller but genuine relics from Egypt such as papyri, mummies in glass cases, jewellery and *shabti* figures. Surrounding the displays were Belzoni's own sketches and watercolour mock-ups of various tombs and statues. With this combination of ancient and contemporary materials, and the flickering lights of strategically placed torches, the distant past was transformed into an immediate, performed space – a carefully selected and mediated formulation of an ancient world (re-)created by modern techniques and special effects. It was a 'new' and 'striking' production of the past and its material traces in the centre of London.

Belzoni's exhibition undoubtedly formed a part of the broader 'shows' culture of the early nineteenth century, which has been catalogued at length in Richard Altick's seminal study, *The Shows of London* (1978). The vast spectrum of popular shows and 'non-theatrical entertainments' that emerged in this period, ranging from waxworks, freak shows and panoramas to electrical and technological displays, was, as Altick demonstrates, a dynamic mixture of information and entertainment that was, in theory, equally accessible to both and literate and non-literate members of the British population. Such events were generally designed to stimulate and excite paying audiences, while at the same time conveying a particular 'reality' or mediated information set. In keeping with this model, shows like Belzoni's contributed to a newly scientific culture of knowledge about the East, while at the same time transforming that culture into a display of new technologies and effects. As Gillen D'arcy Wood argues in *The Shock of the Real* (2001), Belzoni's considerable commercial success was dependent not upon his exhibition's aesthetic value, but upon its striking 'effects', and the creation of an apparently authentic experience through the 'presentation of the artefacts on display not as art but as real'.[1] Through the physical labours and technical ingenuity of showmen such as Belzoni, history and reality merged with spectacle and sensation, as nineteenth-century Londoners were able to move through the spatial realities of ancient Egypt and encounter the remnants of antiquity. Not only was the ancient suddenly new, exciting and spectacular, but, as the *London Literary Gazette* explained, it was materially available and might be easily stepped into from within the British metropolis:

> Who could contemplate all these things without a feeling of wonder and admiration? We are, by ascending a short stair-case, transported back 3,000 years; we are in a tomb of a monarch of the most ancient times; we are surrounded by the characters of an unknown language, the visible signs of a lost religion; hieroglyphicks [*sic*] which unintelligibly denote to our sense the learning of the primal world; sacrifices, possessions, combats, and all the busy pomps and turmoils of life – of

life which has ceased so long, that a hundred generations of our species have since existed, the remotest moiety of whom belong almost to the realm of oblivion.[2]

Attendees at this exhibition were, in effect, virtual tourists, whose fantastic subterranean experience paralleled (at least to a point) Belzoni's own moments of discovery. In recreating the European traveller's experiences in the East, the theatrical spaces of the Egyptian Hall provided a physical equivalent to closing the eyes or opening works of fiction and travel writing in order to indulge in wonderful dreams and fantasies from within the structures of British industrial and technological modernity. Like the controlled dreaming of Alice's sister in *Alice in Wonderland*, discussed in the previous chapter, the viewer enters and exits this self-enclosed enclave of their own accord, and takes a distinct pleasure in the movement between the other and the everyday, or between fantasy and reality. There is a sense here in which one no longer needs to travel to Egypt and the Middle East in order to encounter the wonders, magic and buried treasures of the Arabian Nights. Within the shows culture of nineteenth-century Britain, this chapter will argue, the ancient world not only had erupted into the present, but had seemingly been magicked into the heart of the British metropolis.

An Archaeological Performance

Belzoni's exhibition at the Egyptian Hall was, first and foremost, a performance, and it was Belzoni's 'mechanical ingenuity and indefatigable diligence', *The Times* enthused, that had enabled him to 'transport to the arena of European controversy, the otherwise immoveable excavations of Egypt'.[3] This, the newspaper insisted, reflected 'no less credit upon him as an artist than his sagacity and success in discovering the subject matter of his extraordinary exhibition has distinguished him above all other European travellers in modern times'.[4] This insistence upon the level of artistry and the sophisticated stagecraft underpinning Belzoni's work was very much in keeping with the highly rhetorical mode in which Belzoni himself presented his exploits. Belzoni recounted the pragmatics of his adventures locating and collecting Egyptian antiquities on behalf of the British Consul between 1815 and 1819 in his *Narrative of the Operations and Recent Discoveries within the Pyramids, Temples, Tombs, and Excavations in Egypt and Nubia,* published in 1820. During this time, he located the bust of Ramses II (known as the Young Memnon) in Thebes, excavated the sand-choked temple of Abu Simbel to find the elaborate tomb of Seti I (the centrepiece of his exhibition in the Egyptian Hall), conducted archaeological digs at Karnak, unearthed six royal tombs in the Valley of the Kings, found the lost city of Berenice, and located the entrance to the second pyramid of Giza, successfully infiltrating its elaborate underground network. In 1820, Belzoni transported the Young Memnon, the alabaster sarcophagus of Seti I, the enormous red granite head and arm of Amenhotep III and many other smaller relics to England. The removal of the Young Memnon, in particular, seized the public imagination in Britain.[5] 'This extraordinary head' was, the *Quarterly Review* declared in 1818, 'without doubt the finest specimen of Ancient Egyptian sculpture which has yet been discovered'.[6] According to Belzoni's own account of its removal, French archaeologists had already attempted to take possession of the statue, separating the head from the rest of the enormous statue by means of an explosion. He notes that he found it near 'the remains of its body and chair, with its face upwards, and apparently smiling on me, at the thought of being taken to England'.[7] This Orientalist gesture towards the salvation of goods and culture implicit in imperial intervention was also clearly a piece of dramatic hyperbole, designed to draw attention to Belzoni's achievement as a kind of performance. Like the fairy-tale castles and subterranean palaces discussed in the previous chapter, this statue had apparently been lying in wait for the arrival of the white European hero, Belzoni.

The granite head of the Young Memnon, now in the British Museum, is approximately 9 feet high and weighs over 11 tons (see Figure 3.1). Belzoni provides a very detailed description of its removal from Egypt in his memoir, explaining how he gathered a team of eighty local men, who levered the statue on to a rolling platform and pulled it a few hundred yards towards the river each day, until they finally reached the banks of the Nile, where it was put on a boat bound for Cairo and then Britain. Noting rather derisively that this method was necessarily simple because 'work of no other description could be executed by these people as their utmost sagacity reaches only to pulling a rope, or sitting on the extremity of a lever', Belzoni emphasises the physical strain of these labours, insisting that

> the hard task they had, to track such a weight, the heavy poles they were obliged to carry to use as levers, and the continual replacing [of] the rollers, with the extreme heat and dust, were more than any European could have withstood.[8]

Figure 3.1 The British Museum, Room 4 - Colossal bust of Ramses II, the 'Younger Memnon'. Author: Mujtaba Chohan. Courtesy of Wikimedia Commons. CC BY-SA 3.0, https://commons.wikimedia.org/w/index.php?curid=1545133

He emphasises, again in a highly theatrical mode, the physical and emotional toll of this undertaking upon himself, noting that during one period of exertion, 'I was seized with such a giddiness in my head, that I could not stand. The blood ran so copiously from my nose and mouth, that I was unable to continue the operation' and 'postponed it to the next day'.[9] His task was, Belzoni makes clear, a truly Herculean exploit, reminiscent of his days as the 'Patagonian Sampson' of Sadler's Wells theatre, when he would lift a large iron frame upon which seven or more members of the company would climb in a human pyramid as he walked around the stage.[10]

Belzoni's famed strength and his talent for stagecraft, which had been sources of popular entertainment and easy revenue in England, were touted as key reasons for his successes in Egypt. An 1851 article on Belzoni in *Household Words*, for example, claimed that his physical strength and facility for the local languages in Egypt gave him the aura of 'a superior being, endowed with magical power'.[11] Ever the performer, his archaeological stunts in Egypt seemed just as deliberately sensational as his exhibition at the Egyptian Hall in London, and Belzoni himself was mythologised as a being of supposedly superhuman 'strength and activity, in the character of a modern Hercules'.[12] He was supposedly 'an encouraging example to all those, who have not only sound heads to project, but stout hearts to execute'.[13] The dynamic co-functioning of archaeology and showmanship apparent in reports of Belzoni's archaeological operations is made evident in an illustration by the Italian painter, decorator and engraver Agostino Aglio (Figure 3.2), who travelled throughout Egypt with Belzoni and provided six plates to accompany his work. Here, the figure of Memnon dominates the foreground and the skyline of Aglio's engraving, its size clearly exaggerated in proportion to the undifferentiated multitude of Egyptian labourers straining themselves to move this colossal object inch by inch towards the unseen river. Interestingly, the giant figure of Belzoni himself is absent from the scene, perhaps emphasising his role as the overseer, or architect/stage manager of the project. There is no other activity: two figures in the distance have paused to

Figure 3.2 'Mode in which Memnon's head was removed by Belzoni and his team of labourers'. *Plates Illustrative of the Researches and Operations of G. Belzoni in Egypt and Nubia.* Agostino Aglio, 1820. Rawpixel free CC0 Image ID: 399667.

watch the drama unfold. The scene as a whole has the appearance of a stage set, effectively converting an ancient relic and the Egyptian landscape in general into a fantastic spectacle.[14]

Being cast as a dramatic 'character' in such exciting Eastern settings meant that Belzoni might be critiqued and understood in terms of the adventures and magic of the Arabian Nights. In a letter to his New York friend Henry Brevoort, written in London in 1820, Washington Irving described the great pleasure of encountering Belzoni and subsequently reading his work, drawing upon the Arabian Nights' tradition of mesmeric storytelling in his observation that 'I have been as much delighted in conversing with him, and getting from him an account of his adventures and feelings, as was ever one of Sinbad's auditors.'[15] Irving's analogy is particularly apt. As a modern-day Sinbad, Belzoni can be removed from the social, political and economic contexts in which he is operating in nineteenth-century Egypt, and celebrated as a brave and valiant traveller, whose series of adventures in magical, ill-defined Eastern locations involved meeting monsters and encountering various supernatural phenomena before returning home to a life of fame with immeasurable treasures. Much like Belzoni, Sinbad recounts his exploits for the entertainment and edification of others and, as the sole European witness to many of the happenings he reports, there is considerable scope for showmanship and imaginative flourishes in his tales. As Sinbad, Belzoni's years of extensive plundering in Egypt become infused with magic and dramatic purpose – his imperialist enterprise is rendered mythical and heroic, and it takes place in a fictional landscape beyond normal, lived experience.

Like the archaeological excavations discussed in the previous chapter, Belzoni's discoveries were also made meaningful by comparison to the fantasies of the Arabian Nights. *Household Words* noted that the temple at Thebes containing the Young Memnon had been 'so completely, and for so long a period, buried in sand, that even its existence remained unsuspected' until Belzoni's wonderful discovery.[16] Like Layard exposing the world of Nineveh, discussed in Chapter 2, this young and virile archaeologist possessed the power to peel back layers of history and to re-animate part of an ancient culture. Further, his find was like the sudden manifestation of an enchanted fairy-tale palace, as *Household Words* went on to note that 'descriptions which travellers give of it, resemble those of the palaces in the "Arabian Nights"'.[17] Later, in 1865, *Chambers's* used similar romantic hyperbole to describe Belzoni's detection of the tomb of Seti I:

> Belzoni and his Arabs, now half delirious with excitement and joy, hurl down the masonry, and burst in. What they see there is like to a vision told in the *Arabian Nights*. There are halls, and secret chambers, and corridors, and staircases of a splendour and on a scale to stagger belief. There are walls all brilliant with vivid colours, fresh as they were thousands of years back, when the workman laid down his brush to die. There are columns and cornices, belaboured with sumptuous carvings and imagery; and all around, thick spread on the rock, gorgeously-pictured allegories, illustrative of deep and awful mysteries.[18]

Use of the present tense in this passage, more than forty years after the event being described took place, conveys the excitement of the characters while emphasising the intensity and the seeming unreality, or perhaps fictionality, of their experience. The immense scale of this underground network, its vivid colours and its well-preserved artwork overwhelm the eye, and create the sense that the entire tomb is in fact an optic illusion. It is a space of fantasy and desire, mediated by an affective connection to a fictional Orient. The imagined and the real belong together in this underground cavern, which is at once the tomb of an ancient pharaoh and an illusory 'vision' of an ethereal palace from the Arabian Nights. Infiltrating the ancient tomb of Seti I is therefore a means by which the fantastic can be unearthed and celebrated in the same manner as the forty thieves' plunder, Sinbad's diamonds or Aladdin's lamp.

Already figured in both theatrical and fantastical terms, Belzoni's exploits in Egypt were easily transferred to a forum for popular entertainment in London, and his 1821 exhibition was a dramatic production intended to simulate the physical and sensory experiences of his adventures in Egypt. It was an opportunity, as the *Gentleman's Magazine* observed, for physical movement into, and exploration of, an artificially created alternate reality:

> It is scarcely possible by description to convey an adequate idea of these subterranean abodes, or of the strange and horrible figures with which they are filled. Most travellers are satisfied with entering the large hall, the gallery, and the staircase; in fact, as far as they can conveniently proceed, but Mr. Belzoni frequently explored the inmost recesses of these extra-ordinary excavations.[19]

There is a blending of reality and representation in this exhibit, which casts it as the kind of 'simulation' later conceptualised by Jean Baudrillard as fundamental to the production of what he calls 'hyper-reality'. The exhibit becomes a 'real without origin or reality' in the sense that any distinction between the representation and its original reference no longer exists.[20] Here, the fantastic landscapes, crypts and relics of the ancient world could seemingly be experienced first-hand – a corollary, I want to argue, to the landscapes, crypts and treasures that comprised the stage settings of theatrical productions of the Arabian Nights in the same period.

New Magic for Old

Like the tomb of Seti I, the many enclosed spaces and subterranean caverns of the Arabian Nights, outlined in the previous chapter, provided ideal theatrical opportunities to display the rich landscapes, domestic interiors and dazzling treasures of the East, within the public spaces of Britain. As Edward Ziter has demonstrated in *The Orient on the Victorian Stage* (2003), the British entertainment industry generally 'followed the lead of the human sciences' in its visualisation and production of the Orient for public consumption, disseminating popularised, dramatic versions of those theories which were emerging in new scientific fields of practice such as ethnology, anthropology, archaeology, and geography.[21] In his reading of Charles Farley's 1824 production, *The Spirits of the Moon; or, The Inundation of the Nile*, at Covent Garden as 'a fantastic parallel to the emerging science of Egyptology', Ziter draws nineteenth-century musicals, entertainments and panoramas together with museums and exhibition halls as readily accessible spaces that seemingly affirmed the imperial gaze upon the apparently dormant, unclaimed riches of the East:

> Deep beneath the surface, the inscrutable meaning of the East resided. The theatre's frequent descent into ancient subterranean crypts was a physical corollary to the antiquarian desire to embrace the interred remnants of antiquity. In the theatre and the exhibition room, one could enter the tomb by lamplight. One could search beneath the surface and contemplate strange sights that only reluctantly yielded their meaning.[22]

Farley's theatrical re-creation of a closed tomb that required forced entry may, Ziter notes, have been consciously informed by Belzoni's recent exhibition in its use of scenery that explicitly included the

'Egyptian Hall'.[23] Both Farley's and Belzoni's productions certainly provided ornately decorated, strategically lit spaces in which an obscure and mysterious Orient might be displayed and studied, and where visitors might actively participate in the adventurer's narrative of discovery, infiltration, exploration and safe return, without leaving England. Significantly, Ziter even uses language of magic and enchantment in his own description of this production, as one that 'conjured British adventurers at the East's occult core', thus emphasising the seeming effortlessness and immediacy of these wonderful theatrical manifestations.[24]

Stories from the Arabian Nights were an ideal vehicle for this physical movement into an imagined East, and in themselves represented the kind of dramatic transformation and the eruption of the wonderful and apparently supernatural into the everyday that early nineteenth-century theatrical culture was striving to achieve. Many of the tales were especially well suited to the growing public appetite for spectacle and sensation that emerged in this period as an alternative to the 'legitimate' rhetorical genres of tragedy and comedy, which were restricted to the theatres of Drury Lane and Covent Garden until the Theatre Regulation Act of 1843.[25] Forbidden the use of the spoken word, or at least of the spoken words of so-called 'legitimate' play texts, the minor playhouses spawned a stimulating cultural pastiche of burlesque, burletta, opera and pantomime, which, as Jane Moody has demonstrated, not only enabled them to skirt the law, but also 'transformed how the contemporary world could be imagined on stage'.[26] Their new 'physical, visceral aesthetic' was driven not by dialogue but by incidental music, song, dance, visual extravagance, experimental stage machinery and set designs, and often highly exaggerated gestures and movements.[27]

Such was the appeal of the Arabian Nights to these dramatic pioneers that almost all the stories from Galland's *Arabian Nights' Entertainments* were performed at least once across the major and minor British theatres of the nineteenth century. Furthermore, they were often performed in accordance with this new aesthetic, even when it was not necessary to do so. Episodes from this diverse collection of tales appeared at regular intervals across the legitimate and illegitimate theatrical world of the nineteenth century as comedy, drama, romance, opera, burlesque, burletta, pantomime, harlequinade, melodrama and ballet, proffering a series of communal, physical encounters with a familiar world of fiction. Treated as spectacle, the stories of the Arabian Nights were a rich source of creative and imaginative engagement, and a stimulus to new productions.

A prevalent concern for spectacle and sensation provoked regular criticism of the poor dialogue and dubious plot lines of many early nineteenth-century productions. Such was the case for one infuriated writer for the *European Magazine*, who declared that the 1826 fairy opera of *Aladdin* performed at Drury Lane was 'the most wretched trash that ever proceeded from a "man of letters"', and insisted that while the scenery was 'remarkably splendid', there should be more to theatrical productions than the current popular appetite for splendour:

> The scenery, as usual, was excellent, admirable, superb. This is *our* drama – scenery, scenery, scenery; and there an end of all that is truly excellent in it. If such people as go to play-houses are content with gazing and gaping, this may be all very right. [The scenic artist Clarkson] STANFIELD will furnish them with a profusion of pictures for the former, and [the playwright George] SOANES plenty of *humour* for the latter. But really when such enormous expences [sic] are incurred, something better, something at any rate a little less despicable ought to be done in the way of poetry and prose.[28]

This derisive dismissal both of the endless production of spectacle at the expense of more sophisticated narrative structures, and of 'such people as go to play-houses' solely to indulge in mindless 'gazing and gaping', points to a growing demand for novelty and sensation that might capture and hold the attention of new, broader and often semi-literate audiences. Such performances clearly sought to induce the kind of shock, awe and 'cheap thrills of immediate response' that Nicholas Daly has associated more exclusively with the changing social, cultural and political landscapes of England in the 1860s.[29] Although undoubtedly less technically advanced than these later productions, early drama none the less aspired continuously to provide new possibilities for experiencing magic and wonder, while at the same time illuminating and enabling the fantasies of British modernity.

Edward Ziter has argued that the perpetual display and consumption of Eastern harems, caverns, tombs and treasures on nineteenth-century stages 'both reflected and helped constitute the British colonial imaginary'.[30] Certainly, there was a distinct possibility for acts of voyeurism through such entertainments, as the enclosed, often subterranean spaces of the East were penetrated and their wonderful interiors displayed. It was a visual aesthetic undoubtedly influenced in the early decades of the century by the controversial figure of Lord Byron, whose three melodramatic Eastern adventures, *The Giaour* (1813), *The Bride of Abydos* (1813) and *The Corsair* (1814), seemingly confirmed the otherness of a highly sensual and sexual feminised Orient, while simultaneously celebrating that otherness as an intoxicating stimulant to the Romantic aesthetic and imagination.[31] Through Byron's Oriental narratives, as Saree Makdisi observes, the landscapes and scenarios of the East become intoxicating spaces into which the Romantic narrator and his prurient reader/viewer might project themselves and acquire an almost mythic status.[32] Despite such trends, however, the Arabian Nights, a work frequently metonymic of childhood innocence and wonder despite its often patently adult content, was not simply a dramatic other against which to define the imperial self; it was, as we have seen, an integral component of that self, its memories and its dreams. At the same time that shows of the Orient were, as Ziter claims, forming and regulating imperialist impressions of the East, they were also, at least in the case of productions of the Arabian Nights, fostering a self-reflective, inward gaze, as an imaginative destination of childhood became a physical space within Britain that might be stepped into and explored. Here, the fantasies of youth might be projected, physically embodied, and (re-)enacted, as a private world of childish responses associated with these stories was rendered a public and communal experience.

From its earliest stage adaptations in Britain, attending a performance derived from the Arabian Nights was not considered a new, unusual or particularly exotic experience; rather, it provided access to familiar childhood narratives in a new, material and visually stimulating format. When the very first English pantomime of 'Aladdin' was produced at the Covent Garden Theatre in 1788, the story was already so well known to London audiences via other media that the *European Magazine*, commending the producer for his recourse to the Arabian Nights, noted that the tale was so familiar as to render any plot summary superfluous: 'The Arabian Nights' Entertainments are in the hands of our readers; to them therefore we shall refer for the story of Aladdin and his Lamp.'[33] Assumed knowledge of the tales is apparent in a great many theatre reviews, which typically provide only a cursory plot summary or none at all. In 1806, for instance, the *Belle Assemblée* review of the *Forty Thieves* at Drury Lane opened by remarking that 'it is unnecessary to enter into a detail of the plot of this piece, as the story on which it is founded, and which it follows with scarcely any deviation, is generally known'; reviewing an opera of *Aladdin* at Covent Garden in 1813, the *Theatrical Inquisitor* noted that 'the story of Aladdin . . . has long been familiar, and a favourite with the nursery'; in 1822, the *Mirror of the Stage* considered it 'useless' to outline the plot of the *Barber of Bagdad* because 'our readers have doubtless read all the tales in the "Arabian Nights," and we therefore need only say, this piece is founded on one of them'.[34] It seems that the tales had already permeated popular culture to such an extent that further detail was simply not necessary.

At times, this act of recalling the scenes of childhood within the theatrical spaces of nineteenth-century Britain incited deeply emotional responses on the part of theatre-goers. For instance, the *New Monthly Magazine* considered the 1814 production of *The Ninth Statue* at Drury Lane 'only interesting in so far as it adheres to its Eastern original', while the following year, the *Ladies' Monthly Museum* noted with disappointment that *Who Wants a Wife* at Covent Garden was 'altered from that inexhaustible treasure, The Arabian Nights'.[35] In 1822, the *Literary Gazette* wrote of the performance of *Cherry and Fair Star; Or, The Children of Cyprus* at Covent Garden that 'our readers will not perhaps care to know how far from or how near to the story of their childhood is the drama in detail', while the 1826 version of the *Barber and His Brothers* at the Adelphi Theatre disappointed one critic because, he claimed, it 'has not adhered very rigidly to the original tale' and 'the scenes [the director] has introduced in place of those he has struck out, are far from being an improvement'.[36] The term 'original' here seems to be conflated with these individual reviewers' own, remembered childhood versions of the tales, whatever that may have been, as a site of psychological and emotional investment and a standard against which all other versions are measured and found wanting.

Theatrical performances based upon or inspired by tales of the Arabian Nights had a disturbing capacity to evoke and disrupt childhood memories simultaneously, and with them the almost sacred status that the tales had occupied in early life. Such was the stance of *Blackwood's Edinburgh Magazine*, which, in an 1819 piece on recent dramas in London, declared the Arabian Nights to be 'the paradise of our boyhood' and insisted that 'the attempt to realise or recal [*sic*], in any adequate manner, the feelings with which we peruse the Arabian Nights, must always be unsuccessful'.[37] One could no longer experience the innocent wonder of the child reader, and *Blackwood's* emphasised the anxieties that might be induced by any attempt to do so:

> They are founded on tales in the Arabian Nights; and, accordingly, they interfere, in a most impertinent and troublesome manner, with some of the very best associations of the best years of our life. They come

floundering, with their clumsy and unhallowed realities, into an ideal world, that our imaginations had built up and peopled in childhood, and disturb the whole fabric and its inhabitants – changing them into something even less fanciful and wondrous than the actual forms by which we are surrounded.[38]

The adaptation of the Arabian Nights for the Victorian stage clearly brought the ideal and the material into conflict, as the magic and wonder contained within the stories must now be convincingly replicated, or engineered. Any attempt to recreate and to populate the imaginative 'fabric' of a treasured and ultimately irretrievable childhood realm consequently demanded the use of the potentially clumsy, 'unhallowed realities' of costuming, set design and construction, trapdoors, mirrors, carefully focused lighting, optical trickery, and a substantial degree of backstage labour. The success or failure of a production largely depended upon the artistic and technological capabilities of its director, designers and stage managers.

Stepping into the treasure-filled caverns, intimate domestic spaces and bustling towns of the Arabian Nights within British theatres and exhibition spaces demanded rich and colourful backdrops of Oriental landscapes, featuring stormy seas, underground labyrinths and magnificent palaces. The desire to recreate those landscapes to some extent drove developments in scenic design.[39] In 1806, for instance, the *Theatrical Journal* noted that the Drury Lane Theatre was making rapid progress in 'the art of scenic decoration', as 'the views of the city of Bagdad, and the surrounding country' afforded by its production of the 'grand operatical romance' *The Forty Thieves* were 'truly *oriental*, both as to architecture and the vegetation'.[40] There seems to be a degree of authenticity being sought here in terms of the visual encounter with the East, despite the fact that the opera was heavily infused with magical events and, according to the *Belle Assemblée; or Court and Fashionable Magazine*, the performance had been 'pressed down by an incumbering [sic] machinery of fairies, genii and hobgoblins' in the attempt to recreate the supernatural through science.[41] Its scenery included a palace, the magnificent interior of a banqueting hall, a fairy lake and a Turkish pavilion, each situated in or around the city of Baghdad. This blending of recognisable, geographical locations and detailed architectural exteriors with enchanted palaces and wonderful fairylands – which was very common to productions of the Arabian Nights – would indicate that, in the opinion of this reviewer, to be 'truly *oriental*' was to be visually spectacular, to capture the supernatural in the everyday, and to realise all the wonders of the Arabian Nights in material, visual form.

The fact that stunning scenery was one of the major attractions of performances from the Arabian Nights is evident from their play bills. In 1828, a bill in the *Theatrical Observer* listed the tragedy of *Virginius*, an opera of *Aladdin* in two acts, and the melodrama of *The Dumb Savoyard* as the evening's entertainments at Drury Lane. Under each title, the principal actors and their characters are listed. Only *Aladdin* includes a list of scenery: it commences with a rather specific setting, the street and city of Isfahan, and then moves to a subterranean passage of rocks, the gardens of the genii of the lamp, royal baths, Aladdin's palace, an African desert, and the hall in the Schah's palace.[42] Similarly, in 1837, the *Theatrical Observer* lists Shakespeare's tragedy of *King John*, a farce entitled *The Happiest Day of My Life*, and a 'new Grand Eastern Romance' from the Arabian Nights called *Noureddin, & the Fair Persian; Or, The Bright Star of Morn* as the evening's entertainments at Covent Garden.[43] Again, only the work drawn from the Arabian Nights lists the scenery, which, in its two acts, comprised twenty separate backdrops including a number of Eastern cities and palaces, a hall of mirrors and a grand assemblage of fairies, again combining the 'real' with the magical. Like the 1806 production of *The Forty Thieves*, these scenes move from specific Eastern cities into sites of magic and wonder, blending the imagined with the 'real' in order to create an Orient for the stage that might be celebrated for both its stagecraft and its accuracy. As one writer for the *European Magazine* made clear in his review of Thomas Dibdin's three-act musical romance, *The Ninth Statue; Or, The Irishman in Bagdad*, which was performed at Drury Lane in 1814, it was the apparent effortlessness of the movement from the real to the unreal, 'the scenery, the magic changes, and all the effects of supernatural potency' that primarily appealed to the audiences of such productions.[44] A reviewer for the *New Monthly Magazine* agreed, noting that 'of the merits of this piece as a dramatic production we can say but little', for in terms of 'dialogue, incident and interest, it is about upon a par with the generality of melo-dramas'; none the less, the materialisation of a seemingly supernatural world within the bounds of Drury Lane Theatre gave rise to great spectacle:

> Considered merely as a spectacle, it is almost impossible to describe its magnificence. We never saw, on any stage, a scene comparable in beauty to that raised by the magician at the end of the first act, where the Genii

of Fire and Water rise to pronounce the oracle, and enjoin him how to obtain the ninth statue; it is unparalleled in richness and variety of colour. The last scene is also most beautiful.[45]

Just as, within the world of the Arabian Nights, enchanted objects, buildings and people are themselves ephemera, with the capacity to change into other forms and to de-materialise and re-materialise in new locations, the transformations that take place on stage must appear immediate, effortless and extraordinarily beautiful. There is a sense that, like Aladdin instructing the genie to build an enchanted palace, one has simply to wish to make such things happen.

There was, of course, a substantial amount of labour and mechanical expertise required in order to achieve this apparently spontaneous eruption of the supernatural into the everyday, comparable to the feats of engineering underpinning Belzoni's dramatic removal of the Young Memnon and his theatrical presentation of artefacts in the Egyptian Hall. At times, as in the case of John Fawcett's melodramatic production of *Cherry and Fair Star* at Covent Garden in 1822, the effect was, by all accounts, mesmerising. *Cherry and Fair Star*, a 'favourite fairy tale . . . filched so prettily from the story in the Arabian Nights' by the Countess Marie-Catherine d'Aulnoy (1650–1705), is an imitation of 'The Story of the Two Sisters who Envied their Younger Sister' and features a burning forest, a sailing ship in the Port of Cyprus and a magnificent fairy vision.[46] While it was noted that 'there was little of plot or interesting incident' in Fawcett's adaptation, the scenery was, according to reviews, 'truly magnificent; and the illusions admirably sustained'.[47]

Not only was the mechanical representation of a burning forest in this performance deemed, in the words of the *London Magazine*, 'too hot to look at', but the arrival of a 'superb galley in the Port of Cyprus' that approached the front of the stage 'after having shown herself in almost every position', and the so-called 'Bower of Illusion' were deemed 'two grand efforts of art' by the *Literary Gazette*.[48] This latter illusion, produced by way of a large mirror and strategically placed lighting, seemed to effect an elaborate transformation of the entire theatre:

> We have never witnessed any similar experiment so brilliantly and effectively made. The Illusion scene is produced by a mirror, which quite fills the stage, at a considerable distance from the lamps. In front of this, aërial figures are suspended, twisting and twining laurel

wreaths, fairies dance and birds flutter: the whole is reflected by the glass; and the ensemble, including the theatre itself and its lights, is at once beautiful, curious, and magnificent.[49]

The genuine pleasure of this reviewer in the skilled artifice of the illusion prompts a celebration of both the Eastern romance itself and the Western technologies capable of capturing and re-producing that fiction. Like the Sultan in his bedchamber at the outset of the Arabian Nights collection, within the self-contained space of the Covent Garden Theatre, the viewer experiences a period of sensory and material separation from the outside world, while immersed in a kind of alternate reality filled with light, colour and motion.

Within the shows culture of the nineteenth century, the tales of the Arabian Nights came to represent a dramatic time and space where one might physically, if momentarily, step into an artificial paradise, behold its treasures, and derive a distinct pleasure from the quality of the illusion. Less successful productions, such as *The Enchanted Courser; Or, The Sultan of Cardistan* at Drury Lane in 1824, demonstrate even more clearly the labours and technical expertise necessary to this movement, and the collision of materiality with the imagination that might ensue. Based upon the 'Story of the Enchanted Horse', this performance apparently was largely intended to exhibit the popular circus entertainer Andrew Ducrow's famous 'stud of horses as performers at this theatre'.[50] Substantially reducing the number of characters and complications in the plot, this version of the tale focused almost exclusively upon the visual impact of the piece, clearly intending that the tale be understood in a disjointed, imagistic way, rather than as an intricate narrative.[51] Objecting to this deliberate attempt to engage a popular audience by way of pure spectacle, *La Belle Assemblée* dismissed the entire production as a mere 'parade of glitter' that assaulted the senses to such an extent that 'we were so often scared from rationality, by the clashing of cymbals and braying of trumpets, that we scarcely knew whether we sat or stood'.[52] Inadequate, overly cumbersome stage effects were apparently even more pronounced in the climactic scene in which the enchanted horse flew across the stage. The *Theatrical Examiner* provides a detailed and disparaging account of how this effect was achieved: a real horse was used on stage with wings attached to its shoulders, and as the Prince galloped off stage, an 'awkward wooden substitute' was seen 'making anything but a winged progress across the upper scenes', to be finally replaced by 'a mere picture, so poorly contrived, that it appeared nothing else'.[53] The failure of that picture to appear as anything but a poorly executed two-dimensional painting was, apparently, 'puerile in the extreme', and represented the failure of the theatrical medium to provide a convincing illusion of magic in this instance.[54]

The *Monthly Magazine*, in a review of the same performance, emphasised the challenges inherent in producing such a fantastic concept 'realistically' when the only point of comparison is imaginary:

> It is very well to talk of a flying horse, for imagination will do wonders, but to represent so termagant a pegasus with effect, seemed to be next to an impossibility. This, however, has been effected by the ingenuity of Mr. [James] Winston, who it appears is the director of all such matters; and they cannot be in better hands, for in point of splendour, of decoration, and wonder of machinery few tales will be found to equal the *Enchanted Courser*.[55]

The visual effect required of this production is, of course, not that of genuine magic or the supernatural, but of an increasingly sophisticated science of stagecraft, which might allow viewers to derive pleasure from the apparent 'reality' of an image, while secure in the knowledge that it is not 'real'. This paradoxical oscillation between the experience of the 'real' and the experience of the theatrical medium, what Jay David Bolter and Richard Grusin have termed the 'double logic of remediation', is precisely what gives rise to a sense of wonder or disappointment in any given performance.[56] 'If the medium really disappeared,' Bolter and Grusin note, 'as is the apparent goal of the logic of transparency, the viewer would not be amazed because she would not know of the medium's presence.'[57] By the same token, if the technologies underpinning an illusion are overly intrusive, as in the case of the flying horse, the medium fails to become transparent and will not incite wonder at all. The *Theatrical Observer*'s conclusion that 'we cannot say that as a *drama* [*The Enchanted Courser*] is likely to produce a magic effect' not only points to the weakness of this particular production, but to the desire of audiences at such performances for a sensation of immediacy, of magic that is known to have been manufactured.[58] In this manner, the wonder and enchantment of the Arabian Nights become inextricably intertwined with the 'wonder of machinery' and technical ingenuity in an industrialising, modernising Britain.

Despite its popularity as a source of spectacle in Britain, continual repetition of the same special effects in producing the Arabian Nights would none the less lead, as one exasperated reviewer noted in relation to the 1826 fairy opera of Aladdin at Drury Lane, to monotony:

> The story of Aladdin we have said is threadbare. It has been brought out over and over again in pantomime and in farce, till the pristine brilliancy it derived from Eastern magnificence and the machinery of genius and fairy, is almost worn off.[59]

Explicitly comparing the British theatre to a factory system, this reviewer makes clear that the endless, mechanical replication of dramatic materials will inevitably have a dulling effect. Continual technological innovation and variation are necessary to realise the fantasies contained within these stories, and to capture and present a world of 'genius and fairy' in more authentic and more exciting ways than any previous medium or production.

Recent scholarship on the role of magic and the supernatural in nineteenth-century literature and culture has indicated that the development of new technologies in this period – and with them the experiences of new phenomena such as 'disembodied voices over the telephone, the superhuman speed of the railway, near-instantaneous communication through telegraphic wires' – did not develop in opposition to constructions of magic and the supernatural, but in fact transformed daily life in Britain by rendering it increasingly 'uncanny'.[60] Throughout the century, the workings of the natural world seemed ever more mysterious and 'full of invisible, occult forces'.[61] The extensive use of technological innovation and showmanship in productions of the Arabian Nights drew upon and celebrated such forces by presenting a collection of tales originating in the East as a type of 'modern enchantment' in Britain (to use Simon During's helpful expression). In his history of secular magic, During argues that, from around 1700, magic 'slowly became disconnected from supernature' to persist in popular culture as the 'self-consciously illusory' performance of conjuring acts, new technologies and new media, stage productions and special effects.[62] In its many iterations on stage and in exhibition halls, the Arabian Nights was undoubtedly a source of such enchantment, of magic made manifest, in nineteenth-century Britain.

It is perhaps no coincidence that 'the first and most spectacular showcasing of the new possibilities of gas lighting on the Parisian stage' was an 'epoch-making production' of Aladdin by Nicholas Isouard, staged by the theatrical innovators Louis Daguerre and Pierre Ciéri at the Salle Le Peletier of the Opéra in 1822.[63] The desire to produce a spectacular Aladdin's palace, in this case a 'Palace of Light', seemed to demand such developments.[64] By the end of the century, the genie of Aladdin's wonderful lamp was even more explicitly aligned with the fuels and energies of European industrialisation in the pantomime of Aladdin at the Grand Theatre, Islington, in 1889–90, entitled *Aladdin; Or the Saucy Young Scamp Who Collected the Lamp*. This production featured, we are told, 'Steam, Gas, Mechanical and Limelight Effects', and the genii encountered by Aladdin were named Fiz-Fiz, Paraffin, Benzoline and Colza.[65] Britain, it seemed, was no longer in need of Eastern magic, for it had developed new powers of its own. These industrial fuels were just as wonderful, and they effected transformations just as magical, as those that might be wrought by any genie. This pantomime was, very explicitly, a celebration of both the fantastic other-world of the Arabian Nights, and the scientific and technological capabilities of British modernity in reproducing that world. Here, magic and science, reason and irrationality were imbricated in ways that were not alien or other but central to British scientific and technological modernity. Such materialisations of the dream-realm of the Arabian Nights on stage were intended to bear witness to the wonder, novelty and imaginative possibilities of scientific principles at work and they became, as the next section of this chapter will demonstrate, provocations for new theatrical and artistic creations.

Sinbads of Soho

During the Christmas period of 1814–15, a farce entitled *The Valley of Diamonds; Or, Harlequin Sinbad* was performed as an afterpiece to each of the main productions at Drury Lane Theatre. Sinbad was already, as the *Belle Assemblée* noted, an immensely popular character, who would be 'interesting in whatever shape he may appear' and so 'he, of course, excited great attention and curiosity' in this first pantomime version of the tale.[66] The production opened with views of a magnificent, unidentified Eastern landscape dominated by large rocks, which were studded with what appeared to be 'the richest gems of the earth', one of the many repositories of treasure that fill the tales of the Arabian Nights.[67] This scene was, however, simply the framing device for moving its audience into a typical theatrical harlequinade. After a few initial altercations between Sinbad and some enormous swooping eagles, the famous sailor encountered the 'fairy of the place' and was immediately turned into Harlequin, his allegorical counterpart, while his daughter (a character introduced solely for the purpose of the pantomime) became Columbine. The figure of the Clown spontaneously emerged from a magic chest on stage. The materialisation of these figures, drawn from the Italian *commedia dell'arte* tradition, marked a clear point of departure from the Arabian Nights narrative, as together they set sail for England and, the performance notes indicate, 'on a sudden the scene shifts to a magnificent view of Blackfriars Bridge, with St. Paul's and the steeples of the city in perspective', a scene readily familiar to the audiences at Drury Lane Theatre.[68] In bringing the action to London, the audience itself becomes a part of the spectacle, and of the joke, while the artificiality of the theatrical performance is underscored. Here, we are told, 'all the usual changes, buffetings, and tumblings of Pantomime [took] place'.[69] The *Belle Assemblée* elaborates upon some of the more 'ingenious' transformations that occurred throughout the ensuing scenes:

> Among the ludicrous tricks was the flight of a candle which was chased by the *Clown* and *Pantaloon*, in order to light their pipes; and the subsequent appearance of the former in a bassoon, which was taken out of the Orchestra. An interesting little girl, who was stated to be only five years of age, who was taken out of a barrel, and who danced a hornpipe admirably, was among the amusing incidents of the piece. Another was the sudden change of *Harlequin* into a skeleton.[70]

While the famous voyages of Sinbad the Sailor clearly provided the impetus for this production, the shift from frame story to harlequinade, and from treasure-laden rockscape to the steeples of London, marks a distinct shift in mood, genre and expectation. Driven almost entirely by swift changes of scene, spectacular tricks and stage machinery, the pantomime created its own contexts and deployed new cultural references, approaching the narrative form as a dynamic and continually evolving set of materials. Drawing a bassoon from the orchestra, revealed to contain the Clown, not only operates as a meta-theatrical element within the production, but, like the later dancing of the hornpipe, openly acknowledges the convergence of the musical, theatrical and narrative traditions involved here. No longer simply an imaginative corollary to archaeological excavation, anthropology and ethnography, this tale was, first and foremost, a field of play and of creative experimentation that might give rise to new configurations and artistic creations.

The mixture of the allegorical with the literal, of the old with the new, was in many ways the quintessence of Victorian pantomime. The early decades of the nineteenth century marked, as David Mayer has demonstrated, a fundamental shift in this genre, from a 'cheerful and somewhat mindless entertainment' to an increasingly pressing means of engagement with the social, economic, political and aesthetic issues of the age.[71] Here, through continual improvisation on the old stock characters, the form 'easily and confidently documented the everyday trivia of its milieu'.[72] On stage, that 'King of English Clowns', Joseph Grimaldi, dubbed an 'urban anarchist' by Jane Moody for his disregard for the law and social convention, repeatedly moved through the world of London streets, filled with shops, placards, billboards and buildings readily recognisable by his audiences.[73] 'London fads', such as coach driving, dandyism, and even scuffles for umbrellas during thunderstorms, made their way into the harlequinades of the theatre, and 'heightened the effect of an exotic, theatrical world giving way to the foibles of ordinary London'.[74] Like the performance of *Harlequin Sinbad* at Drury Lane, borrowings from the Arabian Nights for the purpose of pantomime generally followed this trend, constantly enacting shifts in place and perspective in the move from frame story to harlequinade, which literally pulled the figures from these tales into the villages and cities of modern Britain.

Harlequin and the Red Dwarf; Or, the Adamant Rock, a pantomime inspired by 'The Story of the Third Calender', which was performed at Covent Garden in 1812, departed even further from Scheherazade's tale in terms of its tone, rhythm and comic scope.[75] Galland's version of this tale – the main version in circulation at the time – opens with Agib, the son of a king, recounting the moment of his shipwreck upon the so-called 'black mountain', a powerful magnetic rock or 'mine of adamant' that draws all metals towards it across the sea. The opening scenes of the tale are an extremely dramatic account of violence and suffering:

> About noon we were come so near, that we found what the pilot had foretold, to be true; for we saw all the nails and iron about the ship fly towards the mountain, where they fixed, by the violence of the attraction, with a horrible noise; the ship split asunder; and sunk into the sea, which was so deep about that place, that we could not sound it. All my people were drowned; but God had mercy on me, and permitted me to save myself by means of a plank, which the wind drove ashore just at the foot of the mountain.[76]

The sole survivor of this tragedy, Agib undergoes a series of fantastic adventures and misfortunes as he locates a brass bow and arrows with which to destroy the statue above the adamant rock, releases a metallic man who will lead him to safety across the sea, lives forty days with a young boy in an underground cavern, spends a year with forty beautiful women in an enchanted palace, and finally loses his right eye in a scuffle with a flying horse. It is a tale of interconnected yet disparate magical episodes that invites digression, bewilderment and bemusement – fitting materials for the endless transformations of place, person and scene that drove nineteenth-century pantomime.

Despite its marvellous content and structural appeal, Galland's version of the tale of the Third Calender underwent substantial dramatic alterations for its appearance on the London stage. *Harlequin and the Red Dwarf* included a romantic dimension absent from the Galland, and altered the characters' names in order to undercut the severity of the tale and maintain a sense of the frivolous and entertaining. In the 1812 stage version, outlined by *The Times*, the hero, Prince Cherry, undertakes a perilous sea voyage to search for his love, the Princess Fair Star, who is being held captive by the Red Dwarf to whom she has been promised in marriage by her parents, the Emperor Longoheadiano and his wife, the Empress Rondabellyiana. In typical pantomimic mockery of physical deformities, the names of the Emperor and Empress were materially represented in the form of over-sized papier-mâché masks – one long and one round – which were worn by the characters in what *The Times* considered to be 'the most ludicrous scene in the whole pantomime'.[77] Shipwrecked by the magnetic force of the Adamant Rock, Prince Cherry is assisted by a Green Bird who leads him to his love, whereupon he frees her with his magic bow and arrows. At this point in the tale, the Green Bird transforms the lovers into Harlequin and Columbine, who flee for England, while the Red Dwarf transforms the Emperor and Empress into Pantaloon and the Clown (played in the 1812 production by Joseph Grimaldi), who set off in pursuit. Sixteen harlequinade chase scenes follow, each set in different, identifiably English, locations, including Ramsgate Pier, the George and Blue Boar in Holborn, Bow marketplace, an auction house, a seaside resort, the Liverpool Museum, and finally Epping Forest, before the lovers are magically restored to their original forms and united in the Green Bird's fairy palace.[78]

Radical changes in plot, character and names notwithstanding, *Harlequin and the Red Dwarf* was readily identified by its reviewers as having been based on a story from the Arabian Nights – a sure sign of the popularity and familiarity of the tales. The pantomime was praised for its deft changes of scene, use of props and the general hilarity of the spectacle, which included a live stag, horses and hounds in the sixteen chase scenes. The *Universal Magazine* noted that 'much might be said in favour of [the performance's] pantomimic machinery', while according to the *European Magazine*, 'The scenery is superb, and the machinery, in almost every part, is entitled to great praise, for the ingenuity with which it is designed, and the ability with which it is executed.'[79] In his accompanying notes to the memoirs of Grimaldi, Dickens was far more temperate in his praise of this particular pantomime, noting that while the scenery was superb, it was in no way as successful as similar productions at Covent Garden. Nevertheless, he deemed the chase in Epping Forest to have supplied 'one of the finest landscapes ever displayed in any theatre'. Here, he noted:

> Horses were introduced – a jolly fat Parson, Pantaloon, and the Clown, took part in the joys of the chase: Pantaloon on a little Shetland pony was followed by Grimaldi on a great cart-horse, aping the Mammoth wonder for size; Joe [Grimaldi], with a long waggoner's whip in his hand and a jockey-cap, the peak of prodigious extent, seemed as anxious to be in at the death as if nothing in the world was comparable to it; his eagerness created a doubt, whether Barnes and his miniature horse would or would not be galloped over by Joe and his Bucephalus – or being trundled over, horse and man, for the popular diversion.[80]

While conceding that the horses behaved better than the dogs and the stag, *The Times* found the behaviour of the animals in this production deeply disappointing, and expressed the hope that the theatre's managers would subsequently 'abandon the hideous absurdity of introducing brutes on the stage'.[81] None the less, the comic value of a large man on a Shetland pony being chased across the stage by a smaller man on a great cart-horse seems to capture for Dickens the essence of the pantomime's humour. This was a physical comedy driven by the instability of bodies and identities, the rapid movement of characters from one world to another, and continual distortions of scale and perspective.

Such pantomimes inspired by the Arabian Nights illustrate the popular conceptualisation of these stories as an inherently unstable, non-linear compilation of colour and movement, repeated motifs, digressions and diversions. A harlequinade chase with horses and hounds in Epping Forest undoubtedly seems far removed from the story of the Third Calender, yet the tales of the Arabian Nights were never limited to a particular text or edition, and were endlessly changing and expanding. Enabling that compilation continually to evolve over time through improvisation, alteration and adaptation not only allowed it to move beyond the imperialist containment of the Orient and its treasures, outlined by Ziter, but it was in many ways in keeping with the dynamic nature of the collection's earlier existence as an oral tradition. It allowed the tales to be positioned within new personal, political and cultural structures while facilitating moments of recognition and recollection within a genre that, as Melynda Nuss has noted, by its very nature, collapsed time and space and exposed the artificiality of its creations:

> Through its two-part structure, the pantomime not only taught its audience how to transition from local worlds into the distant and exotic world that could be created by more elaborate staging techniques, it actually taught them that the seemingly distant and exotic world could dissolve at any moment into the world they knew every day. The grand personages of the frame narrative, for all their pretensions and exotic settings, are 'really' the allegorical Harlequin and Columbine, Pantaloon, Lover, and Clown.[82]

Through pantomime, British audiences found themselves transported to other, wonderful realms, only to be swiftly returned to their own, which had been made wonderful by the experience. This imaginative journey explicitly invited viewers to compare and contrast the worlds they encountered, and to reflect upon the nature not only of the elusive and illusive other, but of the nature of the modern self in a rapidly changing world.[83] That the imagined realm of the Arabian Nights might at any moment 'dissolve' into the familiar and the everyday was, I would argue, deeply suggestive of its latent presence in contemporary nineteenth-century experience.

At times, the new titles given to theatrical adaptations of the Arabian Nights reflected their propensity to mutate and adapt to new contexts and conditions. The 1814 production of *The Ninth Statue; Or, the Irishman in Bagdad* at Drury Lane, for example, explicitly presented an intermingling of cultures in its bipartite title. Although it is unclear from reviews of this performance exactly how an Irishman figured in the narrative, the title none the less inculcates a sense of the European traveller's imaginative movement into new spaces and times. The production also featured two traditional Irish melodies, further emphasising its hybrid nature. The resulting 'heterogeneous compound of pantomime and farce', officially referred to as a 'New Musical Romance', was, the *Monthly Theatrical Reporter* contemptuously declared, 'a kind of mongrel, non-descript' dramatic production – literally the result of different traditions – drawn from the Arabian Nights and '*got up* (to speak technically), for scenic representation'.[84] Occasionally, the transformations undergone by the tales were such that they were presented as new creations rather than adaptations. The burlesque entitled *You Must Be Buried*, performed at the Haymarket in 1827, and the opera entitled *The Spirit of the Bell*, performed at the Lyceum in 1835, for instance, offered no indication that they were re-workings of the tales of Aladdin and Sinbad, respectively. Transported across time, space and culture, the stories of the Arabian Nights were so widely diffused in British culture that, at times, a production might simply refer to an adamant rock, a Barmecide Feast or a wonderful lamp in order to add new dimensions to a work or its characters by way of familiar intertextual references.

Driven by a desire for immediacy while simultaneously evoking memories of well-known narratives, such productions were both forward- and backward-looking, aptly demonstrating the process of dramatic (re-)creation through repetition, outlined by Elin Diamond in *Performance and Cultural Politics* (1996). A performance, Diamond notes, necessarily 'embeds traces of other performances', but at the same time 'it also produces experiences whose interpretation only partially depends on previous experiences'.[85] It is through this uneasy tension between replication and innovation, between 'the pre-existing discursive field' and the 'performative present', that the possibility emerges of 'materialising something that exceeds our knowledge, that alters the shape of sites and imagines other as yet unsuspected modes of being'.[86] In the case of the Arabian Nights, the frequent re-working of familiar materials through new technologies and literary and cultural frameworks rendered those materials new, spectacular and fundamentally modern within the shows culture of nineteenth-century London.

Increasingly embedded in British literary and theatrical traditions, the Arabian Nights continued to maintain its topicality. The 1844 production of *Aladdin* at the Lyceum Theatre, for example, introduced in the advertisements of the *Theatrical Advertiser* as an 'entirely Original, and much better than new, Grand, Operatic, Melo-dramatic, Cabalistic, Burlesque Extravaganza', was an amalgamation of several generic, musical and dramatic traditions.[87] The play's somewhat extravagant claim to originality seems to rest with its attempts to 'modernise' the story of Aladdin through specifically

British references and contexts. The opening scene is identified in the accompanying pamphlet as the secret study of Abanzar, 'the real magician of the East'.[88] As the curtain rises, solemn music plays and the sound of ringing bells is heard while the magician is seen sitting in the darkness before a desk containing a large book, an hourglass, an owl and a goblin. Despite this somewhat sinister and occult setting, the opening lines place this scene not in an exotic Eastern location, but in Central London: 'St Paul's confirms the fact, 'tis three o'clock, And I may soon expect the great Orlock.'[89] Again, distance is transformed into proximity as the mystical and mysterious are located within the same urban space as the play's audience.

The play then progresses through a series of extremely short scenes with little dialogue and occasional musical accompaniment, including polkas, ballets and solo songs, as the audience is transported from the dark room in London to a bustling street scene in China, then to an elaborately adorned apartment in the palace of the Chinese Princess Badroulbadour and, at the end of the first act, to the subterranean cavern in China that holds the wonderful lamp. These rapid shifts around the globe are reflective of the magical transformations and relocations that drive the tale of Aladdin, enabling continual movement and action while at the same time fostering a sense of wonder, or even confusion, as to the means by which such transformations are achieved. In the Lyceum's production, the speed with which Aladdin's palace is built by a genie, relocated to Africa, and then returned to China, is seemingly matched by the rapid spread of information across national borders by the periodical press. In the second scene, as the evil magician endeavours to impress upon Aladdin the far-reaching reputation of his late father, he turns for evidence to the daily newspapers, as the predominant vehicle for the transmission of information around the world:

> Than your late sire, no tailor e'er was wiser,
> The *Pekin Times*, the *Post*, and *Advertiser*,
> Proclaimed his fame in language most pathetic,
> Moses and Son were never so poetic.[90]

Similarly, in the opening moments of the third scene, the despondent Chinese Princess is approached by one of her maids, who attempts to cheer her by asking 'What can we do to dissipate your vapours? / Pray, has your highness seen the morning papers?' Despite her location, the Princess's reply is clearly informed by topical allusions to British society and its increasingly fast-paced news cycle:

> Yes, every one; I've read them through and through,
> 'Tis always the same thing, there's nothing new;
> Letters from constant readers – dull debates,
> With vestry meetings, about parish rates.
> Statues in *status quo* for want of cash,
> Gigantic fountains that don't make a splash;
> Suspension bridges far too long suspended,
> Unending lists of monuments unended;
> And streets stopped up for horse and carriage movements,
> By so called metropolitan improvements;
> Each is so dreary, that I fain would choose,
> To hang the editor in his own *news*.[91]

As readers of periodicals, which were themselves a sign of the new steam-powered age, both the African magician and the Chinese princess are situated within an emerging world of new media technologies and information exchange. In this context, distanced individuals are brought into contact with one another by way of increasingly rapid communication across material networks. None the less, Badroulbadour, like many commentators of the period, decries the effects of this deluge of unordered, piecemeal information, which she finds both overwhelming and strangely numbing.[92] An educated member of the reading public conversant with the latest political debates, scientific discoveries and marvels of modern architecture and engineering, the Princess seeks relief from this ongoing rhythm of mechanical production and consumption, and she is ultimately rescued from her boredom by involvement in Aladdin's quest. Her audience, similarly, is drawn from the physical, social and technological structures of London into a world of magic and the supernatural – a world that has been actively produced by and embedded within those structures.

In 1826, *Oxberry's Dramatic Biography and Histrionic Anecdotes* declared the 'long-expected operative romance' of Aladdin playing at Drury Lane Theatre to be 'in so imperfect a state, as to be an insult to the public, and a disgrace to the theatre'.[93] Again, the principal cause for complaint was not the spectacle itself, but the dramatic content, as the work's composer was allegedly 'shackled by utter nonsense' and the 'villainous lines to which he was condemned to put to music'.[94] Tellingly, however, the writer betrays an abiding affection and, indeed, a sense of loyalty to the story itself. Aladdin, we are told, 'hung heavily; and perhaps, national feeling alone prevented its utter condemnation'.[95] Here, the tales, as early as 1826, are already understood to be a national product, and a part of the British literary and cultural landscape. In 1839, *Chambers's Edinburgh Journal* was even more explicit in its location of the Arabian Nights within the British canon, declaring, in an article entitled 'What English Literature Gives Us', that 'The Arabian Nights' Entertainments are not ours by birth, but they have nonetheless taken their place amongst the similar things of our own which constitute the national literary inheritance.'[96] Outlining some of the tales that comprise this 'dreamy romantic grandeur', the author declares the work a 'glorious book, and one to which we cannot well show enough of respect'.[97] This identification of the Arabian Nights as a part of the British canon not only points to the profound impact of the work upon British literature and culture, but is an attitude that, as Abdulla Al-Dabbagh has observed, is somewhat unusual in that it paradoxically regards 'a *translated* work as indistinguishable from a native, literary tradition', and there are certainly some potentially pejorative connotations to such an assumption of ownership over an Eastern narrative tradition.[98] The Arabian Nights, however, has a tendency to resist such attempts at control and containment. It spills over the pages of its various texts, continually re-inventing itself, and, as this chapter has shown, driving new creative, technological and dramatic practices. Situating productions of the tales within the British literary canon recognises their evolution within new personal, political and cultural structures and contexts, and demonstrates the extent to which they contribute to, were embedded in and were produced by those contexts.

Notes

1. Wood, *The Shock of the Real*, p. 2.
2. Anon., 'Egyptian Antiquities', p. 268.
3. Anon., 'The Discovery Ships Are Completely Ready to Leave Deptford', p. 3.
4. Ibid. p. 3.
5. The head of the Young Memnon is often supposed to have inspired Percy Shelley's poem, 'Ozymandias'. On the relationship between Shelley and this statue, see John Rodenbeck 'Travelers from an Antique Land: Shelley's Inspiration for "Ozymandias"' (2004).
6. Anon., 'Narrative of an Expedition to Explore the River Zaire, usually called the Congo, in South Africa, in 1816', p. 368.
7. Belzoni, *Narrative of the Operations and Recent Discoveries within the Pyramids, Temples, Tombs, and Excavations in Egypt and Nubia*, p. 39.

8. Ibid. pp. 43–4, 50–1.
9. Ibid. p. 50.
10. Anon., 'Town Talk', pp. 309–12; Anon., 'Stage Silhouettes', pp. 257–8.
11. Anon., 'The Story of Giovanni Belzoni', p. 551.
12. Anon., 'John Baptist Belzoni', p. 181.
13. Anon., 'The Story of Giovanni Belzoni', p. 552.
14. This scene seems to have retained its performative qualities in the cultural imagination. In his 2003 biography of Belzoni, Stanley Mayes describes the removal of the Young Memnon in the same highly theatrical language that had been used by the nineteenth-century periodical press. He writes of 'sweating, half-naked Arabs hauling on the tow-ropes, chanting a work-song as the colossal head moved forward a few inches at a time; the face of Memnon smiling inscrutably into the eye of the sun; and Giovanni standing there overburdened with clothes, his head burst in that terrible heat, anxiously watching every movement of the stone as it strained against its palm-fibre bonds'. See Mayes, *The Great Belzoni*, p. 130.
15. Irving, *The Life and Letters of Washington Irving*, vol. 2, p. 386.
16. Anon., 'The Story of Giovanni Belzoni', p. 551.
17. Ibid. p. 551.
18. Anon., 'Tomb of Sethi, Descendant of the Sun', p. 733. Emphasis in the original.
19. Anon., 'Antiquarian Researches. Mr Belzoni's Exhibition of the Egyptian Tomb', p. 450.
20. Baudrillard, *Simulacra and Simulation*, p. 1.
21. Ziter, *The Orient on the Victorian Stage*, p. 10.
22. Ibid. p. 79.
23. Ibid. p. 80.
24. Ibid. p. 79.
25. This 1843 regulation brought an end to the patent monopoly by laying out a nationwide system of licensing. Under this new system, theatres might apply for a licence from the Lord Chamberlain that would enable them to perform drama.
26. Moody, *Illegitimate Theatre in London, 1770–1840*, p. 117.
27. Ibid. p. 79
28. Anon., 'Drama', *European Magazine, and London Review*, pp. 637, 638. Emphasis in the original.
29. Daly, *Sensation and Modernity in the 1860s*, p. 8.
30. Ziter, *The Orient on the Victorian Stage*, p. 3.
31. On the political and ideological implications of Byron's Orientalism, see Butler, 'Byron and the Empire in the East', pp. 63–81, and McGann, '"My brain is Feminine": Byron and the Poetry of Deception', pp. 63–76.
32. Makdisi, *Romantic Imperialism*, p. 133. For an overview of the proliferation of the harem trope in nineteenth-century British theatre, see Ziter, *The Orient on the Victorian Stage*, pp. 54–93.

33. Anon., 'Theatrical Journal', *European Magazine, and London Review* 14 (December 1788), p. 470.
34. Ibid. p. 470; Anon., 'Drury Lane', *Belle Assemblée*, p. 169; Anon., 'Theatre Royal Covent-Garden', p. 252; Anon., 'Surrey', p. 110.
35. Anon., 'Dramatic Register', p. 553; Anon., 'Covent-Garden Theatre', *Ladies Monthly Magazine*, p. 288.
36. Anon., 'Drama. The London Theatres', p. 236; Anon., 'Dramatic Criticisms. Covent-Garden', p. 190.
37. Anon., 'Notices of the Acted Drama in London', p. 320.
38. Ibid. p. 320.
39. In general, however, the growing importance of detailed painting and set design was largely due to the fact that stages were becoming more and more brightly illuminated by gas lighting and limelight.
40. Anon., 'Theatrical Journal', *European Magazine, and London Review* 49 (April 1806), p. 289. Emphasis in the original.
41. Anon., 'Drury Lane', *Belle Assemblée*, p. 170.
42. Anon., 'Advertisement, Theatre Royal, Drury Lane', p. 4.
43. Anon., 'Advertisement, Theatre Royal, Covent Garden', p. 3.
44. Anon., 'Theatrical Journal', *European Magazine, and London Review* 66 (Dec. 1816), p. 523.
45. Anon., 'Dramatic Register', *New Monthly Magazine*, pp. 552–4 (p. 553).
46. Anon., 'The Drama', *London Magazine*, p. 484. Ellipses in the original. In Galland's version of this tale, each time the Sultan of Persia's wife gives birth, her sisters set the baby adrift in the canal and claim that she has given birth to a dog, a cat and a mole, respectively. The three children – two boys and a girl – are rescued by an attendant in the Sultan's gardens. Several years later, the young princess is visited by a mysterious old woman who tells her that her house requires three things: a talking bird, a Singing Tree and the 'Yellow Golden Water'. The Princess's brothers attempt and fail to capture these ornaments, but the Princess herself succeeds. Their wonderful possessions soon gain the attention of the Sultan, to whom the talking bird relates the tale of the children's survival. The Sultana is then liberated from a long imprisonment and the family is united in the Persian capital amidst great celebrations.
47. Anon., 'Theatrical Register. New Pieces', p. 366.
48. Anon., 'The Drama', *London Magazine*, p. 484; Anon., 'Drama. The London Theatres', p. 236.
49. Anon., 'Drama. The London Theatres', p. 236.
50. Anon., 'The Drama. Drury-Lane Theatre', p. 342. For more information on Andrew Ducrow and the use of horses in stage productions, see Saxon, *The Life and Art of Andrew Ducrow* (1978).
51. In Galland's tale, a young Indian man presents the King of Persia with a magic horse, demanding in exchange to be married to his daughter. The King's son is outraged at this impertinence and insists upon riding

the horse in order to verify its powers. He is soon transported to Bengal, where he falls in love with a princess and brings her back to Persia on the horse. The Indian, however, abducts both the horse and the Princess of Bengal, fleeing to Cashmere, where he is later killed. The Princess discovers that the Sultan of Cashmere now wants to marry her and feigns insanity until the Prince of Persia, who has been travelling in search of her, finally rescues and marries her.

52. Anon., 'English Theatricals. Drury-Lane', p. 265.
53. Anon., 'Theatrical Examiner', p. 694.
54. Ibid. p. 694.
55. Anon., 'Drury-Lane Theatre', *Monthly Magazine*, p. 359.
56. Bolter and Grusin, *Remediation*, p. 157.
57. Ibid. p. 157.
58. Anon., 'Drury Lane Theatre', *Theatrical Observer*, p. 1. Emphasis in the original.
59. Anon., 'The Overture and the Whole of the Music in Aladdin', p. 243.
60. Bown et al., 'Introduction', p. 1.
61. Ibid. p. 1. On the so-called 'magic of the mechanical' in the context of the history of electrical experimentation, see Sconce, *Haunted Media* (2000).
62. During, *Modern Enchantments*, p. 14.
63. Saglia, 'Theatre, Drama, and Vision in the Romantic Age', p. 759.
64. In her chapter, 'Why Aladdin?', Marina Warner reflects on the various characteristics of this story, which have sparked theatrical innovation and consistently rendered it attractive as an opportunity for spectacle on a lavish scale. See Warner, *Stranger Magic*, pp. 357–70.
65. Warner, *Fantastic Metamorphoses*, p. 149.
66. Anon., 'The Theatres. Drury-Lane', p. 41.
67. Ibid. p. 41.
68. Ibid. p. 40.
69. Ibid. p. 40. On the origins of pantomime's allegorical characters, see McKee, *Scenarios of the Commedia Dell'Arte* (1967).
70. Anon., 'The Theatres. Drury-Lane', p. 41. Emphasis in the original.
71. Mayer, *Harlequin in His Element*, p. 8.
72. Ibid. p. 8.
73. Moody, *Illegitimate Theatre in London, 1770–1840*, p. 209.
74. Nuss, *Distance, Theatre, and the Public Voice, 1750–1850*, p. 18.
75. This production is examined by John O'Brien as a classic example of Regency-period pantomimes in 'Pantomime', pp. 103–14.
76. Galland, *Arabian Nights' Entertainments*, p. 107.
77. Anon., 'Covent-Garden Theatre', *The Times*, p. 3.
78. Ibid. p. 3.
79. Anon., 'Theatrical Recorder', *Universal Magazine*, p. 144. Anon., 'Theatrical Journal', *European Magazine, and London Review* 63 (January 1813), p. 45.

80. Grimaldi, *Memoirs*, p. 88.
81. Anon., 'Covent-Garden Theatre', *The Times*, p. 3.
82. Nuss, *Distance, Theatre, and the Public Voice*, p. 19.
83. Jennifer Schacker has made this claim about fairy-story collections more generally in nineteenth-century England, which, she argues, prompted imaginatively liberating flights of fancy while raising larger questions about the transformation of popular culture and 'the nature of "Englishness" in the midst of rapid social, cultural, and technological change'. See Schacker, *National Dreams*, p. 12.
84. Anon., 'Theatre-Royal, Drury-Lane', *Monthly Theatrical Reporter*, p. 137. Emphasis in the original.
85. Diamond, *Performance and Cultural Politics*, p. 2.
86. Ibid. p. 2.
87. Anon., 'Advertisement, Theatre Royal, Lyceum', p. 4.
88. Anon., *Aladdin and the Wonderful Lamp; or, New Lamps for Old Ones*, I, i, 1–2.
89. Ibid. I, i, 1–2.
90. Ibid. I, ii, 15–18.
91. Ibid. I, iii, 6–17. Emphasis in the original.
92. Thomas Carlyle, for example, in his 1829 essay 'Signs of the Times', lamented the new lack of direct contact with society and nature caused by the intervention of machinery in every aspect of life, and expressed his concern that, as print publications were fast becoming the principal medium of public debate and influence, they were shaping and distorting human learning and communications. John Stuart Mill heartily agreed, insisting in his 1836 essay 'Civilization' that the new cacophony of voices across the periodical press disempowered individual writers, who found themselves increasingly lost in a glutted marketplace of ideas, opinions, adverts and quacks.
93. Anon., 'Dramatic Criticisms. Drury-Lane Theatre', p. 71.
94. Ibid. p. 71.
95. Ibid. p. 71.
96. Anon., 'What English Literature Gives Us', p. 1.
97. Ibid. p. 1.
98. Al-Dabbagh, *Literary Orientalism, Postcolonialism, and Universalism*, p. 30. Emphasis in original. Al-Dabbagh makes this observation in response to Martha Conant's study of the Arabian Nights and the Oriental tale in eighteenth-century England.

Chapter 4

Magic and Machines at the Great Exhibition

During the summer of 1851, a thirty-five-year-old Charlotte Brontë travelled to London to visit the Great Exhibition of the Works of Industry of All Nations at Hyde Park. She wrote of the experience in a letter to her father:

> It is a wonderful place – vast – strange new and impossible to describe. Its grandeur does not consist in *one* thing but in the unique assemblage of *all* things – Whatever human industry has created – you find there – from the great compartments filled with Railway Engines and boilers, with Mill-machinery in full work – with splendid carriages of all kinds – with harness of every description – the glass-covered and velvet spread stands loaded with the most gorgeous work of the goldsmith and silversmith – and the carefully guarded caskets full of real diamonds and pearls worth hundreds of thousands of pounds.[1]

The first international exhibition of manufactured products, the Great Exhibition was indeed vast. From 1 May to 15 October 1851, over 100,000 objects from more than 15,000 contributors were displayed within its 900,000 square feet of internal floor space. This plethora of objects was supposedly representative of the entire globe: its raw materials, decorative manufactures, mechanical inventions and sculptures.[2] Here, engines, boilers and industrial machinery, exhibited in full operation, might be examined alongside precious jewels, caskets and the intricate work of gold and silver-smiths. It was, Brontë is clear, the strange mix of things, and the unexpected juxtapositions of such an assemblage, that led to a sense of wonder and bewilderment.

Brontë was far from alone in finding the range of materials that vied for her attention disorienting. Visitors to the Great Exhibition were thrust into a profound encounter with the world of objects, where they beheld an extensive array of things that circulated within, were used by, and structured the organisations and habits of different societies around the world. Removed from the social and cultural conditions of their production, objects of extraordinary diversity existed here in what Andrew Miller has termed an 'intermediate space', held separate from the processes of exchange between producer and consumer, which 'juxtaposed goods from all points in the globe, eliminating their original contexts and constructing new meanings in its austere space'.[3] The exhibition was, as Brontë says, 'strange new and impossible to describe', because this great mass of disparate materials seemed to resist attempts to represent it in words. 'Every one who has seen it', declared *Chambers's Edinburgh Journal*, 'will have felt the impossibility of giving an account of either the fabric or its contents ... all are felt to be beyond the reach of words.'[4] Moving through the palace was an emotional, 'felt' experience, rather than a linguistic phenomenon. This posed, as Verity Hunt has argued, an interesting problem for language: 'How best to narrativize the miles of international displays and their seminal glass home?'[5] Such a 'depthless, abstract space', as Miller argues, 'encouraged its own patterns of behaviour and thought'.[6]

One imaginative model for drawing out those patterns and figuring the exhibition in narrative form was, this chapter will argue, the ever-proliferating tales of the Arabian Nights. Not only did this story-cycle provide a useful structure for conceptualising and understanding the dazzling manifestation of discordant materials within the Crystal Palace, but, through such comparisons, the objects on display became charged with new meanings and exercised new powers over their beholders. Further, infusing this event with an aura of magic and wonder provoked reflections on the mysterious workings of modern machinery and industry, and the comparative values of old and new, hand-crafted and mechanical, and exotic and domestic wares.

The World in a London Park

The Crystal Palace was a monumental structure of British industry where peoples and objects of the world seemed magically to converge and coalesce. Thackeray's exuberant 'May-Day Ode', written on the opening of the exhibition and published in *The Times* on 30 April, emphasised the building's other-worldly aura:

> As though 'twere by a wizard's rod
> A blazing arch of lucid glass
> Leaps like a fountain from the grass
> To meet the sun!
> A quiet green, but few days since
> With cattle browsing in the shade,
> And lo! long lines of bright arcade
> In order raised;
> A palace as for fairy Prince,
> A rare pavilion, such as man
> Saw never, since mankind began,
> And built and glazed![7]

Thackeray's evocation of fairies and wizards was typical of many reactions to the speed with which the Crystal Palace was constructed. Reports of the building emphasised its seemingly supernatural arrival in Hyde Park and its appearance of magical unreality. Charles Knight, in an article in *Household Words*, described the palace by way of comparison to that familiar moment in the Arabian Nights 'when Aladdin raised a palace in one night, whose walls were formed, not of layers of bricks, but of gold and silver'.[8] The *Leader* believed that work on the building's rapid construction 'goes on magically, and day after day new objects of wonder are revealed' as if by 'some invisible agency'.[9] *The Times* was particularly effusive in its review of the palace's seemingly immaterial form in contrast to the surrounding, concrete city of London:

> The vast fabric may be seen, by any one who visits that part of town, in its full dimensions – an Arabian Night's structure, full of light, and with a certain airy unsubstantial character about it which belongs more to an enchanted land than this gross material world of ours. The eye, accustomed to the solid heavy details of stone and lime or brick and mortar architecture, wanders along those extended and transparent aisles with their terraced outlines, almost distrusting its own conclusions on the reality of what it sees, for the whole looks like a splendid phantasm, which the heat of the noon-day sun would dissolve, or a gust of wind scatter into fragments, or a London fog utterly extinguish.[10]

A fantastic construction that, like Aladdin's own palace, promised access to magic objects and distant kingdoms, this 408 foot high, modular, wrought-iron and glass structure designed by Joseph Paxton was, in reality, as one of its guidebooks declared, a supremely 'industrial palace of glass, iron, and wood'.[11] Although imbued with an aura of enchantment, its rapid construction in just nine months had been made possible by the prefabrication of all its component parts in factories in the Midlands, before their assemblage on site by a large labour force that numbered up to 2,000 men a day. The Crystal Palace was innovative technologically, and it made use of the industrial skills and inventions of its time. The new mass production of glass after the lifting of the glass tax in 1845 had led to the development of plate-glass technology by Robert Lucas Chance, whose factory in Smethwick produced all 300,000 panels for the palace in the largest size ever made. Communication between locations was facilitated by telegraphy and the use of the railway, while steam engines on site were used to cut the wooden glazing bars, as well as the 24 miles of Paxton's patent guttering, that held the glass in position.[12]

The notion of an Aladdin's palace suddenly materialising out of thin air was not a particularly unusual frame of reference for such moments of seemingly rapid relocation or transformation in nineteenth-century literature and culture. Dickens, for example, deploys the construction throughout his writing. In 'A Visit to Newgate', one of the *Sketches by Boz* (1836), he reflects on the human force of habit, such that 'if Bedlam could be suddenly removed like another Aladdin's palace, and set down on the space now occupied by Newgate', scarcely one man in a hundred would bestow even a hasty glance upon it.[13] Later, in *Our Mutual Friend* (1865), modern English architecture is imbued with a sense of instability and impermanence when the narrator notes that the schools where Kent and Surrey meet were, at the time the novel is set, 'newly built, and there were so many like them all over the country, that one might have thought the whole were but one restless edifice with the locomotive gift of Aladdin's palace'.[14] Such material transformations appear to be immediate, effortless and apparently amoral. As a narrative device, this enables continual movement and action, while fostering a sense of wonder, or even confusion, as to the means by which such transformations are achieved. Moreover, people, as well as buildings, may find themselves magically transported in this manner, as they enjoy momentary experiences of joy and delight that appear illusory, or unreal. Elsewhere in the same fiction, we are therefore told that the *nouveaux-riches* Veneerings, 'bran-new people in a bran-new house in a bran-new quarter of London', seek to advance in the social world by impressing influential people around them, and so 'they have a house out of the Tales of the Genii and give dinners out of the Arabian Nights', the illusory nature of which is ultimately confirmed when they have been left bankrupted by the end of the novel.[15]

A more extended metaphor is deployed in *The Old Curiosity Shop* (1841), when the unscrupulous young Dick Swiveller awakes after a serious illness, feeling well rested and happier, with the Marchioness playing cribbage at a nearby table. In this moment of confusion, Dick draws on the popular understanding of the Arabian Nights as a space of fantasy and dreaming, as discussed in Chapter 2, to speculate that 'if this is not a dream, I have woke up by mistake in an Arabian Night instead of a London one'.[16] Initially associating his altered physical state and surroundings with an altered consciousness, Dick becomes increasingly convinced of the reality of his new environment, and then explicitly draws upon the tale of Bedreddin Hassan to describe the abrupt transformation he has undergone:

> 'It's an Arabian Night, that's what it is,' said Richard. 'I'm in Damascus or Grand Cairo. The Marchioness is a Genie, and having had a wager with another Genie about who is the handsomest young man alive, and the worthiest to be the husband of the Princess of China, has brought me away, room and all, to compare us together. Perhaps,' said Mr Swiveller, turning languidly round upon his pillow, and looking on that side of his bed which was next the wall, 'the Princess may still – No, she's gone.'[17]

In 'The Story of Noureddin Ali, and Bedreddin Hassan', while he is sleeping by his father's tomb, the young Bedreddin is magically transported to Cairo by a genie and a fairy who have decided that he is the most beautiful of mortals and therefore deserves to marry a delightful young Cairene woman. This allusion underlines Dick's experience, at least from his own perspective, as sudden and inexplicable, while illuminating the role that wealth and the possibility of material gain have played in his decisions about matrimony. Although the opportunistic Dick, who has always enjoyed imagining himself in a state of luxury, sought to marry Little Nell in order to enjoy her supposed inheritance, he will ultimately, as this scene suggests, marry the Marchioness. He thus effects a more permanent change in his life circumstances than that achieved momentarily here, as if by magic.

Use of the Arabian Nights as a metaphor of magical transformation was, as Isobel Armstrong has noted, a 'frequent and seemingly banal analogy' of the nineteenth century.[18] In broader cultural constructions, these tales came to represent a dramatic time and space of 'ideal happiness', to use George Eliot's phrase, 'in which you are invited to step from the labour and discord of the street into a paradise in which everything is given to you and nothing claimed'.[19] The Crystal Palace appeared in many accounts as one such transformative space. A new and innovative architectural form, it challenged the viewer's vision, judgement and sense of scale to such an extent that recourse was made to the familiar language of magic and enchantment in an effort to represent its unfamiliar effects. The palace and the objects it contained had apparently materialised within nineteenth-century London like the stuff of dreams, seemingly conjured by the rub of a magic lamp. It was, Charlotte Brontë wrote,

> as if magic only could have gathered this mass of wealth from all the ends of the Earth – as if none but supernatural hands could have arranged it thus – with such a blaze and contrast of colours and marvellous power of effect.[20]

An enchanted space, it was 'such a Bazaar or Fair as eastern genii might have created' that even 'the multitude filling the great aisles seems ruled and subdued by some invisible influence'.[21]

Despite its wider presence as a rhetorical strategy, Eva Badowska, in an analysis of Charlotte Brontë's *Villette* (1853) in the context of the Great Exhibition, has rightly drawn our attention to the potential dangers that may be implicit in such slippages between the fictional and factual. While showcasing the hypnotic power of the exhibition, Brontë's allusion to bazaars and genii also, Badowska argues, slips into an Orientalist rhetoric that is instantly troubling in its capacity to erase the human labour and the movement of capital involved in the production and accumulation of goods:

> For to describe commodities as conjured up by a genie is to mask the movements of capital that really made things happen. To suggest that magic collected things from 'all the ends of the earth' is to eclipse the geographic reaches of the empire that made Brontë's hyperbole only somewhat fanciful.[22]

Badowska situates this imagery exclusively within the ideology of global capitalist and colonial expansion, of which the exhibition was undoubtedly, in her words, 'an unabashed celebration'.[23] While 'on the one hand a strategy of misrecognition' that located the objects of the East within an ethereal fantasy space that was somehow removed from scenes of colonial intervention and appropriation, this rhetoric may also, as Isobel Armstrong argues in her study of the emergent glass culture of Victorian England, contain coded references to such violence, for 'Aladdin is indeed a tale of theft and riches'.[24] It is also a tale, we might add, of the capture and command of incarcerated beings, and as such, it had further political and cultural resonances in the period. There was, as Marina Warner has shown, an 'obsessive multiplication of slaves in the story of Aladdin' in theatres of the nineteenth century, during Britain's struggles over the slave trade, which communicated the 'soulless, dehumanised condition of enslavement decried by the abolitionists'.[25] In the context of the Great Exhibition, the slaves of the lamp were, in effect, Britain's own labour force.

'Let us consider', declared Charles Knight after his opening allusion to the Aladdin's palace construction in *Household Words*, 'how many Slaves of the Lamp have been employed in constructing the Palace of Industry.'[26] While the 'Genii of the Lamp' – which Knight uses here to mean both the intellectual power or 'genius' behind the operation, as well as those spirits capable of granting wishes when summoned – were at hand 'in the form of skilful manufacturers and wise statesmen', the amount of manual labour involved in its production was immense.[27] In fact, he declares, 'the labour employed upon our Palace of Industry, as compared with the labour which raised the [Great Pyramid of Egypt], is as one to two thousand'.[28] Further, in stark contrast to those 'supernatural hands' that Brontë believed must have arranged it, Knight's description of the varied industry within the building is suggestive of intense physical toil amongst a chaotic mass of disparate materials:

> It is no exaggeration to say that there were thousands intensely occupied, each with his own work of unloading or unpacking. The great struggle was in the centre of the western aisle, where the heavy British articles of models, or machinery, were deposited. In the Foreign department, the allotted spaces were filled with chests, bearing inscriptions in English, French, German, and Italian. Fragments of sculpture, heads and feet of colossal statues, were spread in wild confusion on the central floor.[29]

This Arabian Nights structure was, as Knight makes clear, a palace produced not by magic but by industry, and the source of Britain's power in conjuring it had been its own labour force. The energy and skills of British industry were akin to the powers of the wonderful lamp, such that it might now replicate or even surpass those fantastical realms contained within the Arabian Nights. Indeed, within this wonderful space, one might supposedly encounter materials from all the realms and cultures of the globe.

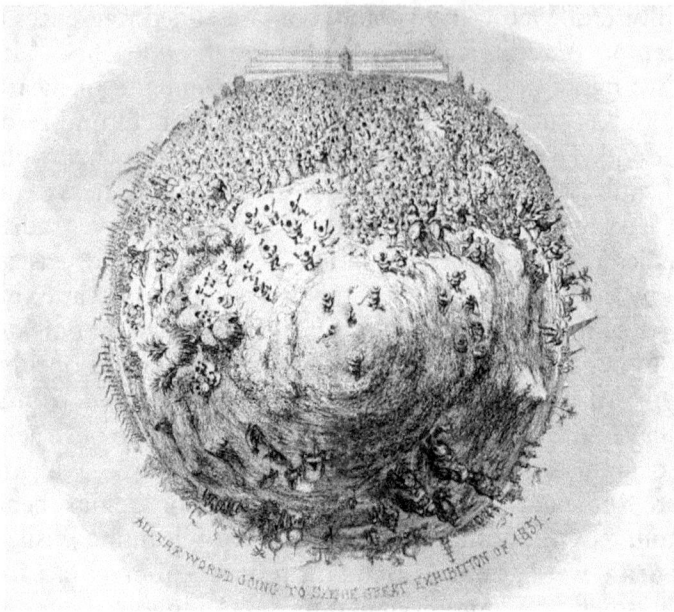

Figure 4.1 'All the World Going to See the Great Exhibition of 1851', George Cruikshank, in Henry Mayhew and George Cruikshank, *1851; Or, the Adventures of Mr. and Mrs. Sandboys and Family, Who Came up to London to 'Enjoy Themselves' and to See the Great Exhibition*. London: David Bogue, 1857. Credit: Internet Archive.

The almost supernatural ability of the Crystal Palace to absorb and to reconfigure the globe is demonstrated by George Cruikshank's famous illustration 'All the World Going to See the Great Exhibition of 1851' (Figure 4.1), which first appeared in Henry Mayhew's comic novel *1851: or, The Adventures of Mr. and Mrs. Sandboys and Family, Who Came up to London to 'Enjoy Themselves' and to See the Great Exhibition* and visualises the claims of the novel's opening line: 'The Great Exhibition was about to attract the sight-seers of all the world – the sight-seers, who make up nine tenths of the human family.'[30] In Cruikshank's image, this multitudinous human family is a social and a material network emanating from the stunning new building located in Hyde Park. Britain is represented solely by the Crystal Palace, a modern architectural triumph positioned out of all proportion across the apex of the globe, drawing crowds of tourists towards it in an increasingly undifferentiated, teeming throng. While there is a general sense of humanity's evolutionary progression in their movement from the barren, atavistic lands at the south of the picture to the modern, crowded city at the north, there is no clear delineation of borders or countries. Rather, each portion of this oddly bulging globe, in keeping with the stated purpose of the exhibition, has been reduced to one or two representative objects: Africa, at the right of the image, is represented by camels and pyramids; Asia is characterised by the people's broad-brimmed hats and the elephants at the bottom of the globe; while the steam-ships at the far left symbolise America.[31] As this tidal wave of people reaches London, it is easily absorbed and contained by a mammoth structure. The clear implication here is that both peoples and cultures are being collected, represented and consumed at the Great Exhibition, which can magically hold the world and its entire contents. This is further illustrated by the English flags that have been planted on both poles, implying that Britain has captured the entire globe.

Barbara Black has argued that Cruikshank's illustration contributes to the nineteenth century's emerging 'fable for museum culture' because it offers 'a geopolitical vision of the world commercially and imperially remapped, with London playing host'.[32] Certainly, this totalising concept of a globe contracted and reconfigured by British influence was replicated in the spatial organisation of the exhibition, which divided the displays between an east wing for foreign exhibits and a west wing for the United Kingdom, its colonies and its dependencies.[33] The *Illustrated Exhibitor* explicitly described the building's layout in terms of the globe, noting that there was 'one long avenue from east to west being intersected by a Transept, which divides the building into two nearly equal portions' and is 'as it were, the equator of the world in Hyde-Park'.[34] Many visitors to the palace recorded their visits as a kind of virtual, whirlwind tour of the world. The Swedish writer Frederika Bremer, for instance, recalled in her memoirs that during the exhibition, 'I wandered therefore hour by hour, from the lands of the west to those of the east, and from the north to the south, from the Polar regions to the Equator.'[35] The *Athenaeum* claimed that 'here is the whole world concentrated in a mere point in space', where 'all man's material is brought for the first time into a single point of view'.[36] *Sharpe's London Journal* included a long piece entitled 'A Journey Round the World in the Crystal Palace', which provided a brief summary of the main displays of the exhibition and the writer's initial impressions of them.[37] Condensed within the palace, within a single point on the globe, was an abstracted and miniaturised world, available for consumption, exploration and entertainment.[38]

The exhibition challenged the spatial and sensory perceptions of many of its visitors. In the palace, the *Athenaeum* insisted, 'the mind becomes impressed with an idea that all the objects are dwarfed – by the vastness of the whole'.[39] According to the *Art Journal Illustrated Catalogue*, 'the eye is completely dazzled by the rich variety of hues which burst upon it on every side' and 'it is not until this partial bewilderment has subsided, that we are in a condition to appreciate as it deserves its real magnificence'.[40] The report in *Sharpe's London Journal* describes the confusion caused by observing the accumulation of so many different objects in one building, where,

> in the first moment of amazement you behold at the same time, in the midst of these confused sounds, carpets from the East, arms from India, a European park with its woods and rivulets, and an innumerable army of equestrian statues around you.[41]

The new proximity of these disparate materials creates 'a new world – and what world is it?'[42] Moving through this space was both disorientating and exhausting. Samuel Warren wrote rather poetically that here 'the Soul was approached through its highest senses, flooded with excitement; all its faculties were appealed to at once, and it sank, for a while, exhausted, overwhelmed'.[43] The *Athenaeum* also emphasised the surreal nature of the diversity and the vast number of collections, claiming that moving through the spaces of the palace was 'like wandering through a realm of dreams' and that the opening ceremony in particular (Figure 4.2) produced a dizzying sense of shifting structures and perspectives:

> The eye also took measures of distance at this point which were among the most curious experiences of the day. Glancing along the greatly narrowed avenue marked by the continuous double line of spectators between whom the Queen was to pass up the southern side, the perspective seemed to stretch infinitely away, – and the termination was a point which the eye could not define. When the procession turned this point, the fact could not be ascertained by unassisted vision – and it had made some progress up the avenue when it was discovered by means of a telescope.[44]

The Great Exhibition challenged the eye and overwhelmed the senses with far more stimuli than could be fully apprehended by the viewer. The question of *how* to look at it was clearly a problem of scale that

Magic and Machines at the Great Exhibition   151

Figure 4.2 The opening of the Great Exhibition by Queen Victoria at Crystal Palace. 1851. Engraved by H. Bibby. Credit: Wellcome Collection. CC BY 4.0.

potentially undermined critical judgement and insight, and gave way to fatigue and bewilderment.

According to several contemporary guidebooks, magnifying glasses were placed on swivels at short intervals along the galleries of the palace in order to assist visitors gazing upon the displays below, by allowing the eye to isolate and examine objects of interest.[45] The sheer multitude of objects on display at the palace necessitated this kind of partial and sequential, rather than comprehensive, approach to the displays. Thomas Richards has argued that the importance of keeping large crowds moving through the confined spaces of the exhibition created a serial rhythm of spectatorship, as visitors were 'virtually forced to acquire a limited attention span'.[46] This allowed visitors to form only a cursory impression of each display as, 'regardless of what you ultimately fixed your gaze upon, the Crystal Palace turned you into a dilettante, loitering your way through a phantasmagoria of commodities'.[47] Richards goes on to argue for the pivotal role of the Great Exhibition in the formation of consumer culture and the transformation of the commodity into a spectacle in Britain. However, his insight into this episodic pattern of seeing and quickly judging each display within the exhibition before moving on to the next also points to a mode of seeing and 'reading' the objects that is in keeping with the instalment mode of the Arabian Nights and the periodical reading culture of Victorian Britain.

A familiar metaphor for the extensive displays and the surreal atmosphere within the palace, it is tempting to speculate that the Arabian Nights also provided a familiar conceptual model for ways of approaching and understanding its vast collections. The Arabian Nights, as Borges noted, 'doubles and dizzyingly redoubles the ramifications of a central tale into digressing tales, but without ever trying to gradate its realities', so that the effect '(which should be one of depth) is superficial, like a Persian carpet'.[48] It was a seemingly endless network of tales that diverted the reader through a fundamentally non-linear style of reading. In the nineteenth century, this intricate creation was admired for its creative artifice and 'the harmony with which the natural is blended with the supernatural', while also criticised because its 'brilliant surface work' was considered to lack depth and so function as a landscape where 'men and women are woven like embroidery into the tissue of the story'.[49] Although divided into geographical sections, the beautiful 'Arabian Nights structure' of the Crystal Palace and its wonderful contents might, like those very stories, be explored, examined and re-examined in any order. A discrete spatial and temporal sphere, detached from the rhythms of the outside world, the collections were interconnected yet disparate. Like Scheherazade's nightly performance, they offered a carefully orchestrated, 'choreographed' experience, which, according to the *Athenaeum*, allowed the visitor to pass by 'endless scenes' as if they were 'arranged by a clever artist for a grand opera'.[50] It was, as John Tallis wrote in his extensive three-volume account of the event, a 'glancing bed of peripatetic flowrets' and 'a kaleidoscope *parterre* of bright hues and tints, shifting and blending, and intermingling like living shot-silk', where 'nobody looks at anything in particular – unless it be somebody else'.[51] The *Leader* even stated that 'the progress of arrangements in Hyde-park reads like a page of the Arabian Nights'.[52] In this way, the tales of the Arabian Nights became a useful tool for approaching, gazing upon and making sense of the modern spaces and objects of the Great Exhibition. However, paradoxically, that tool also allowed the objects on display to assume an abstract, imaginary status as starting points for fiction and fantasy.

The Power of Things

Amidst the great clutter of things at the exhibition, re-framed and refracted by continual reference to the Arabian Nights, certain objects drew and focused the viewer's gaze. Displayed prominently in the nave of the palace's eastern transept, the infamous Koh-i-Noor diamond, which had been presented to Queen Victoria by the East India Company less than a year earlier, was an extremely popular attraction. Initially contained within a gilded, birdcage-like structure, and then re-displayed within a small tent arranged with gas lamps and mirrors, the jewel received mixed reactions, as many visitors expressed disappointment in its size and lustre. None the less, its potency as a symbol of the magic and romance that India held for Britain was captured by way of allusion to the Arabian Nights. In May 1851, *Punch* included a short piece that reflected upon the stone as a source of repeated pleasure and Oriental fantasy:

> Ever since the 1st of May, I've driven directly after early breakfast to the Palace of that great Jin, PAXTON, in Hyde Park, where for hours I've done nothing but think myself a great Princess of the Arabian Nights, with the Koh-i-noor my own property, whenever I liked to wear it.[53]

This precious stone, according to *Allen's Indian Mail*, 'enclose[d] within its impenetrable bosom the spirit of one of those princes of the Arabian Nights whose humanity was liable to metamorphosis', and it speculated as to 'what stories it might not tell of all the scenes it has witnessed'.[54] Through such allusions, Armstrong notes, 'the Koh-i-noor's violent history of colonial expropriation can dissolve like the mists'.[55] There is, as Armstrong tells us, something 'knowing' about these references, as, drawn into a history of enchanted objects seen, represented and re-imagined through literature, the gem is rendered fundamentally unstable, and liable to abuse by those with whom it comes into contact. At the same time, however, in holding the spirit of an Arabian prince, this diamond, like many of the enchanted rings, jewels and lamps in the Arabian Nights, occupies an ambiguous status between person and object. Through this allusion to an Eastern fable, it is granted agency, even subjectivity, and its own impenetrable spirit presence. There is a suggestion, too, that it cannot quite be safely contained and may exert a power, or cast a spell, over its beholders.

In keeping with the array of objects that are revealed to possess magical properties in the stories of the Arabian Nights, even the most mundane household goods and furnishings on display at the exhibition were made meaningful by such comparisons. In a lengthy description of a 'large earthen wine or oil jar, from Alentejo', in Portugal, which 'had probably been introduced into Spain by the Moors, as similar vessels are found among the Arabs of Mount Atlas', the exhibition catalogue goes on to note that 'the oil jars of the Forty Thieves in the Arabian Nights were probably of this description'.[56] A reviewer for the *London Journal* similarly declared that, while wandering the Asiatic quarters of the exhibition, 'One looked at the tickets, expecting to see that they were "worked in the households of Cogia Hassan and Ali Baba"'.[57]

Apparently dematerialised from the realms of the Arabian Nights and re-materialised within the Crystal Palace, such objects are, in the words of *Sharpe's London Journal*, 'stolen from the golden country of the "Thousand-and-one Nights"', and they occupy a problematic ontological status between the real and the imaginary.[58] The allusion is an apt one: the stories of the Arabian Nights teem with all manner of material objects. Some are inanimate wares that contribute to the collection's surplus of narrative detail and colour. Others, be they lamps, treasures, books, statues, amulets, talismans, potions, carpets or even severed heads, are profoundly animate. They talk, move, alter in size and shape, and exercise power over the world around them. In Marina Warner's words, they 'ignite and speak, move and grow, pulse and radiate, displaying sentience and expressing feelings and developing attachments to their owners'.[59] Frequent comparisons to the rich material repository of the Arabian Nights in the context of the Great Exhibition explicitly invoked these properties, imbuing the items on display with the same vitality and energy, and, significantly, with the same power to affect their beholders. It was an association that, to draw upon the rubric set out by Bill Brown in his elucidation of 'Thing Theory', distinguished such items as 'things' rather than mere 'objects':

> You could imagine things ... as what is excessive in objects, as what exceeds their mere materialization as objects or their mere utilization as objects – their force as a sensuous presence or as a metaphysical presence, the magic by which objects become values, fetishes, idols and totems.[60]

When perceived as 'things', material objects exceed both their practical uses and their perceived intrinsic values to signify in new, often unexpected, ways. Such, as Arjun Appadurai has observed, are the 'idiosyncrasies of things' as they circulate in society and are ascribed meaning.[61] Removed from their social and cultural contexts and 'normal' uses, and relocated to the Crystal Palace, objects on display at the Great Exhibition were strangely out of place, re-imagined as magical, and subjected to the kind of 'fetishistic overvaluation or misappropriation' and the 'irregular if not unreasonable reobjectification of the object' that, Brown insists, precipitate 'thinginess'.[62]

The distinction that Brown upholds between objects and things is not dependent upon any inherent qualities of the thing in question, but rather upon its reception by the viewer. The 'magic' by which objects take on new meanings and serve as symbols, idols and totems is facilitated almost exclusively by the context in which they are situated and the ideas and memories that they stimulate. In this, the thing shares the dual nature of the fetish, which, as Peter Pels has argued, is both a material object and an evocative sign to its beholder, both 'discursive creation and material reality'.[63] The object itself remains the same but it takes on new layers of meaning, triggers personal and/or cultural memories and elicits imaginative interpretations. William Pietz has emphasised the 'intensely personal' nature of this process, which he believes is 'experienced as a substantial movement from "inside" the self . . . into the self-limited morphology of a material object situated in space "outside"'.[64] The object itself is thus regarded as the material expression of an internal psychological or emotional state. We see an example of this emotionally charged animation of objects in *Sharpe's London Journal*, which imagined the materials of popular Eastern fiction having been 'cast' into the halls of the Great Exhibition, spilling over from their texts to be found amongst the disorientating assemblage of objects on display:

> Picture to yourself, on either side, prospects stolen from the golden country of the 'Thousand-and-one Nights', two galleries, apparently interminable, covered from top to bottom with the most perfect produce of the human genius, and all natural curiosities from Canton to Peru, and from New Zealand to Greenland. Imagine entire miles of carpets of every colour, sparkling crystals, furniture of incredible richness, bronzes, velvets, jewels worthy of Cleopatra, silks, silver, pearls, diamonds; all appear cast at a venture into this bazaar of universal genius.[65]

Framed as an act of theft, the furniture, silks and jewels that this writer beholds by the famed crystal fountain generate powerful associations with the treasure troves protected by magic words, the enchanted palaces, flying carpets, and lamps and bottles containing genii that have been known in various contexts and configurations since childhood. Countries as far flung as Peru, Egypt, Greenland and New Zealand, as well as the diverse products of their industry, are subsumed by this sweeping narrative gesture, to become metonymic of that mythical, dream-like 'golden country' that enriched the animistic realm of childhood. Even common household goods and furnishings, as the *London Journal* demonstrates, might be transformed and made meaningful in this space, not by animistic beliefs or superstitions, but by personal attachment and memory:

> It was pleasant, too, to stroll in the Asiatic quarters, reviving the days of one's childhood and the 'Arabian Nights'. The coffee-cups and embroidered napkins, the trays, the saddle-housings, the mats, the cloth of gold and silver, just the same as Haroun Alraschid used, and Lady Mary Montague described ages afterwards. . . . All the Eastern novels one ever read came rushing on the mind. All was musky and oriental.[66]

The personal past is revived by these objects, as they prompt recollections of earlier, imaginative encounters with such things in the tales of Haroun Alraschid. Understood as material relics of childhood, these materials become infused with the life and the vitality that, as noted in Chapter 1, are granted to inanimate things through childhood acts of play. The subject thus recognises the potential power that they allow the thing to exert over them, while recognising the possibility that it carries a life of its own.[67] The power of things in the realm of the Arabian Nights is thus extended to the halls of the Great Exhibition, as the history of those enchanted objects seen, represented and re-imagined through literature and theatre becomes imbricated in the manufactured objects of industry. This uneasy co-habitation of the fictional and the material was, it seems, most pronounced in the Indian displays, where, the next section of this chapter will demonstrate, an anxious meta-narrative emerged about the nature of modern production and consumption.

The Many Meanings of an Oriental Rug

The Indian collections at the exhibition, assembled by the East India Company, were, according to *Allen's Indian Mail*, resplendent with all manner of wonderful objects, 'second only in attraction to the

Koh-i-Noor'.[68] Of particular note was an elaborate Indian tent display, which held an immensely fine collection of Indian workmanship, including carpets, tapestries, gold cloth caps, an ivory throne, carved chessmen, containers of ivory and silver, and a number of hookahs and intricately detailed shawls.[69] Immensely popular, this display 'dr[e]w the multitude to its portals every day'.[70] Visitors to the exhibition were not permitted to enter or move through the tent, but were restricted to gazing upon it in its entirety from the opening, 'reading' it en masse as a stage setting or an Oriental 'scene' to be populated with figures from the imagination. There was, perhaps, something of Scheherazade's seraglio in this liminal space and its evocation of the (absent) Oriental potentate, and it prompted explicit comparisons to the Arabian Nights, a well-known standard against which to measure the scene's successful re-creation of magic and wonder. One guidebook to the exhibition enthused:

> The leading object among the Indian collection is, undoubtedly, the magnificently-fitted tent, which realizes all our notions of the exquisite luxury of Oriental despotism. . . .The exquisite rugs in green and crimson velvet, adorned with sun-like radiated shields of gold, which adorn the walls; the rich carpets placed above the mattings, the superbly-carved sideboard in black wood, the fans and fly-flappers of every design, and the bland odour of the sandal-wood, remind us of the haughty potentates of the 'Arabian Nights'. We can almost see the king of the Indies, and the intelligent ape (the transformed kalendeer [sic], as Mr. Lane *will* call him), playing at chess together.[71]

Memories of the Arabian Nights, easily brought before the mind's eye, are triggered by these objects, rendering the display both personally meaningful and strangely ahistorical. Removed from social and cultural contexts, and understood as the physical realisation of a fictional space, the tent becomes a possible material landscape for any number of wonderful tales in the Arabian Nights, which were themselves formed across different countries and time periods.

For the *Illustrated Exhibitor*, the narrative possibilities of this tent display also included the tales of Haroun Alraschid and the story of Noureddin and the Fair Persian:

> In such a tent might the Peri Banou have spread her carpet – in such a tent might fabled genii have done homage to Solomon – in such a tent might the Caliph Haroun Alraschid have listened to the heedless merchant who flung the date-stones [in the tale of 'The Merchant and the Genie'] – in such a tent might have passed the loves of Noureddin and the fair Persian.[72]

For centuries, the Oriental carpet has been endowed with magical properties, supposedly defying the physical laws of the universe to hover above the ground and offer its flyer new vantage points and routes of travel or escape. Here, the carpet spread across the floor of the Indian tent is explicitly connected to King Solomon's flying carpet, which was made from green silk and, in a number of Islamic legends, gifted to Solomon from God to allow him to command the wind. It is also connected to the fairy Peri Banou's magic carpet, which was created by fairies and carried the young Prince Ahmed into the heart of fairyland itself.[73] 'Whoever sits on this piece of tapestry', Ahmed is told, 'may be transported in an instant where-ever he desires to be, without being stopped by any obstacle.'[74] In the same story, a tent, too, is endowed with magical properties as it shrinks or expands as needed. Another gift from the fairy Peri Banou, it is 'a pavilion large enough to shelter [the prince's father], his court, and army, from the violence of weather, and which a man may carry in his hand'.[75] In the Arabian Nights, such objects as carpets and tents are able to fulfil wishes and offer new perspectives and experiences. Aligning the tent and carpet in the Indian display with their fantastic counterparts rendered them, too, the stuff of dreams – enchanted objects offering access to distant magical kingdoms.

This particular tent and carpet were, in fact, products of the Jabalpur School of Industry for Reformed Thugs, located in the Mahakaushal region of Madhya Pradesh. The display appears in the exhibition catalogue under the East Indies section dedicated to 'Arms, Ordnance, and Accoutrements', which states that the carpet and tent were

> the work of reclaimed murderers, who only a few years ago subsisted on their fellow-men, and of their progeny, who, but for the measures of a benevolent government, would assuredly have followed the same trade.[76]

The term 'Thug' or 'Thuggee,' taken from the Hindi word for 'thief', was the name given to the cult of men who, for centuries, had allegedly travelled in large groups across India, disguised as travellers, pilgrims and merchants. Joining fellow travellers, they supposedly earned their confidence before robbing and ritualistically strangling or garrotting them. This secret organisation first attracted public attention in England in 1836, when William Henry Sleeman, a British officer in the East India Company, published a guide to Ramaseeana, the language of the Thugs. The following year, Edward Thornton published his *Illustrations of the History and Practice of the Thugs*, which was drawn largely from Sleeman's work, and in 1839, Philip Meadows Taylor's sensationalist three-volume narrative, *Confessions of a Thug*, was enthusiastically embraced by a morbidly fascinated public.[77] British periodicals seized upon the sensation caused by reports of the Thuggee cult, declaring the Thugs to be 'marked by a cruelty, treachery, and ferocity unknown to Europe', and a striking illustration of 'the dark character of heathenism, and the power of a false religion to pervert and silence'.[78] The Thugs were deemed a 'vast and organized society' whose 'sole profession is to murder in cold blood every human being whom circumstances enable them to over-power'.[79] Further, the *Examiner* insisted, this 'fraternity of murderers, consisting of many thousands of persons . . . has every year destroyed multitudes of victims'.[80]

Just as the exhibition catalogue declared the carpet and tent on display to be material evidence of the positive outcomes of British intervention, the atrocities allegedly committed by Thugs were frequently referenced as justification for British rule in India.[81] In 1829, two officials of the East India Company, T. C. Smith and William Henry Sleeman, were given permission by the India Office systematically to remove the threat of the Thuggee cult. According to British records, by the end of the 1830s, 3,026 men had been found guilty of the crime of Thugging and subjected to various forms of punishment, including imprisonment, transportation and public execution by strangulation. In 1839, Sleeman declared that the previously extensive 'system' of the Thuggee had been 'eradicated' in India, and that the Thuggee and Dacoity Department would continue to prevent its re-emergence.[82] One of Sleeman's methods for preventing the re-emergence of the Thuggee was his so-called School of Industry, which opened in the centre of the town of Jabalpur in 1837 for the reformation of 'approvers' (a term used for men who were pardoned or given lesser sentences in exchange for providing testimony about the cult) and children whose fathers had been imprisoned or hanged as suspected Thugs. Regarding Thuggee as a dominant hereditary condition, or a form of contagion that must be rendered extinct, British officers endeavoured to prevent the sons of Thugs from marrying or procreating, and encouraged them instead to redirect their energies towards what they considered more Christian and socially productive ends. Inmates at the school were not taught to read or write but were instructed in practical skills that put their knot-tying abilities to proper use, including the manufacture of ropes, carpets and tents. It was hoped that with new practical skills, inmates would abandon their ancestral ties to the Thuggee cult and become useful members of a British-ruled Indian society. The continuity of an often idealised ancient Indian craft tradition across new generations was thus facilitated and overseen by imperial Britain itself.

The Thug School of Industry speaks to a strange and bitterly contested aspect of Indian history, which draws together the overtly imperialist project of the regeneration and salvation of so-called Indian 'savages', with a much disputed narrative of cult murders and brutality, and an ancient Indian craft tradition that had been distinctly modernised.[83] The ornate products of this complicated system of 're-education' in Jabalpur were assigned a monetary value, assumed a commodity status and circulated throughout the empire, prone to fetishist treatment. According to Mike Dash's history of the Thuggee cult, by the time of the Great Exhibition, the Thugs at Jabalpur were producing more than 130 tents and 3,300 yards of Kidderminster carpet each year, and the school's annual revenue exceeded 35,000 rupees.[84] The school supplied tents to the Indian army and gifted an enormous seamless carpet weighing over 2 tons to Queen Victoria (now displayed in the Waterloo Chamber of Windsor Castle); their work was shown at both the Great Exhibition of 1851 in London and the later Paris Exhibition of 1867.

Through their association with the Arabian Nights, the Thuggee tent and carpet on display at the Great Exhibition were re-conceived as the products of magic and the spirits, rather than of violence and enforced labour. This was, in some ways, a testament to the beauty and intricacy of the products themselves, which British manufacturers could not match in either aesthetic beauty or precision of execution. According to the *Examiner*:

> Splendid as these jewels are, there is even greater attraction in the gorgeous tent which the East India Company have fitted up on the northern side of the nave as a receptacle for the choicest objects of Indian workmanship that could be gathered together. This tent realises every idea of Oriental magnificence. It is like a scene from the Arabian Nights. The tapestried walls are one blaze of glistening metal, wrought, nevertheless, in the loom. On the ground, heaped-up masses of velvet and brocade carpets, piled into throngs for Oriental potentates; screens and chairs of state, marvels of cunning carved work; models and devices – all breathing of the East.[85]

Part of the wonder that infuses this scene with fantasies of enchantment and the Arabian Nights is, it seems, generated by the knowledge that the 'cunning carved work' of the furniture is entirely handcrafted, and the tapestry that appears to be made of 'glistening metal' has been 'wrought, nevertheless, in the loom', a pre-industrial and, in the view of this reviewer, rather rudimentary, tool. There is something impossible, or even magical, about these extremely refined works of machine-like perfection that have been produced not by modern machine, but by the virtuosity of the artisan. So splendid are the results that they emulate the 'Oriental magnificence' of the enchanted palaces of the Arabian Nights. They are therefore re-located from their history of violence and imperial intervention to the realm of magic, credited to the effortless creations of fairies and genii in an anxious meta-narrative about the nature of modern production.

Lara Kriegel has noted that one means of facilitating the celebration of an idealised British labour force at the Great Exhibition was to highlight the 'strangeness, poverty, and effeminacy' of Oriental labourers in comparison.[86] This tactic was undoubtedly employed in the Indian courts. Amongst the array of raw materials, crafted wares, jewels, precious stones, arms and elephant trappings that filled the 30,000 square feet of floor space dedicated to India was a collection of over 150 miniature clay figures, which the Exhibition Catalogue notes were assembled by a Captain P. Reynolds. These figures represented various traditional Indian crafts and trades such as cotton-spinners, weavers, blacksmiths, cooks and labourers. The Thuggee cult were also represented here, and their violent operations were illustrated in a series of five vignettes: in the first, they are sitting smoking and conversing with an unsuspecting traveller; in the second, a horseman successfully defends himself from an attack by Thugs; in the third, Thugs conceal a corpse in a well, having previously mutilated its features with a knife in order to prevent its recognition; in the fourth, Thugs strangle a rider on horseback; in the fifth, they are murdering a pedlar, who has tripped and fallen, and thus become easy prey.[87] Collectively, this group of figurines inspired the morbid fascination, disgust and sheer disbelief of British reviewers. The exhibition reporter Edward Concannen was genuinely horrified by this collection of 'distorted', thin Indian bodies, which he described as 'poor, half-clad [and] rice-fed'.[88] The official catalogue testified to the inertia and effeminacy of these figures and the frailty of their bodies, affirming that 'the soft and delicate limbed-Bengallee' was well represented amongst the models, as was the 'tall and slender inhabitant of Southern India'.[89] The *Examiner* described these figurines even more severely as 'a lean, starved-out regiment of squalid beggars, three-parts naked, or with scanty folds of coarsest cotton flung around their wasted limbs'.[90] Miniaturised and transformed into objects of aesthetic contemplation and morbid fascination, these frail and grotesque figures appeared to stand in stark contrast to their exquisite artistic creations.

As the distance between civilisations was collapsed within the enclosed space of the exhibition, the competing ideologies surrounding production by machine and by hand were brought into sharp relief.[91] The *Examiner* regarded the Indian collection as 'an admirable study of the East in all that relates to the handiwork of man', and it seems that handiwork entered into an ongoing dialectic about the productive process with the nearby machines and their creations.[92] Next to the looms of Lancashire, to use Kriegel's pertinent example, 'the jaw-bone of the boalee fish and the iron spinning roller – two implements used in the production of cotton on the subcontinent – appeared particularly primitive', and the loom itself appeared particularly advanced.[93] *Chambers's Edinburgh Journal* confidently noted that 'the rude and tiny apparatus for weaving which dangles from the boughs of a tree [in the Indian court] will be compared with the power-loom of recent invention' and, further, that 'the process of two women grinding at the mill, will not only recall a passage in Scripture', but it will 'mark the vast stride which has been made in the industrial arts'.[94] Indian tools, largely unchanged since biblical times, 'the germ, as it were, of those arts which, by aid of capital and machinery, have attained such magnitude in modern Europe', emerge as an antiquated standard against which to measure the progress of British technology and industrialised labour.[95] None the less, while the 'thousand iron monsters' that Mayhew described as 'snorting and clattering' amongst the British exhibits in the northern transept sent their noise and vibrations throughout the building, the startling incongruity of the figurines of Indian labourers with their antiquated tools, and the delicate results of their industry, was noted with shock and awe.[96] The *Examiner* instructed viewers on this disparity: 'Look into the glittering pavilion; you will fancy yourself in fairy land. Look outside – examine the model population ranged all round that gorgeous marquee, and you will dream of a horde of squalid, starved barbarians.'[97] It seemed that the only possible way to unite the beautiful Indian objects of the display with the Indian subjects who had produced them was to insist upon the agency of magic. Thus, the *Illustrated Exhibitor* declared that the Indian artisans' skills in creating such beautiful products from such rough implements was truly 'one of the marvels of the exhibition'.[98] The *Examiner*, too, further considered the real significance of the 'wondrous pieces of barbaric splendour' within the Indian tent display to be the seeming impossibility of their production by the craftsmen featured outside the tent:

> Can these be the people who have woven these magnificent fabrics, who have carved these wonderful ornaments in scented wood, in ivory, and in gold . . . labouring with the rudest, roughest implements – the weaver sitting in holes in the earth before the handful of rickety sticks which constitute the loom; the cook toiling with his pot of ghee and his dish of rice; the snake-charmer piping to the hooded cobra; the musician dolefully thrumming his tum-tum; the potter squatted beside his wheel; the husbandman standing upon the bullock-drawn harrow, so as to force the wooden teeth into the ground; the women, always by twos, grinding the corn in the rude, rough hand-mill. . . . And still the wonder is, how such people and such tools produce such results as we have seen.[99]

At once primitive and superior, the outmoded tools and practices of Indian handicraft cannot simply be consigned to the past because they offer such extraordinary products, which flourish alongside the operations of British technological modernity. Casting those products within a framework of magic and the Arabian Nights was, I would suggest, a part of the rhetoric of that modernity. It made the comparison between nations and their wares more palatable to the British viewer, while at the same time generating wonder both for the hand-crafted, magical productions of allegedly primitive barbarians, and for the technological and mechanical advancements of British civilisation.

The Genie of the Loom

In a lengthy reflection on the construction and nature of the Crystal Palace, the *Athenaeum* draws a comparison between the achievements of both Eastern magic and Western industry, before pitting the one against the other in an apparently 'friendly' competition:

> Since the young imagination, fired with tales of sprites and genii, conjured up visions of Eastern palaces, adorned with the splendour of Arabian fiction, there has been nothing to compare with it for grace, lightness, fancy and variety of effects as the sun is crossed by moving clouds. That this edifice has been raised and completed in five months – that in November last not a pillar had been erected, and now the whole structure is finished, to the minutest point of decoration – is a fact to impress the

stranger with a magnificent conception of our industrial resources. How curious it is to reflect that in a palace which almost seems to have arisen in a single night by magic, the sober and practical Saxon has invited the workers of the whole earth to a friendly trial of strength under the verdict of the fine old Saxon institution of the jury! How the romantic and practical seem here to have met and shaken hands![100]

The magnificence of Britain's industrial resources become truly apparent only by way of comparison. The space within the Crystal Palace is one of intense inter-cultural contact, driven by the kind of 'poetics of relation' that Édouard Glissant argues is fundamental to 'the immeasurable intermixing of cultures'.[101] As Susan Stanford Friedman notes, 'heightened hybridizations, jarring juxtapositions, increasingly porous boundaries both characterize modernity and help bring it into being'.[102] Modernity itself is, of course, a relative term, often predicated on a break with the past across social, cultural, political and economic institutions, and conferred by historians as a means of determining major shifts in orientation. However, it is also a self-referential concept, employed and applied within any given era by those seeking to express and explore what they regard as new conditions in the social, political and economic order. It is the latter that is at play here, as the *Athenaeum* evokes the old, the Other, the magical and the traditional in order to distinguish itself as both 'new' and 'now'. The Arabian Nights serves a crucial intermediary role in this process of negotiation, as the splendours it contains provide a gauge of the extent to which Britain has realised the impossible. Interestingly, the question of a final verdict on this 'friendly trial' remains unresolved: it is the meeting, the mix of old and new, magical and mechanical, that defines this exhibition space.

For the multitude of visitors to the Great Exhibition, the sight of the mechanical devices displayed and operating in the Hall of Machinery was a source of amazement as overwhelming as the Oriental courts. The exhibition organisers were, the catalogue claims, eager to present an 'overwhelming impression of speed and power in industrial machinery', and had included within the Crystal Palace complex an external engine house containing stationary steam engines, which generated steam that ran through pipes into the palace itself and to the machinery.[103] Visitors could witness the spectacle and experience the noise and the vibrations made by machines in operation. There were, according to one witness, 'thousands of little machines, which well deserved the epithet of beautiful . . . hard at work and ingeniously occupied in the manufacture of all sorts of useful articles from knife handles to envelopes'.[104] These machines also included a large hydraulic press, steam-powered cranes, several small mechanical looms, a sizeable jacquard loom, and various instruments of construction such as steam hammers and forging irons. Clare Pettitt has argued that the 'Machinery in Motion' at the Great Exhibition was a conscious attempt on the part of the Commissioners to represent those 'processes of production' that were 'growing increasingly difficult for non-experts to understand'.[105] It was this 'knowledge-gap', which Pettitt argues was 'creating a society which was becoming rapidly less legible to ordinary people', that, I would suggest, was so frequently represented, or perhaps filled, by the language of magic and enchantment.[106] The apparent autonomy of such machines, which operated with very little or no human intervention, was a source of great wonder. The envelope-folding machine invented by Warren de la Rue and Edwin Hill, for example, seemed to operate by way of a 'magic finger'.[107] In an account of the 'cotton machinery' at the exhibition, the scientist and photographer Robert Hunt describes the magic of an 'iron arm' that 'never slackened or tired' as it worked:

> Several thousand spindles may be seen in a single room, revolving with inconceivable rapidity, with no hand to urge their progress or to guide their operations, drawing out, twisting, and winding up as many thousand threads, with unfailing precision, indefatigable patience, and strength – a scene as magical to the eye that is not familiarised to it, as the effects have been marvellous in augmenting wealth and population.[108]

In the seeming absence of any human bodies or human agency, Hunt imagines the machine itself to demonstrate qualities of patience and strength, while describing its mechanical action almost as though it is a wonderful dance. Henry Mayhew provides a similarly telling account of the excitement inspired by various such machines in motion:

> The people press, two and three deep, with their heads stretched out, watching intently the operations of the moving mechanism. You see the farmers, their dusty hats telling of the distance they have come, with their mouths wide agape, leaning over the bars to see the self-acting mills at work, and smiling as they behold the frame spontaneously draw itself out, and then spontaneously run back again. . . . Indeed, whether it be the noisy flax-crushing machine, or the splashing centrifugal pump, or the clatter of the Jacquard lace machine, or the bewildering whirling

of the cylindrical steam-press, – round each and all these are anxious, intelligent, and simple-minded artisans, and farmers, and servants, and youths, and children clustered, endeavouring to solve the mystery of its complex operations.[109]

Like Hunt, Mayhew presents the modern machine as a disorientating visual and aural phenomenon whose mysterious operations give its viewers great pleasure. The notion that the 'self-acting' mill's mechanism is a 'spontaneous' running movement, and that the operations of the steam press constitute a rather 'bewildering whirling' grant these objects, too, an active agency, emphasising the disembodied, mechanised nature of British industry while attributing a sense of magic to that progressive industry.

Such a magic of the mechanical has recently been taken up by Jeffrey Sconce in *Haunted Media: Electronic Presence from Telegraphy to Television* (2000), which traces the metaphors of 'presence' that electrical technologies have spawned from the nineteenth century's electric telegraph to the virtual realities of the twenty-first century, claiming that a causal relationship exists between electricity and paranormal interests. In the context of the Great Exhibition, the magic of a pre-industrial craft tradition with the capacity to produce Arabian Nights-like wonders in the form of apparently magical tents and carpets is complemented and challenged by the magic of, for instance, the 'magnificent and costly engines' for locomotion, or a 'stupendous wide-gauge engine' and various other 'beautiful engines' designed for express travelling.[110] Interestingly, it is precisely this metaphor that enables the southerner Mr Hale to glimpse the extraordinary powers of industrial machinery, as they are extolled by the mill owner Mr Thornton in Elizabeth Gaskell's *North and South* (1855):

> She ... fell back into her own thoughts – as completely forgotten by Mr Thornton as if she had not been in the room, so thoroughly was he occupied in explaining to Mr Hale the magnificent power, yet delicate adjustment of the might of the steam-hammer, which was recalling to Mr Hale some of the wonderful stories of subservient genii in the Arabian Nights – one moment stretching from earth to sky and filling all the width of the horizon, at the next obediently compressed into a vase small enough to be borne in the hand of a child.[111]

In order to elucidate the operations of Thornton's cotton-mill, Gaskell, who was herself well versed in the tales of the Arabian Nights, evokes an other, magical mode of production.[112] Steam-driven machinery is, in effect, what Thornton terms a 'practical realization of a gigantic thought'.[113] The science by which the material world is able to be manipulated is a source of power akin to that which may be harnessed by one who releases the genie of the lamp in Oriental romance and effects change in their material circumstances.[114]

In Edgar Allan Poe's 'The Thousand-and-Second Tale of Scheherazade' (1845), the young storyteller furnishes her listeners with a further history of Sinbad the Sailor, in which Sinbad circumnavigates the globe and encounters a series of extraordinary natural phenomena and industrial wonders. In England, he discovers 'a nation of the most powerful magicians' who have performed extraordinary feats:

> One of this nation of mighty conjurers created a man out of brass and wood, and leather, and endowed him with such ingenuity that he would have beaten at chess, all the race of mankind with the exception of the great Caliph, Haroun Alraschid. Another of these magi constructed (of like material) a creature that put to shame even the genius of him who made it; for so great were its reasoning powers that, in a second, it performed calculations of so vast an extent that they would have required the united labor of fifty thousand fleshy men for a year.[115]

In addition to Maelzel's chess-player and Babbage's calculating machine, referenced in this passage, Sinbad encounters a range of technological marvels, including the Great Western Railway, the electrotype, the daguerreotype and the electric telegraph, each of which provides further evidence of the magical supremacy of this group of men. These phenomena are, in fact, so extraordinary that the Sultan, frustrated with the absurdity of Scheherazade's tale, recalls his murderous designs on womanhood and has her violently garrotted.[116] 'Truth is stranger than fiction', declares the subtitle to Poe's story, and certainly, it seems that the wonders of the modern world are stranger, greater and far more absurd than any tale the Sultan has heard throughout his thousand and one nights with Scheherazade.

The notion that Britain's technological progress was so great as to outstrip any marvel dreamed up by Scheherazade was made explicit in the context of the Great Exhibition in a story published in the *Leisure Hour* in 1852 entitled 'Aladdin at the Crystal Palace; Or, Science Versus Fairy-Land'. Again establishing a framework of competition between romance and reality, the tale opens with the editor's declaration that 'the marvels of modern science far excel, in wonder and interest, the oriental fables which were wont to consume . . . so many of the golden hours of youth'.[117] The ensuing narrative details Aladdin's return to an unidentified Eastern land after taking a wonderful journey through Britain, which included a tour of the Crystal Palace guided by a jinn known as 'Paxtoni'. Aladdin recounts the marvels he has seen to his royal wife and concludes by telling her that, after viewing the extraordinary glass structure and 'all the internal wonders of this surpassingly wonderful palace', he was overcome by its beauty and surrendered his own magic lamp to the superior magicians of the West:

> I once more turned to my powerful conductor. 'Here', said I, 'take this my once valued lamp; its powers are far, very far surpassed by your powers. The Genii of Steam and of Electricity are much more powerful than the Genie of the Lamp!' So I delivered it up to the genie Paxtoni, who, as he took it, impressively replied, as he disappeared amongst the crowd, 'Remember, Aladdin, that KNOWLEDGE IS POWER.'[118]

Though obviously a very light-hearted piece, the assumed power struggle between fantasy and modernity represented through the figures of Paxton and Aladdin in this tale encapsulates the friction, rivalry and potentially stimulating dialogue produced by the mix of old and new in the space of the Great Exhibition. The language of magic and the Arabian Nights becomes integral to this vision of modernity, as Aladdin's surrender of his wonderful lamp to the British 'genie' not only signifies Britain's presumed superiority to the wonderful achievements of Eastern fantasy fiction, but uses those very narratives to illustrate its own magical prowess. The Crystal Palace thus becomes a modern space in which the magic objects of the Arabian Nights can be remembered, explored and celebrated while, at the same time, rendered obsolete.

Notes

1. Brontë, 'Charlotte Brontë to the Revd Patrick Brontë, 7 June [1851]', pp. 630–1. Emphasis in the original.
2. These are the four main categories of the official three-volume catalogue.
3. Miller, *Novels Behind Glass*, pp. 52, 51.
4. Anon., 'A Glance at the Exhibition', p. 337.
5. Hunt, 'Narrativizing "The World's Show": The Great Exhibition, Panoramic Views and Print Supplements', p. 115. Hunt posits the panorama as one of the imaginative models used in figuring the exhibition.

6. Miller, *Novels Behind Glass*, p. 53.
7. Thackeray, 'May Day Ode', p. 5.
8. Knight, 'Three May-Days in London', p. 121.
9. Anon., 'Progress at the International Exhibition', p. 382.
10. Anon., 'The Crystal Palace', *The Times*, p. 5.
11. Anon., *Guide Book to the Industrial Exhibition; with Facts, Figures, and Observations on the Manufactures and Produce Exhibited*, p. 8.
12. For a detailed discussion of the design and construction of the palace, see Hobhouse, *The Crystal Palace and the Great Exhibition* (2002), pp. 1–80. On the emergence of glass as a fundamentally modern material of the period, see Armstrong, *Victorian Glassworlds* (2008).
13. Dickens, *Sketches by Boz*, p. 201.
14. Dickens, *Our Mutual Friend*, p. 219.
15. Ibid. p. 219.
16. Dickens, *The Old Curiosity Shop*, p. 476.
17. Ibid. p. 478.
18. Armstrong, *Victorian Glassworlds*, p. 142.
19. Eliot, *Middlemarch*, p. 351. Eliot deploys the Arabian Nights within the deeply domestic, realist mode of this novel in order to warn her readers of the illusive nature of Tertius Lydgate's fantasies of marital bliss with Rosamond Vincy.
20. Brontë, 'Charlotte Brontë to the Revd Patrick Brontë, 7 June [1851]', p. 631.
21. Ibid. p. 631.
22. Badowska, 'Choseville: Brontë's "Villette" and the Art of Bourgeois Interiority', p. 1511.
23. Ibid. p. 1511.
24. Armstrong, *Victorian Glassworlds*, pp. 142, 143.
25. Warner, *Stranger Magic*, p. 364.
26. Knight, 'Three May-Days in London', p. 121.
27. Ibid. p. 121.
28. Ibid. p. 122.
29. Ibid. p. 122.
30. Mayhew, *1851; Or, the Adventures of Mr. and Mrs. Sandboys and Family*, p. 1.
31. My interpretation of these representative objects is indebted to the notes accompanying the image in the Museum of London's print collection.
32. Black, *On Exhibit: Victorians and Their Museums*, p. 13.
33. For detailed analyses of the construction and layout of the exhibition space, see Auerbach, *The Great Exhibition of 1851: A Nation on Display* (1999), and Davis, *The Great Exhibition* (1999).
34. Anon., 'The Transept', p. 9.
35. Bremer, 'Impressions of England in the Autumn of 1851', p. 193.
36. Anon., 'The Great Industrial Exhibition', p. 478.
37. Anon., 'A Journey Round the World in the Crystal Palace', pp. 250–6.

38. The visual and spatial arrangement of the world within the Crystal Palace conforms to the method of ordering and viewing the world conceptualised by Timothy Mitchell as the 'world as picture' or 'world as exhibition' gaze. According to Mitchell, the notion that there was a privileged, objective viewpoint from which to discern 'structures of meaning' prompted the Western tourist's search at various Eastern locations for the correct, elevated position from which to achieve a panorama of the surrounding landscape, as well as the creation of 'bird's-eye view' maps of the East, and the incorporation of viewing platforms into British galleries and exhibitions. This was the case in a metaphorical sense at the Great Exhibition, which sought a 'bird's-eye' – or, in fact, British – view of the globe from within the Crystal Palace. See Mitchell, *Colonising Egypt*, pp. 18–23.
39. Anon., 'The Great Industrial Exhibition', p. 478.
40. Anon., *The Art Journal Illustrated Catalogue: The Industry of All Nations, 1851*, p. xxv.
41. Anon., 'A Journey Round the World in the Crystal Palace', p. 250
42. Ibid. p. 250.
43. Warren, *The Lily and the Bee*, p. 10.
44. Anon., 'The Great Industrial Exhibition', p. 477.
45. This is also discussed in Glen, *Charlotte Brontë*, p. 222.
46. Richards, *The Commodity Culture of Victorian England*, p. 35.
47. Ibid. p. 35.
48. Borges, 'When Fiction Lives in Fiction', p. 160.
49. Ochlenschlaeger, 'Aladdin', p. 620; Anon., 'The People of the Arabian Nights', p. 329. For further reading on the seemingly atemporal amplification of the narratives of the Oriental tale delivered within the seraglio, see Grosrichard, *The Sultan's Court*, pp. 79–80.
50. Anon., 'The Great Industrial Exhibition', p. 478.
51. Tallis, *History and Description of the Crystal Palace and the Exhibition of the World's Industry in 1851*, III, p. 53. Emphasis in the original.
52. Anon., 'Progress at the International Exposition', p. 382.
53. Anon., 'How We Hunted the Prince', p. 222.
54. Anon., 'India at the Great Exhibition', p. 333.
55. Armstrong, *Victorian Glassworlds*, p. 143.
56. Commissioners for the Exhibition of 1851, *Great Exhibition of the Works of Industry of All Nations. Official Descriptive and Illustrated Catalogue*, vol. 3, p. 1317.
57. Anon., 'The Exhibition', p. 77.
58. Anon., 'A Journey Round the World in the Crystal Palace', p. 250.
59. Warner, *Stranger Magic*, p. 199.
60. Brown, 'Thing Theory', p. 5.
61. Appadurai, 'Introduction: Commodities and the Politics of Value', p. 36.

62. Brown, 'The Secret Life of Things (Virginia Woolf and the Matter of Modernism)', pp. 1–2.
63. Pels, 'The Spirit of Matter: On Fetish, Rarity, Fact, and Fancy', p. 101.
64. Pietz, 'The Problem of the Fetish', pp. 11–12. Pietz offers the example of human tears as one such intensely personal material expression of an internal state.
65. Anon., 'A Journey Round the World in the Crystal Palace', p. 250.
66. Anon., 'The Exhibition', p. 77.
67. Marina Warner has taken up this argument in exploring the power of things in a world of 'personal, electronic prostheses – mobiles phones, iPods, and laptops', to contend that Oriental storytelling 'in the fashion of the *Nights*, underlies this modern strain of animism, and its vision both foreshadows the eerie cybernetics of our hardware media and gives a way of understanding our relationship with them' (Warner, *Stranger Magic*, pp. 204–5).
68. Anon., 'India at the Great Exhibition', p. 362.
69. Ibid. p. 362.
70. Ibid. p. 362.
71. Anon., *A Guide to the Great Exhibition; Containing a Description of Every Principal Object of Interest, With a Plan, Pointing out the Easiest and Most Systematic Way of Examining the Contents of the Crystal Palace*, pp. 113–14. Emphasis in the original.
72. Anon., 'India and Indian Contributions to the Industrial Bazaar', p. 319.
73. For a detailed discussion on the roles of the carpet in Eastern culture, see Abidi, 'The Secret History of the Flying Carpet', pp. 141–8, and Warner, *Stranger Magic*, pp. 59–83.
74. Galland, *Arabian Nights' Entertainments*, p. 823.
75. Ibid, p. 853. Charlotte Brontë draws on the same magic tent to indicate the ineffable nature of Lucy Snowe's unrequited love for Graham Bretton in *Villette* (1853): 'I kept a place for him, too – a place of which I never took the measure, either by rule or compass: I think it was like the tent of Peri-Banou. All my life long I carried it folded in the hollow of my hand – yet, released from that hold and constriction, I know not but its innate capacity for expanse might have magnified it into a tabernacle for a host.' See Brontë, *Villette*, p. 457.
76. Commissioners for the Exhibition of 1851, *Great Exhibition of the Works of Industry of All Nations. Official Descriptive and Illustrated Catalogue*, vol. 2, p. 912.
77. For an excellent overview of the English public's reception of this novel, see Poovey, 'Ambiguity and Historicism: Interpreting *Confessions of a Thug*', pp. 3–21.
78. Anon., 'Indian Assassins', p. 218; Anon., 'Ramaseeana; or, A Vocabulary of the Peculiar Language Used by the Thugs', p. 359.

79. Anon., 'The Secret Societies of Asia – The Assassins and Thugs', p. 229.
80. Anon., 'The Thugs, a Fraternity of Murderers in India', p. 71.
81. For a detailed outline of the legal procedures involved in opposing the Thuggee, see Radhika, *A Despotism of Law*, pp. 168–228.
82. Sleeman, *Report on the Depredations Committed by the Thug Gangs of Upper and Central India*, p. 19.
83. In 1848, the School of Industry acquired a Brussels loom and a skilled young carpet maker from Kidderminster to facilitate the modernisation of their processes.
84. Dash, *Thug: The True Story of India's Murderous Cult*, p. 274.
85. Anon., 'The Great Exhibition', p. 313.
86. Kriegel, 'The Pudding and the Palace: Labour, Print Culture, and Imperial Britain in 1851', p. 233.
87. Anon., *Reports by the Juries on the Subjects in the Thirty Classes into Which the Exhibition Was Divided*, vol. 4, p. 1446.
88. Concannen, *Remembrances of the Great Exhibition*, n.p.
89. Commissioners for the Exhibition of 1851, *Great Exhibition of the Works of Industry of All Nations. Official Descriptive and Illustrated Catalogue*, vol. 2, p. 930.
90. Anon., 'The Great Exhibition', p. 313.
91. In *Novel Craft: Victorian Domestic Handicraft and Nineteenth-Century Fiction* (2011), Talia Schaffer reminds us that this was an ideological tension already firmly entrenched within Victorian society. Analysing domestic handicraft practices in four Victorian novels, Schaffer approaches what she terms the 'craft paradigm' as a means of critiquing the modern mass-produced commodity and subverting the socio-economic changes wrought by industrialisation.
92. Anon., 'The Great Exhibition', p. 314.
93. Kriegel, 'Narrating the Subcontinent in 1851', p. 159.
94. Anon., 'A Glance at the Exhibition', p. 339.
95. Ibid. p. 339.
96. Mayhew, *1851; or, the Adventures of Mr. and Mrs. Sandboys and Family, Who Came up to London to 'Enjoy Themselves' and to See the Great Exhibition*, p. 137.
97. Anon., 'The Great Exhibition', p. 313.
98. Anon., 'India and Indian Contributions to the Industrial Bazaar', p. 319.
99. Anon., 'The Great Exhibition', p. 313
100. Anon., 'The Great Industrial Exhibition', p. 478.
101. Glissant, *Poetics of Relation*, p. 138.
102. Friedman, 'Unthinking Manifest Destiny: Muslim Modernities on Three Continents', p. 71.
103. Commissioners for the Exhibition of 1851, *Great Exhibition of the Works of Industry of All Nations. Official Descriptive and Illustrated Catalogue*, vol. 1, p. 210.

104. Harvard Gibbs-Smith, *The Great Exhibition of 1851, A Commemorative Album*, p. 80. Ellipses in the original.
105. Pettitt, *Patent Inventions: Intellectual Property and the Victorian Novel*, p. 95.
106. Ibid. p. 95.
107. Ibid. p. 95.
108. Hunt, *Hunt's Hand-Book to the Official Catalogues*, vol. 2, p. 509.
109. Mayhew, *1851; or, the Adventures of Mr. and Mrs. Sandboys*, p. 161.
110. Commissioners for the Exhibition of 1851, *Great Exhibition of the Works of Industry of All Nations. Official Descriptive and Illustrated Catalogue*, vol. 1, p. 210.
111. Gaskell, *North and South*, p. 81.
112. On the influence of the Arabian Nights on Gaskell's literary œuvre, see Cook, 'The Victorian Scheherazade: Elizabeth Gaskell and George Meredith', pp. 197–217.
113. Gaskell, *North and South*, p. 81.
114. Interestingly, the 2004 BBC adaptation of *North and South* introduced a scene in which several of the novel's central characters travel by railway from Milton to London to visit the Great Exhibition. Although not included in Gaskell's novel, it is certainly in keeping with its interest in the social and cultural impact of industrialisation. For further discussion of such anxieties, see Scholl, 'Moving Between *North and South*: Cultural Signs and the Progress of Modernity in Elizabeth Gaskell's Novel', pp. 95–106.
115. Poe, 'The Thousand-and-Second Tale of Scheherazade', p. 115.
116. On the troubling gender politics of Poe's narrative, and his decision to address a largely female readership through a woman narrator who is violently garrotted, see Pangborn, 'The Arabian Romance of America in Poe's "Thousand-and-Second Tale of Scheherazade"', pp. 35–57.
117. Anon., 'Aladdin at the Crystal Palace; or, Science Versus Fairy-Land', p. 261.
118. Ibid. p. 262.

Chapter 5

Epilogue: A New Arabian Nights

> But the great city was new to him; he had gone from a provincial school to a military college, and thence direct to the Eastern Empire; and he promised himself a variety of delights in this world for exploration. . . . It was a mild evening, already dark and now and then threatening rain. The succession of faces in the lamplight stirred the Lieutenant's imagination; and it seemed to him as if he could walk for ever in that stimulating city atmosphere and surrounded by the mystery of four million private lives. He glanced at the houses, and marvelled at what was passing behind those warmly-lighted windows; he looked into face after face, and saw them each intent upon some unknown interest criminal or kindly. 'They talk of war,' he thought, 'but this is the great battlefield of mankind.'
>
> Robert Louis Stevenson, *New Arabian Nights*, 1882

In Robert Louis Stevenson's 'The Adventure of the Hansom Cabs', one of a sequence of stories in his *New Arabian Nights* (1882), the minor English celebrity Lieutenant Brackenbury Rich arrives in London for the first time, having distinguished himself in 'one of the lesser Indian hill wars'.[1] Dedicated to a life of excitement and adventure, the Lieutenant is thrilled to behold the complexity and potentially perilous mysteries of this new city. Beneath his gaze, both the landscape and the inhabitants of London become ideal material for romantic episodes and terrible crimes. This fantasy of the modern, urban environment as a place of exoticism and novelty unlike any in the East is soon confirmed when Rich hails a hansom cab at random and is delivered by it at astonishing speed to an unfamiliar country house filled with strange guests, who have been similarly collected by cabs and brought to attend a party whose host and purpose are unknown. The fact that, ultimately, there is a very reasonable explanation for this mystery only reinforces the fictitious nature of Stevenson's project. Like Scheherazade, his tales are a charade, intended to distract and amuse his audience. In his hands, however, late nineteenth-century London becomes the scene of a 'new', British, modern Arabian Nights. It has replaced Delhi, Cairo and Baghdad as a city of enchantment and as a source of potentially infinite, wonderful stories, and it is a fertile environment for the advent of the detective story.

Stevenson's own childhood delight in his 'fat, old, double-columned volume' of the Arabian Nights, and his belief in the transformative power of these tales upon the world and the mind of the child was noted in Chapter 1.[2] In his essay, 'A Gossip on Romance', he elaborates upon the source of his attraction to these tales, giving some intimation of the intentions underlying his new version. Declaring that the purpose of reading, far being from moral or intellectually enlightening, should always be 'absorbing and voluptuous', he insists that 'we should gloat over a book, be rapt clean of ourselves, and rise from the perusal, our mind filled with the busiest, kaleidoscopic dance of images, incapable of sleep or of continuous thought'.[3] For Stevenson, the Arabian Nights epitomises the dynamics of desire and mental excitement implicit in the act of reading:

> There is one book, for example, more generally loved than Shakespeare, that captivates in childhood, and still delights in age – I mean the *Arabian Nights* – where you shall look in vain for moral or for intellectual interest. No human face or voice greets us among that wooden crowd of kings and genies, sorcerers and beggarmen. Adventure, on the most naked terms, furnishes forth the entertainment and is found enough.[4]

Character and conversation are rejected in favour of incident and excitement, and it is this kind of 'naked', raw adventure that Stevenson seeks to discover and to celebrate in the cosmopolitan streets of Paris and London. His *New Arabian Nights* is a dark and at times macabre series of seven interconnected stories, featuring the recurring character of Prince Florizel of Bohemia and subdivided under two main categories: *The Suicide Club*, comprising three stories (including 'The Adventure of the Hansom Cabs') that move from London to Paris and then back to London, and *The Rajah's Diamond*, comprising four stories, equally divided between London and Paris. In his extensive study of Stevenson, G. K. Chesterton has noted the 'singular sort of texture' and 'singular sort of atmosphere' that this relocation of the Arabian Nights facilitated: 'It is partly like the atmosphere of a dream; in which so many incongruous things cause no surprise. It is partly the real atmosphere of London at night; it is partly the unreal atmosphere of Baghdad.'[5] Robert Irwin has suggested that the surreal nature of the city may in part be due to the fact that while writing the tales, Stevenson was taking opium in order to reduce the effects of his ill health and that, like Scheherazade, his narrative enterprise was designed to ward off death.[6] Beyond this parallel, however, the tales are part of a broader re-enchantment narrative that situates the magic of the Arabian Nights almost exclusively within an absurdist and grotesquely comic, modern world. Stevenson's *New Arabian Nights* is not an adaptation but a recreation, striving to present the British metropolis as at once modern and magical.

This book has largely focused on the first half of the nineteenth century – the period identified by Edward Said as the true beginning of Orientalism – as a historical moment in which the Arabian Nights, propagated by new and evolving print and media cultures, mutated and multiplied across British social, cultural and psychological institutions. It has shown that an array of characters, objects and concepts from the Arabian Nights permeated nineteenth-century culture, and provided a compelling imaginative framework for shifting negotiations with and definitions not only of the Eastern other, but also of the British self. The Arabian Nights entered the bloodstream of British culture and, as it mutated and proliferated in an almost viral way across different media, its captivating stories and well-known magic objects came to expose, and often to represent, the fluctuating boundaries between childhood and adulthood, history and fantasy, and the material and imagined.

It has not been my aim to chronicle the many and varied manifestations of the Arabian Nights and Arabian Nights-inspired materials across British culture in this period, but rather to track some of the ways in which those tales were deployed, as the Victorians sought to make sense of their own, rapidly changing environment. The Arabian Nights offered different ways for the British reader to interpret and to frame their experiences. These stories, as we have seen, were conflated at various moments with childhood, travel, theatre and exhibitions, and they provided a paradigmatic space and time of fantasy, which was serially delved into and at least partly created by the Victorian psyche. The notion of a *New Arabian Nights*, deliberately relocated to London for readers in the latter decades of the century, as well as new translations of the tales from the Arabic by John Payne and Richard Burton in the 1880s, signals a significant shift in the collection's representative status. It testifies to a cultural need to re-create and re-possess the tales in new and evolving contexts.

Such late-Victorian engagements with the Arabian Nights continued the tradition of identification with the magic of these tales, but they also frequently registered the removal of such fantastic spaces from a distant Orient to the very landscape of London itself. The transmigration of these narratives to British culture illustrates the progress of its own fantastical elements within industrial and technological modernity. This centre of commerce, industry and science in many ways *became* the new Arabian Nights: an exciting hub of mystery, enchantment, sensuality and stories that now functioned and evolved largely independently of its Eastern other.

In January 1883, the *Westminster Review* published a scathing review of Stevenson's new tales. Objecting to the relocation of these stories to contemporary Paris and London, it considered Stevenson's association of his work with the Arabian Nights to be no better than fraudulent:

> Mr. Stevenson's tales are Arabian only in name, the suicides, robberies and murders, which form their subject matter are perpetrated in our own day, not further off than London or Paris, and the treatment and colouring are essentially modern and realistic. Consequently in our opinion they too much resemble glorified and mundane 'Penny dreadfuls' – with royal princes, general officers, physicians, and clergymen for *dramatis personae* – to be regarded as legitimate successors of 'The Arabian Nights'.[7]

There is, the *Westminster Review* signals, an important generic shift implicated in Stevenson's new Arabian Nights fantasy. The contemporary setting and often grisly subject matter of the tales are, it seems, more akin to cheap sensation fiction intended for the rapidly expanding urban working classes, than to any beloved Oriental romance. The tales are, in essence, too 'realistic' to be magical. However, it is this very tension between and knitting together of enchantment and disenchantment that, for Stevenson, defines the modern city.

George Meredith had rendered the magic of the Oriental romance ridiculous in his first novel, *The Shaving of Shagpat: An Arabian Entertainment* (1856). In this ironic pastiche of the Arabian Nights, the Arab Empire is enchanted by a single hair on the head of the cruel tyrant Shagpat, and the hero is a barber who must destroy evil talismans, avoid the curses of a malicious genie and fulfil several other magical tasks before he can shave the tyrant's beard. Stevenson, however, draws such materials into the space and fabric of London, and celebrates them as simultaneously ridiculous, impossible and commonplace. We are told, for example, that Prince Florizel, who was 'hurled' from the throne of Bohemia in consequence of his 'edifying neglect of public business', has successfully established himself as a businessman in the streets of London:

> His Highness now keeps a cigar store in Rupert Street, much frequented by other foreign refugees. I go there from time to time to smoke and have a chat, and find him as great a creature as in the days of his prosperity; he has an Olympian air behind the counter; and although a sedentary life is beginning to tell upon his waistcoat, he is probably, take him for all in all, the handsomest tobacconist in London.[8]

This dramatic reversal of fortunes, a familiar trope to readers of the tales of Aladdin, or the Sleeper Awakened, is relocated to the middle classes of London, where it becomes rather more absurd than fantastic. No longer wrought by the machinations of interfering genii or by the recitation of magic words, such an occurrence is caused by political unrest, and it becomes both comical and strangely wonderful in its apparent normalcy. The city has become a milieu of commerce, industry and infinite possibilities, where figures from the Arabian Nights and the exotic East live and work alongside their British inhabitants. Thus, the character of Gilbert in Oscar Wilde's essay, 'The Critic as Artist', suggests to Ernest that they go out into the night, for 'Thought is wonderful, but adventure is more wonderful still. Who knows but we may meet Prince Florizel of Bohemia, and hear the fair Cuban [in 'The Story of the Fair Cuban' in Stevenson's *More New Arabian Nights*] tell us she is not what she seems?'[9] No longer does the East occupy spaces embedded in modernity; it is diffused within the modern urban landscape itself.

The importance of the city as an arena for secrets and fantastic characters permeates Stevenson's tales, in which reason and law, and mystery and the fantastical manage to co-exist. This is, arguably, the same binary structure that defines the genre of classic detective fiction and it reverberates with G. K. Chesterton's famous defence of detective fiction as a kind of poetry of the city:

> The first essential value of the detective story lies in this, that it is the earliest and only form of popular literature in which is expressed some sense of the poetry of modern life. . . . No one can have failed to notice that in these stories the hero or the investigator crosses London with something of the loneliness and liberty of a prince in a tale of elfland, that in the course of an incalculable journey, the casual omnibus assumes

the primal colours of a fairy ship. The lights of the city begin to glow like innumerable goblin eyes, since they are the guardians of some secret, however crude, which the writer knows and the reader does not. Every twist of the road is like a finger pointing to it; every fantastic skyline of chimney-pots seems wildly and derisively signalling the meaning of the mystery. . . . Anything which tends, even under the fantastic form of the minutiae of Sherlock Holmes, to assert this romance of detail in civilisation, to emphasise this unfathomably human character in flints and tiles, is a good thing.[10]

Chesterton's realisation of the city as an enchanted wilderness filled not only with symbolic, mythological figures but with a hidden series of urban hieroglyphs resonates with later twentieth-century fiction and, in particular, with the post-modern novel.[11] However, the role of the detective/hero in exposing the secrets of the city and its inhabitants, and uncovering the traces of past crimes and human characters, is critical to earlier phases of the classic detective story. Like Prince Florizel in the cigar shop, we find an Oriental presence, and sinister Oriental conspiracies, in nineteenth-century tales of crime and detection, such as Wilkie Collins's *The Moonstone* (1868), and Arthur Conan Doyle's *The Sign of Four* (1890), as well as many of his shorter Sherlock Holmes stories. In such texts, exotic adventures occur in the heart of London, as the Orient imparts an element of romance and adventure to the city, which becomes imbued with the spirit of older, wilder and more wonderful realms.

The last decades of the nineteenth century saw significant material and social changes in the landscape of London, which were, for the most part, the effects of Britain's imperial activities in the preceding centuries. At once an industrial city containing one of the world's busiest ports, a centre of international finance, and the symbolic and physical centre of government and power, it was a space of escalating immediate contact with 'others' and a rising globalisation of culture. Here, the liberal politician Charles Masterman writes, was an 'immeasurable city' and a '*terra incognita*, as utterly unknown to the people who talk, think, or chatter, as the interior of China', while General William Booth's treatise, *In Darkest England* (1890), claimed that the slums of London were violent, primitive wildernesses.[12] Joseph McLaughlin has argued that the prevalent metaphor of the 'urban jungle', derived from a contingent moment in imperial history and the increasing permeability of national boundaries, re-created London not as the antithesis of colonial and imperial places and peoples, but as their 'curious doubles'.[13] He cogently summarises

London's position in the British Empire by the time Stevenson came to write his Arabian tales:

> London was just as much an imperial stage as India or Africa or any other number of exotic locales; it was an amalgamation of frontiers; it was that 'vast cesspool' of Dr. Watson; it was the capital of General Booth's 'darkest England'; it was an exotic market of pleasures and delights from the poor streets of [Margaret] Harkness's Whitechapel to the sumptuously oriental interiors of the West End described by Oscar Wilde in *The Picture of Dorian Gray* (also in 1891).[14]

According to McLaughlin, these writings approached the metropolis with a kind of double vision that overlaid urban geography with an imagined geography drawn from representations of the British colonies as wild and exotic. The familiar and unfamiliar, and discourses of the imperial and the metropolitan, were continually shifting as the city itself became a mysterious urban labyrinth demanding to be read and interpreted.

The Arabian Nights was a part of this dominant discourse and it helped to fashion the peculiar literary and psychic landscape of London in these decades. Thus, Watson and Holmes encounter a striking array of Oriental characters and returned colonials in their cases across London, including a contorted ex-soldier who owns a terrifying Indian mongoose, a dwarfish, poison-toting Andaman aborigine known only as Tonga, and a 'crooked' man who was betrayed into the hands of Indian mutineers and now seeks revenge on his former friends on the streets of London.[15] In this overwhelming assemblage of exotic and sinister individuals affected by their time in the Orient, the Arabian Nights provides a familiar interpretative framework and a means of expressing both wonder and confusion. In 'The Adventure of the Noble Bachelor', for example, Dr Watson is attended by two men who, 'having laid out all these luxuries . . . vanished away, like the genii of the Arabian Nights'.[16] In 'The Adventure of the Three Gables', Holmes and Watson find themselves 'in an Arabian-Night drawing room, vast and wonderful', in the West End of London, where they encounter a 'tall, queenly, a perfect figure'.[17] The Arabian Nights has imbued London with surprise, amazement and the comically grotesque.

The 'Arabian Entertainment' contained within the classic mode of the detective story illuminates the role of fiction in providing both distraction and delight. The detective discourse is, as Elaine Freedgood has claimed, an area in which things not only have to be read, but are expected to hold significant meanings as evidence for the case at hand.[18] The author, the real 'culprit', must deliberately arrange all the seemingly haphazard details and things in the story in order to mystify the reader while enabling the sleuth to interpret events. Like the Arabian Nights, it is a self-consciously fictive genre. Stevenson's own mysteries draw upon the self-reflexive structure of the Arabian Nights in order to call attention to the artificiality of his fiction and to the role of his tales as diversions. The tales are presented by a supposedly omniscient narrator known only as the 'Arabian author', but they are mediated by the voice of an editor who comments upon and occasionally disapproves of the author's behaviour. Thus, when the Arabian author 'breaks off' the story of 'The Young Man in Holy Orders', the editor declares that '*I regret and condemn such practices; but I must follow my original.*'[19] Elsewhere, however, he admits to making amendments to the source text, which he considers '*highly pertinent in the original, but little suited to our occidental taste*'.[20] The tension created here between Occidental editor and Oriental narrator epitomises the complex relationship between the source and receiving culture. It highlights the many transformations that the Arabian Nights has undergone in this new context while proclaiming the status of the whole as nothing more than an entertaining charade.

In 'The Adventure of the Hansom Cabs', the empty fiction of the mysterious party in the country house is further highlighted when its setting is gradually dismantled and Lieutenant Brackenbury begins to question whether the entire establishment is in fact a farce:

> The flowering shrubs had disappeared from the staircase; three large furniture waggons stood before the garden gate; the servants were busy dismantling the house upon all sides; and some of them had already donned their great-coats and were preparing to depart.[21]

Like Scheherazade interrupting her story each day to call attention to the breaking dawn and the Sultan's need to resume his daily responsibilities, Stevenson alerts his readers to his own role in imagining and giving shape to this magical world. The Arabian Nights has become a source of wonderful events and illusions within the complex maze of modern life.

Such poetic treatment of London as a fantastical city of the Arabian Nights is a testament to the symbolic power of the literary imagination and it implies a new appreciation of the Arabian

Nights as a fiction rather than a history or a source of social, cultural and ethnographic knowledge about the East. Identification with the figure of Scheherazade as a producer and consumer of stories distinguishes Britain itself as a new source of fable and narrative. It is significant, too, that Stevenson's *New Arabian Nights* and his later collection of *More New Arabian Nights: The Dynamiter* (1885) almost coincided with the English poet John Payne's new ten-volume translation of the Arabian Nights, which was published between 1882 and 1884, as well as the Orientalist Richard Burton's subsequent rendition – which relied extensively on Payne's work – between 1885 and 1886. These translators returned to the Arabic texts in search of more than the extensive annotations on Egyptian life and culture that Edward Lane had furnished nearly fifty years earlier, and they rendered far more poetic versions of the tales, including many that to date had never appeared in English.

While Payne did not expurgate the many erotic episodes of the Arabian Nights, as many of his European forebears had done, Burton nevertheless complained that much of his translation work was far too restrained. Burton's own version of the Arabian Nights and his subsequent six-volume collection of *The Supplemental Nights to the Thousand Nights and a Night* (1886–8) both celebrated and exaggerated what he considered to be the vital, erotic elements of the tales. The resulting collection of stories, attacked by the *Pall Mall Gazette* as 'esoteric pornography', was a very explicit exposition of sexual relations and preferences in the East, with extensive footnotes for the prurient reader on a range of sexual practices including bestiality, sodomy and miscegenation.[22] This other kind of new Arabian Nights fantasy, published by the secretive Kama Shastra Society and sold exclusively through private subscription, unapologetically revelled in the poetic and the sensual, and was very firmly situated in London's subterranean world of erotic literature and pornography.

Forced into such underground channels by the Obscene Publications Act of 1857, the Kama Shastra Society was an organisation founded by Burton and Forster Fitzgerald Arbuthnot in 1882 with the intention of publishing classics of Indian erotica while protecting its producers from prosecution. This society printed Burton's translation of *The Kama Sutra* in 1883 and *The Ananga Ranga* in 1885, and it would later print *The Perfumed Garden of the Sheikh Nefzaoui* (1886), *The Beharistan* (1887) and *The Gulistan* (1888).[23]

Epilogue: A New Arabian Nights 183

In such company, the Arabian Nights and its familiar tales of magic and wonder, known and remembered since childhood, now included shocking scenes of sexual violence and explicit references to sexual activities and nudity, and it was plunged into the first public literary debate in England about pornography, sexuality, purity and state regulations.[24]

Keenly aware of Britain's ongoing social, cultural and psychological entanglement with various tales of the Arabian Nights, Burton endeavoured to pre-empt distress over his erotically charged transformation of what was by now a distinctly English classic by offering a defence of his work in its foreword. Justifying the sexual content of his new translation on the grounds of cultural and historical relativism, Burton urges his readers to 'remember that grossness and indecency, in fact *les turpitudes*, are matters of time and place', that 'what is offensive in England is not so in Egypt'.[25] Further, he insisted, 'what scandalises us now would have been a tame joke *tempore Elisoe*'.[26] Bearing this in mind, he thus claims that his work is of substantial anthropological and Orientalist value in instructing and enlightening his readers and dispelling England's 'ignorance concerning the Eastern races with whom she is continually in contact'.[27] This ignorance, he believes, has been the cause of England's past political failures, revealed in the Afghan Wars (1839–42; 1878–80) and in the bloody aftermath of the 1882 occupation of Egypt, and it is the aim of his work to correct it:

> Hence, when suddenly compelled to assume the reins of government in Moslem lands, as Afghanistan in times past and Egypt at present, she fails after a fashion which scandalises her few (very few) friends; and her crass ignorance concerning the Oriental peoples which should most interest her, exposes her to the contempt of Europe as well as of the Eastern world.[28]

Burton never clarifies exactly how specialist knowledge of Eastern sexual practices might be drawn upon to advance an imperialist British cause, and his rhetoric undoubtedly characterises the tales as a stereotypical Orientalist demonstration of a silent, passive, highly sexualised East actively embracing Western penetration and domination.[29] This is certainly the complaint of Rana Kabbani, who charges Burton with constructing the Orient 'chiefly as an illicit space' and its women as 'convenient chattels who offered sexual gratification denied in the Victorian home for its unseemliness'.[30] This realm of unrestrained sexuality is, however, celebrated by

Burton as both honest and liberal, and he uses it to comment upon the dishonesty and corruption of his own society:

> Subtle corruption and covert licentiousness are utterly absent; we find more real 'vice' in many a French roman ... and in not a few English novels of our day than in the thousands of pages of the Arab. Here we have nothing of that most immodest modern modesty which sees covert implication where nothing is implied, and 'improper' allusion when propriety is not outraged; nor do we meet with the Nineteenth-Century refinement; innocence of the word not of the thought; morality of the tongue not of the heart, and the sincere homage paid to virtue in the guise of perfect hypocrisy.[31]

The East's sexual honesty and openness about its practices highlight the hypocritical prudery of the West, and the psychological consequences of such prudery in British life. Dane Kennedy identifies this 'oblique commentary on [Burton's] own society' and the 'repressive moral regime that ruled British society' in his biographical study, *The Highly Civilized Man* (2005).[32] According to Kennedy, Burton was well aware that his uninhibited translation of the Arabian Nights would stir controversy and, considering himself an 'agent of enlightenment', he welcomed the debates that it would spark.[33] This included seizing upon the occasional references to homosexual practices in the Arabian Nights in order to launch a serious enquiry into the practices and ethics of same-sex relationships in his 'Terminal Essay' in an 'unprecedented account of the historical, geographical, and sociological dimensions of homosexual love'.[34]

Within the social and geographical fabric of Victorian London lay a hidden, repressed world of sensuality, sexuality and desire that, for Burton, might be represented by and channelled through the tales of the Arabian Nights. The erotic fantasies represented in his tales became once again a vehicle for self-actualisation in Britain. Though far removed in style and tone from Robert Louis Stevenson's absurd tales of mystery and magic, Burton's own *New Arabian Nights* nevertheless exhibits a similar desire for poetry, adventure and wonder within the vicissitudes of modern British life. His fantasies of the exotic and the magical within Britain are clearly highly sexualised but, here too, the city becomes a complex palimpsest of hidden spaces, Oriental mysteries and possibilities, which comprise both an enchanted wilderness and the modern metropolis: a dynamic, cosmopolitan space of magic and infinite mysteries.

Considering the role of the Arabian Nights in the context of imperial Britain's participation in Orientalist fantasies of the East, Saree Makdisi and Felicity Nussbaum claim that the evolution of these tales within nineteenth-century British culture reflects the continually evolving, ongoing relationship between an imagined Orient and a modernising, industrialising Occident:

> Thus the gap between Galland's edition in the early eighteenth century and, say, Burton's edition in the late nineteenth – and between both of those texts and the various editions circulating to this day in Arabic itself – offers a kind of measure of the shifting nature of the political and cultural relationships between Europe and the Arab world.[35]

This approach to the Arabian Nights as a rich source of material for the maintenance of difference between East and West undoubtedly had currency in the nineteenth century, and it is a model that, in many ways, has continued to underpin global economic and political relations. Culturally, however, the Arabian Nights were, and continue to be, a far more complex site of emotional, psychological and imaginative investment and exchange.

The story of Schahriar's gradual moral transformation through an ongoing engagement with narrative models the act of reading as a pleasurable abandonment of the self in favour of immersion in the realm of fantasy and the other. The Sultan's final declaration that 'you can never be at a loss for these sort of stories to divert me', and therefore 'I renounce in your favour the cruel law I had imposed of myself' demonstrates the storyteller's ability not only to distract and detain, but also to transform her auditor and to effect material change beyond the bounds of the narrative itself.[36] In the nineteenth century, the tales of the Arabian Nights offered a space for fantasy, creativity, disinvestment of the self and experimentation with multiple identities. Alongside its role as a potential gauge of nineteenth-century geopolitical relations, it equally became a kind of measure of the shifting nature of nineteenth-century Britain itself, and a complex marker of personal and cultural identities, dreams and preoccupations. Writing in a moment of intensifying polarisation between nationalism and globalism, it is perhaps increasingly important to recognise such moments of exchange, and the receptivity and openness that engaging with such texts can offer.

Notes

1. Stevenson, 'The Adventure of the Hansom Cabs', p. 76.
2. Stevenson, 'A Penny Plain and Twopence Coloured', p. 218.
3. Stevenson, 'A Gossip on Romance', p. 247.
4. Ibid. p. 262.
5. Chesterton, 'Robert Louis Stevenson', vol. 18, p. 107.
6. Irwin, 'Foreword', p. 12.
7. Anon., 'Belles Lettres', p. 284.
8. Stevenson, 'The Adventure of Prince Florizel and a Detective', pp. 181–2.
9. Wilde, 'The Critic as Artist', p. 248.
10. Chesterton, 'A Defence of Detective Stories', pp. 158–60.
11. Reading and interpreting the urban labyrinth is, for example, central to the work of writers such as Thomas Pynchon, Peter Ackroyd, Iain Sinclair and Paul Auster.
12. Masterman, *From the Abyss*, p. 96.
13. McLaughlin, *Writing the Urban Jungle*, p. 5.
14. Ibid. p. 5.
15. For excellent readings on the threat of reverse colonisation in the Sherlock Holmes stories, see Siddiqi, 'The Cesspool of Empire: Sherlock Holmes and the Return of the Repressed', pp. 233–47; and Harris, 'Pathological Possibilities: Contagion and Empire in Doyle's Sherlock Holmes Stories', pp. 447–66.
16. Doyle, 'The Adventure of the Noble Bachelor', p. 251.
17. Doyle, 'The Adventure of the Three Gables', p. 1067.
18. Freedgood, *The Ideas in Things*, pp. 150–2.
19. Stevenson, 'Story of the Young Man in Holy Orders', p. 141. Italics in the original.
20. Stevenson, 'Story of the Physician and the Saratoga Trunk', p. 75. Italics in the original.
21. Stevenson, 'The Adventure of the Hansom Cabs', pp. 83–4.
22. Sigma, 'Pantagruelism or Pornography?', p. 2.
23. Sometimes known as Lord Campbell's Act, the Obscene Publications Act permitted authorities to issue warrants in search of pornographic publications, and imposed severe penalties on those individuals found guilty of possessing them. On the history of English laws against obscenity in the nineteenth century, see Roberts, 'Making Victorian Morals? The Society for the Suppression of Vice and its Critics, 1802–1886', pp. 157–73.
24. For an outline of this debate and the public reception of Burton's translation, see Colligan, '"Esoteric Pornography": Sir Richard Burton's *Arabian Nights* and the Origins of Pornography', pp. 31–64.
25. Burton, 'The Translator's Foreword', p. xv.
26. Ibid. p. xv.
27. Ibid. p. xxiv.

28. Ibid. p. xxiii.
29. For a detailed social history, following Said, of the sexual dynamics that underscored the operation of empire, see Hyam, *Empire and Sexuality* (1990).
30. Kabbani, *Europe's Myths of Orient*, p. 7.
31. Burton, 'Translator's Foreword', p. xvii.
32. Kennedy, *The Highly Civilized Man*, pp. 221, 246.
33. Ibid. p. 232.
34. Ibid. p. 238.
35. Makidisi and Nussbaum, 'Introduction', p. 3.
36. Galland, *Arabian Nights' Entertainment*, p. 892.

Bibliography

Primary Sources

Anonymous, 'A Glance at the Exhibition', *Chambers's Edinburgh Journal* 387 (31 May 1851), pp. 337–40.

Anonymous, 'A Journey Round the World in the Crystal Palace', *Sharpe's London Journal* 14 (July 1851), pp. 250–6.

Anonymous, 'Advertisement, Theatre Royal, Covent Garden', *Theatrical Observer* 4768 (30 March 1837), p. 3.

Anonymous, 'Advertisement, Theatre Royal, Drury Lane', *Theatrical Observer* 1994 (2 May 1828), p. 4.

Anonymous, 'Advertisement, Theatre Royal, Lyceum', *Theatrical Observer* 7119 (17 October 1844), p. 4.

Anonymous, *A Guide to the Great Exhibition; Containing a Description of Every Principal Object of Interest, With a Plan, Pointing out the Easiest and Most Systematic Way of Examining the Contents of the Crystal Palace* (London: George Routledge, 1851).

Anonymous, *Aladdin and the Wonderful Lamp; or, New Lamps for Old Ones: In Two Acts; as Performed at the Lyceum Theatre* (London: W. S. Johnson, 1844).

Anonymous, 'Aladdin at the Crystal Palace; Or, Science Versus Fairy-Land', *Leisure Hour* 1.17 (22 April 1852), pp. 261–2.

Anonymous, *Aladdin; Or, The Wonderful Lamp; Sindbad the Sailor; Or, The Old Man of the Sea; Ali Baba; Or, the Forty Thieves*, Rev. Mary Elizabeth Braddon (London: John and Robert Maxwell, 1880).

Anonymous, 'Antiquarian Researches. Mr Belzoni's Exhibition of the Egyptian Tomb', *Gentleman's Magazine, and Historical Chronicle* (May 1821), pp. 447–50.

Anonymous, *Arabian Nights Entertainments Translated into French by M Galland and Now Done into English*, 4 vols (London: C. D. Piguenit, 1792).

Anonymous, *Arabian Nights Entertainments Translated into French by M Galland and Now Done into English*, 4 vols, 10th edn (London: Harrison, 1785).

Anonymous, 'Austen Henry Layard', *Illustrated Review* 5.65 (20 March 1873), pp. 293–302.
Anonymous, 'Bazaars of Constantinople', *Chambers's Edinburgh Journal* 208 (23 January 1836), pp. 412–13.
Anonymous, 'Belles Lettres', *Westminster Review* 119.235 (January 1883), pp. 272–95.
Anonymous, 'Caves', *Chambers's Journal of Popular Literature, Science, and the Arts* 850 (10 April 1880), pp. 230–3.
Anonymous, 'Covent-Garden Theatre', *Ladies' Monthly Museum, or Polite Repository of Amusement and Instruction* 3 (May 1816), pp. 288–9.
Anonymous, 'Covent-Garden Theatre', *The Times* (28 December 1812), p. 3.
Anonymous, 'Delhi', *Chambers's Edinburgh Journal* 32 (8 September 1832), pp. 252–3.
Anonymous, 'Drama', *European Magazine, and London Review* 2.10 (June 1826), pp. 634–46.
Anonymous, 'Drama. The London Theatres', *Literary Gazette* 273 (13 April 1822), pp. 235–6.
Anonymous, 'Dramatic Criticisms. Drury-Lane Theatre', in *Oxberry's Dramatic Biography, and Histrionic Anecdotes*, vol. 5 (London: George Virtue, 1826), pp. 71–2.
Anonymous, 'Dramatic Criticisms. Drury-Lane Theatre', in *Oxberry's Dramatic Biography, and Histrionic Anecdotes*, vol. 6 (London: George Virtue, 1826), pp. 189–90.
Anonymous, 'Dramatic Register', *New Monthly Magazine, and Universal Register* 2 (1 January 1815), pp. 552–4.
Anonymous, 'Drury Lane', *Belle Assemblée; Or, Court and Fashionable Magazine* 1.3 (April 1806), pp. 169–70.
Anonymous, 'Drury-Lane Theatre', *Monthly Magazine, or, British Register* 58.402 (November 1824), p. 359.
Anonymous, 'Drury Lane Theatre', *Theatrical Observer* 910 (29 October 1824), p. 1.
Anonymous, 'Early Adventures in Persia, Susiana, and Babylonia, including a Residence among the Bakhtiyari and other Wild Tribes before the Discovery of Nineveh', *Edinburgh Review* 167.342 (April 1888), pp. 519–53.
Anonymous, 'Egyptian Antiquities', *London Literary Gazette, and Journal of Belles Lettres, Arts, Sciences* 223 (28 April 1821), pp. 268–9.
Anonymous, 'English Theatricals. Drury-Lane', *Belle Assemblée; Or, Court and Fashionable Magazine* 30.195 (December 1824), pp. 264–5.
Anonymous, 'Eternal Lamps', *Household Words* 8.187 (22 October 1853), pp. 185–8.
Anonymous, *Guide Book to the Industrial Exhibition; with Facts, Figures, and Observations on the Manufactures and Produce Exhibited* (London: Partridge and Oakey, 1851).

Anonymous, 'How We Hunted the Prince', *Punch* 20 (1851), p. 222.

Anonymous, 'India and Indian Contributions to the Industrial Bazaar', *Illustrated Exhibitor* 8 (4 October 1851), pp. 317–28.

Anonymous, 'India at the Great Exhibition', *Allen's Indian Mail, and Register of Intelligence for British and Foreign India, China and All Parts of the East* 9.174 (3 June 1851), pp. 333–4.

Anonymous, 'Indian Assassins', *London Journal* 26.667 (5 December1857), pp. 217–18.

Anonymous, 'John Baptist Belzoni', *Ladies' Monthly Museum, or Polite Repository of Amusement and Instruction* 22 (October 1825), pp. 181–7.

Anonymous, 'Literae Orientales', *Dublin University Magazine* 10.57 (September 1837), pp. 274–92.

Anonymous, 'Narrative of an Expedition to Explore the River Zaire, usually called the Congo, in South Africa, in 1816', *Quarterly Review* 18.36 (January 1818), pp. 335–79.

Anonymous, 'Notes, During a Visit to Egypt, Nubia, the Oasis, Mount Sinai, and Jerusalem', *Eclectic Review* 21 (January 1824), pp. 1–33.

Anonymous, 'Notices of the Acted Drama in London', *Blackwood's Edinburgh Magazine* 5.27 (June 1819), pp. 317–22.

Anonymous, 'Old Cairo and Its Mosque', *Household Words* 3.66 (28 June 1851), pp. 332–4.

Anonymous, 'On the Tales and Fictions of the East', *New Annual Register, or, General Repository of History, Politics, and Literature* (1 January 1812), pp. 222–34.

Anonymous, 'Progress at the International Exhibition', *Leader* 2.57 (26 April 1851), p. 382.

Anonymous, 'Ramaseeana; or, A Vocabulary of the Peculiar Language Used by the Thugs', *Edinburgh Review* 64:130 (1 January 1837), pp. 357–95.

Anonymous, *Reports by the Juries on the Subjects in the Thirty Classes into Which the Exhibition Was Divided*, 4 vols (London: Spicer Brothers, 1852).

Anonymous, 'Some Account of the City of Isfahan', *Saturday Magazine* 5.149 (25 October 1834), pp. 161–8.

Anonymous, 'Stage Silhouettes', *Bow Bells: A Magazine of General Literature and Art for Family Reading* 25.323 (9 March 1894), pp. 257–8.

Anonymous, 'Surrey', *Mirror of the Stage* 1.7 (4 November 1822), pp. 110–11.

Anonymous, 'The Alhambra, in Spain', *Mirror of Literature, Amusement, and Instruction* 19.549 (26 May 1832), pp. 337–42.

Anonymous, *The Art Journal Illustrated Catalogue: The Industry of All Nations, 1851* (London: George Virtue, 1851).

Anonymous, *The Book of the Thousand Nights and One Night, from the Arabic of the Aegyptian M. S.*, trans. Henry Torrens (Calcutta and London: W. H. Thacker, 1838).

Anonymous, 'The City of Damascus', *Mirror of Literature, Amusement, and Instruction* 6.170 (26 November 1825), pp. 364–5.

Anonymous, 'The Court of Egypt', *Chambers's Edinburgh Journal* 26 (28 July 1832), p. 207.

Anonymous, 'The Crystal Palace', *The Times* (15 January 1851), p. 5.

Anonymous, 'The Discovery Ships Are Completely Ready to Leave Deptford', *The Times* (30 April 1821), p. 3.

Anonymous, 'The Drama', *London Magazine* 5.29 (May 1822), pp. 481–4.

Anonymous, 'The Drama. Drury-Lane Theatre', *Ladies' Monthly Museum, or Polite Repository of Amusement and Instruction* 20 (December 1824), p. 342.

Anonymous, 'The Electric Telegraph', in Dionysius Lardner (ed.), *The Museum of Science and Art*, vol. 3 (London: Walton and Maberly, 1854), pp. 113–208.

Anonymous, 'The Exhibition', *London Journal* 14.345 (4 October 1851), pp. 77–8.

Anonymous, 'The Great Exhibition', *Examiner* 2259 (17 May 1851), pp. 313–14.

Anonymous, 'The Great Industrial Exhibition', *Athenaeum* 1227 (3 May 1851), pp. 477–9.

Anonymous, *The History of Aladdin, or the Wonderful Lamp* (London: J. Limbird, Mirror Press).

Anonymous, 'The Overture and the Whole of the Music in Aladdin, or the Wonderful Lamp, a Fairy Opera, in Three Acts, Composed by Henry R. Bishop, Composer to the Theatre Royal, Drury Lane, and Professor of Harmony and Composition at the Royal Academy of Music', *Quarterly Musical Magazine and Review* 8.30 (April 1826), pp. 242–52.

Anonymous, 'The Peasants of British India', *Household Words* 4.95 (17 January 1852), pp. 389–93.

Anonymous, 'The People of the Arabian Nights', *Littell's Living Age* 793 (6 August 1859), pp. 327–43.

Anonymous, 'The Secret Societies of Asia – The Assassins and Thugs', *Blackwood's Edinburgh Magazine* 49.304 (February 1841), pp. 229–47.

Anonymous, 'The Selector, and Literary Notices of New Works', *Mirror of Literature, Amusement, and Instruction* 13.360 (14 March 1829), pp. 189–92.

Anonymous, 'The Story of Giovanni Belzoni', *Household Words* 2.49 (1 March 1851), pp. 548–52.

Anonymous, 'The Theatres. Drury-Lane', *Belle Assemblée; Or, Court and Fashionable Magazine* (February 1815), pp. 40–1.

Anonymous, 'The Thugs, a Fraternity of Murderers in India', *Examiner* 1513 (29 January 1837), p. 71.

Anonymous, 'The Transept', *Illustrated Exhibitor* 1 (7 June 1851), pp. 9–12.

Anonymous, 'Theatre Royal Covent-Garden', *Theatrical Inquisitor, and Monthly Mirror* 2 (May 1813), pp. 252–4.

Anonymous, 'Theatre-Royal, Drury-Lane', *Monthly Theatrical Reporter* 1.4 (January 1815), pp. 136–40.

Anonymous, 'Theatrical Examiner', *Examiner* 874 (31 October 1824), p. 694.
Anonymous, 'Theatrical Journal', *European Magazine, and London Review* 14 (December 1788), pp. 468–71.
Anonymous, 'Theatrical Journal', *European Magazine, and London Review* 49 (April 1806), pp. 288–91.
Anonymous, 'Theatrical Journal', *European Magazine, and London Review* 63 (January 1813), p. 45.
Anonymous, 'Theatrical Journal', *European Magazine, and London Review* 66 (December 1816), pp. 522–5.
Anonymous, 'Theatrical Recorder', *Universal Magazine* 19.111 (Feb 1813), pp. 143–6.
Anonymous, 'Theatrical Register', *Gentleman's Magazine, and Historical Chronicle* (December 1814), p. 672.
Anonymous, 'Theatrical Register. New Pieces', *Gentleman's Magazine, and Historical Chronicle* (April 1822), p. 366.
Anonymous, 'Tomb of Sethi, Descendant of the Sun', *Chambers's Journal of Popular Literature, Science and Arts* 99 (18 November 1865), pp. 732–36.
Anonymous, 'Town Talk', *The Drama; Or, Theatrical Pocket Magazine* 1.6 (October 1821), pp. 309–12.
Anonymous, 'What English Literature Gives Us', *Chambers's Edinburgh Journal* 365 (26 January 1839), pp. 1–2.
Barrie, J. M., *Margaret Ogilvy* (New York: Charles Scribner's Sons, 1896).
Bartlett, William Henry, *The Nile Boat, or, Glimpses of the Land of Egypt*, 2 vols (London: Arthur Hall, 1849).
Belzoni, Giovanni, *Narrative of the Operations and Recent Discoveries within the Pyramids, Temples, Tombs, and Excavations in Egypt and Nubia* (London: John Murray, 1820).
Blanchard, Laman (ed.), *The Life and Literary Remains of L. E. L.*, 2 vols (London: Henry Colburn, 1841).
Braddon, Mary Elizabeth, *Lady Audley's Secret*, ed. Lyn Pykett (Oxford: Oxford University Press, 2012 [1862]).
Bremer, Frederika, 'Impressions of England in the Autumn of 1851. From the Letters and Memoranda of Frederika Bremer', *Sharpe's London Journal of Entertainment and Instruction. For General Reading*, vol. 15 (London: Virtue, Hall and Virtue, 1852), pp. 193–201.
Brontë, Charlotte, 'Charlotte Brontë to the Revd Patrick Brontë, 7 June [1851]', in Margaret Smith (ed.), *The Letters of Charlotte Brontë, with a Selection of Letters by Family and Friends, Volume 2, 1848–1851* (Oxford: Clarendon Press, 2000), pp. 630–1.
Brontë, Charlotte, *Jane Eyre*, ed. Sally Shuttleworth (Oxford: Oxford University Press, 2000 [1847]).
Brontë, Charlotte, *Villette*, ed. Tim Dolin (Oxford: Oxford University Press, 2000 [1853]).

Brontë, Charlotte, Anne Brontë, Branwell Brontë and Emily Brontë, *Tales of Glass Town, Angria, and Gondal: Selected Writings*, ed. Christine Alexander (Oxford: Oxford University Press, 2010).

Burton, Richard F., 'The Translator's Foreword', in *The Book of the Thousand Nights and a Night*, trans. Richard F. Burton, 10 vols (London: Kama Shastra Society, 1885–6).

Carlyle, Thomas, 'Signs of the Times', *Edinburgh Review* 59 (June 1829), pp. 439–59.

Carroll, Lewis, *Alice in Wonderland* (Ware, Hertfordshire: Wordsworth Classics, 2001 [1865]).

Chateaubriand, 'Description of an Eastern Caravan', *Mirror of Literature, Amusement, and Instruction* 1.24 (12 April 1823), pp. 381–2.

Chesterton, G. K., 'A Defence of Detective Stories', *The Defendant* (London: J. M. Dent and Sons, 1914), pp. 155–62.

Chesterton, G. K., 'Robert Louis Stevenson', in George G. Marlin, Richard P. Rabatin and John L. Swan (eds), *The Collected Works of G.K. Chesterton*, vol. 18 (San Francisco: Ignatius Press, 1999), pp. 39–148.

Coleridge, Samuel Taylor, 'Kubla Khan: Or, A Vision in a Dream', in *The Complete Poems of Samuel Taylor Coleridge*, ed. William Keach (London: Penguin, 1997 [1816]), pp. 249–52.

Coleridge, Samuel Taylor, *Selected Letters*, ed. H. J. Jackson (Oxford: Clarendon Press, 1987).

Collins, Wilkie, *The Moonstone*, ed. John Sutherland (Oxford: Oxford University Press, 1999 [1868]).

Commissioners for the Exhibition of 1851, *Great Exhibition of the Works of Industry of All Nations. Official Descriptive and Illustrated Catalogue*, 3 vols (London: Spicer Brothers, 1851).

Concannen, Edward, *Remembrances of the Great Exhibition* (London: Ackerman, 1852).

Cooper, Reverend, *The Oriental Moralist, or the Beauties of the Arabian Nights Entertainments, Translated from the Original and Accompanied with Suitable Reflections Adapted to Each Story* (London: E. Newbery, 1790).

Curtis, George William, *Nile Notes of a Howadji* (New York: Dix, Edwards, and Co., 1856).

Dalziel, Edward, and George Dalziel, *Dalziels' Illustrated Arabian Nights' Entertainments*, rev. Henry William Dulcken (London: Ward, Lock, and Tyler, 1865).

De Quincey, Thomas, *Autobiographic Sketches: 1790–1803* (Edinburgh: Adam and Charles Black, 1862 [1853]).

Dickens, Charles, *A Christmas Carol and Other Christmas Book*, ed. Robert Douglas-Fairhurst (Oxford: Oxford University Press, 2006 [1843]).

Dickens, Charles, 'A Christmas Tree', *Household Words* 2.39 (1850), pp. 289–95.

Dickens, Charles, *American Notes for General Circulation*, ed. Patricia Ingham (London: Penguin, 2000 [1842]).
Dickens, Charles, *A Tale of Two Cities*, ed. Richard Maxwell (London: Penguin, 2000 [1859]).
Dickens, Charles, *Dombey and Son*, ed. Alan Horsman (Oxford: Oxford University Press, 1982 [1848]).
Dickens, Charles, *Hard Times*, ed. Kate Flint (London: Penguin, 2003 [1854]).
Dickens, Charles, 'Manchester Men at their Books', *Household Words* 8.195 (17 December 1853), pp. 377–9.
Dickens, Charles, *Martin Chuzzlewit*, ed. Margaret Cardwell (Oxford: Oxford University Press, 2009 [1844]).
Dickens, Charles, 'Mr Barlow', *All The Year Round* 1.7 (16 January 1869), pp. 156–9.
Dickens, Charles, *Our Mutual Friend*, ed. Adrian Poole (London: Penguin, 1997 [1865]).
Dickens, Charles, *Pictures from Italy*, ed. Kate Flint (London: Penguin, 1998 [1846]).
Dickens, Charles, *Sketches by Boz* (Oxford: Oxford University Press, 1957 [1836]).
Dickens, Charles, 'The Ghost in Master B.'s Room', *All the Year Round* (13 December 1859), pp. 27–31.
Dickens, Charles, *The Old Curiosity Shop*, ed. Norman Page (London: Penguin, 2000 [1841]).
Dickens, Charles, 'The Thousand and One Humbugs', *Household Words* 11.267 (5 May 1855), pp. 313–16.
Dodwell, Henry Herbert, *The Founder of Modern Egypt: A Study of Muhammad Ali* (Cambridge: Cambridge University Press, 1931).
Dorsett, Lyle W., and Marjorie Lamp Mead (eds), *C. S. Lewis's Letters to Children* (New York: Touchstone, 1995).
Doyle, Arthur Conan, 'The Adventure of the Noble Bachelor', in *The Original Illustrated 'Strand' Sherlock Holmes* (Ware: Wordsworth, 1996 [1892]), pp. 243–56.
Doyle, Arthur Conan, 'The Adventure of the Three Gables', in *The Original Illustrated 'Strand' Sherlock Holmes* (Ware: Wordsworth, 1996 [1926]), pp. 1059–70.
Doyle, Arthur Conan, *The Sign of Four*, ed. Ed Glinert (London: Penguin, 2001 [1890]).
Eliot, George, *A Writer's Notebook, 1854–1879, and Uncollected Writings*, ed. Joseph Wiesenfarth (Charlottesville: University of Virginia Press, 1981).
Eliot, George, *Adam Bede*, ed. Carol A. Martin (Oxford: Oxford University Press, 2008 [1859]).
Eliot, George, *Middlemarch*, ed. Rosemary Ashton (London: Penguin, 1994 [1871]).

Elwood, Anne Katharine, *Narrative of a Journey Overland from England, by the Continent of Europe, Egypt, and the Red Sea, to India, Including a Residence There, and Voyage Home in the Years 1825, 26, 27 and 28*, 2 vols (London: Henry Colburn and Richard Bentley, 1830).

Galland, Antoine, *Arabian Nights' Entertainments*, ed. Robert L. Mack (Oxford: Oxford University Press, 1995).

Gaskell, Elizabeth, *North and South*, ed. Patricia Ingham (London: Penguin, 1995 [1855]).

Gaskell, Elizabeth, *The Life of Charlotte Brontë*, ed. Angus Easson (Oxford: Oxford University Press, 2009 [1857]).

Grimaldi, Joseph, *Memoirs of Joseph Grimaldi, Edited by 'Boz'*, rev. Charles Whitehead (London: Richard Bentley, 1846).

Henniker, Frederick, *Notes, During a Visit to Egypt, Nubia, the Oasis, Mount Sinai, and Jerusalem* (London: John Murray, 1823).

Hunt, Leigh, 'New Translations of the Arabian Nights', *London and Westminster Review* 33.1 (October 1839), pp. 101–37.

Hunt, Robert, *Hunt's Hand-Book to the Official Catalogues: An Explanatory Guide to the Natural Productions and Manufactures of the Great Exhibition of the Industry of all Nations, 1851*, 2 vols (London: Spicer Brothers, 1851).

Irving, Pierre (ed.), *The Life and Letters of Washington Irving*, 3 vols (London: Richard Bentley, 1862).

Knight, Charles, 'Three May-Days in London', *Household Words* 3.58 (3 May 1851), pp. 121–4.

Landon, Letitia Elizabeth, 'Captain Cook', in *The Poetical Works of Miss Landon* (Philadelphia: E. L. Carey and A. Hart, 1838), pp. 337–8.

Landon, Letitia Elizabeth, *Traits and Trials of Early Life* (Philadelphia: E. L. Carey and A. Hart, 1837).

Lane, Edward William, *An Account of the Manners and Customs of the Modern Egyptians*, 2 vols (London: Charles Knight, 1836).

Lane, Edward William, *Description of Egypt*, ed. Jason Thompson (Cairo: American University in Cairo Press, 2000).

Lane, Edward William, *The Thousand and One Nights, Commonly Called, in England, The Arabian Nights' Entertainments*, 3 vols (London: Charles Knight, 1841).

Lane-Poole, Stanley, *Life of Edward William Lane* (London: Williams and Norgate, 1877).

Layard, Austen Henry, *Autobiography and Letters from His Childhood until His Appointment as H. M. The Ambassador at Madrid*, ed. William N. Bruce, 2 vols (London: John Murray, 1903).

Layard, Austen Henry, *Nineveh and Its Remains*, 2 vols (London: John Murray, 1849).

Lewis, C. S., 'On Juvenile Tastes', in *On Stories: And Other Essays on Literature*, ed. Walter Hoope (London: Harvest, 1982), pp. 45–51.

Martineau, Harriet, *Eastern Life, Present and Past*, 3 vols (London: Edward Moxon, 1848).

Masterman, Charles, *From the Abyss: Of Its Inhabitants by One of Them* (London: R. B. Johnson, 1902).

Mayhew, Henry, *1851; Or, the Adventures of Mr. and Mrs. Sandboys and Family, Who Came up to London to 'Enjoy Themselves' and to See the Great Exhibition* (London: David Bogue, Fleet Street, 1851).

Meredith, George, *The Shaving of Shagpat: An Arabian Entertainment* (London: Chapman and Hall, 1856).

Mill, John Stuart, 'Civilization', in *The Collected Works of John Stuart Mill*, ed. John M. Robson and Jack Stillinger, vol. 18 (Toronto: University of Toronto Press, 1977), pp. 117–47.

Ochlenschlaeger, Adam, 'Aladdin', *Blackwood's Edinburgh Magazine* 36.228 (November 1834), pp. 620–41.

Poe, Edgar Allan, 'The Thousand-and-Second Tale of Scheherazade', in *The Complete Tales and Poems of Edgar Allan Poe* (London: Penguin, 1982 [1845]), pp. 104–17.

Poole, Sophia Lane, with Edward Lane, *The Englishwoman in Egypt: Letters from Cairo, Written During a Residence there in 1842, 3, and 4*, 2 vols (London: Charles Knight, 1844).

Rich, Claudius James, *Memoir on the Ruins of Babylon* (London: Longman, 1818).

Rousseau, Jean-Jacques, *Émile, ou de l'Éducation*, trans. Barbara Foxley (London: J. M. Dent and Sons, 1974 [1763]).

Shelley, Mary, *Frankenstein*, ed. Maurice Hindle (London: Penguin, 1985 [1818]).

Sherer, Joseph Moyle, *Scenes and Impressions in Egypt and in Italy* (London: Longman, 1824).

Sigma, John Morley, 'Pantagruelism or Pornography?', *Pall Mall Gazette* 42 (14 September 1885), pp. 1–3.

Sleeman, William Henry, *Report on the Depredations Committed by the Thug Gangs of Upper and Central India, from the Cold Season of 1836–37, Down to Their Gradual Suppression, under the Operation of the Measures Adopted against Them by the Supreme Government, in the Year 1839* (Calcutta: G. H. Huttmann, 1840).

Smith, Alfred Charles, *The Nile and Its Banks*, 2 vols (London: John Murray, 1868).

Stephens, Frederic George (writing as Laura Savage), 'Modern Giants', *The Germ* 1.4 (1850), pp. 169–73.

Stevenson, Robert Louis, 'A Gossip on Romance', *Memories and Portraits*, 13th edn (London: Chatto and Windus, 1906 [1882]), pp. 247–74.

Stevenson, Robert Louis, 'A Penny Plain and Twopence Coloured', *Memories and Portraits*, 13th edn (London: Chatto and Windus, 1906 [1884]), pp. 213–27.

Stevenson, Robert Louis, 'Child's Play', *Cornhill Magazine* 38.225 (September 1878), pp. 352–9.

Stevenson, Robert Louis, *More New Arabian Nights: The Dynamiter* (New York: Henry Holt, 1885).
Stevenson, Robert Louis, *New Arabian Nights*, int. Robert Irwin (London: Capuchin Press, 2011 [1882]).
Stevenson, Robert Louis, 'Story of the Physician and the Saratoga Trunk', in *New Arabian Nights*, int. Robert Irwin (London: Capuchin Press, 2011 [1882]), pp. 48–75.
Stevenson, Robert Louis, 'Story of the Young Man in Holy Orders', in *New Arabian Nights*, int. Robert Irwin (London: Capuchin Press, 2011 [1882]), pp. 125–41.
Stevenson, Robert Louis, 'The Adventure of Prince Florizel and a Detective', in *New Arabian Nights*, int. Robert Irwin (London: Capuchin Press, 2011 [1882]), pp. 175–82.
Stevenson, Robert Louis, 'The Adventure of the Hansom Cabs', in *New Arabian Nights*, int. Robert Irwin (London: Capuchin Press, 2011 [1882]), pp. 76–97.
Tallis, John, *History and Description of the Crystal Palace and the Exhibition of the World's Industry in 1851*, 3 vols (London: John Tallis, 1851).
Thackeray, William Makepeace, 'May Day Ode', *The Times* (30 April 1851), p. 5.
Thackeray, William Makepeace, *Vanity Fair*, ed. Helen Small (Oxford: Oxford University Press, 2015 [1848]).
Tylor, Edward Burnett, *Primitive Culture: Researches into the Development of Mythology, Philosophy, Religion, Language, Art, and Custom*, 2 vols (London: John Murray, 1871).
Warner, Charles Dudley, *Mummies and Moslems* (Toronto: Belford, 1876).
Warren, Samuel, *The Lily and the Bee: An Apologue of the Crystal Palace* (Edinburgh: William Blackwood and Sons, 1851).
Wilde, Oscar, 'The Critic as Artist', in *Oscar Wilde: The Major Works*, ed. Isobel Murray (Oxford: Oxford University Press, 2000 [1891]), pp. 241–98.
Wilkinson, John Gardner, *Manners and Customs of the Ancient Egyptians* (London: John Murray, 1837).
Wilson, George, *Electricity and the Electric Telegraph* (London: Longman, Brown, Green, and Longmans, 1852).
Wordsworth, William, 'The Prelude', in *William Wordsworth: The Major Works*, ed. Stephen Gill (Oxford: Oxford University Press, 1984), pp. 375–590.

Secondary Sources

Abidi, Azhar, 'The Secret History of the Flying Carpet', *Meanjin* 63.2 (2004), pp. 141–8.
Ablow, Rachel, 'Introduction', in Rachel Ablow (ed.), *The Feeling of Reading: Affective Experience and Victorian Literature* (Ann Arbor: University of Michigan Press, 2010), pp. 1–10.

Ahmed, Leila, *Edward W. Lane: A Study of his Life and Works and of British Ideas of the Middle East in the Nineteenth Century* (London: Longman, 1978).

Al-Dabbagh, Abdulla, *Literary Orientalism, Postcolonialism, and Universalism* (New York: Peter Lang, 2010).

Alexander, Christine, 'Autobiography and Juvenilia: The Fractured Self in Charlotte Brontë's Early Manuscripts', in Christine Alexander and Juliet McMaster (eds), *The Child Writer from Austen to Woolf* (Cambridge: Cambridge University Press, 2005), pp. 154–72.

Alexander, Christine, and Margaret Smith, *The Oxford Companion to the Brontës* (Oxford: Oxford University Press, 2003).

Ali, Muhsin Jassim, *Scheherazade in England: A Study of Nineteenth-Century English Criticism of the Arabian Nights* (Washington, DC: Three Continents Press, 1981).

Al-Musawi, Muhsin, 'The Taming of the Sultan: A Study of Scheherazade Motif in *Jane Eyre*', *Abad al-Rafidian* 17 (1988), pp. 59–81.

Altick, Richard, *The Shows of London* (Cambridge, MA: Belknap Press, 1978).

Appadurai, Arjun, 'Introduction: Commodities and the Politics of Value', in Arjun Appadurai (ed.), *The Social Life of Things: Commodities in Cultural Perspective* (Cambridge: Cambridge University Press, 1986), pp. 3–63.

Appadurai, Arjun (ed.), *The Social Life of Things: Commodities in Cultural Perspective* (Cambridge: Cambridge University Press, 1986).

Armstrong, Isobel, *Victorian Glassworlds: Glass Culture and the Imagination, 1830–1880* (Oxford: Oxford University Press, 2008).

Auerbach, Jeffrey A., *The Great Exhibition of 1851: A Nation on Display* (New Haven, CT: Yale University Press, 1999).

Badowska, Eva, 'Choseville: Brontë's "Villette" and the Art of Bourgeois Interiority', *PMLA* 120.5 (October 2005), pp. 1509–23.

Ballaster, Ros, *Fabulous Orients: Fictions of the East in England, 1662–1785* (Oxford: Oxford University Press, 2005).

Ballaster, Ros, 'Playing the Second String: The Role of Dinarzade in Eighteenth-Century Fiction', in Saree Makdisi and Felicity Nussbaum (eds), *The Arabian Nights in Historical Context: Between East and West* (Oxford: Oxford University Press, 2008), pp. 83–102.

Ballaster, Ros, 'The Sea-Born Tale: Eighteenth-Century English Translations of *The Thousand and One Nights* and the Lure of Elemental Difference', in Philip F. Kennedy and Marina Warner (eds), *Scheherazade's Children: Global Encounters with the Arabian Nights* (New York: New York University Press, 2013), pp. 27–52.

Barfoot, C. C., and Theo D'Haen (eds), *Oriental Prospects: Western Literature and the Lure of the East* (Amsterdam: Rodopi, 1998).

Baudrillard, Jean, *Simulacra and Simulation*, trans. Sheila Faria Glasner (Ann Arbor: University of Michigan Press, 1994).

Beer, Gillian, *Alice in Space: The Sideways Victorian World of Lewis Carroll* (Chicago: University of Chicago Press, 2016).
Beer, Gillian, *Open Fields: Science in Cultural Encounter* (Oxford: Oxford University Press, 1996).
Bernfeld, Suzanne Cassirer, 'Freud and Archaeology', *American Imago* 8.2 (1 June 1951), pp. 1107–29.
Black, Barbara J., *On Exhibit: Victorians and Their Museums* (Charlottesville: Virginia University Press, 2000).
Bodenheimer, Rosemarie, *Knowing Dickens* (Ithaca, NY: Cornell University Press, 2007).
Bolter, Jay David, and Richard Grusin, *Remediation: Understanding New Media* (Cambridge, MA: MIT Press, 1999).
Borges, Jorge Luis, *Seven Nights*, trans. Eliot Weinberger (London: Faber, 1986).
Borges, Jorge Luis, 'The Translators of *The Thousand and One Nights*', in Eliot Weinberger (ed.), *Borges: Selected Non-Fictions*, trans. Esther Allen, Suzanne Jill Levine and Eliot Weinberger (New York: Viking, 1999), pp. 92–109.
Borges, Jorge Luis, 'When Fiction Lives in Fiction', in Eliot Weinberger (ed.), *Borges: Selected Non Fiction*, trans. Esther Allen, Suzanne Jill Levine and Eliot Weinberger (New York: Viking, 1999), pp. 160–2.
Bown, Nicola, Carolyn Burdett and Pamela Thurschwell, 'Introduction', in Nicola Bown, Carolyn Burdett and Pamela Thurschwell (eds), *The Victorian Supernatural* (Cambridge: Cambridge University Press, 2004), pp. 1–19.
Bridgwater, Patrick, *De Quincey's Gothic Masquerade* (Amsterdam: Rodopi, 2004).
Brown, Bill, *A Sense of Things: The Object Matter of Victorian Literature* (Chicago: University of Chicago Press, 2003).
Brown, Bill, 'Reification, Reanimation, and the American Uncanny', *Critical Inquiry* 32 (2006), pp. 175–207.
Brown, Bill, *The Material Unconscious: American Amusement, Stephen Crane and the Economies of Play* (Cambridge, MA: Harvard University Press, 1996).
Brown, Bill, 'The Secret Life of Things (Virginia Woolf and the Matter of Modernism)', *Modernism/Modernity* 6.2 (1999), pp. 1–28.
Brown, Bill, 'Thing Theory', *Critical Inquiry* 28.1 (2001), pp. 1–22.
Butler, Marilyn, 'Byron and the Empire in the East', in Andrew Rutherford (ed.), *Byron: Augustan and Romantic* (Basingstoke: Macmillan, 1990), pp. 63–81.
Caracciolo, Peter L., 'Introduction: Such a Store House of Ingenious Fiction and Splendid Imagery', in Peter L. Caracciolo (ed.), *The Arabian Nights in English Literature: Studies in the Reception of the Thousand and One Nights into British Culture* (London: Macmillan, 1988), pp. 1–80.

Caracciolo, Peter L., 'The House of Fiction and *Le Jardin Anglo-Chinois*', *Middle Eastern Literatures* 7.2 (2004), pp. 199–211.
Caracciolo, Peter L., 'The Shakespearean Nights of Robert Louis Stevenson', in William Baker and Isobel Armstrong (eds), *Form and Feeling in Modern Literature: Essays in Honour of Barbara Hardy* (Abingdon: Routledge, 2013), pp. 20–2.
Cecire, Maria Sachiko, Hannah Field and Malini Roy (eds), *Space and Place in Children's Literature, 1789 to the Present* (London: Routledge, 2016).
Clot, André, *Harun al-Rashid and the World of the Thousand and One Nights* (London: Saqi, 2005).
Colley, Linda, *Captives: Britain, Empire and the World, 1600–1850* (London: Vintage, 2010).
Colligan, Colette, '"Esoteric Pornography": Sir Richard Burton's *Arabian Nights* and the Origins of Pornography', *Victorian Review* 28.2 (2002), pp. 31–64.
Cook, Cornelia, 'The Victorian Scheherazade: Elizabeth Gaskell and George Meredith', in Peter L. Caracciolo (ed.), *The Arabian Nights in English Literature: Studies in the Reception of the Thousand and One Nights into British Culture* (London: Macmillan, 1988), pp. 197–217.
Daly, Nicholas, *Sensation and Modernity in the 1860s* (Cambridge: Cambridge University Press, 2009).
Daly, Suzanne, *The Empire Inside: Indian Commodities in Victorian Domestic Novels* (Ann Arbor: University of Michigan Press, 2011).
Damrosch, David, *What Is World Literature?* (Princeton: Princeton University Press, 2003).
Dash, Mike, *Thug: The True Story of India's Murderous Cult* (London: Granta, 2005).
Davis, John R., *The Great Exhibition* (Stroud: Sutton, 1999).
Davis, Philip, *The Oxford English Literary History: The Victorians. Volume 8: 1830–1880* (Oxford: Oxford University Press, 2002).
Diamond, Elin, *Performance and Cultural Politics* (London: Routledge, 1996).
Díaz-Andreu, Margarita, *A World History of Nineteenth-Century Archaeology: Nationalism, Colonialism, and the Past* (New York: Oxford University Press, 2007).
Douglas-Fairhurst, Robert, *The Story of Alice: Lewis Carroll and the Secret History of Wonderland* (London: Vintage, 2016).
Douglas-Fairhurst, Robert, 'Working Through Memory and Forgetting in Victorian Literature', *Australasian Journal of Victorian Studies* 21.1 (2016), pp. 1–13.
During, Simon, *Modern Enchantments: The Cultural Power of Secular Magic* (Cambridge, MA: Harvard University Press, 2002).
Fisher, Philip, *The Vehement Passions* (Princeton: Princeton University Press, 2002).

Flint, Kate, 'The Middle Novels: *Chuzzlewit*, *Dombey*, and *Copperfield*', in John O. Jordan (ed.), *The Cambridge Companion to Charles Dickens* (Cambridge: Cambridge University Press, 2001), pp. 34–48.

Flint, Kate, 'Traveling Readers', in Rachel Ablow (ed.), *The Feeling of Reading: Affective Experience and Victorian Literature* (Ann Arbor: University of Michigan Press, 2010), pp. 27–46.

Freedgood, Elaine, *The Ideas in Things: Fugitive Meaning in the Victorian Novel* (Chicago: University of Chicago Press, 2006).

Friedman, Susan Stanford, 'Unthinking Manifest Destiny: Muslim Modernities on Three Continents', in Wai Chee Dimock and Lawrence Buell (eds), *Shades of the Planet: American Literature as World Literature* (Princeton: Princeton University Press, 2007), pp. 62–99.

Fritzsche, Peter, *Stranded in the Present: Modern Time and the Melancholy of History* (Cambridge, MA: Harvard University Press, 2004).

Fulford, Tim, 'Coleridge and the Oriental Tale', in Saree Makdisi and Felicity Nussbaum (eds), *The Arabian Nights in Historical Context: Between East and West* (Oxford: Oxford University Press, 2008), pp. 213–34.

Gallagher, Catherine, *The Industrial Reformation of English Fiction: Social Discourse and Narrative Form, 1832–1867* (Chicago: University of Chicago Press, 1985).

Gerhardt, Mia, *The Art of Story-telling: A Literary Study of the Thousand and One Nights* (Leiden: Brill, 1963).

Gérin, Winifred, *Charlotte Brontë: The Evolution of Genuis* (Oxford: Oxford University Press, 1969).

Glen, Heather, *Charlotte Brontë: The Imagination in History* (Oxford: Oxford University Press, 2002).

Glen, Heather, 'Configuring a World: Some Childhood Writings of Charlotte Brontë', in Mary Hilton, Morag Styles and Victor Watson (eds), *Opening the Nursery Door: Reading, Writing and Childhood, 1600–1900* (London: Routledge, 1997), pp. 215–34.

Glissant, Édouard, *Poetics of Relation*, trans. Betsy Wing (Ann Arbor: University of Michigan Press, 1997).

Grant, Allan, 'The Genie and the Albatross: Coleridge and the *Arabian Nights*', in Peter L. Caracciolo (ed.), *The Arabian Nights in English Literature: Studies in the Reception of the Thousand and One Nights into British Culture* (London: Macmillan, 1988), pp. 111–29.

Gregory, Derek, 'Scripting Egypt: Orientalism and the Cultures of Travel', in James S. Duncan and Derek Gregory (eds), *Writes of Passage: Reading Travel Writing* (London: Routledge, 1999), pp. 114–50.

Grenby, Matthew, *The Child Reader, 1700–1840* (Cambridge: Cambridge University Press, 2011).

Grosrichard, Alain, *The Sultan's Court: European Fantasies of the East*, trans. Liz Heron (London: Verso, 1998).

Harris, Susan Cannon, 'Pathological Possibilities: Contagion and Empire in Doyle's Sherlock Holmes Stories', *Victorian Literature and Culture* 31.2 (2003), pp. 447–66.

Harvard Gibbs-Smith, Charles, *The Great Exhibition of 1851, A Commemorative Album* (London: Victoria and Albert Museum, 1950).

Henes, Mary, and Brian H. Murray (eds), *Travel Writing, Visual Culture and Form, 1760–1900* (Basingstoke: Palgrave Macmillan, 2015).

Henson, Louise, 'Investigations and Fictions: Charles Dickens and Ghosts', in Nicola Bown, Carolyn Burdett and Pamela Thurschwell (eds), *The Victorian Supernatural* (Cambridge: Cambridge University Press, 2004), pp. 44–63.

Hobhouse, Hermione, *The Crystal Palace and the Great Exhibition: Art, Science and Productive Industry* (London: Athlone, 2002).

Hodder, Ian, *Reading the Past: Current Approaches to Interpretation in Archaeology* (Cambridge: Cambridge University Press, 1986).

Hodder, Ian, *The Meaning of Things: Material Culture and Symbolic Expression* (London: Unwin Hyman, 1989).

Holmes, John, 'Pre-Raphaelitism, Sciences, and the Arts in *The Germ*', *Victorian Literature and Culture* 43.4 (December 2015), pp. 689–703.

Hunt, Verity, 'Narrativizing "The World's Show": The Great Exhibition, Panoramic Views and Print Supplements', in Joe Kember, John Plunkett and Jill A. Sullivan (eds), *Popular Exhibitions, Science and Showmanship, 1840–1910* (London: Routledge, 2012), pp. 115–32.

Hyam, Ronald, *Empire and Sexuality: The British Experience* (Manchester: Manchester University Press, 1990).

Ingham, Patricia, *The Brontës* (London: Longman, 2003).

Irwin, Robert, 'Foreword', in Robert Louis Stevenson, *New Arabian Nights* (London: Capuchin Press, 2011), pp. 9–14.

Irwin, Robert, *The Arabian Nights: A Companion* (London: Tauris Parke, 1994).

Irwin, Robert, 'The *Arabian Nights* and the Origins of the Western Novel', in Philip F. Kennedy and Marina Warner (eds), *Scheherazade's Children: Global Encounters with the Arabian Nights* (New York: New York University Press, 2013), pp. 143–53.

Irwin, Robert, *Visions of the Jinn: Illustrators of the Arabian Nights* (Oxford: Oxford University Press, 2010).

Jasanoff, Maya, *Edge of Empire: Lives, Culture, and Conquest in the East 1750–1850* (New York: Alfred A. Knopf, 2005).

Kabbani, Rana, *Europe's Myths of Orient: Devise and Rule* (London: Macmillan, 1986).

Keene, Melanie, *Science in Wonderland: The Scientific Fairy Tales of Victorian Britain* (Oxford: Oxford University Press, 2015).

Kennedy, Dane, *The Highly Civilized Man: Richard Burton and the Victorian World* (Cambridge, MA: Harvard University Press, 2005).

Khan, Jalal Uddin, *Readings in Oriental Literature: Arabian, Indian, and Islamic* (Newcastle Upon Tyne: Cambridge Scholars, 2015).

Killeen, Jarlath, *The Emergence of Irish Gothic Fiction: Histories, Origins, Theories* (Edinburgh: Edinburgh University Press, 2014).
Killen, Andreas, *Berlin Electropolis: Shock, Nerves, and German Modernity* (Berkeley: University of California Press, 2006).
Knipp, C., 'The "Arabian Nights" in England: Galland's Translation and Its Successors', *Journal of Arabic Literature* 5 (1974), pp. 44–54.
Knowles, Nancy, and Katherine Hall, 'Imperial Attitudes in *Lady Audley's Secret*', in Jessica Cox (ed.), *New Perspectives on Mary Elizabeth Braddon* (Amsterdam: Rodopi, 2012), pp. 37–58.
Kofman, Sarah, *The Childhood of Art: An Interpretation of Freud's Aesthetics*, trans. Winifred Woodhull (New York: Columbia University Press, 1988).
Kriegel, Lara, 'Narrating the Subcontinent in 1851: India at the Crystal Palace', in Louise Purbrick (ed.), *The Great Exhibition of 1851: New Interdisciplinary Essays* (Manchester: Manchester University Press, 2001), pp. 146–78.
Kriegel, Lara, 'The Pudding and the Palace: Labour, Print Culture, and Imperial Britain in 1851', in Antoinette Burton (ed.), *After the Imperial Turn: Thinking With and Through the Nation* (Durham, NC: Duke University Press, 2003), pp. 230–45.
Krips, Valerie, *The Presence of the Past: Memory, Heritage, and Childhood in Postwar Britain* (New York: Garland, 2000).
Kuspit, Donald, 'A Mighty Metaphor: The Analogy of Archaeology and Psychoanalysis', in Lynn Gamwell and Richard Wells (eds), *Sigmund Freud and His Art: His Personal Collection of Antiquities* (New York: N. Abrams in conjunction with London: Freud Museum, 1989), pp. 133–51.
Lamb, Jonathan, *Preserving the Self in the South Seas, 1680–1840* (Chicago: University of Chicago Press, 2001).
Leask, Nigel, *British Romantic Writers and the East: Anxieties of Empire* (Cambridge: Cambridge University Press, 1992).
Leask, Nigel, *Curiosity and the Aesthetics of Travel Writing, 1770–1840: 'from an Antique Land'* (Oxford: Oxford University Press, 2002).
Levine, Caroline, 'Strategic Formalism: Toward a New Method in Cultural Studies', *Victorian Studies* 48.4 (2006), pp. 625–57.
Levine, Philippa, *The Amateur and the Professional: Antiquarians, Historians and Archaeologists in Victorian England, 1838–1886* (Cambridge: Cambridge University Press, 1986).
Lindskoog, Kathryn Ann, *Surprised by C. S. Lewis, George MacDonald and Dante: An Array of Original Discoveries* (Macon, GA: Mercer University Press, 2001).
Lovett, Charles C., *Lewis Carroll Among His Books: A Descriptive Catalogue of the Private Library of Charles L. Dodgson* (Jefferson, NC: McFarland, 2005).
McClintock, Anne, *Imperial Leather: Race, Gender, and Sexuality in the Colonial Contest* (London: Routledge, 1995).

McGann, Jerome J., '"My brain is Feminine": Byron and the Poetry of Deception', in Andrew Rutherford (ed.), *Byron: Augustan and Romantic* (Basingstoke: Macmillan, 1990), pp. 26–51.

Mack, Robert L., 'Cultivating the Garden: Antoine Galland's *Arabian Nights* in the Traditions of English Literature', in Saree Makdisi and Felicity Nussbaum (eds), *The Arabian Nights in Historical Context: Between East and West* (Oxford: Oxford University Press, 2008), pp. 51–81.

McKee, Kenneth, *Scenarios of the Commedia Dell'Arte: Flaminio Scala's Il Teatro delle Favole Rappresentative*, trans. Henry F. Salerno (New York: New York University Press, 1967).

McLaughlin, Joseph, *Writing the Urban Jungle: Reading Empire in London from Doyle to Eliot* (Charlottesville: University of Virginia Press, 2000).

Madden, William A., 'Framing the Alices', *PMLA* 101.3 (May 1986), pp. 362–73.

Mahdi, Muhsin, 'The Sources of Galland's *Nuits*', in Ulrich Marzolph (ed.), *The Arabian Nights Reader* (Detroit: Wayne State University Press, 2006), pp. 122–36.

Makdisi, Saree, *Romantic Imperialism: Universal Empire and the Culture of Modernity* (Cambridge: Cambridge University Press, 1998).

Makdisi, Saree, and Felicity Nussbaum, 'Introduction', in Saree Makdisi and Felicity Nussbaum (eds), *The Arabian Nights in Historical Context: Between East and West* (Oxford: Oxford University Press, 2008), pp. 1–23.

Malley, Shawn, *From Archaeology to Spectacle in Victorian Britain: The Case of Assyria, 1845–1854* (Farnham: Ashgate, 2012).

Manley, Deborah, and Peta Rée, *Henry Salt: Artist, Traveller, Diplomat, Egyptologist* (London: Libri, 2001).

Marzolph, Ulrich (ed.), *The Arabian Nights in Transnational Perspective* (Detroit: Wayne State University Press, 2007).

Marzolph, Ulrich, Richard van Leeuwen and Hassan Wassouf (eds), *The Arabian Nights Encyclopedia*, 2 vols (Santa Barbara: ABC-CLIO, 2004).

Mayer, David, *Harlequin in His Element: The English Pantomime, 1806–1836* (Cambridge, MA: Harvard University Press, 1969).

Mayes, Stanley, *The Great Belzoni: The Circus Strongman Who Discovered Egypt's Treasures* (London: Tauris Parke, 2003).

Miller, Andrew H., *Novels Behind Glass: Commodity Culture and Victorian Narrative* (Cambridge: Cambridge University Press, 1995).

Mitchell, Timothy, *Colonising Egypt* (Cambridge: Cambridge University Press, 1988).

Moody, Jane, *Illegitimate Theatre in London, 1770–1840* (Cambridge: Cambridge University Press, 2000).

Nance, Susan, *How the Arabian Nights Inspired the American Dream, 1790–1935* (Chapel Hill: University of North Carolina Press, 2009).

Nishio, Tetsuo, and Yuriko Yamanaka, *The Arabian Nights and Orientalism: Perspectives from East and West* (London: I. B. Tauris, 2005).
Norcia, Megan, 'Playing Empire: Children's Parlor Games, Home Theatricals, and Improvisational Play', *Children's Literature Association Quarterly* 29.4 (2004), pp. 294–314.
Nuss, Melynda, *Distance, Theatre, and the Public Voice, 1750–1850* (New York: Palgrave, 2012).
O'Brien, John, 'Pantomime', in Jane Moody and Daniel O'Quinn (eds), *The Cambridge Companion to British Theatre, 1770–1830* (Cambridge: Cambridge University Press, 2007), pp. 103–14.
O'Connor, Ralph, *The Earth on Show: Fossils and the Poetics of Popular Science, 1802–1856* (Chicago: University of Chicago Press, 2007).
Ormond, Leonée, 'Victorian Romance: Tennyson', in Corinne Saunders (ed.), *A Companion to Romance: From Classical to Contemporary* (Malden, MA: Blackwell, 2004), pp. 321–40.
Pangborn, Matthew, 'The Arabian Romance of America in Poe's "Thousand-and-Second Tale of Scheherazade"', *Poe Studies* 43.1 (2010), pp. 35–57.
Pearson, Mike, and Michael Shanks, *Theatre/Archaeology* (London: Routledge, 2001).
Pels, Peter, 'The Spirit of Matter: On Fetish, Rarity, Fact, and Fancy', in Patricia Spyer (ed.), *Border Fetishisms: Material Objects in Unstable Spaces* (New York: Routledge, 1998), pp. 91–121.
Pettitt, Clare, *Patent Inventions: Intellectual Property and the Victorian Novel* (Oxford: Oxford University Press, 2004).
Pettitt, Clare, 'Peggotty's Work-Box: Victorian Souvenirs and Material Memory', *Romanticism and Victorianism on the Net* 53 (2009), <https://doi.org/10.7202/029896ar> (last accessed October 2018).
Pietz, William, 'The Problem of the Fetish', *Res* 9 (1985), pp. 5–17.
Plotz, John, *Portable Property: Victorian Culture on the Move* (Princeton: Princeton University Press, 2008).
Plotz, Judith, 'In the Footsteps of Aladdin: De Quincey's Arabian Nights', *Wordsworth Circle* 29.2 (1998), pp. 120–6.
Poovey, Mary, 'Ambiguity and Historicism: Interpreting *Confessions of a Thug*', *Narrative* 12.1 (January 2004), pp. 3–21.
Rabinbach, Anson, *The Human Motor: Energy, Fatigue, and the Origins of Modernity* (New York: Basic Books, 1990).
Radhika, Singha, *A Despotism of Law: Crime and Justice in Early Colonial India* (Oxford: Oxford University Press, 1998).
Richards, Thomas, *The Commodity Culture of Victorian England: Advertising and Spectacle 1851–1914* (Stanford: Stanford University Press, 1990).
Ricoeur, Paul, *Freud and Philosophy: An Essay on Interpretation*, trans. Denis Savage (New Haven, CT: Yale University Press, 1970).

Roberts, M. J. D., 'Making Victorian Morals? The Society for the Suppression of Vice and its Critics, 1802–1886', *Historical Studies* 21.83 (1981), pp. 157–73.

Rodenbeck, John, 'Travelers from an Antique Land: Shelley's Inspiration for "Ozymandias"', *Alif: Journal of Comparative Poetics* 24 (2004), pp. 121–48.

Rose, Jacqueline, *The Case of Peter Pan, or the Impossibility of Children's Fiction* (London: Macmillan, 1984).

Saglia, Diego, 'Theatre, Drama, and Vision in the Romantic Age: Stages of the New', in Paul Hamilton (ed.), *The Oxford Handbook of European Romanticism* (Oxford: Oxford University Press, 2016), pp. 752–70.

Said, Edward, *Orientalism* (London: Penguin, 2003 [1978]).

Said, Edward, *The World, the Text and the Critic* (Cambridge, MA: Harvard University Press, 1983).

Salisbury, Laura, and Andrew Shail (eds), *Neurology and Modernity: A Cultural History of Nervous Systems, 1800–1950* (Basingstoke: Palgrave Macmillan, 2010).

Sallis, Eva, *Sheherazade through the Looking Glass: The Metamorphosis of the Thousand and One Nights* (London: Curzon, 1999).

Saxon, A. H., *The Life and Art of Andrew Ducrow and the Romantic Age of the English Circus* (Hamden, CT: Archon Books, 1978).

Schacker, Jennifer, *National Dreams: The Remaking of Fairytales in Nineteenth-Century England* (Philadelphia: University of Pennsylvania Press, 2003).

Schacker-Mill, Jennifer, 'Otherness and Otherworldliness: Edward W. Lane's Ethnographic Treatment of the Arabian Nights', *Journal of American Folklore* 113.448 (2000), pp. 164–84.

Schaffer, Talia, *Novel Craft: Victorian Domestic Handicraft and Nineteenth-Century Fiction* (Oxford: Oxford University Press, 2011).

Schivelbusch, Wolfgang, *The Railway Journey: The Industrialization of Time and Space in the 19th Century* (Berkeley: University of California Press, 1986).

Scholl, Lesa, 'Moving Between *North and South*: Cultural Signs and the Progress of Modernity in Elizabeth Gaskell's Novel', in Lesa Scholl, Emily Morris and Sarina Gruver Moore (eds), *Place and Progress in the Works of Elizabeth Gaskell* (London: Routledge, 2016), pp. 95–106.

Sconce, Jeffrey, *Haunted Media: Electronic Presence from Telegraphy to Television* (Durham, NC: Duke University Press, 2000).

Shuttleworth, Sally, *The Mind of the Child: Child Development in Literature, Science, and Medicine, 1840–1900* (Oxford: Oxford University Press, 2010).

Shuttleworth, Sally, 'The Psychology of Childhood in Victorian Literature and Medicine', in Helen Small and Trudi Tate (eds), *Literature, Science, Psychoanalysis, 1830–1970: Essays in Honour of Gillian Beer* (Oxford: Oxford University Press, 2003), pp. 86–101.

Siddiqi, Yumna, 'The Cesspool of Empire: Sherlock Holmes and the Return of the Repressed', *Victorian Literature and Culture* 34.1 (2006), pp. 233–47.

Slater, Michael, 'Dickens in Wonderland', in Peter L. Caracciolo (ed.), *The Arabian Nights in English Literature: Studies in the Reception of the Thousand and One Nights into British Culture* (London: Macmillan, 1988), pp. 130–42.

Speaight, George, *The History of the English Toy Theatre*, rev. edn (London: Studio Vista, 1969).

Spence, Donald, *The Freudian Metaphor: Towards Paradigm Change in Psychoanalysis* (New York: Norton, 1987).

Steward, Paul Jay, 'Caves in Fiction', in John Gunn (ed.), *Encyclopedia of Caves and Karst Science* (New York: Fitzroy Dearborn, 2004), pp. 421–4.

Steward, Paul Jay, 'Folklore, Myth, and Legend, Caves in', in William B. White and David C. Culver (eds), *Encyclopedia of Caves*, 2nd edn (Waltham, MA: Elsevier Science, 2012), pp. 321–3.

Stewart, Susan, *On Longing: Narratives of the Miniature, the Gigantic, the Souvenir, the Collection* (Durham, NC: Duke University Press, 1993).

Thomas, Julian, *Archaeology and Modernity* (London: Routledge, 2004).

Thomas, Julian, *Time, Culture and Identity: An Interpretative Archaeology* (London: Routledge, 1996).

Tilley, Christopher (ed.), *Interpretive Archaeology* (Oxford: Berg, 1993).

Tilley, Christopher, *Material Culture and Text: The Art of Ambiguity* (London: Routledge, 1991).

Tilley, Christopher, *Metaphor and Material Culture* (Oxford: Blackwell, 1999).

Tucker, Nicholas, 'Fairy Tales and Their Early Opponents: In Defence of Mrs Trimmer', in Mary Hilton, Morag Styles and Victor Watson (eds), *Opening the Nursery Door: Reading, Writing and Childhood, 1600–1900* (London: Routledge, 1997), pp. 104–16.

Turner, Mark W., 'Periodical Time in the Nineteenth Century', *Media History* 8.2 (2010), pp. 183–96.

Warner, Marina, *Fantastic Metamorphoses, Other Worlds: Ways of Telling the Self* (Oxford: Oxford University Press, 2002).

Warner, Marina, *Stranger Magic: Charmed States and the Arabian Nights* (London: Chatto and Windus, 2011).

Warwick, Alexandra, and Martin Willis, 'Introduction: The Archaeological Imagination', *Journal of Literature and Science* 5.1 (2012), pp. 1–5.

Whitlark, James, *Illuminated Fantasy: From Blake's Visions to Recent Graphic Fiction* (Rutherford, NJ: Fairleigh Dickinson University Press, 1988).

Williams, Raymond, *The Country and the City* (Oxford: Oxford University Press, 1973).

Wolfreys, Julian, *Dickens's London: Perception, Subjectivity and Phenomenal Urban Multiplicity* (Edinburgh: Edinburgh University Press, 2012).

Wood, Gillen D'arcy, *The Shock of the Real: Romanticism and Visual Culture, 1760–1860* (Basingstoke: Palgrave, 2001).

Yeazell, Ruth Bernard, *Harems of the Mind: Passages of Western Art and Literature* (New Haven, CT: Yale University Press, 2000).

Yegenoglu, Meyda, *Colonial Fantasies: Towards a Feminist Reading of Orientalism* (Cambridge: Cambridge University Press, 1998).

Zimmerman, Virginia, *Excavating Victorians* (Albany: State University of New York Press, 2008).

Ziter, Edward, *The Orient on the Victorian Stage* (Cambridge: Cambridge University Press, 2003).

Index

antiquities, 7, 8, 26, 41, 62, 63–4, 65, 67, 72–3, 74, 76, 82, 108, 110–11, 116; *see also* archaeology; caves
Arabian Nights
  in archaeology, 61–2, 66–7, 68–70, 71–4, 75–6, 80, 114–15
  in British literary canon, 135–6
  child readers of, 11, 13, 20, 21–4, 26, 31–2, 32–3, 41, 42–4, 45–8, 48–51, 61, 120–1
  children's editions of, 48–50
  eroticism, 9, 35, 182–4
  in ethnography, 62, 95–8
  fictional readers of, 20, 54–5
  as metaphor, 3–4, 7, 13, 32–3, 35, 38, 46, 47, 61, 62–3, 91, 104n, 105n, 142, 144–7, 152, 166
  as metonymic of childhood, 20, 31, 33, 35, 42–3, 52, 61
  narrative structure, 4, 6, 9, 15, 20, 98, 106n, 152, 170n, 176, 181
  proliferation of, 4–6, 6–7, 15, 20–2, 31–2, 83, 86–7, 89, 182, 185
  Romantic conception of, 20, 34–9
  on stage, 117, 119–35
  in travel writing, 13–14, 61, 62, 66–7, 83–5, 86–8, 89–92, 115
Arabian Nights characters
  Abon Hassan, 90–1, 92
  African Magician, 27, 30, 36–7, 38, 75, 134–5
  Aladdin, 8, 30, 38, 68, 69, 71–2, 78–9, 80, 82, 123, 143, 144, 147; *see also* magic lamp
  Ali Baba, 41, 47, 68, 70, 82, 90, 154
  Bedriddin Hassan, 145
  Cassim Baba, 40

Dinarzade, 41
Haroun Alraschid, 29, 46, 57n, 83, 91, 156, 157, 167
Morgiana, 53
Peri Banou, 68, 157, 158, 171n
Prince Agib, 69, 129, 130
Princess Badroulbadour, 24, 26, 30, 134–5
Scheherazade, 4, 5, 6, 15, 23, 24, 29, 30–1, 41, 42, 68, 76, 86, 94, 98, 106n, 152, 157, 167, 173n, 176, 181, 182
Sinbad, 51, 70, 73, 78, 82, 88, 90, 114
Solomon, 2, 157, 158
Sultan Schariar, 4, 9, 15, 41, 49, 79, 185
Arabian Nights stories
  'The History of Aladdin, or the Wonderful Lamp', 2, 4, 5, 24–6, 27, 29–30, 35–7, 38, 48, 57n, 74, 75–6, 104n, 134, 139n, 147, 167–8, 178
  'The History of Prince Zeyn Alasnam', 35, 68
  'The History of Sinbad the Sailor', 35, 49, 69, 74, 87, 91, 115, 128, 133, 167
  'The History of the Second Calender', 49, 87
  'The History of the Third Calender', 69, 87, 129–30, 132
  'The History of the Young King of the Black-Isles', 41, 79–80
  'The Story of Ali Baba, and the Forty Thieves destroyed by a Slave', 4, 5, 17n, 40, 46, 53, 57n, 74, 154

Arabian Nights stories (*cont.*)
  'The Story of Amine', 50
  'The Story of Noureddin and his Son', 98, 145, 157
  'The Story of Prince Ahmed and the Fairy Pari Banou', 17n, 48, 68
  'The Story of the Barber's Sixth Brother', 87
  'The Story of the Enchanted Horse', 51, 124–5
  'The Story of the Little Hunchback', 43, 59n
  'The Story of the Sleeper Awakened', 17n, 91, 178
Arabian Nights theatrical productions
  Aladdin, Covent Garden (1788), 119
  Aladdin, Covent Garden (1813), 119
  Aladdin, Drury Lane (1826), 118, 126, 135–6
  Aladdin, Drury Lane (1828), 122
  Aladdin, Lyceum (1844), 133–5
  Aladdin: Or, The Saucy Young Scamp Who Collected the Lamp (1889–90), 127
  Aladdin, Salle Le Peletier (1822), 126–7
  Barber of Bagdad, Surrey (1822), 120
  Cherry and Fair Star; Or, the Children of Cyprus, Covent Garden (1822), 120, 123–4
  Forty Thieves, Drury Lane (1806), 119, 121–2
  Harlequin and the Red Dwarf; Or, the Adamant Rock, 129–31
  Noureddin and the Fair Persian; Or, the Bright Star of Morn, Covent Garden (1837), 122
  The Barber and his Brothers, Adelphi (1826), 120
  The Enchanted Courser; Or, The Sultan of Cardistan, Drury Lane (1824), 124–5
  The Ninth Statue; Or, the Irishman in Bagdad, Drury Lane (1814), 120, 122–3, 132
  The Spirit of the Bell, Lyceum, 133
  The Valley of Diamonds; Or, Harlequin Sinbad, 127–9
  Who Wants a Wife, Covent Garden (1815), 120
  You Must Be Buried, Haymarket (1827), 133
archaeology, 61, 63, 67, 80
  excavation sites, 64, 75, 76, 110–11, 114–15
  and fairy tales, 65–6, 70–1, 75, 114
  interpretive archaeology, 64–6
  and showmanship, 112–14
  and the subconscious, 76–7
  see also antiquities; caves
autobiography, 19, 32, 33, 34, 35, 37–8, 44, 61, 89, 111, 131

Baghdad, 4, 8, 29, 35, 36, 73, 83, 90, 91, 121, 175, 176
Barrie, J. M., 32, 47–8
Belzoni, Giovanni Battista, 71, 108–16, 117, 123
Borges, Jorge Luis, 4, 60n, 152
Braddon, Mary Elizabeth, 104n
  Lady Audley's Secret, 78–80
Brontë, Charlotte
  and the Great Exhibition, 141–2, 146–7
  Jane Eyre, 19–20, 21, 41–2, 44, 46, 50–1
  Villette, 146, 171n
Brontë family, 20, 22, 26–8
Burton, Richard, 8, 176, 182–5
Byron, Lord George Gordon, 34, 118–19

Cairo, 4, 8, 83, 84, 89–92, 93, 95–6, 99, 145, 175; *see also* Egypt
carpets, 11, 46, 47, 150, 152, 154, 155, 156, 157–60, 166, 172n; *see also* magic objects
Carroll, Lewis, 47–8
  Alice's Adventures in Wonderland, 76, 80–3, 110
caves, 25, 36–7, 62, 65, 67, 68–70, 71, 74, 75, 78–9, 80, 108, 110, 115, 116–17, 118–19, 121; *see also* archaeology
chapbooks, 24–6, 44, 45; *see also* miniature books
childhood
  connection to Orient, 39–40, 42, 55
  definition of, 33–4
  material souvenirs of, 11, 20, 23, 26, 40, 44–8, 156

Index

psychology of, 39–40
Romantic conception of, 34–7, 47
time and space of, 20, 27–8, 31, 33–4, 39–40, 42, 43, 47–8, 48–55
children's literature, 31–3, 47–8
China, 13, 15, 72, 94, 103n, 134, 145, 179
Coleridge, Samuel Taylor, 34–5, 36, 72–3
Cruikshank, George, 148–9
Crystal Palace, 8, 14, 142–4, 146, 148, 149, 151, 152, 154, 155, 163–4, 167–8, 170n; *see also* Great Exhibition

De Quincey, Thomas, 20, 35–9
Delhi, 8, 84, 175; *see also* India
detective fiction, 175, 178–9, 180–1
Dickens, Charles, 2, 5, 20, 22, 29, 31, 46–7, 52, 57n, 58n, 85, 105n, 131
A Christmas Carol, 47, 90
'A Christmas Tree', 40–1, 42
American Notes, 87
David Copperfield, 21
Hard Times, 52–4
Household Words, 2, 52, 85, 91, 92, 112, 114, 143, 147
'Manchester Men at their Books', 52
Martin Chuzzlewit, 47
'Mr Barlow', 51
Our Mutual Friend, 144–5
Pictures from Italy, 87–8
Sketches by Boz, 144
'The Ghost in Master B's Room', 29
The Old Curiosity Shop, 145
dreams, 10, 15, 37, 45, 46, 52, 54, 62, 66, 73, 76, 81–2, 101, 110, 146, 150, 158

Egypt, 4, 6, 7, 13, 62, 63, 64, 65–6, 71, 72–3, 82–3, 84, 90, 91–2, 92–4, 95–9, 100, 101, 108, 109, 110–17, 156, 182–3; *see also* Cairo
Egyptian Hall, 108, 110, 111, 113, 117, 123
Eliot, George, 145–6
Adam Bede, 100
exhibitions *see* Great Exhibition; shows of London

fairy-tales, 5, 14, 47, 65, 66, 69, 82, 111, 114, 140n
Freud, Sigmund, 77, 80

Galland, Antoine, 4, 22, 25, 68, 72, 79, 94, 99, 117, 129, 130, 138n, 185
Gaskell, Elizabeth, 26
Cranford, 21
North and South, 166, 173n
genii, 2, 3, 27, 35, 49, 68, 79, 96, 121, 122, 123, 127, 145, 146, 147, 156, 157, 161, 163, 166, 167, 168, 178, 180
Gothic, 37, 77
Great Exhibition, 8, 14–15, 141–68
architectural structure, 14–15, 143–4
arrangement of displays, 142, 149–52, 170n
Indian exhibits, 156–8, 160–3
magical aura, 142–4, 145–9, 150
mechanical exhibits, 141, 164–7
objects from Arabian Nights, 153, 154–6, 157, 160–1
see also Crystal Palace
Grimaldi, Joseph, 129, 130, 131

handicraft, 15, 142, 161, 162, 163, 172n
Henniker, Sir Frederick, 65, 72–3

imperialism, 3, 7, 8, 9, 10, 11, 12, 20, 30, 38, 66, 74, 79, 83, 85–8, 99, 111, 114, 116, 119, 132, 146–7, 149, 153, 160–1, 179, 180, 183, 185
India, 6, 10, 13, 15, 85, 88, 94, 150, 153, 156–63; *see also* Delhi

Johnson, Richard, 49–50
juvenile drama *see* toy theatres

Knight, Charles, 143, 147
Koh-i-noor diamond, 153, 156–7

Landon, Letitia Elizabeth (L. E. L.), 22–3, 45–6
Lane, Edward William, 92, 182
Account of the Manners and Customs of the Modern Egyptians, 93–4, 95–7, 99, 100
Arabian Nights, 4–5, 94–5, 96–9
'Description of Egypt', 92–3

Layard, Austen Henry, 61–2, 63, 66–7, 74, 75–6, 114
Lewis, C. S., 48

magic, 1–4, 6, 8, 13–15, 26, 45, 47, 49, 50, 66, 68, 70, 71, 72, 74, 75–6, 79, 89, 90, 95, 99, 100, 110, 114, 117, 118, 121–2, 125, 130, 135, 142, 143, 144, 145–7, 149, 153–8, 160–3, 164–8, 176, 177–8, 181, 183, 184–5
magic lamp, 2, 3, 11, 15, 24–5, 27, 36–7, 41, 46, 47, 51, 71, 101–2, 115, 127, 133, 146, 147, 154, 167, 168; see also Arabian Nights characters: Aladdin
magic objects, 8, 10, 11, 40–1, 47, 65, 76, 79, 84–5, 90, 123, 142, 143, 146, 152, 153, 154, 155, 156, 158, 166, 168, 176; see also carpets; magic lamp
magical thinking, 9–10, 14, 63, 100–2, 126–7, 171n
memoir see autobiography
memory, 11, 12, 20, 23, 24, 29, 31, 38, 44–6, 52, 54, 61, 63, 67, 70, 73, 75, 81, 85, 95, 99, 156
Meredith, George, 177
miniature books, 26–7, 33; see also chapbooks
modernity, 2, 3, 7, 10, 15, 16, 24, 39, 54, 63, 72, 75, 76–7, 80, 81, 82, 99, 110, 118, 127, 163, 164, 168, 176, 177, 178

Newbery, John and Elizabeth, 49
nostalgia, 29, 31, 44

opera, 117, 118, 119, 121, 122, 126, 133, 135
Orientalism, 7–8, 8–10, 85–7, 111, 146–7, 153, 176, 179
  and Eastern veil, 92–3
  Romantics and, 34, 38–9, 88, 118–19
  and theatricality, 91–2

pantomime, 117, 119, 126, 127–33
Paxton, Joseph, 143, 144, 153, 168

Payne, John, 8, 176, 182
Persia, 4, 62, 64, 83, 94
Poe, Edgar Allan, 167, 173n
print culture, 4–6, 18n, 20–1, 31, 74, 134, 135, 140n, 152, 159

Ramses II see Young Memnon
reading, history of, 11, 12–13, 16
  embodied reading, 22–3, 26, 55
  serial reading, 12, 15, 18n, 23, 81, 151, 152, 176
Rousseau, Jean Jacques, 33–4, 35

Said, Edward, 7, 8, 31, 85, 91, 98, 176
Shelley, Mary, *Frankenstein*, 77–8
shows of London, 108–10, 116–17
slaves, 2, 53, 147
stagecraft, 7, 14, 109, 110, 112, 120–7
Stephens, Frederic George, 1–2, 3
Stevenson, Robert Louis, 20, 22, 29, 175
  'A Penny Plain and Twopence Coloured', 28, 43–4
  'Child's Play', 40
  New Arabian Nights, 8, 174–6, 177–9, 181–2

Tennyson, Alfred Lord, 20, 22
Thackeray, William, 20, 21, 142–3
  Vanity Fair, 105n
Thing Theory, 10–11, 154–5; see also magic objects
Thugs, 158–60, 161–3
toy theatres, 28–31, 44
travel writing, 63–7, 82–92

Wilde, Oscar, 178, 180
wonder, 2, 3, 6, 14, 15, 41, 42, 45, 52, 62, 67, 69, 70, 73, 76, 101, 109, 110, 118, 119, 120, 121–2, 125, 127, 134, 141–2, 144, 157, 160–1, 163, 165, 166, 167, 180, 183, 184
Wordsworth, William, 28, 34, 36, 38
  The Prelude, 23–4, 26, 45, 74

Young Memnon, 111, 112, 113, 114, 136n, 137n

EU representative:
Easy Access System Europe
Mustamäe tee 50, 10621 Tallinn, Estonia
Gpsr.requests@easproject.com

www.ingramcontent.com/pod-product-compliance
Lightning Source LLC
Chambersburg PA
CBHW070353240426
43671CB00013BA/2479